More praise for Dora

"This touches on one ~~the strengths of the novel that it~~ is both plot driven – as well as an intimate portrait of a young woman's painful journey toward maturity.....This is a page turner with heart and deserves to find a wide readership"

— www.sffmedia.com

"If you enjoy accessible sci-fi/fantasy (or even if you don't, because I thought I didn't) this book is a ton of fun!"

— www.lindamaubooks.com/blog/

"Machado's writing is as competent as her characterization, being vivid and often poetic. The plot itself is well devised and generally moves along at a good pace... There are quite a few surprises... I was surprised to find that the novel was often a little darker than I expected, and there are one or two quite brutal moments that add a nice (dare I say it) gritty feel, without coming across too heavily. Machado's world also comes across well in her writing."

—www.speculativehorizons.blog-spot.com

"Once in a while, a new fantasy/adventure comes out that doesn't travel well-worn paths in the genre but instead gives us a vivid new world, an exciting set of original characters, and page after page of non-stop intrigue, action, twists, revelation, and fun. STONEWISER is the best to appear in years."

—Barnes & Noble review

Spotlight Book for June 2008
—http://fantasybookcritic.blogspot.com

Stonewiser: The Heart of the Stone
— A 2009 ForeWord Book of the Year Finalist

STONEWISER
The Call of the Stone

The STONEWISER Series

STONEWISER
The Call of the Stone

Dora Machado

Mermaid
PRESS

Map art by Dora Machado
Cover and interior design by Mayapriya Long, Bookwrights
Cover and text art by Duncan Long
Stonewiser™ is a trademark of Dora Machado

ISBN: 978-0-9799682-2-8
Library of Congress Control Number: 2009921612

Mermaid Press is an imprint of Mermaid Publishing, LLC
www.merpress.com

Mermaid Publishing, LLC
P.O. Box 5480
Spring Hill, FL 34611

Printed in the United States of America

To VAR and MPA
Who taught me to wise tales out of lives
and lives out of tales.

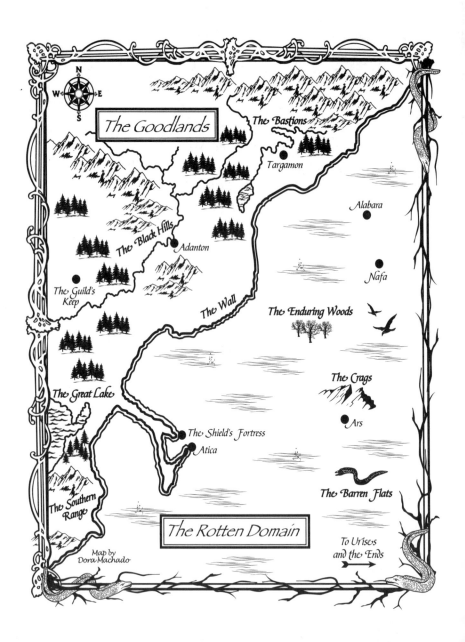

The Goodlands

The Bastions

Targamon

Alabara

Nafa

The Black Hills

Adanton

The Guild's
Keep

The Wall

The Enduring Woods

The Great Lake

The Crags

Ars

The Shield's Fortress

Atica

The Barren Flats

The Southern
Range

The Rotten Domain

To Urises
and the Ends

Map by
Dora Machado

One

SARIAH WAS WITH her pupils when the executioners came. They arrived on her deck without warning or fanfare, slipping in through the door one after the other, until twelve of them crammed her stonewiser's deck. Twelve. They had been warned about her. They took care to block the door and windows before they stripped the dark mantles they wore to conceal their garb. The sight of their red robes was worse than a rotfish fang to her gut. Dread squelched all of the day's promises and numbed Sariah to death's bold announcement.

A bulky fellow with a face as cracked as the mud flats stepped forward. "Stonewiser, you are called to the nets."

It was a measure of the fear Sariah inspired that the voice of the grizzled veteran shook faintly when he addressed her.

She called on her practiced discipline to avoid the man's pitfall. "Has it been decided?"

His smile was just another crevice on his weathered face. "We raced to beat the messengers. You die tomorrow at sunrise. Don't worry. We'll make great good of your death."

Tomorrow. She chided herself for sending her guard away to aid with the blood month's butchering. At the time, it had seemed like the fair decision. Every able hand was needed and no word about her fate had been expected until next year. Besides, she couldn't very well keep the runners around when she intended a brief private foray of her own. She eyed the bag she had packed the night before. Her little journey would have to wait now.

Young Mia stood up, considering the executioners with the leery stare of a stalking cat. With a muted swoosh, a dozen swords rushed out of the executioners' sheaths and aimed at the girl.

Perhaps they had heard about Mia as well. The little girl's freckled face darkened with the power gathering in her. Her sparkling blue and green eyes queried Sariah, pleading for permission. Such great insight in a twelve-year-old. Such great power and sorrow.

Restraint was the only guard against useless death at the moment. Keeping her eyes on the executioners and moving slowly to avoid startling them, Sariah inched closer to the girl, speaking softly. "Not now, Mianina. Remember, a deck can't withstand your flow. And you can't punish good people for doing their jobs."

The executioners' dangerous mood eased a bit, but Mia was still on edge. Sariah loathed what she had done to the child, what she'd had to do. She pressed her palms on Mia's bony shoulders, closed her eyes and thought of the Barren Flats at dawn. It took a moment, but her determination to avoid disaster lent her the strength to concentrate. *Calm.* She infused Mia with as much of it as she could muster. *Peacefulness.* She tried to quench the anger rumbling in her creation's little body. She sensed Mia rally around the kinder emotions.

"That should last you a while, Mianina. Take the other children and go home."

Blond spiraling curls tickled Sariah's nose when she planted a kiss on the top of Mia's head. The girl didn't want to go, but she did, leading the other children out of Sariah's deck, dripping a little black flow from her palms, but only a little. Sariah was proud of her.

The executioners allowed the children to pass without trouble. It had been nice, this little hiatus in her life, these few months of exploration and study. But she was a child of the Guild and knew better. Fate couldn't be escaped or skipped. Trespasses always caught up with the guilty. The executioners had found her. Now she had to find a way to thwart the Domain's justice and deny fair men their rightful dues.

"May I change?" she asked on the odd chance she might yet gain an advantage or two.

"You come as you are," the chief executioner said. "You need nothing fancy to die. Search her." He motioned with his head to one of the others. "Be careful."

The other man hesitated before approaching. He patted her down with exaggerated care. He took her knife and the sling she wore at her belt. He found the other knife she kept tucked in the back of her boot and emptied her pockets of the assorted stones she liked to carry with her. The little pouch she wore tied as a garter around her thigh tripped his fingers. He rolled it down her leg and over her boot, and then shook three small stones out of the pouch. Guild-raised and owned, she lived safely in Ars, but even here, she hadn't been able to shed her wariness.

The executioner unhooked the leather string and removed her memory stone from her neck. He added it to the little pile growing on the floor. He handled the stones as if they were scalding hot, as if they were capable of singeing his soul. "Will they—?"

"If I want them to."

The hair on the man's arms stood on end. Under his companions' anxious gazes, he scooped up the stones and sidled across the deck one cautious step at a time. He lost his nerve at the last moment, broke out into a contrived trot, and ended up throwing the stones out the window with a desperate pitch. Fools. She had no taste for useless blood.

"Ready?" the chief executioner said.

"A moment, please." Sariah stepped before the small mirror nailed to one of the shelter's posts. She made a show of straightening her tunic and fixing her hair. Even in the Domain, vanity was a commonly accepted vice, a perfect screen to take quick stock of her situation.

The Domain's brutal sun had darkened her skin and streaked her brown hair with golden highlights that matched her eyes' caramel hue. In defiance of the Guild's laws, she wore her hair longer now, in a thick braid that hung down between her shoulder blades, a practical form of heresy. She fussed over the plait and tucked her long bangs behind her ear. The time served her well to collect her thoughts and modulate her emotions. She was as ready as she could be.

"The comely and the homely die all the same," the chief executioner said. "Trust Petrid. I've seen many die. Conceit has no place at the nets."

"And so it doesn't." Sariah offered her wrists.

Petrid bound them together with a competent set of knots.

By the time Sariah walked out of her deck shelter, Ars had heard of the executioners' arrival. The decks and bridges were lined with somber people she had come to know during the last few months. A wide range of emotions played on their familiar faces: fear, relief, regret, resentment. Losing her, the stonewiser they had paid so much to bring to Ars, was a blow to the entire settlement. But they knew, just as she knew, that her fate was unavoidable and lawful.

Torana met her at the last bridge, surrounded by her brood of children, although Mia was wisely not among them. "I've sent for them," she said when Sariah walked by. "Have courage."

Sariah stopped dead in her tracks. "They mustn't come. Do you hear me? Tell him I said *not* to come."

Petrid yanked at the ropes. Sariah stumbled behind him. Was Torana mad? This was Sariah's trouble and she would deal with it. She didn't want anyone else hurt or killed on her account.

They stopped only long enough for her to don a weave to protect her legs from the rot's acid brew. The Barren Flats lay before her, the vast desert of shallow, corrupted water where the Domainers made their home. The executioners plunged into the knee-high dead water and, dragging her along, trekked ahead. Their red-weave mantles trailed behind them like spilled blood.

The line of Ars's rule was clearly marked by a throng of people who waited just outside the settlement's boundaries. She didn't know exactly how Domainers knew this sort of thing. There were no markers, no signs, no warnings and yet every person in the Domain knew where a settlement ended and the free range began.

Sariah had never been to a Domainer execution before. She had not anticipated that the executioners had a large following. A rowdy crowd gathered around a sprawling flotilla of traveling decks. A trinket trader floated his wares before wading customers.

Peddlers fought over shoppers and a mountebank exhorted the merits of his cure-all from the top of his shelter's roof. Compared to the clean order of Domain settlements, the site belonged among the Goodlands' raunchy towns. Yet it was here, in the Domain, substituting decks for houses, knee-high dead water for streets, and peopled with a good number of cross-eyed varlets and slovenly wenches, some of them harlots crying out the prices of the remarkable deeds they offered to perform.

Sariah stumbled when the first blow struck her on the side of the head.

"You like that, you bloody wench?" a man yelled. "That's for messing with the New Blood."

A strike between her shoulder blades knocked the air out of her lungs.

"Kill the witch," someone screeched. "To the nets."

"Tomorrow," Petrid shouted. "Come tomorrow for the show."

Sariah dodged the next shot. She already reeked with the dead water's mud. Clumped together, the mud made for surprisingly convincing projectiles—flammable ones—she remembered.

Someone's aim failed and hit one of the executioners instead. "It was meant for the Shield's whore."

Meliahs help her. They had reason to claim that too.

By the time they arrived at the executioners' deck cluster, Sariah was soiled and sore. A circle of decks opened to allow her party's passage and then closed quickly behind them. They waded among the cluster, until they arrived at the center, where a sturdily built deck held a round cage divided into five slivers of cells. The executioners secured her hands and feet with locked irons. It was only after the door slammed shut that they began to smile and congratulate each other on a bloodless capture.

Sariah sat with her back to the bars and her feet wedged in the middle of the cage, where the chains had been locked to a massive center post. She didn't like small spaces, but she recognized she was safer in the cell than among the hostile crowd.

"Hey, you," a man called from the cell opposite to hers. "Got any food? They don't feed us any here. No reason to feed the dead, is there?"

The man didn't look like he needed fare, stout and portly with a swollen belly and a double chin that veiled any attempt at a neck. "No food? My luck. Figures."

Sariah wiped the mud from her cheek and made a show of listening to the man's protestations while she watched the executioners. They were many, a whole tribe of them, and they were cautious, taking turns guarding the prisoners. Stacked six deep, their tightly roped-together decks acted like a veritable fortress around the cage. Even if she managed the chains and the padlock, she wouldn't make it alive through those decks. The executioners had taken her weave. She couldn't very well run the water without it, not for very long anyway.

"Me? I'm innocent," the man was saying. "A hideous misunderstanding has brought me here. I mean, what else but a malicious plot can put me in the nets with the likes of you and her?"

Her? A cell over from the empty cell next to Sariah's, a third prisoner stirred beneath a tattered blanket.

"Hello, Sariah," the woman said. "It gives me a measure of comfort to know that you and I will die together."

Sariah stared, too stunned to say anything. The fair hair was a little longer now, but she recognized the woman well enough. The lively face reminded her that beauty wasn't always honest. She had once trusted that blunt mismatched gaze. Not anymore.

Enita, ex-marcher for Atica, offered a mocking grimace for a smile. "Are you surprised to see me? Don't be. You and I, we were judged at the same justice gathering. Both of our arguments proved insufficient to save our lives."

Rage boiled in Sariah's veins. "You traitor."

"You must mean *us* traitors. Had I known you would manage the deed so easily, I wouldn't have bothered. Word is you delivered him to the quartering block."

"I didn't betray him."

"Is that what he thinks?" Enita smirked. "I suppose that's his right. The justice gathering must have thought differently. I'm sure the carnage he suffered is one of the reasons you're here."

Sariah couldn't bear to remember. Enita's treason had been too dangerous to forget, too painful and horrifying to forgive. She wouldn't mind witnessing the justice of Enita's punishment. She wouldn't mind it at all.

"It's not fair," the man said. "The executioners get paid twice for our deaths, by the justice gathering and by the crowd. We ought to get something, for being the entertainment."

"You're gonna die," Enita said. "What does coin matter to you now?"

"I don't deserve to die with you two."

"Because you're so virtuous?" Enita snickered. "You killed your mate and your brother, and when your mother came to see about the ruckus, you killed her too. Kin slayer. You die well with us."

"She was cuckolding me," the man said. "She deserved to die. And what's three deaths compared to the thousands of deaths you two contrived? You betrayed the Domain. She broke the wall."

The wall. Aye. By far the most terrible of Sariah's deeds. Death would be an easy reprieve for such trespass, the easiest of all the choices she had made thus far. She couldn't argue with the man, and she had nothing to say to the likes of Enita, who watched Sariah like a gull eyeing the fish bucket. Sariah settled to think in silence. The morning would bring the easy choice for sure. The hardest set of choices, the alternatives to dying—those she would have to fashion herself.

Two

THE SUN'S BLOODIED birth on the Barren Flats' horizon harbored
the day's festivities. The executioners' camp was in full swing. The
shops were open for business. Food for sale was cooking on the
grills. By the time Sariah and the other two prisoners were led
from their cells, peddlers, beggars, pickpockets and harlots were
already working the crowds.

Hungry, stiff and sore from her night in the cell, Sariah recognized the accents of people from a dozen different settlements. It
was a chaotic gathering, like a fair or a market, where people came
to chat, laugh, shop, and in this case, watch the killings. Nothing
attracted the curious as surely as death.

Although the water was still calm, the nets were fully cast.
They were anchored on four of the executioners' decks. The edges
of the nets were marked by brightly painted buoys which floated
above the water line, connecting the decks and marking the square
perimeter. Sariah and the other two prisoners were poled to the
nets' center. Three tiny platforms bobbed on the dead water at
equal intervals. Sariah cringed as she stepped on the creaky deck.
It was small, no more than two paces on each side, flimsily built
with thin twine and rotting wood, and disturbingly unsteady to
the sensibilities of her inner ear. She planted her feet apart and
found her balance. The little deck wasn't very reliable, but then
again, it wasn't intended to be.

Strong and athletic, Enita managed well enough, but the man
was less assured. He squatted on the little deck like a pig stranded
after the floods. He wouldn't last very long that way. None of the
prisoners wore weaves, and that bode badly for them. A brief contact with the dead water burned, but a few moments in the rot's

brew meant the excruciatingly painful dissolution of skin, muscle and bone, the loss of a limb or two, and shortly thereafter, death.

Business was booming on the decks gathered around the nets. Some of the executioners were collecting the watching fees from the crowd. Others were crying out the odds and recording the wagers. A wager for death always held the better odds. Enita was the favorite to last to the end. She flashed Sariah a defying grin. Sariah gave the woman credit for her poise because at the moment, fear was rattling her knees rather violently.

But even Enita paled when the executioners pulled the nets taut. The water boiled with life. The parts of the nets sticking out of the water were piled with astonishing numbers of long contorting creatures, some brown, some black, some mottled or streaked. The larger ones were splotched with algae and encrusted with barnacles. They were as thick as Sariah's legs and as long as she was tall, with elongated snouts equipped with quivering suckers and serrated teeth.

She'd had nightmares about the giant eels, rulers of the Barren Flats. These were bred and raised for the executioners' purposes, made ready with days of hunger. Maddened by the brutal exposure to air, they flapped and slithered in the nets, convulsing and contorting around Sariah like a sinister garden.

An eel sank its teeth onto the squatting man's shoe. The man stomped and screamed. The beast bit through his shoe and tore off a chunk of his toe. The scent of blood unleashed a rave. The water boiled with a frothy surf of eels.

Sariah rode the swells as well as she could. She concentrated on keeping her balance. The crowd was laughing and clapping, pelting her and the others with chunks of refuse, egging on the eels. The executioners dropped the net, allowing the beasts additional depth to launch. Sariah slapped the things off her legs as they came, but one of them latched onto her calf. It took her several attempts to get rid of it. She finally snatched it by the tail, swung it over her head, and slammed it on the water, but not before the enterprising eel ripped off a chunk of her legging, leaving a bloody trail behind.

On his teetering deck, the man tilted from one side to the other, swinging wildly until he lost his balance to the barrage of eels fastened to his feet. The crowd cried in horrified delight. He staggered in the water, tripping on the nets, gaining his footing briefly, only to fall back into the dead water. The eels tore into his legs voraciously. At the same time, his skin began to crackle and ooze. He wailed a continuous shriek of agony. Sariah didn't know how she could help him, but she reached out for his outstretched hand anyway. That's all she grabbed, a scalded hand which she dropped in shock as soon as she realized it was no longer attached to his body.

His death was a flash of blood, suckers, teeth, chunks of flesh. The eels dug into his belly and wriggled in place as if his guts were his body's choicest portion. Every part, every particle floating in the bloody water was snatched and consumed.

Meliahs help her. If she was going to survive this day, she had to act now. She groped for her plait and found the stone she had hidden there tangled in her hair. It had been a shrewd precaution, the only one of her weapons undiscovered by the executioners' search. She pushed and pulled and managed to untangle the stone just as a huge eel bumped her deck.

She staggered and almost fell. She barely kept her balance. Like a veritable leviathan, the huge eel lunged out of the water and chomped down on the side of her hand. Her fingers went into spasms. Her hand opened reflexively. Despite the crowd's uproar, all she heard was the sickening sound of her stone as it dropped in the dead water with a final *plop*.

Still, she tried to make the damn stone burst. But her mind couldn't reach through the water's thickness. Swaying violently on the deck, Sariah stared at her empty hand. Curse her rotten luck. She had done what no stonewiser had done before. She had forsaken her lease, quit the Guild, escaped the keep, traveled to the Domain, wised the forbidden seven twin stones to reveal the Guild's deceit, and joined in kin with Ars. And now she was going to be dinner for a bunch of eels?

A vicious hit struck her hard in the ribs. Sariah managed to stay on her feet. What now? She craned her neck to look at the crowd.

"They're upping their profits," Enita shouted from her wobbly deck. "They're adding stones to their game."

A line was forming to purchase the right to shoot at them. To load the sling with the bigger stones cost more, but there were plenty of takers ready to pay. She had to do something. Rocking from side to side, she shuffled her little deck to the farthest point away from the shooters. Enita followed Sariah's lead, grunting every time a slingshot hit her. With her heart pumping like a pewter mallet, Sariah could have shuffled her deck all the way to the wall. But the executioners acted quickly, lifting the edge of the nets high above the water, an impossible barrier between her and the Barren Flats. Sariah's knee smarted with a well-aimed blow. Could she manage to jump the net?

Enita must have been thinking the same thing. She was an amazing jumper and a fit marcher with formidable legs whose strength Sariah could never hope to match. If anybody had a chance at jumping the nets, it was Enita.

Still, Enita asked, "Do you have any other tricks up your braid, wiser?"

A stone. Sariah needed another stone. The sling shooters. Could she catch one of the stones they aimed at her and transform it in time?

Sariah focused on the next shooter. He was a burly fellow with a stubbly beard and a nose as thick as a cudgel. He bought four shots. He took his time twirling the sling. He snarled when he released the shot. The stone came at her with incredible speed. Sariah tried to snatch it in the air. It missed her hand altogether.

The shot that struck Sariah on the side of the head darkened the day for a long moment. The pain. It flared down her spine like a raging fire. She stayed upright out of pure wiser discipline, teetering in the spinning darkness. She couldn't die just now. Not yet. She forced herself to look at the crowd through watery eyes.

"Triple my bet," the bull-nosed shooter shouted. "I'll take her out with my next shot."

The executioner counted the man's coins. "Go ahead."

Another shot from him would kill her. Sariah cringed when he loaded a fist-sized stone in his sling. He didn't waste any time. He whirled the sling above his head and aimed. Sariah whispered a prayer and braced for the lethal impact.

Three

ONE MOMENT THE shooter was on his feet whirling his sling. The next instant he was on his knees, crying a string of obscenities, clutching his mangled hand. Balancing precariously on the rickety deck, Sariah couldn't quite understand what had happened, until she registered the man standing in the dead water halfway between the nets and the spectators' decks. The familiar figure was tall and broad of shoulders, dangerously poised and holding his sling ready for another shot if necessary.

Meliahs curse him. No, nay, no, Meliahs bless him. Sariah stomped on the eel that landed between her feet and kicked it off the little deck. How dare he endanger himself for nothing? He couldn't beat a full tribe of executioners. He couldn't make war on them either. She would have his hide for this, despite his damn good timing.

He didn't spare her the slightest look. He stood there like a petrified giant, drawing the crowd to silence with his wordless presence's defiance. The noise of laughter and chatter died out. The deadly day came to a standstill.

Enita had shuffled her little deck close to Sariah's and now stood next to her, gaping. "What is *he* doing here?"

Sariah held her breath.

The newcomer unwrapped his scarf, baring his face for all to see, breathing heavily, although when he spoke his voice was steady as the morning's calm breeze. "I'm Kael, Son of Ars. Forgive the interruption, executioners. I mean you no harm or disrespect. I regret the shooter's pain and offer retribution." He nodded at the squirming man and then returned his attention to Petrid. "We acknowledge your rights to collect these fees and to kill this woman.

Everyone has a right to make a living in the Domain, and yours is no less than ours."

The chief executioner hesitated before sheathing his sword, but Kael's words had their intended effect. The other executioners, who had taken to the water and surrounded Kael, followed Petrid's example and lowered their weapons. That was all very good progress, but not fast enough. Sariah's views about her need of rescue were changing rapidly. Since Kael had come despite her warning, and given that she didn't have any stones and the eels were industriously chewing at the deck's unraveling twine, he might as well hurry up and get her out of the nets.

It was only then that the others arrived, making their way between the crowded decks. Marcher Metelaus, Kael's older brother, and Lazar, his younger brother, were wheezing like busted stallions after what must have been a desperate run. Lazar carried a basket strapped to his back, and in it, Sariah recognized half-man Malord, the Domain's gathering wiser and her advocate before the justice gathering. Sariah couldn't guess at their plans, but whatever they were going to do, they needed to do it quickly. The eel rave was in no waiting mood.

"If you don't come to challenge our rights, why are you here?" Petrid asked.

"I'm here to purchase the right of atonement for this woman," Kael said.

The crowd gasped. Sariah had no idea what Kael was talking about, but she wished he would talk faster.

"Atonement?" Petrid looked dubious. "The woman wishes to beg forgiveness from Meliahs' nine sisters?"

"She does."

"That's a mighty expensive right."

"And highly profitable, I understand. For you." Kael flashed his ferocious smile, the one capable of freezing Meliahs' rot pits and chilling a raging fire.

"What about me?" It was Enita speaking. "Are you going to purchase atonement for me? You've known me a lot longer than you've known Sariah. You and I, we share the same Blood. I know things, about Atica, about the Shield, things that can help you rule the Domain."

Kael spoke to Petrid exclusively. "What will you lose if you take the stonewiser out of the nets for a few moments while we talk? If you don't like what I have to say, you can return her to the nets and finish feeding your eels."

That was a grand idea for a rescue. Sariah would have to congratulate him for the brilliant thought later. She slapped another eel from her ankle. Hurry now.

"Why would you want to save her?" Enita said. "She lies. She cheats. She betrayed you. For Meliahs' sake, she delivered you to the Shield's quartering block!"

Kael's stare skewered Enita like a killing arrow. "You'll never understand an oath."

Enita flashed a bitter grin. "May your damn oaths kill you."

She leapt, powerful, agile and lithe, a spectacular showmanship of the Domainer art of the jump that Sariah couldn't help but envy at the moment. She somersaulted high over the nets and shot sideways. Sariah thought she was going to make it.

She heard the shooter's telltale grunt at the same time the stone whizzed by. The shot hit Enita at the base of the skull. Her neatly tucked body unraveled in the air. Her arms and legs flung out convulsively. Sariah hoped Enita was already dead when she plummeted headfirst into the water and got tangled at the edge of the nets. Her body quivered like a fly caught in a giant spider web. Her head bobbed limply at the waterline. The crowd was going wild, celebrating the killing shot, exchanging wagered money. A new bet began. How much longer could Sariah last?

The eels fell on Enita's listless body, fighting among themselves for chunks of her face. A few sported beards of Enita's fair hair as they scurried away with scalp hunks between their fangs. In the feeding frenzy, the eels stirred the water into a turbulent rage, buffeting Sariah's little deck with the strength of a sudden gale. Sariah slipped, lost her balance and almost fell. It didn't seem possible she would last another moment.

"There's no deal for carcasses if the stonewiser falls." Kael's voice carried clearly across the water. "Those eels of yours are blood-mad and she's just a Goodlander weakling looking feeble on that deck."

Weakling? Sariah reclaimed her balance and stood erect on the deck. *Feeble?* As if she hadn't endured for a good two hours against the eels and the crowd, outlasting two others? She held on out of pride and spite.

The chief executioner took his time making the decision. Kael matched his equanimity without the slightest show of haste. It seemed to Sariah that a hundred chills had turned before Petrid finally spoke.

"Fetch her," he commanded. "We'll talk, Son of Ars."

The crowd started to boo, but the jeering wilted as Kael's terrible glower swept over the chastened spectators. The executioners who were coming to fetch her seemed to pole with the speed of lame tortoises digging uphill. Sariah used the last of her strength to jump to their deck as soon as it came within her reach. She landed on her knees, because now that she was away from the eels, her legs refused to stand her weight.

Free of its load, the little deck overturned and bobbed in the water briefly. The beasts finished ripping it apart. Sariah watched the eels' ferocity with a sense of numb horror. She wiped the sweat from her brow and breathed what felt like her first real gulp of air in two days. It struck her then that Kael's taunting had had a clear purpose—her wounded pride had lent her the strength to endure a few more moments.

"I haven't had a good reason to sell a right of atonement in, let's see..." Petrid's forehead furrowed. "Thirty chills or so."

"The wiser there, she's no danger to Domainers," Kael said. "Two chills living in Ars without trouble prove that. She's a good reason for you to sell atonement and make great profit."

After a life of despising the Guild's mercenary ways, had Kael turned into a Guild trader overnight?

"But the scope of her offenses..." Petrid's pregnant pause said it all.

"Atonement is not granted based on the gravity's scope but rather on the valuable nature of the proposed reparation."

"I see that you know a great deal about my business."

Kael flashed his fierce grin. "I've made it my business to learn about yours."

Sariah was glad he knew what he was talking about, because she understood only a little about the Domainers' ways and even less about the executioners and their business. The two men spewed technicalities at each other, a slow deliberate dance over the fragile notion of her life.

Kael was a sight to behold, imposing, proud, maybe even arrogant in his stance. She had to will herself to look at him without shuddering in fear for his life. His fair hair was plastered against his skull and his black and green stare scoured his surroundings with lethal competence. She didn't have to be close to him to recognize the determination on the stern lines of his face. Under the broken eyebrow, the discordant black pupil dominated his glare, gleaming dangerously with a promise of violence.

"I don't understand how you can claim atonement," the executioner said. "She betrayed us. She revealed the location of our demesnes to the Shield. She started a war. She loosened the rot on good land. She broke the wall. Do you contest these charges?"

"Her intent was good," Kael said. "Atonement is her right."

"Who knows the witch's purpose?"

"I do." There was no hesitation in Kael's voice, no doubt and no allowance for disagreement or protest.

"Yet the justice gathering found her guilty."

"Ah." It was always an infuriating sound coming from Kael. "A point of law. And one which must be addressed." Kael motioned to his brothers. "Stonewiser Malord?"

Malord somehow rose, although his legs had defected long ago in deference to the quartering block's ax. He was the gathering's lead, the most knowledgeable wiser in the Domain, the only man Sariah knew who could rise without legs, looking dignified and superior while stuffed in a basket strapped to another man's back. Cinnamon dark, long of face and sharp-featured, his deep voice carried the weight of his authority.

"The justice gathering had no means at its disposal to spare her life," Malord said. "It can only declare innocence or guilt, but you know that, Petrid."

"So what?" The executioner spat to the side. "You expect us to take up your burden?"

"You have your trade's leeway," Malord said. "Don't be fooled, the gathering realizes this wiser's importance to the Domain. Didn't she wise a tale of Domainer redemption out of the seven twin stones? Is that not enough to grant her atonement?"

"Redemption?" Petrid scoffed. "How can you call this state of catastrophic disaster redemption? There's war in the Goodlands and it threatens to spill over to the Domain. Has the Shield gone away? No. It has gotten crueler and more savage. Has the Guild stopped hunting us? No. It kills us with ever more pleasure."

"Sariah's unprecedented wisings showed that we didn't commit the crimes for which we were execrated to the Rotten Domain," Malord said. "Her wisings freed us from the accusation that we brought the rot to the land."

"Perhaps she proved us innocent of that, but only to prove us guilty of worse crimes. Ask anybody in the Domain and they'll tell you they would prefer to remain guilty but proud, execrated but separate from the filth of the Goodlands."

And that was the very reason why she had to die. Because to these beleaguered Domainers, the redemption she had discovered had turned out to be a more hideous charge than they could bear.

"It will take time to sort out matters," Malord said. "What we need is a way for all the Blood to come together."

"Goodlanders and us?" Petrid laughed. "You're mad if you think they'll share the land with us."

"We can't give up hope. It's our purpose. Perhaps they can be persuaded. If there's a tale out there that can help bring us together, if she could find it—"

"You think she can do that?"

"It's our only hope."

Meliahs only knew how hard she had been trying to find such a tale, quietly, unbeknownst to those who wouldn't want her to find it under any circumstances. Now it was out in the open, an impossible undertaking revealed to a mostly hostile crowd.

"Her claims have given us a chance," Malord said, "a shot at a better future."

"Her claims are disputed by many," Petrid said.

"Precisely. Will you kill the only person in the Domain who can affirm our rights?"

The executioner flinched. The Domainers were far from convinced of Sariah's claims but after centuries of oppression living in the Barren Flats, they craved a better life as much as they wanted good land and uncorrupted water. The executioners were a people unto themselves, but they also lived in the harshness of the Domain and shared in the Domainers' hopes. Perhaps they understood what was at stake. On the other hand, with matters as they were, with the hatred of the Bloods simmering to a raging boil, who in the Domain would really favor the truth?

The chief executioner huddled with his peers in whispered discussion. Petrid listened, petting his left arm absentmindedly. Sariah noticed movement along his sleeve. The face of a brown-spotted miniature monkey darted from his ruffled cuff, a quick show of black eyes and tiny fangs, along with a chattering bark.

Lazar flashed Sariah one of his brilliant, reassuring smiles. Metelaus nodded, cautioning her for patience with a stern purse of lips from the depths of his salt-and-pepper beard. Kael kept his back to her, his eyes on the executioners and his hands poised on his loaded weapons belt.

"Will the justice gathering support atonement?" Petrid asked.

"That's why I'm here," Malord said. "They will be pleased by a reprieve."

Sariah understood Kael's complicated maneuvering now. He hadn't just been biding his time and waiting for the outcome of the gathering throughout the last few months after all. He had been engaged in a convoluted effort to preserve her life. It explained some of his sudden absences and journeys. It certainly explained this last trip as well. He hadn't gone to check on Ars's demesnes, as she had believed. He had gone to the gathering himself. She should have seen it sooner, but she had been too busy plotting on her own. Aye. Leave it to Kael to take his oath of protection before the justice gathering and beyond.

As her advocate, Malord hadn't been able to convince the justice gathering of her innocence. No one could have. But even after she had been found guilty, Kael and Malord had conspired to find a way in which the gathering could support the executioners' decision to sell atonement. It was no small accomplishment when considering her situation.

"Even if we were willing to sell atonement, other issues must be addressed," Petrid said. "It's unprecedented. She's a Goodlander with matching eyes. She's not of the Domain."

"She's my kin by the way of the blanket," Kael said. "She's my blood now."

It was shocking to hear their forbidden union proclaimed brazenly aloud, but it was also liberating, gratifying and thrilling, like the nights spent together in bodily conversations brimming with passion. She blinked away a rush of old fear.

The executioner still hesitated. "Will you stand for her if necessary?"

"I'll serve atonement with her."

The crowd murmured. Some familiar faces from Ars jeered. Sariah didn't know how exactly, but she knew Kael was giving beyond his own rights. She started to protest. Kael's hand was already in the air, forbidding her to speak.

"Are you sure the woman has the coin to purchase atonement?" the executioner asked.

Kael patted his pack. "I have the coin right here with me."

A whole pack full of coin? Sariah gaped. Kael had never measured wealth in coin and although she never lacked anything she needed in the Domain, she had never seen much coin among Kael's wares. Poverty was rampant in the Domain. Her wising profit was barely enough to purchase vellum and ink. Where had Kael found so much money?

It had to come from his lifelong roaming and land-healing earnings. It had to be next to everything he had. She couldn't let Kael do it. She couldn't let him spend all his coin on the likes of her. She got up, but before she could protest, a heavy hand landed on her shoulder.

"Don't you dare spoil Kael's negotiations," Metelaus whispered. He had materialized next to her, no doubt at Kael's silent behest. The brothers had an irritating way of working wordlessly in complete tandem. Sariah swore to herself that she would make it right. She would find a way to repay Kael her price.

The sight of the ready coin seemed to be the most persuasive argument thus far.

"Who will avow for the woman's compliance?" Petrid asked.

"I avow with my wiser's authority," Malord said.

"I avow with my marcher's right," Metelaus said.

"I avow with my runner's lead," Lazar said.

"The woman is lucky to have eminent friends and kin such as you," the executioner said. "What assurances will you grant?"

Malord's swarthy features darkened. "Is our eminence not good enough to grant you plenty of assurances?"

"Atonement is only granted for profit," Petrid said. "Death, on the other hand, is free for the woman."

Malord grimaced as if he had tasted sour limes. "I pledge the stone of Iluim to her cause."

Was the old stonewiser losing his wits?

"I pledge my runner's deck," Lazar said.

"And you?" the executioner asked Metelaus.

He hesitated. He had a wife and a host of children who could be rendered homeless by such an oath. Sariah didn't think he should imperil his family. She tried to say so, but he jumbled her protests with a stern hand over her mouth. "I pledge too."

Sariah groaned. It would do Metelaus good if Torana beat him senseless for the deed. They were all recklessly crazy, kin-sworn, noble and steadfast to her cause, but clearly mad. Anyone could see that.

"Will you be quiet now?" Metelaus withdrew his hand, testing her, knowing she was capable of betraying herself easily.

Sariah slumped down next to him in grudging concession.

"We're willing to grant atonement," the executioner said. "One month for each of Meliahs' nine sisters as is customary. The wiser must find this tale which can unite the Bloods. And she must bring it before us or she forfeits her life as decreed."

Too little time for too great a task. Sariah knew a bad deal when she heard one. She had been looking for just such proof for the last year. Yet she saw Kael's wisdom in the proposal. It had to be done. Nothing less would satisfy the executioners, the justice gathering, and ultimately, the Bloods.

"If she defaults, you forfeit your pledges," Petrid said. "We take great risk on this venture. Therefore we need further assurances to protect ourselves from default, potential losses and probable death. You are Sons of Ars. No other house is as praised or admired in the Domain. If the wiser defaults, we require Ars's earnings for three years *and* the Crags."

The crowd gasped. Metelaus growled like a wounded beast. Lazar paled, and even Malord, who was not of Ars, looked aggrieved. Sariah loathed the executioner. His smile was as chilling as his monkey's snarl. She understood he had a job to do, but did he really need to unleash his greed blindly on her kin?

"Fine." Kael spat the word as if it were poisonous.

Her life wasn't worth Ars's earnings, let alone the settlement's unique and profitable placement as guardians of the Crags, the best good water source around. It was also one of the few ranges of solid stone that remained unconsumed by the rot in the Domain, populated with valuable herds of goats which made life sustainable for Ars's people.

"I won't have it," she said.

Kael's first look at her was an incinerating glower that could have melted her bones as effectively as the rot. "Pay no heed to her," he said between clenched teeth. "She has no voice in the Domain. I speak for the woman."

The damn fool. But he was right. A Goodlander by birth, she had no rights in the Domain and was a mere spectator in the matter of her own life and death.

"Kael knows what he's doing," Metelaus whispered.

"I won't be the cause of Ars's ruin," Sariah whispered back.

"Then listen, so you can meet your obligations and we can all get out of here alive."

"The executioners are setting up this deal so that I'll fail. Can't you see? Why would they want me to return with the tale when they stand to make huge profits from my failure?"

"Don't you think Kael knows that?"

"It's not right, Metelaus. Give me a few moments of distraction and I'll be gone."

"Look around. You'll be dead before you blink. What good will you be then?"

"Kael is mad putting out Ars like that."

"If I were he, and Torana were you, I'd do the same thing."

Sariah sunk her face in her hands. She had made her share of bad deals before, but this one promised to be the most costly of all. It was just a fast way for the executioners to enrich themselves, of trumping prosperous Ars and overtaking its prominence. No matter how kind they were, people in Ars were going to be furious with her for putting their livelihoods at risk, for threatening to destroy what they had built since the execration. Sariah couldn't bear the thought of ruining the only kin she had ever known, the very people who had granted her a home.

"It's done then." The executioner accepted Kael's pack. "Remember. Nine months to the sunrise. One last thing. A sentence for a sentence. We require an irrevocable condition to the entire agreement in the form of an edict."

"An edict. Of course." Rage burned in Kael's gaze and simmered in Sariah's soul like a twin.

The executioner smiled in naked triumph. "I hereby decree the wiser banished from the Domain."

Four

PETRID WIELDED THE banishment bracelet with a snake charmer's deliberate care. At first sight, it seemed to be no more than an intricately ornamented band adorned with precious stones, the type of ancient trinket the wealthy and the powerful liked to flaunt to each other in the Goodlands. Nine square links connected to each other by smaller round hinges made up the sinuous gold bracelet. Each link was filigreed and decorated with different and elaborate designs. Stunning opalescent red crystals of a kind Sariah had never seen before were expertly inlaid on each link.

Sariah had never worn anything like it. She had never fancied rich dress or ornamental jewels. She was a stonewiser, for Meliahs' sake, pledged to the stones' austere ways. But she had to admit to the bracelet's outstanding workmanship, to its exuberant if gaudy beauty, to the shock that the mere sight of it provoked. It evoked the Blood's sumptuous past, the luxury and prosperity of the Old World, the catastrophic losses to the rot. The bracelet was not only incongruent with herself. Like a knife to the heart, it struck a painful contrast between the promising past and the barren present.

When Petrid laid it carefully on her arm, Sariah realized she had allowed herself to be misled by the bracelet's striking appearance. It was by no means a harmless trinket. It was an object of treachery. It didn't feel like any metal Sariah knew. On the contrary, if felt warm and malleable, oddly resolved to cling to her skin and peculiarly heavy.

Whispering a ritual prayer in the old language, Petrid brought her wrist close to his mouth. His lips hovered over the bracelet's ornate clasp, a tenth link, smaller than the rest, shaped like a striking red-pupiled eye. He kissed the golden pin dangling from the little chain with a lover's passion, with a believer's zealous faith. Then he slid the pin into the clasp's hinges and pressed it into place.

What happened next was more than strange. It was astounding. In one subtle pulse, the eye on the clasp disappeared under a silvery lid. The bracelet's round hinges contracted and vanished. Like a coiled serpent settling to feed on its kill, the bracelet fit itself snugly around her wrist.

What mysterious force fueled the remarkable bracelet? Sariah couldn't begin to guess. She didn't believe in magic. Instead, she believed in ignorance, a condition which rendered people vulnerable to the unexplained. Could there be a wising on the bracelet? Where stones lurked, wisings could easily hide. Aye. It had to be. She couldn't wait to discover how the bracelet worked.

The chief executioner exhaled a long breath, all too glad to finish the job. "Nine months to honor Meliahs' nine sisters," he said. "Nine months to find and submit the tale you seek. Pray thus for their gifts to Pride, Courage, Strength, Hope, Shrewdness, Loyalty, Generosity and Faith. But never trust on the last of the nine, Mercy, for she squanders her gifts on others and has little compassion for her bearer. When the time comes, she will not hesitate. She'll suck you dry of your essence before abandoning you to your sworn fate."

Sariah couldn't repress the shiver that ran the length of her spine. She didn't understand Petrid's strange words, but she remembered every one of them. She would have to think more on that later. The gaudy bracelet felt too heavy on her arm. It was a mark of her banishment, a warning to all Domainers that she was nonexistent in their world and that a meeting with her, however brief, was liable to cause great losses.

"My brothers will complete the transaction," Kael said in a flat tone, as if he was vying for a sack of flour or a load of potatoes. "We'll be taking our leave now."

"Not just yet." The broad-nosed, bearded man who had shot at Sariah stood on the executioner's deck blocking their path. "I want my turn at her."

"If I recall correctly," Kael said, "you shot your last stone and killed the other woman."

"I paid to shoot at *this* woman."

Kael's eyes narrowed on the man's face. "I know you."

"What if you do?" The man squared his bulky shoulders.

"You're Josfan. You used to be a roamer, until Leah ran you out."

"That was a while back," Josfan said. "I follow the executioners now."

"I can't imagine you had many options after the roamers' gathering upheld Leah's view."

"What does that have to do with anything? I demand my shot."

"I'm afraid it can't be. I have no quarrel with you, but we've struck a settlement with the executioners. The execution is off. Stand aside."

"I paid good coin for four shots at her. I'm still owed one."

"My brothers will refund your coin."

"Do you think coin will buy her way out of this?" The man's spiked club bounced against his palm. "Think again, Son of Ars. Princes and lords are a thing of the past in the Domain. I'm afraid they're all dead."

It happened too fast. A blur of half-moon swords exploded from Kael's weapons belt. The clash of steel prevailed over the crowd's cries. The man's club flew from his bleeding hand. His belt dropped to the ground in lieu of his guts. When it was over, he writhed at Kael's feet with twin swords angling at his throat.

"Next time, take the coin," Kael said. "Princes and lords are a thing of the past, but I am here to stay."

He wiped his swords on the man's tunic and returned the weapons to his scabbards. Before Sariah could say a word, he plucked her from the executioners' deck and, heaving her over his shoulder, carried her through the grumbling crowd. Without a weave to protect her legs from the dead water, Sariah had no option but to accept the favor.

The rabble was even more incensed than before. Some were bitter because they had been denied the spectacle of her death. Some were mad because they had lost their bets or their chance for profit. Some were friends of the defeated shooter and some were simply angry at the injustice. Yet they didn't dare pelt her openly as they had done before, mostly because they respected and feared Kael.

Kael's traveling deck was just arriving, pulled by some of his fastest runners, loaded and ready to go. Kael dumped her feet-first on the deck and pointed toward the shelter. "Don't come out unless I say so." He turned and huddled with the runners, whispering muted orders.

Sariah swallowed an angry retort and did what she was told, only because she realized the situation was precarious. She didn't have to wait long. Kael wore his pulling harness when he entered. He ignored her thoroughly, going about the shelter with his usual methodical efficiency, inspecting the goods stored there with a measure of haste.

He must have known that the executioners didn't feed their wards, because he dropped a skin full of the strong drink Domainers favored on her lap. The spicy brew soothed her parched throat and warmed her empty stomach. He also produced a huge chunk of dark bread and a wedge of buttery cheese from his pack. Sariah didn't realize how hungry she was until she bit down on the glorious offering.

He poured water from the barrel in a bucket and parked it in front of her. "Clean those eel bites. They like to fester. Eat and rest. We have hard going ahead."

He was gone from the shelter right away. The deck began to move, first slowly and then increasingly faster, until it ran at a good clip. Daft man, not overly expressive either. No sense in complaining, though. He had come.

She took stock of the shelter while she ate. Kael must have arranged to have provisions retrieved from Ars before he came to the executioners' camp. She was glad to see some of her things as well, the few garments she owned, her pack, her stones, her leatherbound engrossments and annotations, her scribing floor desk and her tool baskets. The man was a stubborn ox, but she had to admit that when it came to planning, he was brilliant.

With a lick of her fingers, she finished her meal. She washed her wounds, and in doing so, discovered the grime of the last two days. She scrubbed herself mercilessly. She may be a rogue stonewiser, but she had always abided by the Guild's cleanliness rules. Besides, she liked to smell fresh.

Clean and fed, she clad herself with a fresh shift from her pack and sat down on the pallet to examine the banishment bracelet. It was an object that defied reason. Its mysterious power evoked the stones, yet it was obviously a thing of the Domain. A number of Domainer coppers could be seen engraved in Generosity's link, a Domainer buckler was emblazoned on Pride's link, and two Domainer half-moon swords were crossed on Courage's link. She found no trace of the hinges and clasps that had been there before. She tried to pull the thing over her knuckles, but it wouldn't fit. On the contrary, it seemed to tighten in proportion to her efforts. Strange. Was her imagination playing tricks on her? Nay. When she fiddled with the bracelet, it stuck to her arm with the grit of a thousand suckers.

Nine links. Nine months. That's all the time she had to find the tale that the executioners' required. At the breaking of the wall, Mistress Grimly, the Guild's Prime Hand, had appropriated the seven twin stones that contained the tale of the Blood's split. By now those stones were buried or worse, destroyed. But what Sariah needed now was different. She needed a tale that would help unify the divided Blood, heal the wounds of a broken world, and build consensus among the fiercest of foes. By Meliahs, she needed a miracle, a stone tale capable of fostering peace on a warring world.

She didn't have much in terms of promising leads, only the work she had done this last year and the fragmented information she had wised from other stones. She also had Zemi's words, the final ranting of the intrusion created by Zeminaya, the most powerful stonewiser of her time. *The justice of the execration ends with me,* the intrusion had said. *The Shield dies with me. The Blood we split and the proof is with the bane of the pure. The rot we made ourselves, because we created simmering fire and flesh, we broke Meliahs' pact, we forsook labor and sweat.*

She remembered the shock of realizing the truth, the desperation of knowing what neither one of the Bloods was likely to accept—that they were both part of the same blood. Old Blood wisers had created the New Blood to labor in its stead. But as the rot destroyed the Old World, the oppressed New Blood had turned on their creators, expelled the Old Blood from the Goodlands, and condemned them to die in the Rotten Domain under the false belief they were the New Blood.

She had known then that the revelation would be hard to accept for both Bloods. What she hadn't known was that both Bloods would find her discoveries beyond disagreeable, untenable. Far from crumbling, the powers that had ruthlessly ruled the world survived to terrorize it. Her formidable foes had doubled and multiplied. The Guild. The Shield. Mistress Grimly. Master Arron. In the throes of a changing world, her enemies, and yes, even some of her friends, favored her death for different if valid reasons. The executioners' bid for her life was just one example of the dangers that stalked her. Kael, the inveterate cynic, had seen it for what it was. Sariah had to be careful. She didn't have Kael's battle-honed instincts.

Was there a lost tale out there, a forgotten stone capable of bringing unity to a divided world? And if there was, would she be able to find it before it was too late? She had one sentence from the intrusion to guide her. *The Blood we split and the proof is with the bane of the pure.* Who were the pure? What and where was their bane? How could it lead her to find the tale she sought?

Unable to find a way to undo the bracelet, Sariah fetched a needle chisel from her tool basket and began to probe the clasp for a weak point.

"Ouch!" She dropped the chisel. Had the bracelet just stung her? With the pain fresh in her mind, she couldn't blame her imagination, but she grabbed the chisel and tried to force open the silvery lid again. The pain returned, like a wasp sting, only worse.

What kind of power did the bracelet conceal? And where was the power hidden? It had to be in the stones. Anticipating a trap, or at the very least, a snaring trance, Sariah braced for a bruising contact. Cautiously, she tapped on one of the red stones. Nothing. Perhaps it needed a firmer contact. She tapped harder. Nothing again. She rubbed the stone against her palm, first lightly, then more firmly. Complete and utter blankness. Odd. Maybe the wising was concealed in one of the other stones?

Surely the stones had to be the key. She tried all the tricks she knew. She queried all the stones individually and then together. She did it gingerly at first, then more forcefully. Nothing. The nine stones on the bracelet were cold and silent like the dead. The eye on the clasp remained stubbornly closed.

She wasn't going to give up so easily. If stonewising didn't give her any answers, she would try something else. She grit her teeth and applied her chisel to the links' junctions. There should have been hinges there, but there weren't any. Instead, the bracelet flowed seamlessly and her chisel found no place for purchase. She even tried to pry out the red crystals. Her pain was for nothing. There was no weakness or leverage to be found on the bracelet. All nine crystals appeared to be one with the cuff.

She tried to saw it off, first with her knife, then with one of Kael's spare rotfish fangs. The bracelet's gold finish didn't yield, not even a tiny chip or a slight dent. Her wrist was a different story. It was bruised and chafed, and it hurt as if she was sawing off her hand. Was she going crazy or was she suffering the bracelet's vengeance on her own flesh?

"Enough of this." She picked up one of Kael's axes, braced her wrist over her writing desk, and landed a well-aimed blow. The pain that exploded in her skull blinded her and left her seeing in shades of black and red.

"What by the rot are you doing?"

Sariah jerked to her feet. She had been so involved in trying to rid herself of the accursed bracelet that she hadn't realized that the deck had stopped moving and that Kael, with his pulling harness still on, had entered the shelter.

"I was trying to get this off." Wasn't it obvious? She was still reeling from the pain.

Kael snatched the ax from her hands. "You're going to kill yourself. You can't get that thing off. Nobody but the chief executioner can. Think, Sariah—what good would it be to them if you, or anybody else for that matter, could take off the bracelet?"

"You mean to tell me that there isn't a way?"

"Not one that involves you surviving the attempt."

"Lovely then. And to think I despise gaudy jewelry."

"Don't make light of this."

Time to face him squarely. "You shouldn't have come." The intensity of his black and green stare locked on her. The harmonious flow of his straight nose, the defined lines of his tightly pressed lips and the sleek construction of his jaw would have made for a beautiful face. But the scarred eyebrow and the discordant black eye broke all sense of facial harmony and added a perpetually fierce expression to his features.

The broken brow lifted on his forehead. "Do you want me to go then?"

"Aye. You should go." And then, "Maybe."

She was all too aware of his nearness, of the irrepressible sense of wholeness that enveloped her when he embraced her, of the inevitable course of his mouth toward hers. Her senses were lost to his intensity. She breathed him, the heated air he exhaled, the distant hint of laurel clinging to his hair, the salty scent of days of travel, toil and sweat, mixed with the smell of the Barren Flats' acid emissions. She could feel the hunger in him, in his shoulders' tension, in his hands' clutch around her waist. Her own hunger was no less rebellious, wanting to burst from where she kept it contained. It was always like this between them, a struggle of wills, a battle with restraint.

"We have very little time." In a swift motion, he pulled the shift over her head, pushed her back on the blankets, and parted her legs with his knee. All the while, his lips were intent on hers, drinking her breath and filling her mouth with the taste of him, as if he knew she needed the strokes of his tongue to survive.

She slid her hands under his shirt and ran them over the contours of his familiar body. He was tall and powerful, but not bulky with the pretentious extravagance of muscle built for show. Instead, his neck, back and arms were strong from pulling his deck through the Barren Flats. His legs were lithe from jumping and running in the dead water. Her fingers tripped over the scars on his chest. No one knew those scars as well as she did, because some of those were her fault too, and always a stark reminder she had almost lost him once.

"It's been too long," he mumbled apologetically while he fumbled with his breeches' ties. "A fortnight. Wicked goddess, I thought I was ailing."

She knew the thirst and suffered it willingly because the emptiness of their separation, terrible as it was, was better than giving him up. Theirs was an unusual bond, tried and tested, as demanding as a twin stone trance and as fundamental to her existence as breathing air. She didn't try to understand it, not anymore. Her wiser's mind was at a loss to comprehend her heart's mysteries. The lust she couldn't explain either, so she acknowledged it in the only way she could, granting him berth.

He didn't bother with the rest of his clothes. He came into her firmly, claiming occupancy of every space he bore in her body's depths. But his hands were tender when they traced the bruise on her forehead, when they spanned her waist and cupped her breasts with a connoisseur's delicacy. The black and green eyes beheld her as if she was a hard-earned prize. She should have been afraid, knowing full well from her years at the Guild that done roughly the sport could cause her injury, but she was not scared.

Her body was the gift she gave him freely. Raised to serve without a mind for the self, it was no small privilege to her. In the ways of the Guild, she hadn't known parents or kin. She had only known the obligations of her leases, the services required by her masters and mistresses, and the use of her body for others' pleasure, a bothersome, most often harmless chore which was a part of her duties. Then she had met Kael and everything changed. She thought she knew why.

"May I?" she whispered in his ear.

"Aye, Sariah. Always when we're together like this."

She pressed her hands against his back. His emotions burned through her palms, reaching out to stroke her mind like the clearest of stone tales. *Need. Lust. Affection.* It had been the flood of his affection that had percolated through the drought of duty and allowed her scorched soul to discover her own reservoir. It was that affection that touched her now, transforming something common and lurid into a gratifying sharing for the generous purpose of each others' free and willful pleasure.

The clips on his pulling harness jiggled at his pace. His weave chafed against her skin. She could feel the struggle in him, the lust advancing on the affection, not suppressing it, not exactly, but teaming up with his need to burst his restraint.

"When I saw you there—" He couldn't finish.

"I'm here now." She smiled at her own uncharitable wickedness, relishing the power that a thrust and a twist granted her body over his, appreciating her own boldness, the shivers that shot through him, the pleasures she unleashed.

His eyes narrowed to slits. The furious grin turned up at the corners of his mouth. He pinned her wrists in his hand, cutting her connection to his emotions. It prevented her from outright witnessing the barbaric surge of the beast she cherished. The inevitable collision loomed in his eyes' luminous horizon. And to think that until she met him, she hadn't known such bliss existed.

She gave herself to the moment, because the moment was all she had. But she knew better. Danger, fear and despair watched undeterred from the dark gallery of her impending fate.

Five

WHEN HER MIND next reclaimed her senses, they were both breathless and tangled in each other's arms, still joined, satisfied and yet starting again, lips engaged with kisses and tongues.

"We have to stop," Kael murmured.

She was lost when their mouths parted as a result of his will power, not hers. Curse Meliahs, claiming her service thrice, to the stones, to the legacy, to the only man she had ever wanted to serve of her own accord. The attachment was as grave as a deadly ailment and as debilitating as the stone madness, and yet she, a wiser trained to care only for the stones, relished him like the rarest stone. It was an unthinkable bias for a stonewiser, but at least it was one she had chosen for herself.

He leaned his forehead against hers and exhaled slowly, reclaiming his discipline and hopefully hers. She sensed him escaping her body's clutch. Then he was gone from her arms and she mourned the loss of his touch.

He inspected the eel bite on her leg. "You skipped the salve."

"Don't fret. It's just a nick. I had a stone, you know. I dropped it like a witless ninny."

"Witless? Nay." He rummaged through his sack. "Witless was to dismiss the runners. Witless was to tell Torana not to fetch me. Witless was to leave Ars before I returned."

"What else did you expect me to do?"

He rolled his eyes, a gesture that always heated Sariah's not-so-tepid blood. "Use your good sense?"

"And blow up our deck and Ars? Get the children killed?"

He pulled out a flat jar from where he scooped a good bit of yellow salve and began to spread it over the eel bite. "Do you know what scares me?"

"Not the executioners, that I know."

"You believe it."

"What?"

"That you can manage on your own. Always. That asking for help, or waiting for it, is somehow wrong."

"The executioners came before their time, that's all."

He worked the salve into her wound until she winced. "You can't go at this alone. You'll die if you try."

It was her burden, her duty. And better she than he. "It's not so good for your lungs to run the water as fast as you did. And your leg, you're still regaining your strength—"

"My lungs and my leg are fine. I can do my duty well enough."

Duty. She hated the word. She had never wanted to be duty to him. Not to him.

He finished with the salve and stuffed the jar back in his bag. "You should have sent for me right away. You should have dallied and delayed. Somebody tipped off the executioners. They knew what they were doing."

"Ars. That's what they want. And you gave it to them."

The black-eyed glower was dark like a bad omen. "Do you think so? You're alive. You're with me. We can manage the rest."

"The deal you made is too expensive, too risky, for you, for your kin, for Ars. We've worked hard, I give you that, but our leads have been weak."

Light twinkled in his eyes.

Sariah's heart raced. "What?"

"You shouldn't hold me in such low regard when I hedge my bets. I learned from the best. You. Remember?"

Did he know? Sariah probed cautiously. "Have you learned something new?"

"Me?" His chuckle was devoid of mirth. "Not me, not really. You, on the other hand..."

Sariah's breath caught in her throat. She hadn't told anyone, especially not him. "How?"

"You're a bad liar to start. And I live with you. Recall that? I knew you were up to something even as I left."

Sariah wished she could deny it, but her face was hot like a chunk of flaming coal.

"There's the small matter of your bag." He gestured toward the pack now stowed among her wares. "The one I found on the stone-wiser's deck, packed nice and tidy with a few days' provisions."

She gulped dryly.

"Never mind that you sent away my runners. That's a small detail, really. Where were you going, Sariah?" he asked softly, a poor attempt at masking his temper.

"I—Well—"

"North, I think. That's why I started pulling this way."

How could he have known?

"You packed your heavy mantle."

"Oh." She felt like the dumbest wench in the Domain.

"I thought Davenhorn at first, seeing you packed for about four days, but then I spoke to Mia and she said you recently visited with Torana's friend, Agatha."

Damn the man, there wasn't a daft bone in the whole of his body. Well, she hadn't done anything wrong. She was free to do as she wished and visiting a friend was not a gravity. Was it?

He stared at her with a stern look of disappointment on his face. She hated that look and she loathed the thought of letting him down, but she had no illusions he would understand her reasoning. For good and for bad, he was too righteous to consider life's little nuances, too virtuous to admit to the usefulness of vice, and too pure of mind and heart to embrace something as corruptive and convenient as a touch of deception here and there.

"Nafa, I think." He startled her out of her thoughts. "Agatha hails from there and you would have wanted to know as much about the settlement as you could. I hope you got good directions, Sariah. The Domain is unforgiving to the unprepared and the foolish."

"Of course I got good directions. Do you think I'm stupid?"

"Only occasionally." He quieted her mounting indignation with a finger to her lips. "Why did you lie to me?"

"I didn't lie to you."

"Even Mia knows better than that. Omission is no less of a lie. Neither does it count as an attempt at half-truth."

He was right, of course, but she wasn't ready to admit it. Besides, she was no mindless wench, no empty-headed scoundrel running scams for profit. She was a stonewiser, albeit a flawed one, but one who understood her duty and the importance of the legacy she had undertaken. She was trapped, angry and unable to do right no matter how much she tried.

"I'm not your lease and you're not my conscience."

"But we are one by way of the blanket. And you, you promised me truth."

Aye, that she had, at death's door, at the foot of the quartering block, no less. For what little credit he gave her, she tried. Misery must have been evident on her face because Kael stopped scolding her and appraised her quietly.

"What's in Nafa?"

"A name." Small as it was, she jumped at the chance to make up for her lie. "I can show you if you'd like."

"Later, for sure." He stood up and began to check the ropes securing their sparse cargo. "We need to go. To Nafa."

"*I* need to go to Nafa. Not you."

"Ah." He crossed his arms and tilted his head, an irritating pose that begged for a good boxing to his ears. "And how will you travel the Domain without me?"

"I was going to hire a puller." Did he expect her to acknowledge that she was woefully ignorant and unable to navigate the Barren Flats alone, useless, like a blind and lame mule trudging through the quicksand dunes? "I don't want to fight with you."

"Me? Fight? Naah. You're already doing that."

"Kael, this isn't your battle. You're needed in Ars."

"They'll have to do without us for a while."

"You can't come. I won't have it."

"You can't stop me." He paused from checking the knots around the water barrel. "Is it that you don't trust me, Sariah?"

She spied the wounded doubt in his gaze, the suspicion she didn't think him fit or able to assist her.

"No, nay, no. It's not that, it's just that—" She had a vision of him on the quartering block. "I can't—I won't have you hurt. Not again."

"I see." The dominance of his black eye softened, allowing the wondrous glimmer of his green eye to overtake his gaze. "It turns out that behind your stonewiser's icy shell, you are made of feathers and roses after all." He stroked her face. "Spiny feathers and thorned roses, mind you, but soft and sweet-smelling nevertheless."

She found herself tucked against his breast. His heart's steady beat and his laughter's muffled sound filtered mutedly through his chest. There was peace in his embrace, and warmth. How could she be willing to part from him when all she wanted was him? But how could she allow him to face his own destruction on her account when she cared only for him?

"I'll be fine, wiser, as long as you are with me."

She never knew what to say when he said things like that to her. "I swear to you. I won't let the executioners have Ars."

"I believe you." He tilted her chin up and met her eyes. "You're the surest bet I know, that is, unless you get yourself killed along the way."

"I'm going to pay you back, Kael. All that coin. In the Guild, a loan is always paid with good profit."

His eyes swooped down on her like a pair of hunting hawks. "You haven't heard a word I said. You share my blankets, you share my coin."

"In the Guild—"

"The Guild rot to dung. I don't give a damn how it was done at the Guild. It's different now. Understand?"

Sariah was startled by his reaction. Truth was, despite her efforts, she didn't always understand him. She had trouble conceiving a world where a stonewiser's worth wasn't measured in coin, where her failures were not penalized with debts and punishment, where her person wasn't someone's means to profit or gratification, and where truth mattered. Meliahs knew she wanted to belong to the kinder world outside the Guild, but sometimes, the break between both worlds seemed too wide to breach.

"I can't go back to Ars, to my pupils, to Mia. Can I?"

"Under a banishment edict you can't live among the Domainers and they can't accept you among them without incurring heavy penalties."

She would miss Mia and the other children. She would miss living free and among kin, even though it was new and often strange for her. A terrible thought occurred to her. "Will you incur those fines if you stay with me?"

"I pledged as I did so that those fines don't apply to me."

She breathed a sigh of relief. "But how can they know if I speak to someone or if someone offers me shelter?"

"They'll know. The executioners mind their stakes and they'll mind you all the better. There are many in the Domain who don't want you to succeed. They would rather live under the shadow of the past than embrace the uncertainties of the future. They're not ready to exchange the old burdens for the new responsibilities. We'll have to be very careful."

Sariah thought of the peril ahead, of the scars he bore, of those days when she thought he was dying. Then she thought of the eels, mostly because her worst fears were stirring all at once.

"It's done and over." Kael kissed the top of her head. "The next time you see an eel, you'll be the one doing the eating."

Sometimes, she swore he could read her thoughts. His mouth was delicious on her lips, a bit too quick for her taste, but liable to linger if she tried.

"You know this is going to be dangerous."

"Aye, love," he mumbled against her mouth. "No way out but forward."

The need boiled in her blood, the pervasive little flame that whooshed to rage when he beheld her with those mismatched eyes of his. Sariah thought she would scream when he stopped mid-kiss and tilted his head to listen. She couldn't detect any sounds, but her belly went to knots when she saw his face's expression.

He scrambled to his feet. "We'd best get going."

It dawned on Sariah that Kael had been uncharacteristically impatient this day, restless, driven and fast at everything he had done, including making love to her, something he usually enjoyed prolonging for his benefit and hers. Weave on hand, she followed him out of the shelter.

"What is it?"

"They're coming." He clipped the pulling ropes to his harness, jumped in the knee-high water and starting pulling.

Sariah shoved her legs in her weave, donned her harness and followed him to the water. He was already pulling hard and fast, a single-minded ox at the plow. She could barely keep up with him.

"Who's coming?"

"The mob."

"What do you mean, the mob?"

"The executioners' followers. They have their rights."

"What rights?"

"As long as they paid their watching fees, once today ends, the executioners' followers can kill you and collect for it."

"What?"

"It's the law. It's complicated, but the gist of it is that the executioners' followers pay dues to run markets and peddle goods during the executions. When an execution is not completed and they don't get a full return on their dues, they have a right to augment their earnings by going after the condemned and selling the corpse back to the executioners."

"But you paid good coin for atonement!"

"You misunderstand atonement. The executioners only agreed because it's so damn profitable for them. We paid for a way out of the nets this day and up to nine months' time. It was the only way to spare your life. There are no assurances. On the contrary. Atonement was granted *after* the executioners' followers paid their dues. That turns them into a very greedy and driven mob. There's a good deal of coin at stake here."

Meliahs help her. Sariah turned to spy the uneven shadows breaking the horizon's straight line. Pockets of people and decks. They were coming. She matched Kael's wide strides as best she could, propelled by dread growing in direct proportion to the night's coming darkness.

Six

NAFA WAS A tidy, orderly settlement, a concentric array of decks surrounding a broken ridge where a sulfurous flow of water bubbled through a travertine basin to the surface. The water flowed scalding hot, Kael had explained, but once cooled, it was safe to drink if not pleasant to taste, granting the settlement a chance to thrive in the inhospitable flats. Sariah stared at the green and purple lights dancing above the settlement's center like the giant flames of an enormous hearth.

"The gas that surfaces with the water combined with the Barren Flats' own vapors account for the play of lights," Kael said.

"Amazing." Beauty abounded even in the most wretched of places.

Kael halted and released the claws to anchor the deck. "This is close enough. We're far away from the main approaches to the settlement here. As long as we keep dark, no one should notice us. Who is it that I'm looking for?"

"We're looking for a man called Leandro. I'll go with you."

"You can't. You're banished, remember? And we don't want to call attention to ourselves, on account of the mob."

The executioners had made an already difficult task even harder with their banishment edict. "But—"

"Trust me. If there's such a man as Leandro, I'll find him. Stay here. Keep your eyes open. Don't allow anyone to approach the deck. Understand?"

"I have my stones ready."

"Good." Kael stole a quick kiss. "I'll be back soon."

The full blow of the banishment sentence struck Sariah as she watched Kael wade through the flats until he was lost in the penumbral shadows. It was early evening. The distant sound of voices

and music teased her. Irked and maybe a little jealous of Kael's
freedom, she went back in the shelter. She made sure the door and
windows were well-shuttered and covered by the thick hangings
before she lit the lamp. No sense in revealing her location to anyone who may be following them. And better to keep busy than to
dwell on her misfortunes. She had work to do.

With practiced ease, she mixed the iron salts with a measure of
tanning and water. She added some gum, soot and a touch of cobalt to make her favorite blue ink. She dipped her brush, tried out
the ink on a piece of used parchment, and found it was too thin
and runny. She added a bit of oil and tried it again. Still too thin.
Every hall in the Guild had its own ink recipe. Sariah turned to her
own hall's secrets, the ingredient that made the Hall of Scribe's ink
the rave of the keep—crumbled spider webs.

She sprinkled a pinch of the dust, stirring quickly, until the ink
turned to the right consistency. She had been delighted to discover
that the rot had no bearing on the host of assorted, impressively
sized bugs that made their home in the Domain, including spiders.
And when it came to web-spinning spiders, Sariah hadn't yet met
one she didn't like.

This time, the ink worked perfectly. She sifted through her
bag of stones and lined up some eleven stones of different colors,
shapes, and sizes. She had acquired these stones through trades
and purchases over the last year. They presented a mismatch of
tales, some more revealing than others, some boring, some exact-
ing, some vague, all different except for one thing—they contained
tales of roamers' explorations, very important because Sariah was
hunting for a particular roamer's tale.

Her reasoning was sound. Before the wall was broken, the only
ones who could have come across the people who called themselves the pure were roamers. Traditionally, roamers were specially
trained Domainers who crossed the wall into the Goodlands in
defiance of the Third Covenant to gather information and negotiate the forbidden trade that kept the tribes alive despite the
execration's forced isolation. Kael was such a roamer. With his
help, months ago, she had begun to look for stones that collected
the oral traditions of the Domainers' favorite tales.

Her search had only become more complicated as stones, like people, began to flow illicitly through the wall's many breaches, but despite the confusion, she had discovered an active market for tales. People from different settlements traded stones which they then took for translation to the few wisers who had survived the Shield's purges in the Domain. In fact, entire festivals were devoted to telling these stories, and tale collections derived from such festivals, while not common, could be found occasionally. She had spent much time and no small amount of coin in locating such festival stones.

Sariah picked up the last of her neatly lined stones. She had wised it before, but she wanted to make sure. It was a smallish stone, a basic black basalt, opaque, unpolished, and rather lumpy, but it reached out to her mind with a nice call that tickled her spine and reminded her of Kael's breath on her neck. With a quiet rustle, the trance welcomed her into the stone tale.

In the tale, a stout, grizzled woman stood before a fire that enlivened the deep furrows on her forehead. "I'm Imal, Primer for Catar's festival, and I hereby give witness to the tales told at the turn of the chill gathering to the best of my recollection."

Imal was a prolific storyteller. The task of reviewing all those tales had been daunting. Sariah had sat for days witnessing Imal's narratives, until she fashioned a new way of skimming through the tales, a skip-and-jump approach which would have drawn a steep fine at the keep but allowed her to go from one tale to the other quickly.

She applied this new method now, as she scanned through hundreds of tales to find the right one. The adventures Imal told were colorful and wide spanning. She had trouble remembering places and names, but she still told a good story. It didn't take Sariah long to home in to the particular tale that interested her. It related a roamer's encounter with the clawed terrors, spawns of beasts that inhabited some distant place where no one dared to go for fear of their lives.

Sariah didn't believe in monsters. Instead, she believed in fear. Any beast, especially if unknown, became a monster in the eyes of the frightened. Imal didn't grant a visual tale of the terrors because she had not seen them, but she did mention that on a roamer's account, these monsters guarded what she translated from the old tongue as the purity of the land.

It was a wild tale, most likely based on hearsay, probably embellished by someone's vivid imagination, but Sariah's heart still raced when she heard it. It was the only allusion vaguely related to the pure she had been able to find, and she had searched hard and thoroughly. If she hadn't been able to confirm a source, she may have overlooked the tale as a coincidence. Instead, she deepened her recognizance.

"Back." She pressed beyond the tale. "Beyond Imal."

It took a great deal of effort and strength to press a tale. It wasn't something the Guild taught. On the contrary, it was a forbidden skill, one she had learned from Zemi, the intrusion who had led her through the seven twin stones' wising. Her efforts were rewarded again. Sariah witnessed the storyteller who had first told the story to Imal, standing on the roof of a deck shelter, surrounded by an attentive audience and reciting the tale of the pure. A mother sheltered her child's ears when the man told about the monsters, but most people grinned and giggled when he spoke.

"Back," Sariah commanded. "Beyond Imal, beyond this storyteller."

A sharp whistle pierced her eardrums and screeched in her mind. Pain stabbed at the back of her eyes. No wonder the Guild prohibited the practice of tale pressing. A less experienced wiser could be fatally hurt. Not Sariah. She would sport a headache akin to a canundro hangover tomorrow, but she would be fine after that.

The tale buckled and swayed, torn from its hinges, revealing a tenuous scene where the storyteller spoke to yet another man, a pale and ashen fellow whose face sported the rough stubble of a scruffy beard and strange, anxious eyes. Indeed, his tightly contracted pupils were encased in small black and gray irises, swimming aimlessly in a web of busted capillaries.

"I tell you the truth," Leandro said. "I saw it with my own eyes. Monsters, I say, to protect the pure."

"Come on, man, you want me to add a wild tale to my range?" the storyteller said. "My audience will know your tale for a fake. My reputation will be ruined."

"It's not fake, I tell you. Truth. All truth."

"Did you find them?" the other man asked. "Did you find the pure?"

Leandro's lips drooped. "Them monsters. Wouldn't let me pass. All truth. All the others. Dead."

"It's a strange tale," the storyteller said, "but I'll be fair, I may use it someday. A little horror always works up a crowd around the fire." He dropped a tarnished coin in the man's dirty hands. "Don't bet the whole of that coin. Get something to eat and hang on to your wits if you can. Be well, my friend." The already tenuous tale blurred. The link began to fade.

"Back." Sariah's mind pressed harder, against the pain, above the screech. "A name. A place."

There was a bump in the link, a halt on the flow and an unhealthy reverse that squeezed Sariah's stomach. The storyteller's face reappeared on the tale like the dead recalled from Meliahs' yonder. His lips moved out of step with the sound. "Be well, my friend," he stuttered. "Be well, my friend, Leandro of Nafa."

□ ■ □

The stone dated to a recent festival. Examining the tale's contents and fashions, the exchange between Leandro and the storyteller seemed recent as well. Sariah exhaled slowly, allowing her mind to relax. She dipped her brush in the ink and set it to the parchment to record her wising. A very faint noise interrupted her concentration.

A ripple's quiet murmur. A silent dribble of drops. A foot, rising slowly out of the water. A year ago, she would have thought nothing of a ripple and a drip in the vast expanse of dead water, but now her ears were attuned to the flats and trained to understand the dangers. The deck swayed imperceptibly. Whoever was coming for her was good. Sariah reached for her rotfish fang dirk, the one Kael had been training her to use. She tucked herself to one side of the shuttered door. A trickle of sweat ran the length of her spine. She waited.

The sudden attack came not through the door, as Sariah expected, but from the side. A long weaved body crashed through the small window and landed in a crouch, facing her. Sariah remembered her basics. Survey your enemy. Find the strengths. Find the weaknesses.

The trouble was the warrior before her seemed to be all strength and no weaknesses. He was a full head taller than she was. Muscles bulged on his upper arms and shoulders. A long lithe leg struck first, aiming at Sariah's dirk. Sariah blocked the kick, but found herself trapped in the corner between the assailant and the wall. A gleaming hatchet descended on her like the belch's rage. Sariah blocked the blow with her forearms. She feinted high but came up from beneath, seeking her opponent's underbelly. Her blade clashed against the hatchet instead.

Sariah barely stepped back in time to avoid a hammer to the head. With blades on one side, a hammer head on the other and topped by a wicked spike, the hatchet was a fearful weapon. Sariah tried to reach for her pocket but the assailant anticipated her move. The ax slashed through Sariah's weave, ripping her pocket open, spilling the stones on the floor. She tried to make the stones burst, but without her palm's recent contact, the stones didn't work. The hatchet's blade bounced off her banishment bracelet, shocking her with a painful jolt. The pain propelled Sariah forward. She managed a fist to her opponent's face. She drew blood in the process.

"So you fight with more than stones, kitten," her opponent rumbled. "Not bad for a Goodlander weakling."

A woman. Sariah now knew she faced a woman. Not that it made any difference, because the woman was obviously a deadly warrior. She launched a fulminating attack—a series of kicks that left Sariah weaponless and pinned under her knee.

Sariah fumbled for a weapon. She singed her fingertips against something hot. It was her little desk lamp, which had tipped over onto the floor. The flammable mud in it still burned brightly. In one swift motion, she snatched the scorching lamp and smashed it against the woman's back.

Flames flickered over her opponent's weave. Sariah dove for her dirk, but even with her weave on fire, the other woman beat her to it. She kicked Sariah to the corner and then crashed back-first against the door shutters, smothering the flames. The back of Sariah's head cracked against the corner post. The world swayed with the deck. The moonlight streaming through the broken window dimmed and blurred in painful sequence. The woman loomed over her, smoldering like a demon crawling out of Meliahs' rot pit. Sariah knew she should be dead by now. The woman was simply too good a fighter. Why then was she still alive?

"You fight good, kitten, but not good enough for Delis," her assailant said in a low raspy voice and a thick accent that lengthened her vowels when she spoke. "It's a pity I have to kill you. I would so like to keep you."

Blue and violet eyes stared at Sariah, feverish with death. The lethal hatchet rose in the air and began its final descent. A whistle broke the silence, and then a solid thump. The woman froze. The hatchet slipped from her hand and clattered on the floor. She toppled over Sariah, trapping her under an avalanche of muscular weight. Sariah struggled to get out from under the woman, trying to understand what had just happened.

Blood. It stained Sariah's hand, but it wasn't her blood. An arrow protruded from her attacker's back. The deck shook with the steps of many feet. Faces peered through the smashed window. A crash shattered what remained of the door's shutter. Four or five people broke into the shelter. With a cursory look at them, Sariah understood. She had gone from bad to worse—the mob had found her.

□ ■ □

The bearded man snorted like a rutting pig. "What do we have here? If it isn't the hawk and the snake sharing the nest?"

The woman stirred. Despite her wound, she pushed herself off Sariah and slumped against the wall, eyeing the newcomers with open hatred. Her hands fumbled for her hatchet. The man took a knee in front of her.

"Delis, darling, is it you?" He peeked under the weave that covered her face. "Thank you for disarming the wiser witch for us. They sent the best after this one, I see. We've paid our fees. We've found our prize. Why is it you insist on stealing our reward?"

Delis snarled. "Up your arse, you peddler's bitch. You'd sell your mother for dung—"

The man cuffed her in the face. "I cannot kill you with my own hands, not for lack of want, mind you, but on account of the law. I won't be blamed for your loss." He called on the other men. "Throw her out into the dead water."

Wounded as she was, Delis kicked and punched and crashed against Sariah before no less than six men were finally able to drag her out of the shelter.

"She's wounded," Sariah said. "She'll die."

"That's the point, you slow-witted slut," the man said. "We'll let the Domain do some of the murdering this night, but don't worry, we won't let it do all of the killing. Fire the deck," he said to his minions. "Let none of her foul witchery survive the night."

Sariah recognized the man's broad nose and the stubbly beard. The mob's leader was the same man who had tried to kill her at the nets and who had defied Kael afterwards. Josfan. That was his name. Coin aside, he was set on eliminating her and all traces of her passing. Two men dragged Sariah to her feet. A shovelful of flammable mud later, the deck ignited with a muted swoosh.

She eyed the flames. "Why are you doing this?"

"It's our right, isn't it? We paid for it and we'll get paid for it too."

"But you, Josfan, you really want me dead. You paid a lot at the nets to shoot at me. Did someone send you after me?"

"Wouldn't you like to know?" Josfan flashed his hideous smile. "Justice it is, wench, that you who broke the wall and tried to destroy the New Blood will end up as a sprinkle of ashes fizzling in the dead water."

"If you burn me, you won't have a body to collect on."

"But I don't need your body to collect my reward. I just need your bracelet."

Of course. The bracelet would offer more than sufficient proof of her death. Sariah struggled with the thugs who tried to stretch out her arm. Her shoulder and elbow ached from the strain. Her forearm ended up splayed on her desk anyway. A serrated saw appeared in Josfan's hand, a big rusting brute of a blade which could have easily belonged to an enduring wood cutter or to one of the Shield's quartering blocks. Josfan wetted his lips and tested the saw's teeth against her forearm.

"I wouldn't do that, if I were you." Sariah unclenched her fist. A black stone gleamed on the palm of her hand. "Step away from me. All of you. Or do you wish to join me in a quick trip to Meliahs' rot pits?"

Josfan froze. The men let go of her and scurried out the door, cursing and making the sign against evil. The stone had been Delis's surprising parting gift. The woman must have lifted it from the floor while resisting Josfan's cronies. She had also used the ruckus to sneak the stone into Sariah's hands. Sariah owed the woman a most unlikely and unexpected debt.

"You witch," Josfan spat. "You wouldn't blow yourself up just to spite us."

"Stay and find out."

The saw wilted in Josfan's hands. He took one step back, and then another, before diving for the door and abandoning the deck. Sariah tracked his retreat as closely as she was tracking the fire. She had only a few moments to act.

"We won't let you out of here alive," Josfan shouted from a safe distance. "We just have to wait until the fire burns you. I'll have your bracelet even if I have to sift through your ashes. You've made a huge mistake. We've got you surrounded. You've worked yourself into a death trap."

Meliahs help her. Perhaps she had.

Seven

THE FLAMES WERE mesmerizing and beautiful, a flowing mane of color and heat that dazzled the eye. The smoke stung her lungs and eyes. She fought the panic and ignored the heat pressing from all directions. She grabbed the stones she had been wising from the floor and stuffed them in her sack, cramming as many of the engrossments and annotations that were not already on fire in the bag as well. Burned deck. No supplies. Long journey ahead. She had to save as much as she could.

She stuffed the sack with whatever garments she could find. She grabbed her own bag, the one she had packed before the executioners came, and reached for Kael's favorite belongings, his winter cloak, his medicine pouch, the jar of wised marbles for his sling. No chance of taking the rest. Shame.

The smoke was too thick. Despite the enduring wood construction and the protective coating, the base of the deck was beginning to burn. She couldn't breathe. She had to get out. They would be waiting for her with slings loaded and bows drawn.

She groped through her bag and found more stones. She hurled a first stone towards the back of the shelter and willed it to explode when it hit the wall. It burst into a mess of fiery weave and shattered wood. She took cover against the arrows aimed at her behind the cargo stacked on the back deck, but the fire was hot and lapping at her weave. She used her sling to launch the second stone. It burst amidst the group shooting at her, unleashing a second explosion of cries and curses. It was her cue to break through.

She was glad she always kept her weave on when they traveled. She leapt over the cargo and landed in knee-high water. She counted five, maybe six decks of followers surrounding her. She chose at random. She hurled her stone at one of the empty decks, crouched as it exploded, and ran through the fallout into the open flats. Nafa. She aimed towards the settlement's lights. She didn't have any other option. She ran the water as fast as she could, but the men assembled a cohesive chase right away, and an arrow skimmed the water's surface too close to her legs. No alternative then. She loaded her sling at a run, then stopped, turned, shot her last stone and commanded it to burst. She didn't wait to see the effects of her defense. She didn't enjoy the thought, either. Meliahs forgive her. She loathed having to misuse stones for violence. She ran as fast as she could, knowing what would happen if the mob caught her.

In the dark, her senses were keen and her heart pumped hard in support of her legs. Raised in the Goodlands, she wasn't the strongest of water runners, but she pushed herself to exceed her body's limits, despite the load she carried. She must have been halfway between her burning deck and Nafa when she saw the hunched shadow stumbling ahead of her. She recognized the shaft protruding from her back. Delis. She fell twice in the dead water before Sariah reached her. The second time, she didn't get up.

"Come." Sariah grabbed the woman's arm, all too aware of the torches gaining ground behind her. "Make haste, we have to run."

She pulled Delis to her feet. The woman was too large and heavy to carry. Her weave was torn and the dead water must have been seeping in and burning her, but Delis threw an arm over Sariah's shoulder and stumbled a few paces forward.

"Damn." The torches were nearing them. "Can they see in the dark?"

"Your bracelet," Delis rasped. "It's the fifth night."

Sariah stared at her wrist in disbelief. The nine stones in the bracelet shone with a crimson radiance, a lucent glow that would be visible in the dark to anyone, even as it was, covered under her weaved glove. She stopped, ripped her other glove and tied it around the bracelet. The glow was less but still visible, a red beacon in the black expanse.

"Take this." Delis tugged at her face scarf. Sariah wrapped it around her arm, concealing the glow under the fabric's multiple layers.

A wild mane of dark hair bloomed around Delis's head like a smoky haze. "The light will burn through the fabric soon."

"Great." Sariah forged ahead, but Delis couldn't keep up. She came to a stop and nearly crumbled.

"Get up," Sariah said. "We have to go."

The woman just stood there, panting like an old cow waiting to die.

"And you called me a Goodlander weakling? The great Delis can't match a kitten's pace?"

Blue and violet eyes flickered with righteous pride. Delis rose, stumbled a few more steps, and then waded with more assurance. Their pursuers were falling behind, fanning out in all directions, unable to locate them in the darkness without the red glow. After a few more moments, the mob halted as if stopped by an invisible line.

"Nafa's boundaries," Delis panted. "Can't follow us."

At last, a break in their favor. She spied the shapes of people from Nafa watching her burning deck. So much for keeping the deck dark. She crouched low over the water, as low as she could go considering that she was loaded, had an entire arm exposed to the dead water without her glove and was trying to support Delis as well. Sariah forded the settlement until she could no longer see her deck. She helped Delis climb an abandoned deck in a quiet part of town. As soon as they were out of the dead water, Delis tumbled over like a broken boulder. Sariah could hardly breathe. Now what?

She needed to get Delis help and then she needed to find Kael and get out of Nafa. The deck was gone. How would they continue their journey without it? Panic. One problem at a time. Delis. Surely Nafa's people would render her assistance.

The old deck had no shelter, but Sariah untied the assortment of sacks and bags she carried and piled them beneath a cover of rotting ropes. She looked around. Light flickered nearby, but for the most part, the area seemed dark and sparsely populated. The air smelled of neglect. It wasn't the most prosperous part of Nafa.

She made up her mind and dragged the senseless Delis over a broken bridge to a more populated lane. The woman weighed more than a bull. The traffic was light, but she waited until no one was around to dump Delis's body on a lit deck. She rapped on the shutters before darting out of sight behind a nearby stack of broken crates. She wondered if this was how babies were gifted to the Guild, abandoned in the darkness at the massive threshold of the keep's gates.

She had done what she could for Delis. Now she had to find Kael. She took a last look to make sure Delis got the help she needed. A man came to the door.

"What do we have here?" He sounded half-drunk.

A woman appeared from inside. "It's a body, that's what it is. Is it your drunk of a brother again?"

"It's a woman. She's stuck with an arrow."

"Why, poor thing. Bring her inside, fetch the healer."

The man's tone had never been kind, but now it was down-right cold. "We ain't gonna spend no coin for a healer on this one. Look." He pointed to Delis's forehead.

From her hiding place, Sariah strained to see. A mark was stamped on the right side of Delis's forehead near her temple, a mark that had been concealed by her wrap before, three diagonal lines crossed by another trio of equal but opposing lines.

"Lightning strike me, it's a net-stamped rot spawn," the man said. "She's one of the executioners' mongrels."

"Don't let the neighbors see it." The woman kicked Delis's inert body. "Bloody bitch, off my deck."

"I'll put her out to the flats. She'll be gone by morn."

The man dragged Delis over the bridge and back the way Sariah had come. Delis's body grated against the wood. Her weave caught an edge and ripped further. The man cursed. Soon thereafter, a splash broke the dead water's calm.

By Meliahs. Delis was of the executioners, sent to kill her so that the mob wouldn't get their due and the executioners could wreck Sariah's search, claim Kael's assurances and Ars. No wonder the mob despised her. She was taking their profit from them. What Sariah had never known was that Domainers, or at least these Domainers, abhorred executioners to the point of refusing aid to a wounded woman. Perhaps they were right to resent someone who performed duties as foul as Delis's, but as much as Sariah despised her assailant, could she walk away knowing the woman was dissolving slowly in the agony of the dead waters?

Sariah waited for the man to return to his deck before retracing her footsteps. She found Delis half-sunk and struggling, holding her head out of the water but too weak to climb out by herself. Sariah grabbed her arms and pulled her back onto the deck with some difficulty. She thanked Meliahs for the night's darkness, the only real protection they had.

Delis was shaking from shock. "Why?"

"Why what?"

"Why are you helping me?"

Why indeed? "Wait here."

The woman clutched Sariah's wrist with unnatural strength. "They'll tear me apart in the morning."

"I'm going to find help. Let go. I promise I'll be back before daylight."

By the woman's expression, Sariah could tell she didn't believe a word she said.

Sariah had barely gone a few lanes when she spotted a group of people coming up behind her, engaged in animated conversation. She tucked herself against the wall of a darkened shelter and waited for them to pass.

"A banished criminal?" a woman was saying. "Here?"

"That's why they've called a search," a man said. "Didn't you hear the explosions?"

"And the flames," someone else said. "Didn't you see the fire? Hurry up!"

Perfect. The survivors of the men who attacked her must have told their story to Nafa's marcher. Now the entire settlement was out searching for her. What else could go wrong this night?

"Look!" One of the men in the group pointed. "Do you see something there?"

The rest of the group turned to look in Sariah's direction.

A brutal push shoved her face-first against the deck shelter. "Don't move."

As if she could.

"I don't see anything," someone said. "Come on. We're missing all the fun."

The group walked on. Sariah dared to breathe.

"Are you all right?" Kael whispered. "You've got rents and burns all over you."

"How did you find me?"

"Stay as you are." She heard him rustling through his shoulder bag, looking for something. "I saw the fire and figured your night was busier than mine. So I thought, if Sariah had to abandon the deck in haste, where would she go? That's how I ended up on this side of Nafa, wondering how by Meliahs' dung heaps I was going to find you. But then, you made it easy for me."

"Easy?"

"You're glowing."

Sariah looked down to see her bracelet's red radiance seeping through the scorched fabric. "By the rot, the light burned through again."

Kael wrapped his summer mantle around her arm, folding it many times over to a good thickness, until her arm felt like an enormous sausage packaged for sale.

"That should hold for a while," he said. "What happened?"

They huddled in the dark while Sariah gave him a quick account of her night. "That group from the mob found me only because Delis broke through the window and allowed the light to escape," Sariah finished.

"They sent Delis?"

"You know Delis?"

"I know *of* Delis. Where is she now?"

Sariah guided Kael to the abandoned deck where the woman lay.

"Wicked goddess, Sariah, the things you do." Kael considered the unconscious woman. "We have no time for this. We've got to go."

"We can't leave her to die."

"She tried to kill you."

"But then she smuggled me a stone. I can't leave her here. They hate her." Just like they hated her.

Kael shook his head. "All right. Let's see what we can do."

"I've got your medicine pouch."

"Good thinking. Pass me the vinegar and the saffron salve."

Sariah helped Kael to rip Delis's weave around the wound. "Did you find him? Did you find Leandro?"

"I found out about Leandro," Kael said, "but he no longer dwells here."

"Curse my luck. Where is he?"

"They weren't sure."

"What do you mean? Who's 'they' and why weren't they sure?"

"They are his family, his daughters, to be sure." Kael moistened a rag with water from his skin and groped about Delis's back, wiping off the crusted blood. "Leandro was taken."

"Taken? By whom?"

"By a traveling healer, they said."

Sariah's belly went to ice. "Was he ill? No. Don't tell me. Is he dead?"

"Not as far as his daughters know, but they haven't heard from him in a while." Kael squinted in the darkness. "Damn, it's dark tonight."

Sariah had an idea. She held her arm over the woman's back and peeled off some of the fabric covering the bracelet. The red glow illuminated the wound.

"That's better," Kael said.

Sariah could barely contain her anxiety. If they couldn't find Leandro, if he was dead, her incipient search was over. "Where did this traveling healer take Leandro?"

"To the atorium, his daughters said. For a curative rest."

"The what?"

"The atorium. A kinder name for the sanatorium, just as the term 'curative rest' is a discreet description of his malady."

"Is he sick?"

"Apparently, Leandro had problems for many years. He failed as a roamer. He was a wagering man, a back alley player whose antics almost bankrupted his family. But that wasn't his only problem. It seems that your Leandro may be missing a twine or two from his deck, if you know what I mean. Would you hold the light steady?"

"Oh." Sariah held out her arm stiffly. Leandro was crazy? Still, she had no other clues. "Do you know where this atorium is?"

"Sort of. There aren't too many of those in the Domain."

"Can you take me there?"

"Either I take you there or I mend this wound," he said. "Can't do both at the same time. The light, Sariah. You've taken your arm away again."

"Sorry." She turned her attention to Delis's wound. What was left of the broken shaft protruded at an angle above the woman's shoulder blade. The arrowhead was burrowed in the flesh.

"What say you?" Kael said. "Do you want it out?"

Sariah hadn't realized that Delis was conscious, but now she noticed the subtle change in the woman's respiration.

Delis rumbled. "What is it to you, whoreson?"

"It's nothing to me." Kael sounded deceivingly placid. "To be truthful, I prefer you dead and out of the way, but she bids me to help you and I heed her wishes."

Delis's blue and violet eyes shifted to Sariah. Sweat drenched the woman's narrow forehead. It dripped along the crooked bone of a long meandering nose and pooled above a narrow mouth and a set of naturally puckered lips.

"Is she yours then?"

A strange question.

"In or out?" Kael asked testily. "We don't have all night."

"Out," Delis said.

"'Out, *please*' will do."

How many hundreds of arrows had Kael extracted from runners and friends over a lifetime of hardship in the Domain? Evidently many. He wiggled the barb and, pressing down at either side of the wound, extracted the point with expert ease. Delis moaned like a calving ox. Sariah wiped the flow of new blood and smeared the salve over the wound.

"Who's there?"

Sariah recognized the voice calling in the dark. It belonged to the man from the deck where she had tried to find help for Delis.

No doubt he was back to check on the woman's demise. Sariah readjusted the cloak to cover the bracelet's glow.

"We have to go." Kael began to tie his harness's ropes to the old deck.

"In this?" Delis said. "Are you mad?"

"Have you any better idea?"

"Not at the moment, no."

"You ought to, since you managed to burn our deck, wench."

"Madame Executioner to you."

Kael snorted. "Not a chance."

"He's coming back," Sariah whispered. "He's got friends."

"She burned our deck and tried to kill you," Kael said. "Are you sure you want to take this miserable waste of a rot spawn with us?"

"We can't leave her here to die."

"This ought to make for an interesting trip." Kael hacked the mooring ropes and took to the water, pulling the rickety deck into the vast darkness of a moonless night.

Eight

"How do you know where we are?" Sariah's voice echoed in a hollow landscape erased by a fog that clogged the lungs, stung the eyes and obscured any semblance of a view. The fog swirled around her almost as thick as the dead water. It felt as if it were permeating her bones and rusting her tired joints.

"I don't know where we are." Kael stopped pulling. "Not exactly, anyway."

"What do you mean?" Kael's precise sense of direction was his roamer's gift, keen, unequivocal and reliable no matter where they went, and even more acute in the Domain. "We aren't lost, are we?"

"Lost? No." He peered into the dense whiteness. "We're where we are supposed to be and yet we are not. Something's wrong. Very wrong."

The chill in Sariah's belly matched the fog's icy cold. A thin crust of ice cracked under her feet. "I didn't think the dead water could freeze. I thought the rot's brew is too warm for that."

"It is." Kael punched through the ice crust and dipped his gloved fingers in the lukewarm water. "Look. The ice is forming over the water's quickly cooling emissions, a layer of ice above a layer of air and vapor. I've never seen this before."

"At least my feet are warm, even though the rest of me is freezing."

"Let me warm you." He took her into his embrace, rubbing her numb arms, forcing her frozen blood to flow. His breath was a comfortable blast of warmth seeping through his face wrap.

"Strange," he said. "The chill has turned months ahead of its time. It's too cold for this time of the year. I doubt the mob would venture to travel in this weather."

"You said we would arrive at the Enduring Woods today."

Kael gave her a last hearty body rub and released her. "I don't understand. By my reckoning, we should be there now. And the time, look at the light. It should be close to midday and yet it's more like twilight."

"So we're lost."

"We're not lost. We're where we should be. It's more like the Barren Flats and the weather are wrong."

Blame the weather for the mess. Couldn't he just admit he was wrong? They pulled a decrepit old deck, a moldy, rotting piece of junk with no shelter, abandoned because of its uselessness. Despite their efforts to re-knot the twines and repair the breaks, it threatened to come apart anytime. They had very few supplies, only what Sariah had managed to save from their burning deck, what Kael had carried in his shoulder bag, and what Delis had in her pouch, all of which included two skins of ale, a few old bannocks and some cheese, not enough food to last the three of them for another day.

Delis had been no help. She lay on her back, pressing her wound against the wood in some kind of masochist feat, mumbling angry, unintelligible words to herself. Sariah and Kael had pulled for three days and nights straight. They needed to find a sturdier deck and food, and they needed to rest.

"There's no shame in admitting we're lost," she said.

The black eye dominated his glare. "I'm telling you, I've guided us true. Something feels funny."

"*Feels* funny?" Feelings were something she drew from Kael occasionally, with much difficulty and only with the help of her craft. "Perhaps we should retrace our steps back to the loop and start anew."

"We don't have a few days to waste. Do we? And if it gets any colder, we don't want to be stranded on the open flats. We go this way." He started to pull again.

"But—"

"We go this way."

The cold wind sliced through Sariah's wet weave as if she were naked, setting her teeth to chatter. Better to talk than to dwell on the misery of pulling.

"Why do they hate her thus?"

"Delis?" Kael shrugged. "It's not just her, although her reputation is among the worst. On account of her deeds. If you kill enough sheep, you'll be called a wolf even if you're something else. But I don't think she's something else. She's the original wolf."

"That bad, eh?" Sariah stole a look at the woman lying on the deck. "She doesn't look that fierce to me."

"She's the best murderess the executioners have put out this generation," Kael said. "She has never missed an assigned kill, or so say the wagging tongues. They say she collects noses and ears—her victims', mind you."

Sariah repressed a shiver. "She's so strong."

"So you like her?" Kael winked.

"No, nay, no. I wish I was as strong as her, that's all. And fearless, too. I wish I didn't mind doing whatever it was I needed to do."

Kael's chuckles carried a definite ring of amusement. "You may lack the bitch's muscles, wiser, but you're no coward."

"She doesn't seem to mind that nobody likes her, that everybody hates her."

"Ah. That might be because she's an executioner."

"You treated the executioners with respect."

"That doesn't mean I like them."

"You said they were within their rights."

"They were. They are a queer people. They have a right to kill by the nets and to thrive by killing. Domainers know someone has to do it, but I won't lie to you, I'm wary of killers in all forms."

"Are executioners born into their tribes?"

"I suppose some are, but the bulk of the executioners are outcasts from the different tribes, men and women who have been run out of their settlements and are not welcomed elsewhere."

Sariah pondered the idea. "I guess it's better than being banished or alone."

"Are you thinking of joining?"

"You never know."

"There." Kael spied something between fast-moving patches of fog. "Do you see them?"

Sariah narrowed her eyes and saw a row of ghastly shadows. Slowly, as if in a dream, enormous shapes began to emerge looming over them like Meliahs' stone giants.

"What are these?"

"We're at the edge of the Enduring Woods."

Against the fog's background, the amorphous shape of a massive set of vaulted roots protruded from the dead water. The roots twisted and blended to form a tuberous swelling the size of a small house. Atop the roots, a single trunk grew to amazing girth and height. Gnarled branches weaved in and out of the fog, twisting like knotted fingers.

Kael made for the colossal tree. "We can rest here."

Sariah was sorely relieved. She was cold and exhausted, and she didn't trust the deck they pulled to last much longer. Kael had said the forester was an old friend. The need to replace their crumbling deck had necessitated the detour. Sariah was hoping Kael's contacts would help them find a decent, affordable deck, something light to pull but sturdy, with a shelter maybe, so they didn't have to suffer the weather's inclemency. She wasn't one to complain, but she was looking forward to a tiny break in their fortunes.

The enormous buttress roots clawed at the Barren Flats like crooked tentacles. A measure of coarse wet mud lay between the roots, creating a few protected coves. Kael chose the most expansive of the lot, only a few paces wide but enough to beach their decrepit deck. After so many days trekking through water, the feel of solid ground under her feet tricked Sariah's senses. Her legs struggled to adjust to the absence of the water's gravity.

"From the rot we rose and to the stone we shall return by way of hallowed land." This little bit of mud under her feet made her appreciate the Domainers' oath even more. She willed her weary bones not to collapse just yet. While Kael scooped some of the flat's flammable mud and made a fire, Sariah examined Delis's back.

"Much better." She spread a new layer of salve on the cleansed wound. "You're healing beautifully."

Delis grunted something incomprehensible under her breath. The woman's foul mood seemed to be the worst of her ills. She was as friendly as a cross-eyed mule. She had trapped her unkempt dark hair in a bushy tail at the base of her skull, a rumpled style which accentuated the contrast between her long nose and her small mouth. She didn't want to speak to Sariah, yet her blue and violet eyes stalked her viciously. Perhaps because of that, Kael insisted on keeping Delis's hatchet on his belt and her hands tied. Sariah was too tired to argue and too cold to think.

The fire thawed Sariah's hands. The bannocks, stale and tasteless as they were, felt like a banquet to her empty stomach. The deck was hard on her back, but she didn't care. She lay down next to Kael. He kept his weapons belt strapped to his waist, a most uncomfortable way to sleep, daring Delis to harm them with a sullen glower which promised to end her troubles and theirs at the first sign of danger. Delis turned around, dismissing him with a loud *tsk*. Despite her attitude, Sariah covered Delis with her executioner's red mantle. No one was going to freeze today.

Sariah slept fretfully. She dreamed she was wising icebergs. A thin layer of dew turned to ice and frosted the mantle covering them, waking her up with a loud crunch every time she moved. She opened her eyes to find her head tucked in the curve of Delis's breast, a generous pillow for her sleep-numbed cheek. The scent of Delis filled her senses, sweet, unlike the woman, a hint of molasses and wild cloves.

Kael's possessive clutch anchored Sariah to him. His leg was thrown over her thighs. His hand was heavy on her breast. Both Kael and Delis were awake and trading hard stares.

"Kael?" His body was strung like a bow.

"Sleep, love, no sense in all of us being awake." He gathered her close to him.

Sariah turned and cuddled against his chest, lodging her face against the crook of his neck. She murmured something about him needing to rest too. Safe in his arms, she drifted back to sleep. Nothing could keep her awake this night.

□ ■ □

"I have to kill you, you know," Delis said.

Apparently, these cheerful words were Delis's best attempt at casual talk. Well, the woman was not very skilled at conversation then—that was freshly proven.

Sariah stopped stitching the rent in her weave and leveled an even stare on Delis. "I still have the bruises from your beating the other day. If those are any indication, you killing me would be rather painful. Is there anything I could say to dissuade you from your purpose?"

Blue and violet eyes narrowed, but the corner of Delis's mouth twitched, a tiny curve up. "You speak your mind," she said. "I like that."

"That's progress, I suppose. Why would you kill someone you like, I wonder?"

"'Cause I swore to."

"Makes sense." Sariah resumed her stitching. "Oaths I understand."

"You do?" The woman seemed perplexed.

"Of course I do. I'm a stonewiser. Do cheer up, Delis. At least you're alive. It's something to celebrate, isn't it?"

The woman dismissed her with a muted *tsk*.

"Here's something I don't understand. If you were sent to kill me, why did you give me that stone to use against the mob the other day?"

"'Cause *I'm* supposed to kill you," Delis said.

She was an odd one, earnest in an impalpable way, yet grim. Sariah was glad Kael had checked the knots on Delis's ties before he left to find the forester's post. She calculated the time. It was early afternoon. He had left at first light, if one could call the green grayness of this day such. Sariah worried, especially because he had left without a deck, claiming he was well weaved and could take refuge on the woods' buttress roots if necessary. The Domain was an unforgiving place even when you wandered it with a deck. If something happened to him...

He would be fine. He had promised. He should be there by now, hopefully safe and talking to his friend, warming himself against a real wood fire, with a cup of hot spiced wine between his hands and a generous bowl steaming in front of him. She found herself salivating at the thought. Delis interrupted her pleasant musings.

"There's a way," she said.

"A way to do what?"

"A way for me not to kill you."

Sariah was curious. "And what would that be?"

"An oath over an oath."

"Would that be like a nail taking out another nail?"

She wouldn't call it quite a smile, but the twitch on Delis's lips was the next best thing.

"I'm of the Inkes. You know the Inkes?"

Not really, but Sariah nodded politely.

"We live by the three oaths. First oath, kin. Second, more important, craft. I'm an executioner. If I had to kill my father I would, because second oath trumps first oath."

"Very interesting."

"Third oath is over second oath. Third oath is to..." she struggled to find the right word.

"To a lease maybe?" Sariah tried to help.

"No, not to a lease. You would have to be *Inkes-donatis* in the old language. Donnis."

"Donnis?" Sariah consulted her memory for any mention of the strange word in the stone tales. "I don't know donnis. Sorry. Is it like an oath of friendship maybe?"

"Friendship?" The woman smiled, the first true smile she had offered since they met. "Sort of like friends, but not quite, although sometimes it is so."

Delis and her Inkes were surely the strangest people Sariah had encountered. "I don't suppose it would be an easy matter to become donnis and end your quest to kill me?"

"Easy, yes. If Delis wants, Delis does. And Delis wants."

Something about the woman's intensity warned Sariah. "It's not like a lease, right? Because I quit my lease some time ago and I don't intend to live like that ever again."

Delis growled like an irritated weasel. "I said no lease."

"Watch your temper, will you?"

"Will you be my donnis?"

She had deep reservations. Delis didn't strike her with her good manners or her unwillingness to explain. "Perhaps it's not such a good idea—"

"Decide."

Sariah's own dirk was at her throat. Delis's ties were gone. She had Sariah pinned down against the buttress roots. How?

Delis must have been working on her ties all day, rubbing the rope against the deck, taking advantage of Kael's absence and Sariah's sloppy good will. She had lessened her vigilance because she believed that, despite her claims to the opposite, the woman was grateful for her help. She had been wrong.

"Decide," Delis said. "Now."

The fanged dirk was cold against her throat. Sariah didn't want to swallow for fear of cutting herself. "You don't want me to swear to something I don't understand."

"If you don't swear, you die."

"I won't honor an oath under duress."

"But I will."

The blade tickled Sariah's mad pulse. A drop of liquid warmth trickled down her neck. The fog parted to reveal the tall tupelo towering above her, branches swaying with a sudden breeze. For four hundred chills the massive tree had survived the rot, defying destruction through accommodation with its lethally changing environs. Under the circumstances, it was a lesson worth noting, even though Sariah didn't think she could stomach accommodation over defiance just then.

"Swear." The woman was shaking like the tupelo's sparing leaves. "I don't want to kill you, kitten, but I will if I must."

Sariah saw the pain in the other woman's eyes, the ingrained sense of duty prevailing over will, the settlement with death, even when death was not desired. She knew the meaning of blind obedience. She understood duty's clash with choice.

"Please? Swear. For me?"

Despite the bile churning in her gut, despite herself, Delis's plea, her familiar pain, trumped Sariah's resolve. "Fine. Have it your way. I swear. To what, who knows, but don't expect me to like it. The blade is no substitute for a free oath, but you know that."

"You swore." Delis dropped the dirk. "You'll live."

Delis hugged her, a violent squeeze that wrenched the breath out of Sariah. She planted a sudden kiss on her lips. "You won't regret your oath, my donnis. I promise."

By Meliahs. A kiss and an oath. A troublesome combination by any measure. Just in case, Sariah grabbed her dirk from the floor and tucked it securely in her belt.

□ ■ □

"You what?" Kael stared at Sariah in disbelief. "The bitch did what?"

"Calm down, Kael, it all has come to naught. I'm fine and Delis is happy, and we won't have to worry about her killing me anymore. Isn't that right, Delis?"

"Of course, my donnis," Delis said, oddly adoringly.

Kael met Delis's defying stare. "You and I. Our day is coming."

"I'm not afraid of you." Delis bared a row of crowded teeth. "You're but an old wasp hanging about the hive seeking to gorge on honey."

"And I suppose you're the honey bee?" Kael said.

Delis was on her feet and ready to pounce.

Sariah snapped. "Stop it, you two."

"As you wish, my donnis." Delis sat back on her haunches, eyeing Kael dangerously.

Kael eased out of his fight stance and turned to Sariah. "Did you really—?"

"Aye, but the oath is of no practical consequence and all is well."

"Ah." Kael shook his head as if dispelling a cloud of the Domain's worse gnats. "Of no practical consequence, you say? Hardly. All is not well, not with you, not with her, and certainly, not with me."

"Whatever do you mean?"

"What's a donnis, Sariah?"

"Oh, that. Well, I don't really understand the notion, but I gather it's something harmless, like a friendship oath, some trick of the Inkes' oath order which frees Delis from her duty to kill me."

"Harmless, you say?"

"Can't you see Delis is no longer our enemy?"

"You mean *your* enemy?"

Had the man turned daft and blind at the same time? "She's no longer a threat to us. She won't harm me. Or you. Won't you, Delis?"

"Of course not, my donnis. Not as long as you wish the old wasp unharmed."

It was hardly an assurance, but it was better than none.

Kael insisted. "Tell me again, Sariah. Do you know what a donnis is? Do you have cause to know the ways of the Inkes?"

"Not really."

"On both counts?"

"On both counts."

The terrible frown lifted from his brow. His mood lightened and the wicked grin made its notorious appearance. He was acting stranger than a tomcat with burnt whiskers.

"Sit, wiser." He pulled her down on his lap. "I won't have you kick the bitch to death."

"She's my donnis," Delis protested.

Kael fired his most contemptuous glare. "You didn't tell Sariah what she should have known before she swore you that mockery of an oath. And you would have killed her. That's enough evil for me."

"Whatever is wrong with you?" Sariah said.

"The old tongue is a tricky language," he said. "There isn't a word that fairly translates the term *donnis* to our speech. However, there is one word in our language which most people readily comprehend and does justice to such a notion. Do you know what it is?"

"Obviously, no."

"Would you like to tell the wiser, Delis?"

Delis sank in her heels, averting her eyes from Sariah.

"Delis?" Sariah was suddenly alarmed.

"*Pet*," Kael spat. "The correct translation for the word *donnis* is 'pet.'"

Nine

SARIAH FINISHED KNOTTING the last of the thickly pleated weave warps to the lower beam. She ran her hands through the tightly strewn warps and tested them for strength. Good. They were tight and sturdy. Her hands ached, her fingers were chapped and blistered, and her fingertips were numb, but instead of taking a rest, she turned her attention to the other side of the frame where Kael had just finished cutting the notches into the side beams. She threaded the first horizontal row through the upper notch and began plaiting it over-and-under the vertically strewn warps, tightening the weft with short, angry pulls.

Kael took a long draft from his new leather flask, a gift from his friend, the forester. "That will make a fine wall for the new deck when you're done with it. Shame you'll have only shreds of your hands left for your wisings."

"I want this damn wall finished and the deck done. We've wasted enough time as it is. At this pace, Leandro will die of old age in his atorium's bed."

"Have a drink." Kael handed her the flask. "It's hotter than a rot pit today."

Sariah choked on the lukewarm ale. "Ugh. It's like drinking soup. How can it be this hot? Just a few days ago, we were freezing. I know the weather is whimsical in the Domain, but this is ridiculous." Sariah capped the flask and returned it to Kael. "I just hope it doesn't get cold again. We need to reach Leandro with all haste."

"We will." Kael took a warp from the lot and threaded the next notch down from the one Sariah was working on. "The shelter will be done as soon as we install this last wall. And now that we have a good deck, we can travel faster."

Sariah took stock of their work thus far. Three walls rose in the middle of the new deck. A half-thatched roof rested beside the frame of the last wall, now in progress. The fragrant scent of recently cut wood perfumed the air, a lovely reprieve from the flat's acid smell.

"The forester was very kind," she said, resuming her work. "No one I know at the Guild would have given us a brand new deck and the fixings to build a shelter without a good amount of coin or a hefty debt."

"The forester is an old friend," Kael said, without looking up from his task. "We've had our share of adventures together."

"Friendship, the next best thing to kin in the Domain."

"What's the matter with her?" Kael had stopped working and was now squinting into the flats, sheltering his eyes from the sun with a hand over his sweaty brow.

"Her?" A frantic Delis was running toward them. "I couldn't care less."

"I don't see traces of eels or rotfish," Kael said, "and I don't smell the belch either. What's wrong with her?"

"Her head," Sariah said crossly. "Anyone who collects you know what for a living is wrong in the head."

"Donnis?"

"Don't even say it."

Sariah was still furious. Kael had taken to assigning Delis tasks like foraging for food and water, keeping her away from Sariah. Surprisingly, Delis complied, eyeing her with a hint of supplication in her eyes, as if teaching her newest pet the virtue of obedience through devout example. Well, let her demonstrate all she wanted. She was no one's damn pet.

As if reading her thoughts, Kael flashed his wickedest grin. Sariah stuck her tongue out at him. He chuckled, but she wasn't confusing his equanimity with tame acceptance. Sariah was unconvinced by his behavior. Although he acted amused by the situation, he also refused to allow her to probe him. What dark emotions stirred beneath his calm demeanor?

Delis was a different story altogether. The change in her was nothing short of remarkable. She seemed free of the burden that had made her so grim before, oddly cooperative, using her well-honed survival skills to their benefit and almost happy, if such a term could be applied to a natural brooder. A part of Sariah was sorry for Delis. She was trying hard to gain her trust, attention and acceptance. Being the focus of Kael's rage was a disgrace, but bearing the wrath of both, Kael and Sariah, that had to be a catastrophe. Well, she didn't care. The woman had earned it many times over.

"Look, look!" Delis pointed at the sky, waving her full net as she ran.

"What... is... it... ?" Kael's eyes narrowed on a tiny spot in the sky.

"A long-legged crane?" Sariah spied a pair of wings in the air. "A gull?"

"Not a crane and not a gull." Kael frowned. "A hawk, I think. A red hawk."

Why would the appearance of a hawk cause such a fuss?

"There have been no hawks in the Domain since the rot took hold." Kael's eyes were glued to the creature's flight path.

Delis reached them, sweating and out of breath. "Did you see it, my donnis?"

"Don't call me that."

"A strange bird," Delis puffed, "not of the Domain. An omen of grace, my donnis. For you. Meliahs' gift."

"What's in your net?" Kael asked.

"I don't know." Delis dumped her net's contents at Sariah's feet. "See? The bird was hunting after these. But I've never seen these in the Domain either."

A half-dozen large fish flapped on the boards. Fish were common to every puddle of water in the Goodlands, even in the keep's ponds, where Sariah had seen them rise to the surface and hunt for bugs during the long summer days. But these were the dead waters. You could hunt eel and rotfish, krill and the occasional bottom feeder. But fish?

At last, she understood the wonderment on Kael's face. As a roamer, he would have seen such creatures in the Goodlands as surely as she had. But to see not one, but two dead species return to the Barren Flats on the same day was nothing less than miraculous.

Kael was on his knees, examining the silvery fish. "Do you know this kind?"

She didn't. It wasn't the kind kept at the Guild's ponds. Kael selected one of the fish. He smelled the quivering thing and then sliced it in half and lay it on the deck, tracing the spine with the point of his knife, poking at its heart, liver, stomach and intestines with deliberate care.

"Not a faulty species," he said. "Not a monster of nature either. Those we find sometimes. But these?"

He poked some more through the entrails and came up with a cluster of tiny black eggs on the tip of his blade. "They're spawning," he murmured, fascinated. "Here. In the Domain."

"Can they be eaten?" Delis asked.

"I don't see why not." Kael turned one-half of the fish around and checked the silver scales. "No boils or growths, no extra eyes or tails or fins."

"Fish, my donnis. Fish!" Delis clapped delightedly. "It's a sign of favor. Of luck."

"Kael, can you explain this?"

He shook his head without taking his eyes from the fish. "Something's either very right or very wrong with the Domain."

"Wrong, I'd say at the moment." Sariah's eyes narrowed on the horizon, where yet another host of creatures stirred, this flock very much natural to its surroundings.

Her throat botched the warning. "It's the mob."

□ ■ □

After spending the last few exhausting days dodging the mob, Sariah's hopes surged when she spotted the atorium breaking the Barren Flats' visual monotony. But her buoyant mood plunged as they came closer. The site where the atorium had once stood was a scene of desolation. The rot bubbled amidst the skeletons of blackened decks and crumbling debris, a fountain of corruption polluting the filthy water and stinking the air. Sariah's eyes watered from both the sting and sheer frustration.

"They must have ignored the rot's rumblings." Her voice broke the eerie silence. "They must have all perished in the eruption."

"It would take a bunch of idiots to ignore the rot's coming," Delis said.

"Atorium, remember? Sick and crazies?"

"But the caretakers—"

"The caretakers acted as such." Kael's soot-stained face popped out from the ruins' center. "They knew what was coming."

"You mean they escaped the rot?" A hint of hope brightened Sariah's heart.

"The rot? No," Kael said. "The Shield."

"You mean to say the rot didn't do this?"

"Of course it did. But only *after* the Shield attacked." Kael stepped out of the rubble holding the blackened point of a barbed pike, the Shield's favored weapon. "The Shield would have been a little harder to foresee than the rot."

"I thought the Shield limited its incursions to the areas nearest to the wall."

"I suspect this place is not as far from the wall as we might think."

"Did anyone—?"

"Survive?" Kael shrugged. "Can't say for sure, but I think there's a good likelihood. The pots are gone."

"The pots?"

"Domainers always take their pots with them wherever they go." Kael picked his way carefully through the incinerated ruins.

"They might have spied the Shield and escaped," Delis said.

"At least some of them." The burnt timber creaked ominously under Kael's feet as he examined what turned out to be a blackened human body speared upright onto a broken deck.

Sariah fought the urge to vomit. "When did it happen?"

"A month. Maybe two. The rot is a recent arrival. It hasn't yet consumed the ruins, but it will. There's something else here."

Kael stuck his finger into the corpse's gaping mouth. The jawbone crumpled. The lower half of the charred face dissolved into a dusty pile of cremated bone, the dead man's final protest. In his hand, Kael held a single gray stone.

Ten

SARIAH TAPPED THE gray stone on the floor with the tips of her fingers, a quick, sequential beat, the only sound breaking the stillness in the deck shelter. The last thing she saw before closing her eyes was a very worried Kael ready to snatch the stone from her hand should it become violent. Sure enough, the dreaded sight flashed in her mind. She recognized the small brown eyes, the full lips, the handsome face and the wide leonine nose, flaring at the mere thought of her.

The shiver ran the length of her spine. "Master Arron."

"He's no longer your master," Kael said.

"I'm free." She found comfort in hearing the words aloud. "Do you think this stone got here before or after the Shield's attack?"

"Hard to tell. But you don't have to wise this one."

"It's too dangerous, my donnis." It was odd to hear Delis agree with Kael.

"Arron can't hurt me." Was she saying these things to ease their fears or hers?

"If you do it," Kael said, "I want to be there with you."

"Only after I know it's safe," Sariah said. "Only once I have defused whatever traps lie waiting."

"Then let's throw it away," Kael said. "We can hurl it into the flats and never see it again."

"No, we can't."

Without allowing herself more time to fear, she clutched the stone in her hand and pressed it to her palm.

□ ■ □

Sariah thwarted the assault of a snaring trance, rushing into the trance in a reverse snatch that neutralized the power in the stone. She had been caught by one of Arron's creations before, a disturbing experience she didn't intend to suffer again. Instead, she took the trance by surprise and seized the links' timing, asserting control over the tale's pace. Her mind moved up and down the links, scouting for tricks, probing for traps and assessing the tale to make sure it was real and not the projection of someone's mind. Strange. With the exception of the snaring trance, a contraption that Arron used often to force his messages on others, the stone seemed harmless enough.

"Let me in." Kael's voice was like a pounding at the door.

"In a moment." Her mind stepped into the tale cautiously.

Arron was pacing back and forth in what looked like some kind of pavilion. Had he finally quit the keep? Had he been expelled from the Guild? The last time she had seen Arron was almost two chills ago at the breaking of the wall. Back then, the Guild's highest ruling body, the Council, had been split into two factions. Arron, the Council's Speaker and second in the line of rule, had been leading a ragtag army against Grimly, the Guild's Prime Hand for the last forty years. Targeted by both factions, Sariah and a badly wounded Kael had barely escaped the battle with their lives. At the time they fled, the Guild's powerful army, the Shield, had been under the Prime Hand's command. What had been the outcome of that battle?

Deep in the Domain's isolation, Sariah didn't know. News from the Goodlands was sparse and often confusing. She wondered if Mistress Grimly was dead. She doubted it. The witch had a proven knack for survival, political and otherwise. Sariah surprised herself pitying the Council, split between its main leaders. She pitied the Goodlands more.

In the tale, the light of a brazier flickered over Arron's features, revealing a pensive expression. He looked heavier, no less imposing than she remembered, but wide at the hips and bulging at the belly. A little extra flesh was a trait of prosperity in the Guild, but obviously, he had been indulging lately. He was alone, twirling the gray stone in one hand while sipping from the horn he clutched in the other. The man liked his luxuries. Sariah had no doubt the wine was of the best vintage.

Arron was imprinting the stone he clutched in his hand as he spoke. "If you are wising this stone, then you are still at large, living like a fugitive among the vermin. Sariah, you aren't made for the hardships of the Rotten Domain. Return to me, my beloved pupil."

Beloved pupil? Sariah had an urge to puke. When had Arron's so-called kindness resulted in anything but pain and frustration? And why was he speaking kindly in the tale, instead of issuing insults and threats like he did in his other messages? With her usual thoroughness, she scouted the stone tale for tricks one more time and, finding none, opened her eyes.

"You've got to see this." She put her hand over Kael's heart, allowing the tale to filter through her mind, body and palm, and into Kael's mind. She could feel his emotions too, the steely resolve he commanded to withstand whatever came, the wariness of the warrior called to battle.

"It's all right." She closed her eyes. "The only trickery so far is this new tone of his."

"Sariah," Arron said. "Your burdened heart may not allow you to consider the consequences of your actions. You have no guidance, no sound counseling. You know your duty. You alone can deliver justice to my cause. And you know, deep inside, none of this would have happened had you not escaped my tutelage, had you not forsaken my lease."

Kael scoffed. As if Arron hadn't been trying to wrestle control of the Council for years. As if his plots and schemes had not been ongoing since well before his ascent to the Council. Sariah was willing to accept responsibility for her acts, but not for Arron's intrigues.

"How long do you think you can hide?" Arron said. "How long can you keep running? My messages before this one may have scared you. They were the lamentations of a wounded teacher. It's my duty to find you. No matter how well you hide, how far you run, I'll find you. And if you don't heed my call, well, you might as well expect the worst."

Kael's emotions surged with the unspoken threat, *hatred, revulsion, violence.* Sariah remembered the type of revenge Arron favored with dread, but she didn't allow his insinuations to terrorize her. The tone of Arron's message was odd. It held none of the angry ranting of his earlier messages, none of the rage he had directed at her in the stones he liked to plant throughout the Domain. Those stones had been like an epidemic, appearing at random sites, sickening Sariah. Compared to his other messages, Arron was being mild, almost polite. That merited some thought.

"I make you a most unusual offer," Arron said. "A truce, a last chance to make it all right."

A truce? Sariah's breath caught in her throat. Kael chuckled in disbelief. Arron was offering *her* a reprieve? Easier to see the sun yielding the day to the moon.

"If you come out of the Domain," Arron said, "if you abandon your efforts to spread the lies you have unleashed and declare your support for me, I'll welcome you back into my service. You'll recant the lies you've told and you'll submit yourself to my will."

Had Arron won the battle? Was he the new Prime Hand? Sariah couldn't help but wonder where Grimly was, who had control of the keep, who the stonewisers at the keep regarded as their leader. She also wondered what parts of her wisings Arron wanted her to recant, since all of them were true. Did Arron really think she would submit herself to him? He was beyond deluded if he thought she would. He was fit for the atorium.

"Face it, Sariah," Arron said. "You and I, we have the same goals. We want peace and prosperity for the Goodlands. We want to return the Guild to its rightful ways. You won't survive long, not with so many going after you, blaming you for the land's demise."

The shock of Arron's next words left Sariah reeling and smarting from the recoil of Kael's emotions.

"Come to me," Arron said. "Allow me to help you. Come find me and wash away your regrets."

□ ■ □

Sariah turned the glowing bracelet around her wrist. Around and around went Hope, Courage, and all Meliahs' sisters. Deep in thought, she was mostly unaware of the pain. The links scuffed and scratched as she twisted them, yet she found the compulsion satisfactory. Defiance came in all forms.

She was startled when Kael's hand entered into the bracelet's spectral glow to still her hand. "You're hurting yourself," he said. "Can't sleep?"

"Sorry if I woke you."

"I was awake."

He lay between Sariah and Delis like one of the Enduring Woods' substantial buttress roots. He leaned on his elbow, watching her with resigned patience, waiting.

Sariah made a show of silence. She didn't want to talk about Arron. Or about the wall. Or the wrecked atorium. In the last week, they had put quite a few leagues between themselves and the ruins. Exhaustion had required this stop tonight, but only for a few hours. Sariah closed her eyes and saw the blackened decks wilting in the rot, the speared man gaping without a jaw.

"We'll find them," Kael said. "Wherever they went, we'll find them. Most likely, they sought out help from the closest settlement, Alabara. The people there must know what became of the atorium's survivors."

"What if Leandro died?" Sariah said. "What if he was one of the bodies we found? Or worse, one of the bodies we didn't find?" The dead water, the rot and the eels had had plenty of chances to consume the bodies before they arrived.

"Wait and see. No need to jump to conclusions."

The man was a pillar of icy pragmatism.

"I know you're worried," Kael said, "but I think Arron is the one stealing your sleep."

So much for keeping her thoughts to herself. "Arron managed a remarkable tale. He actually sounded concerned at times."

"Do you believe him?"

"Do you think I've gone dumb all of a sudden?"

"Just asking." He was quiet for a moment. "Going to Arron would be madness, Sariah. We've got to concentrate on finding the tale."

"I know. But I'm worried. His message. The setting. The assurances. He feels powerful, more powerful than before. I think

Arron may have defeated Grimly. I think Arron might have become the Guild's Prime Hand. *You must declare yourself for me.* What else could he possibly mean?"

"He needs you," Kael said. "He needs you as much as he wants you."

Sariah was unable to repress the shiver that shook her.

Kael pulled her close. "He won't have you, we won't let him, but the reality is he thinks you can be of use to him."

Sariah recalled Arron's words. "*You alone can deliver justice to my cause.* What justice? Everybody in the land wants me punished and dead."

"Not everybody." He kissed her forehead and then settled on her mouth to scatter her worries into complete disorder.

Sariah tried to disentangle herself from his enterprising lips. "Not now."

"Then where and when?" His lips fluttered over her throat and settled over the breast he had liberated from her shift.

"We can't—"

"She's not watching."

"Yes, I am," Delis piped up.

"Meliahs' dung," Kael cursed. "Mind your business, wench."

"I mind my donnis."

"I'm *not* your donnis."

Delis ignored Sariah's remark. "My donnis doesn't want you to—"

"Watch yourself," Kael said. "My patience with you is at an end."

"Your patience?" Delis hissed. "What about *my* patience?"

They both sprang to their feet and faced each other like quarreling bears. Delis swiped a fist a Kael. Kael blocked it and grabbed Delis by the neck. With her eyes bulging and her face nearly blue, Delis still managed to clamp her powerful legs around Kael's waist and pummel his liver with her heels.

"Enough," Sariah cried. "Stop it."

Delis wasn't the executioners' best murderess without good reason. It took Kael a few moments to disentangle from the woman's thighs without tearing her limbs apart bone by bone. When he was done, Sariah was fairly sure Delis would be limping and Kael would have a backache tomorrow.

"What do you say, wiser?" Kael asked. "Do you want her out of this shelter? I know I do."

The woman looked pleadingly at her, but Sariah was in no mood to be charitable. Delis had deceived her, and she was not anyone's donnis. Plus, she realized shamelessly, she wanted to lay with Kael, even if it was for a short moment. Sariah gathered Delis's blankets and dumped them outside the shelter. Delis limped out the door. The dejection on her face made Sariah feel guilty, but she got over it quickly.

Kael wiped a bit of blood from his nose. "What have we come to? Now I have to fight the wench to bed you?" He sounded sullen, but he was grinning.

"You know what they say." Sariah stamped a kiss on his lips. "All in the spirit of conquest."

"Aye, well, and you know what they say too." He took her hand and rubbed it against his groin. "Violence is the best aphrodisiac."

"Your liver might be shot, but I see the best of you is working hugely well."

"Let's attend to it promptly."

Delis cleared her throat at the door. "My donnis?"

Kael groaned. "Go away."

"Sorry, my donnis. But you better come and look. We've got company."

Eleven

A lamp swung from side to side in the darkness, the Domainers' signal for peaceful approach. Kael swung their lamp in response, but not before donning his weapons belt and tossing her hatchet back to Delis. Sariah fingered the stones in her braid. But it was Lazar who emerged from the night. His handsome smile was brilliant under the light of Kael's lamp. His blond curls were drenched with perspiration from pulling the heavy traveling deck behind him.

"What are you doing here?" Kael jumped in the water and hugged his brother, helping him to pull the last few steps to their deck.

"A charge from Metelaus, I fear." Lazar greeted Sariah and took a grateful swig from the skin she offered. "I've run a new record, I think. You've been difficult to track."

"Uncle, Auntie!" Mia leapt from Lazar's deck to theirs, seizing Sariah with a lung-crushing embrace.

"What are you doing here?" A surprised Sariah hugged the child to her breast.

"The better question is, what is *she* doing here?" Lazar's blue and green eyes were fixed on Delis's net-stamped temple.

"It's a long story," Kael said. "Don't mind her."

"Don't mind an executioner?"

"The wench has been defused."

"Really?" Lazar's tone bore little conviction.

Delis circled Lazar, peering into his deck. Abruptly, she pounced into the shelter and wrestled with something in the darkness. "There's more in here!"

"Stop, Delis," Sariah shouted above the noise of a fierce scuffle. "Stop it, I tell you."

Delis emerged from the shelter clutching a squirming bundle. "Here's treachery, my donnis. Should I kill it?"

"It?" Malord twisted in Delis's hands like a fiend cat caught.

"Let him be."

"Sorry, my donnis." Delis dropped Malord on the deck like a sack of overripe turnips.

Lazar gasped. "Donnis?"

"I'll tell you about it later," Kael said.

Sariah rushed to Malord's side. "Are you all right?"

"Manhandled like a rotten cask by a rot spawn?" Malord straightened his weave with an angry tug. "Of course I'm not well. A fortnight of the flats and now this?"

"Why are you here?" Kael asked.

"We saw your burnt deck at Nafa," Lazar said. "We feared the worst, until we met with the forester—"

"I pledged my cause to Sariah's search," Malord said. "I was there when you needed me, and I fought with you at the wall. And now you snub me, leaving me behind?"

For Meliahs' sake. "Malord, we didn't leave you behind. I had to leave and not because I wanted to." She shook the banishment bracelet under his nose. "Have you two gone mad bringing this innocent child here, knowing my circumstances?"

"Innocent?" Malord mumbled. "Ha."

"He spurns you, my donnis. Should I remove him from your deck?"

"Of course not," Sariah said.

Lazar turned to his brother, frowning. "Who is whose donnis?"

"Sariah pledged to Delis."

"I didn't," Sariah snapped. "Not knowingly, anyway."

"We'd best go inside." Kael smothered his lamp and bid Lazar to do the same. "Just in case."

"Surely you don't mean the rot spawn also?" Malord said.

"Better a whole rot spawn than a half-man," Delis snarled.

Malord slapped her legs. "Get out of my way."

"If you touch me again, I'll kick you back to the top of the Crags."

"Not with two broken legs you can't."

"Auntie." Mia was jumping up and down like a mad rabbit. "Auntie!"

Sariah rubbed her temples, sensing the wrath of an impending headache swooping down on her.

"Well, well. What a sweet family reunion, I see."

A woman Sariah didn't know stepped out of Lazar's shelter, a striking figure as tall as Kael and as svelte as Delis, although notably more curvaceous. As if the spirit of concord had arrived in the flesh, her appearance froze the incipient fray. The newcomer's sleeveless tunic displayed her shoulders' smooth ebony skin. It was generously cut to showcase the admirable swell of her breasts and the strength of long and shapely legs.

"Hello, Kael. *Kaelin*," the newcomer said. "I'm glad to see you again. Will you be so kind and make the introductions? There are some here I don't recall meeting before."

The woman's smile was just another stroke of perfection on a flawlessly crafted face, endowed with a luxurious pair of sculpted lips and large yellow irises that almost matched in the purity of her eyes' bright whites. It was remarkable. For the first time since Sariah had met Kael, he blushed like an eight-year-old, stammering through a feeble attempt at an introduction.

She put an end to that quickly. "I'm Sariah. Who might you be?"

The woman's grip was harsh like the snatch of a hang rope. "I'm the Lady Eda, the forester."

◻ ◼ ◻

"I can't believe you burnt your father's deck, Mianina," Kael said while slicing a strip of dried eel, meticulously salting it, and passing it on to Eda. "How did it happen?"

Eda flashed a splendorous smile of overdone gratitude. In the safe enclosure of their shuttered shelter, the gesture seemed particularly intimate to Sariah. She wondered what was wrong with her this night, why she liked Eda so little when everybody, except Delis perhaps, seemed to adore the woman. Why did she have a sudden urge to punch the forester in the nose on account of a salted strip of eel?

"I didn't mean to burn the deck," Mia said with her mouth full. "It was an accident. It just happened."

"My, my," Eda said. "It seems like a very bad year for the Ars brothers' decks. We might have to grow a new forest just for you and your brothers, Kaelin. But don't worry. I'll give Metelaus a great price on his timber. A kinship special, you may call it."

The men in the shelter laughed as if someone was tickling their toes. Sariah didn't think Eda was funny. She didn't like the way she used Kael's nickname so frequently, ending with a quick lick of pink tongue over sumptuous lips, as if his name was a spoonful of molasses melting between her lips.

Lazar set his drink aside. "Since Sariah left, Mia has been experiencing these bouts. She's unable to contain her powers. She tried, poor thing, but she can't."

"I was sad," Mia said. "I was angry."

"At first, short bursts of unexpected flow escaped her, singeing a thing or two," Lazar said. "But then, the bouts got worse. They began to happen more often, until she couldn't control them at all. After his deck burned, Metelaus thought it would be too dangerous to keep Mia away from Sariah for much longer."

"There's a special link between a stonewiser and her breaker," Malord said. "Sariah, you broke Mia. It's very possible the child is too young to be separated from you."

Sariah put her arm around Mia, stroking her skinny shoulders. Sariah's palms were warm, infusing Mia with calmness, appeasing the child's emotions as she had done since the first day Mia had been broken. But even as she was able to draw peacefulness from her inner reserves to comfort Mia, Sariah was troubled. A link that strong was likely to cause great suffering. An attachment developed to such extent could tap into Sariah's weaknesses, cause the child serious injuries, maybe even kill her.

She had not wanted to break Mia. But Mia had been at death's door and Sariah had had no choice. She couldn't abandon the child to suffer the consequences of her breaking on her own. She had to find a way of helping Mia to overcome the attachment. She considered the little girl, cuddled with her head on her lap. Mia's eyes grew heavy with Sariah's infusion. She promptly fell asleep.

"Has she had any other bouts lately?" Kael asked.

"A few, when we first set out," Lazar said. "Fewer as we neared you and none since a few days back. She gained more control as we came closer to you."

"How did you find us?" Kael asked. "We took great pains to avoid leaving any tracks."

"That, too, it's a bit of a mystery," Lazar said. "The forester helped."

Another one of Eda's smiles launched gracefully toward Kael. Sariah's blood boiled a few degrees warmer. She didn't like the bitterness unsettling her stomach and turning the good food before her into an unappetizing heap of dung.

"But it was Mia who found you," Malord said. "The child can sense Sariah. The closer we came to you, the more accurately she could pinpoint your whereabouts."

Sariah was shocked. "Sense me? How?"

"I'm not sure," Malord said. "I can feel the attachment in her, but I can't follow where it reaches. Perhaps when you probe her, you'll understand better than I can. It's nothing I've seen before."

Sariah repressed an urge to groan. If Malord, the wisest stonewiser in the Domain, couldn't understand this, how was she going to fix it?

"Now, now, we mustn't be all dreary and down." Eda patted Kael's thigh. "Surely you've made some progress with your search for this Leandro, haven't you?"

"You told her?" Sariah stared at Kael, seeing a reckless blabbering fool she had never known before.

"I thought the forester could help."

Of course he did.

"Kaelin, I wished you had stayed for a few more days," Eda said. "After you left, the Enduring Woods came to bloom. The flower clusters were a feast to the eye. And the harvest, you wouldn't believe the harvest. The pericarps were glorious—"

"The what?" Sariah said.

"The pods," Kael explained. "Enduring woods yield their seed in pods instead of fruit, like peas and beans."

"Poor wiser," Eda said. "She doesn't understand what we're

talking about. It must be hard for you to follow when Kael launches into one of his long land-healing monologues."

Kael may have bored Eda with such monologues, but not her. Sariah wondered if that was good or bad. Bad, she decided promptly.

"I was telling you about the flowers. The perfume we extracted, Kaelin, it could come straight from Meliahs' gardens. Here, take a whiff." The woman stretched her elegant neck toward Kael, an irresistible offer. "Isn't it exquisite?"

Someone's nose was at risk. Kael's? Eda's? Sariah didn't know whose yet, but the injury was imminent. Sariah didn't know much about the woman's occupation, but shouldn't a forester have brawny arms and rough hands from felling trees and stripping bark, instead of shapely limbs and manicured nails?

She stared down at her own hands. They had been nice to look at before she left the keep, unornamented, long fingered and always well-kept as required by the Guild's strict tidiness rules. Not now. The gaudy bracelet looked like a harlot's trinket. The raw skin around her chafed wrist reminded her of a dog with the mange. Her palms were scarred by the twin stones' searing touch. Her fingers looked stubby and callous. She picked at the jagged nail on her thumb, the one she had accidentally bruised yesterday. And she wasn't even a forester.

"What does a forester do anyway?" she asked. "I mean, you don't exactly look like a timber laborer."

Eda's chuckles rang like the chimes of a merry bell. "I forget you're not of the Domain. I'm the custodian of the last of the Enduring Woods. I handle the harvesting, production and sale of the woods' derivatives—perfume, gum, bark and sap—but I don't fell the trees myself. We've got laborers who do that."

"The forester is an ancient name in the Domain," Malord said. "Eda's family has watched over the woods since before the rot."

Sariah supposed she should be awed by the distinction. Eda was a woman of the greatest noble blood, who still endured in the Domain with title, good name, and obviously, coin, since she seemed to know her business well.

"And you came along because...?" The suddenness of Sariah's

question silenced the shelter. She felt mildly ashamed, as if she had committed a breach of courtesy.

"I thought I would assist Lazar in his search for Kael," Eda said. "Since I had given Kael directions, I knew where he was heading. I do enjoy getting out of my woods every so often."

Her woods. Eda smiled and everybody smiled, and then she said something funny again, and all the men were laughing. The effect of her smile on the opposite sex was astonishing. What was it about the other woman that bothered her so? Eda had not been mean to her, or unkind. She had not been rude, as Sariah had been, or distant, despite her high status. Yet something had Sariah seething, boiling like a neglected kettle on a hot fire every time Eda's yellow-tinged gaze caressed Kael with the length of her amazing eyelashes. Sariah had never doubted Kael. She knew his emotions, his trueness, the extent of his affections. Yet despite all that, this woman still disturbed Sariah, stirring her basest emotions. Why?

Because Eda wasn't a wanted fiend, or a scrawny fugitive, or a rogue wiser with a heart of stone. Because Eda wasn't a weary soul or a well-used, stone-pledged servant. Because instead, she was a match to Kael's merits—earthy, lovely, noble, wealthy, fine of body and character, and high on heat. Because Eda was the kind of woman that belonged with Kael.

It was Kael's grip that brought Sariah back to the conversation, the inquiry of his fingers reaching to interlace with hers, the subtle plaiting of her five cold digits to his four warm fingers. The loss of his middle finger hadn't weakened his grasp. Its absence still pained Sariah, and yet the intimacy was overriding, for he offered his left hand to no one but her.

"Malord, perhaps you ought to return with Lazar," Kael was saying. "I can't say ours will be an easy road."

"I know," Malord said, "but Sariah might yet have need of me. I'm staying, but Lazar here must go back right away."

Lazar's smile alerted Sariah to news. "Do tell."

"Kemere," Lazar said. "She's with child."

Sariah wasn't blind to the undercurrent of emotion exchanged between the brothers. A sense of quiet awe traveled between Kael and Lazar, wordless joy that spoke of pride and delight. Lazar was beaming. The expression on Kael's face was so honest and raw, so vividly happy for his brother that Sariah found herself wishing foolishly that she could be the source of such joy.

She had done all she could, although only she knew that. She had drunk the last of the potion months ago. In an intricate, cunning trade, she had managed to trick the Guild's Prime Hand into relinquishing one of the Guild's best kept secrets, the Mating Hall's own brew, the only concoction known to unlock a stonewiser's repressed reproduction cycles.

Sariah had no idea if it had worked. She was no ignorant adolescent. On the other hand, her stonewiser biology differed from that of the average woman. She had no helpful experience in matters of pregnancy and birth, which were among the many prohibited topics at the keep. Besides, these days, she wasn't sure having a child was a good idea. Her world was too dangerous, a poor offering for a helpless baby.

It had been Kael's notion, to grow a family in the generations' traditions, to gift a child with the parents' labor and sweat, Meliahs' ways. Like most of Kael's ideas, it was infectious. Lying with him, she had discovered her own little dreams too, delusions, if one believed the ways of the Guild, but at least they were *her* delusions. She didn't need to worry. The Prime Hand's potion had probably been as rancid and spoiled as it tasted, and her womb continued to be as lethal to life as it had always been.

"Kemere's six months' gone," Lazar was saying. "That's why I want to return soon. Wouldn't want to miss a day if I could, but Metelaus was busy with the distributions, and he wouldn't trust anyone with Mia but you and me, Kael."

"You must be off soon then," Kael said, "tomorrow at the latest. You never know how long the road is going to be in the Domain. Meliahs forgive you, if you take too long and Kemere's time comes—"

"She'll kill me."

"And for good reason."

Kael and Lazar broke out into the quiet laughter the grown children of Ars shared with each other, a very private sound, an honest, contagious chuckling that Sariah loved to hear.

"A toast." Eda raised her cup. "To the Ars brothers. May they outlast the rot, may they return to the land."

Resigned to the fate of the barren, Sariah drank to the progress of Ars. She was thinking, though. The forester had come for a purpose. And Kael's dreams deserved to come true.

Twelve

SARIAH WAITED UNTIL both decks were filled with the quiet noises of sleep before she tiptoed over Delis and Mia and stepped out to meet the unspoken summons. The stars were ablaze. For a moment, the woman was part of the night, but then she turned to face Sariah, and her eyes, knowing and two-toned yellow, revealed her as the earthly creature she was.

"You've come." She patted the place next to her on the deck. "I wasn't sure you would. You seemed too aloof to care most of the time."

Aloof? Not when her blood was straining through her veins like thickly clotted cream.

"Why did you come?" Eda asked.

Not for the fun, of that Sariah was sure. "I guess I was curious."

"About Kael and me, I suppose."

Sariah envied the woman's confidence in her body's beauty, in her femaleness's devastating supremacy. She allowed the woman's words to sink in, to sting like the most venomous of poisons, to burn until she wanted to scream in frustration.

Eda flashed her devastating smile. "The tales I could tell you. You mustn't be resentful about the inevitable."

We've had our share of adventures together. Kael never lied.

"He won't be distracted by the ordinary," Eda said. "He's only suitable for the extraordinary."

Sariah had no doubt of their respective placement on Eda's ordinary and extraordinary lists. It hurt; she couldn't deny it, every word and nuance. But wasn't pain the most obvious sign of life to the wounded?

What would it be like to be the forester? To have no curse

tainting your blood, no craft haunting your life, no pledges to serve but those made to the self? What would it be like to exist for your own sake, to seek only your own progress, to reign supreme over your body and know it? For an instant, Sariah allowed herself to wallow in her imagination's indulgence. For an instant also, she hated, envied and cursed the woman who had all she didn't have. Then the moment passed and she was her disciplined stone-pledged self again.

"He's no simple fare," Eda was saying. "You ought to know that—"

"Do you smell that?" Sariah whiffed the night's balmy air. "I never knew it stunk."

"Excuse me?"

"The female estrus," Sariah said. "The fragrance of racing mares."

Eda's eyes flamed like fire arrows. "I've been told you are a little... odd."

"You, on the other hand, are nothing less than sensational. Capitulation is the only reasonable option. Supremacy by awe."

"You said you wanted to know—"

"I said I was curious."

"About Kael and I?"

"About you."

"So you don't want to—"

"No."

An instant of panic flashed in Eda's golden eyes. She was momentarily thrown off course, a fake retreat. But she was by no means easy to snare. Her lovely shoulders straightened. Her breasts rose and sank in quiet provocation. Most people would mistake the woman for a peacock, dazzling with its brilliant plumage, but Eda's beauty was not idle adornment—it was deadly camouflage.

"So tell me," Sariah said. "Who told you?"

"Who told me what?"

"About me. You said you were told I was odd. A very knowledgeable source then."

"I have no idea what you're talking about."

A man would have believed her. Sariah was sure of that. The

yellow eyes blinked, brimming with warm and sudden innocence. Sariah wished she could do that, stun people into a break of the senses, erase the question with a flare of beauty and a hint of a suggestion.

"Beautiful. Powerful. Influential," Sariah said. "You probably tried to take Kael away from me first. When that failed, you gave us a new deck. Thank you for that. I wouldn't want to seem ungrateful. You're too proud to stoop to stalking, so you must have a very good, logical reason to be here this night. And if Kael falls to you, as he eventually must, that's very good too."

The forester was not used to defiance. "If I really wanted to, I could have him."

"Oh, I believe you. Truly, I do. But that's beside the point. Tell me. Why are you here?"

"I've already told you—"

"But it wasn't the truth," Sariah said. "Your crew. How far away are they?"

Eda opened her mouth and closed it without saying a word.

"Well, there must be a crew. You're too far away from your woods to do this by yourself."

Eda's gaze turned cold and appraising.

"But they can't be too close," Sariah said. "Lazar has a good eye, day and night. They must be posing as part of the mob. Aye. You wouldn't risk revealing your hand. It's not compatible with your *other* purposes."

Eda scoffed. "What do you know of my purposes? What do you know of the ways of the Domain?"

"Not much. I fear you're going to have to tell me."

"Beware, Sariah. The forester is one of the Domain's last noble houses. So is the house of Ars. In the times before the execration, we were the most powerful of all houses. Ours was a prosperous world. We were the lords and ladies of a healthy land."

Sariah could see it with her mind's eye, a world in which the likes of Kael and Eda ruled over thousands in justice and wealth; a world of cultivated fields, banquets and celebrations; a dead world, long gone. Did Eda know?

"You of the Guild, you can't begin to understand the meaning of nobility," Eda said. "You only acknowledge your cursed blood's power and your trade's importance. But I heed the past. I honor my ancestors. I'm no traitor. My house stands fast with the house of Ars."

"But it's not Ars you're after, is it? It's me you want."

"Don't overestimate your importance in the great scope of things."

"And you must want me alive, because your crew is out there, my liver is currently free of your blade, and you're still here."

Eda waved her sculpted chin in the general direction of the deck shelter. "You must be feeling quite smug with that snotty brute of yours, keeping watch over you at all hours like a faithful mastiff."

Sariah caught a glimpse of Delis coiled on her haunches, staring from the darkness beyond the threshold like a stalking wolf. She smiled. "I suppose there are advantages to all misfortunes."

"You're odd." Eda chuckled. "Entertaining, but odd."

"It's up to you," Sariah said. "Whether you keep the peace you cherish with the house of Ars, whether your noble reputation comes out unscathed from this meeting. I wonder how the Domainers will feel when they learn their trusted forester has been playing games with the enemy. Think Eda. Do they really need to know? Does Kael need to know?"

The yellow eyes widened. "You wouldn't dare."

"He ought to know your game."

"He wouldn't take your word over mine."

"I'm willing to see. Either way, I doubt he would like you much afterwards."

Had the woman been a mare, she would have been foaming at the mouth.

"Who wants me and why?" Sariah asked. "Answer me truthfully, and I won't tell Kael."

"All I have to do is lie in wait," Eda said. "All I have to do is wait for you to be trapped or killed. The way of things, it will happen very soon."

"Be careful, forester, because Kael could be trapped or killed in the bargain, and you could lose your prize. If you're not helpful to me, if you're not forthcoming, I'll make sure that if and when I'm gone, he'll never, ever return to you."

Eda wasn't easy to shake and yet Sariah needed to know everything she knew. Sariah's tongue was heavy as lead but she pressed on. "A time may come when Kael might want something I can't give. If you came out of this without fault in his eyes, if you left here tomorrow with your intentions secret and your name intact, it could very well be you who could give him what he wants most."

The realization was slow in Eda's yellow eyes, but when it came, it burned like the summer sun. "Do you swear on your wiser's oath you won't tell Kael about my role in this?"

"If you tell me the truth and leave with Lazar tomorrow morning."

The woman hesitated. She stared into the Barren Flats wistfully, as if seducing the night to whisper all the future's secrets in her ear. When she finally spoke, she did it abruptly, without bothering to conceal her irritation. "A few weeks back, a man came to the forest."

"Was he a burly, bearded man with a wide nose?"

"No, he was a matching eyes like you, clean shaven."

"He wanted to buy your timber, I bet."

"He bought enough timber and at a good premium." Eda lifted her chin proudly. "He said the Guild was looking to retrieve you. He said he would pay well for you."

The forester was the logical choice. She was at the center of the Domain's business, trading with all the Domain's settlements, and possibly with a few towns on the other side of the wall, if Sariah had judged Eda fairly as an avid entrepreneur. Noble blood or not, coin was difficult to refuse in the Domain's direness. And, if someone had been tracking Sariah's progress—or lack thereof—they would have known her deck burned at Nafa and anticipated her need for a new one. Aye. The forester was the ideal contact.

"Did he leave a stone for me?" Sariah asked.

"A stone? No."

Not Arron, then. He loved his little monsters, his snatching stones. "Did this man have a name?"

Despite the exquisitely sculpted lines of Eda's face, beauty had a way of turning ugly in defeat. "I'm sure you understand. Considering the kind of business we did, he didn't mention a name and I didn't ask. But he did say he would return for you. He said they needed you. He said Mistress Grimly, the Guild's true and only Prime Hand, was looking for you."

□ ■ □

Alabara was by far the most inaccessible of all of the Domain's tribes. An active rot pit besieged the settlement year round. The only way in or out was a slim dead water lane carved on a beam of crumbling sandstone. It spanned the rot flow and connected with the few narrow ribs of red stone that anchored the odd-looking settlement.

Sariah leaned on the channel's ledge, making a show of taking a rest. Porous and easily eroded, sandstone wasn't a particularly good guardian for truth or a trustworthy depository for lasting wisings. Yet Sariah could sense the faint call of the wising protecting the stone surrounding the channel. The temptation was too hard to resist.

She laid her palms on the stone. The call echoed through her like a gust of cool wind. It had been a while since she had encountered wised stone of this magnitude. The links in the stone were loose and distant, the core felt hollow, and the wising was by no means as strong as it should be, but the sheer joy of the contact flooded her like a rush of fresh water, until she was beaming with the amazing sensation and brimming like a full reservoir.

"Sariah?" Kael's voice recalled her to the heat of the waning day. He had to shake her a little before she heard him. "Sorry, but you're smiling like a fool. In this wretched line, it's bound to attract attention."

With a pang of regret, Sariah released the trance and joined Kael pulling the deck forward. They managed no more than three or four steps before they had to stop again. It was hard, tedious, muscle-wrenching, calf-bruising work getting the deck to start moving, only to have to stop it again right away. They had been in line all day to enter Alabara. The sun was low on the horizon, and yet they were still stuck in the traffic-choked channel.

She looked back to see that their collective disguise as a family was working well. Whoever was looking for Sariah expected two people, not five. That's why they had decided to come to Alabara together, not to mention there weren't any places on the way where they could have dropped off Malord, Mia and Delis.

Malord played the grandfather fittingly, loitering by the door under the shade of the roof's overhang. To avoid recognition, he had shaped himself a pair of bulky limbs by stuffing some rolled blankets under the one he spread over his lap. Sariah wagered he had his heavy mace stuffed under the blankets as well. He was playing snakes and scorpions with little Mia, who had been told in no uncertain terms to be quiet, obedient, and to restrain her power at all costs, a feat that didn't seem hard for her as long as Sariah was nearby and nobody threatened their lives. Meliahs help them all.

Delis knelt by the brazier like a dutiful wife, stirring something, probably dinner, although what she could cook was not clear to Sariah. Delis's face was wrapped, hiding the mark on her temple. Sariah supposed she ought to be grateful for the stench that poisoned the air. In addition to wearing the face wrap, the Alabarians wore translucent, colorful veils to protect their eyes from the sting in the air. The veil didn't hide her features, but the color of Sariah's matching eyes was fairly diffused by it.

For further protection, Sariah had decided to wear male clothing under her weave. Her braid was tucked beneath a young man's cap. She had bulked up her shoulders a bit, toying with the proportions of her tightly bound chest. Her one arm also looked the part, but that was only because of Delis's attempt at concealing her banishment bracelet.

It had happened the night before, as they camped in the flats, waiting for their turn to go into Alabara. They had been discussing the plan that would allow them to enter undetected.

"I will go, regardless," Sariah was saying.

"You can't go," Kael said. "If that thing begins to glow, you'll get yourself killed."

"I must speak to Leandro."

"You can't come."

"Do you think you're my lease?"

Delis stiffened with Sariah's indignation. Her eyes darted to Sariah's face. She had the distinct impression that Delis sought some instruction from her, some wordless command that would enable her to pummel Kael, or at least try.

"I can make the glow go away," Delis said.

"You can? Why didn't you say so before?"

"My donnis didn't ask."

"I'm not your donnis," Sariah said for the millionth time. "But if you can do as you say, then I'm asking you."

Delis worked on a concoction of mud from the flats, mixed over the brazier's low fire with a measure of flour and some boiled flax from their newly acquired stores. Sariah watched the woman work, taking note of the ingredients. Delis toiled tirelessly through the night over the steaming pot, stealing glances at Sariah when she thought she wasn't looking. Long strands of coarse wild hair escaped the severity of Delis's tail, framing her face in dark waves.

When the concoction was ready, Delis slapped it over Sariah's wrist, covering the bracelet. It took several layers. As the mixture dried, it looked as if Sariah's arm had been colonized by bees and turned into a hive. But by the time Delis finished, the bracelet's red glow was invisible.

Kael inspected Delis's handiwork. "Will the glow leak through?"

"After a few hours," Delis said.

"More than enough time for our little excursion," Sariah pointed out.

Her triumphant smile echoed on Delis's face. Kael stared from one woman to the other, no doubt wondering if these two had purposely conspired against him. It had been an odd moment at best, but Sariah had mouthed a quick word of thanks to Delis when Kael wasn't looking. So far, the cover was intact over the bracelet. Sariah prayed it would remain so for a little longer.

"We're coming to the gate," Kael said.

"At last," Sariah said.

"Don't be too happy. Alabara is a strange place, as hard to

escape as it is to enter. We'll have to have our wits about us if we want to do well in there."

"Truth be told, it looks like something out of Meliahs' nightmares. It reminds me of a giant's rotting corpse, you know, like in the story of Meliahs' rape."

"No doubt one of the Guild's favorites," Kael said. "I don't know that story."

"Surely you've heard about the time when the evil Menodor imprisoned Meliahs for forty days and nights and forced her to lay a stone egg from his seed in exchange for her freedom? When it hatched, a giant emerged from the broken shell, tall as Meliahs' boulders. Menodor was joyous to have a new powerful son to follow in his wicked ways. But Meliahs wasn't pleased with Menodor *or* his ways."

"And we all know what happens when Meliahs isn't pleased."

"Indeed," Sariah said. "She destroyed her giant son before it could take its first step. I think that Alabara looks like the rotting skeleton of the evil giant rising from the broken egg."

"We try to remember Meliahs' blessings on this side of the wall," Kael said. "On the other hand, the tale fits."

The settlement before them was an uneven jumble of decks built on top of each other, ten or twelve stories high connected with hundreds of ladders. The structure's wooden carcass rose from an enormous crater edged by a thin cracked shell of eroded red rock. As they made their way slowly towards the gate, Sariah pressed her hand over her veil.

"The stench of the place."

"It's not just the rot," Kael said. "It's the red dye."

"The red dye?"

"Alabara's treasure. Its reason to exist. No other dye is as highly valued for cloth and paint, in the Domain or in the Goodlands. It comes from the caves in the sand rock."

"That's why the stone felt hollow. That's why the links are so brittle and distant. They're excavating the rock. It's a wonder the settlement stands."

"Believe me, it's a more like a miracle." Kael eyed the higher stories with suspicion. "You should hear the tragedies. It falls apart all the time."

"You'd think the marcher here would care to make it safe."

"You'd think."

"Let's hope we don't have to go very high or stay very long. Look at all these people."

"It's hard to believe, but there's a lot less people trying to enter Alabara today. There's usually many more."

"Why do they come here?"

"Some are dye traders, those you know by their mercenary faces. The rest live here."

"Why would they want to live in this rickety dung pile?"

"Think, Sariah. Alabara is the hardest settlement to access in the Domain and that makes it the safest refuge. As close as the settlement is to the wall, no Shield assault has ever succeeded against Alabara."

"Look at those thugs, harassing people for entrance. I didn't think this type of abuse happened in the Domain."

"That's because you don't know Orgos," Kael said. "He is marcher here."

Three decks ahead, a dozen armed guards were taunting a poor woman and her scrawny children, demanding payment.

"But sir," the woman pleaded, "my brother lives here. As soon as he hears I've come, he'll run down and pay our fees."

"Get out of here," the guard shouted. "Take your whelps with you, idle mouths wanting to eat us out of our food."

"Please, sir, call my brother, on the fourth level. He'll pay for our keeping. I swear."

Sariah seethed. "He's a bully. I know the type."

"His name is Alfred," Kael said. "He's Orgos's lackey."

"You know him?"

"I remember him. Let's hope he doesn't remember me."

The blood drained from Sariah's veins. "Why do I get the feeling there's something you're not telling me?"

Kael's gaze was focused ahead. "I think that woman is going to need our help."

"Back to the flats," Alfred was saying.

"But sir, I've waited three days for entry." The woman sobbed. "We have no more food left. We'll die on the flats. Please, sir. My brother—"

"Leave," Alfred barked. "Or I'll cut your deck's twine myself. See how you like the flats without a deck."

"Mia," Kael called. "I need you to run an errand for me."

The girl hopped down from the deck and joined them in the channel. A knowing smile lit up her freckled face as she listened to Kael's careful instructions. Sariah held her breath. Mia did as she was told, reaching the woman's deck, blending in with the anguished woman's children, and dropping a few coins in her weathered hand.

"Uncle sends the entrance fee," Mia whispered before she disappeared into the crowd, leaving the woman shocked but visibly relieved. Mia slipped out of the deck and then blended with the multitudes piling at the gates. Sariah lost sight of her in the sea of people. She must have circled wide and far, because much to Sariah's anxiety, a few long moments passed before she popped up undetected next to Kael.

"Well done, Mianina." Kael ruffled her veil. "You've done that woman and her family a good deed today."

"You too, Uncle." She smiled.

"Go in the shelter and wait there until we pass the gates," Kael said. "We wouldn't want any of those thugs recognizing you."

Sariah watched the girl go. Despite her lethal power, Mia was learning to do right.

Ahead of them, the woman was allowed passage and the line of decks began to move again. Sariah and Kael pulled in unison, advancing slowly. But something about their earlier conversation bothered Sariah.

"So you know this Alfred thug?" she asked. "And the marcher here, Orgos?"

"A little."

It smelled like carrion, and it wasn't just the rot or the dye. "Kael, son of Ars, is there something you want to tell me?"

"Not particularly." He wore the blank face that aggravated her beyond reason.

"Are you in danger here?"

"I doubt anybody remembers."

The stink was only getting worse. "You better tell me what happened."

"It was a few years back," he said. "I was going to roam the Goodlands and I came here to purchase a bit of red dye, a wise investment for all good roamers. Did I tell you? It trades better than coin in the Goodlands—"

"You said that. Go on."

"I guess Orgos didn't like me much on account of some disruption or another. I'm not a big fan of his methods. I didn't like his price either. I thought it excessive. He was outraged when I refused to pay it."

The deck in front of them came to another stop. Sariah and Kael dug their feet in the mud and braced to break their deck's momentum with the back of their legs.

"I take it you didn't part friends?"

"Friends? No. I wouldn't say so."

"But all ended well in the end?"

Kael began to pull again. "He wanted what he wanted and I didn't want to give it."

"Just tell me, Kael. Why does Orgos have a problem with you?"

"I sort of burned down his place."

Sariah stared at him open-mouthed.

"And I killed a few of his men."

"A few?" She took in the armed thugs at the gates.

"And I cut him, just a little."

"You... cut... Orgos? You wounded him?"

"Sliced off his ear cleanly."

"Stop grinning, you fool. It's not funny. You should have told me before we came. You're in danger here!"

She scanned the long deck line, looking for the quickest way out. They were locked in traffic, trudging toward to the gate, cattle routed to the slaughter.

"This is exactly why I didn't want you to come with me," she babbled, close to hysteria. "You can't go into Alabara. We have to turn around. We've got to get out of this line. Run back. Find a place on one of the waiting decks. We'll pick you up on the way out."

"And leave you alone in this? I think not."

"For Meliahs' sake. You cut the man's ear!"

"I doubt he misses it. He was never a good listener."

"You can't go in there. We have to change our plans."

"Why do you insist in making my choices for me?"

Sariah could hardly believe her ears. "I don't—"

"Aye, you do, and it bothers the liver out of me."

"You'll be missing your damn liver if we go in there, and your senseless head."

"They're mine to lose."

"Don't you give me this load of bull—"

"Don't you treat me like your lease."

"My lease?" Sariah gaped. "You're not my lease. You're my blanket mate and you shouldn't be out here risking blood for the sake of stones."

"But I get to do as I please."

"Really?" Sariah wanted to murder him at the moment. "In that case, I do as I please too."

She waded in front of the oncoming traffic, trying to turn the deck around, pulling like a rebellious mule. Kael just stood there, anchoring the deck with his body like the steadiest of piers. He pulled on the rope and dragged her back to his side, until they were nose to nose.

"Since when do you shy your duty, wiser?"

"Since your life started getting in the way."

"I'm not so sour on life as to give it up easily," he said. "I'm not dumb or stupid, but I understand, as you must, that to be free sometimes means you have to suffer or die."

"What by the rot pits are you talking about?"

"Do you know why I'm here? Why I came?"

"Because of your damn oath?"

"That too. But mostly, I'm here because of you and me, not just you, but me. Our lives. After this. When it's all over."

Sariah had never looked that far ahead.

"We get this done and we're free. You and I, free to do as we like, free of duty. Free."

An end to the endless. Freedom to the lifelong bound. No, Sariah didn't think she could understand the notion, but she was suddenly very glad to consider it.

"Don't you understand, Sariah? There is no other way but forward. Let's do this as quickly as we can. Let's do it together, for the future's sake and move on to that future."

The future was such an alluring, elusive, terrifying notion, one day there, the next day gone, along with someone's existence.

"Let's turn around, Kael. I have a bad feeling about this."

"I think it's too late for that," he said softly. "We've arrived at Alabara's gates."

Thirteen

The man called Alfred was broader than a wagon and taller than a camel. He looked like a camel too, with nostrils wider than the flats and flaccid lips which ruminated obscenities in place of cud.

"No beggars allowed," he bellowed. "What's your business?"

"We've come to deliver a load of flax to the weaver." Kael kept his gaze down and his voice low like a humble laborer, but Sariah knew that every part of him was engaged in tracking the thugs at the gates.

"Cargo's double." Alfred extended a filthy hand. "Me and my friends charge insurance to get you in."

Kael shelled out half of his purse's contents. Alfred pocketed the coins and snatched the purse from Kael's hands. Good thing Kael had anticipated the abuse. He had stored the rest of their coin safely away before entering Alabara. Sariah repressed an urge to kick the thug in the knees.

Alfred jumped down from the ledge and waded to the back of their deck, where the flax was piled in small bundles. Sariah feared the people in the upper stories of Alabara could hear her heart hammering. The day before, Kael had scoured the decks waiting to be admitted into Alabara and managed to purchase a small amount of threshing flax for the deception. They had propped up the flax bundles on a bed of less expensive straw. Thankfully, Alfred didn't seem to know the difference. He didn't seem to recognize Kael either.

"What weaver are you delivering to?" Alfred demanded.

Sariah sensed Kael's hesitation. For a moment, she feared he didn't know the name of the settlement's weavers.

"Katrina."

Meliahs be thanked. Kael had been thorough in his research. "Katrina on the fifth level? Good." Alfred ripped a bunch of bundles out of the small lot. "She's not bad looking. You tell the little bitch to come see me if she wants her full load. She knows what to do."

Sariah caught the warning in Kael's eyes. *Hold your tongue,* it cautioned. She realized Kael's reluctance to utter the weaver's name stemmed not from ignorance, but from concern. He knew these men. He had tried to protect the innocent from the vultures' attention. Too late now.

"Move!" Alfred struck Sariah's butt as if she was an ox, and like a good ox, startled her into pulling. "Do you think you're the only ones who want in before nightfall?"

Sariah pulled like a maniac to get out of the man's way. A kick in the knees, that's what the filthy brute needed. She would be glad to do the honors.

They pulled the deck under the settlement's massive structure, a dead water maze of decks, wooden pillars and ladders, choked with gutweed and trash. It took a while, but at last, they found a place to moor their deck, a corner near a bank of ladders, supported by a thick pillar in good repair and not too far from the gates.

Kael didn't bother stripping his weave or his pulling harness. "Shall we go find your Leandro?"

"Quickly, please. This place gives me the shivers."

Around them, the enormous structure shifted and groaned, straining under the massive weight like a loaded beast.

"It's lasted two hundred chills," Kael said. "It should last us another day."

"That might be," Sariah said. "But I can't help the feeling we are stuck in the very belly of Menodor's giant."

□ ■ □

The inhabitants of Alabara scurried ahead of the night. As the sun set, people trekked up and down the ladders in hurried hordes. Sariah had been worried about someone recognizing her, or worse, Kael, but nobody paid them heed as they climbed from one level to the next, carrying bundles of flax on their backs.

"There has to be a better way of taking things up," Sariah puffed, when they reached the third level.

"There are pulleys around." Kael patted the locked wheel standing beside the ladder. "But you get to pay Alfred's men for those and it seems that tonight, even Alfred and his minions have gone to bed early."

"Strange. There's less and less people on the lanes by the moment."

"Let's see if we can find out what's going on. Excuse me, sir," Kael asked a man hurrying up the ladder. "Might you be able to help us with directions?"

"It's late," the man barked without stopping. "Go inside."

"So much for the Domainers' reputed hospitality," Sariah said. "There's someone else coming. Stop, madam, a question, if you will?"

"Mind your business. I mind mine." The woman disappeared down the next set of steps.

"Alabara." Sariah sighed. "The happiest place in the Domain."

"That was foolish." Kael tackled the next ladder.

"What?" Sariah followed.

"You talked to the woman. Thank Meliahs she was too busy to notice the contrast between your voice and your garb."

Ooops. "Sorry. But by the look of things here, I could be wearing only the bracelet and nobody would notice."

"I'd notice." Kael flashed his best roguish grin. "I'd like to notice."

"Five people to a deck make for piss-poor chances. You've got better odds of getting a welcoming banquet in Alabara than of bedding me any time soon."

"We'll have to improvise," Kael said. "If we don't, I'll be doubling over on my knees and useless from protracted wanting. And you, you'll be kicking thugs and wiseasses in the knees like a discombobulated mule. Don't think I'm missing the signs."

Sariah laughed. "Cool yourself and embrace the kicking and the braying. We can't and we won't until we find Leandro and get out of this accursed place."

They rode yet another rickety ladder to the fifth level.

"There." Sariah spied the weaver's sign. "Let's see if she'll talk to us."

"Let me speak."

"But I might be able to—"

"Our deal was that I'll speak or you go back to the deck."

"Fine, but you better get something from her. With the ale-houses closed and the people gone from the lanes, she's our only chance."

Kael knocked on the door.

"It's after dark," a woman's voice said. "Go away."

"We only need a moment of your time," Kael said.

"I'm closed, be off with you."

"We've got flax for you. A gift, if you'll talk to us."

The door cracked open just enough for a pair of eyes to survey the lane first, then Kael and the bundles they brought.

"Free, you said?"

"Free."

A long nose poked out of the door crack, followed by a pudgy face. "Why?"

"We need information."

"Why bring your trouble to me?"

"Flax is all I have."

"And all I need." She considered Kael broodingly. "You wouldn't be one of Orgos's thugs, would you?"

"No, madam. We're not from here."

"Like I couldn't tell. Hurry. Give me the flax. You fools ought to be inside. What is it you want to know?"

Kael handed her a bundle at a time. "I'm looking for the care-takers who used to run the atorium out in the flats. It seems the place burned down and they've come here. Do you know where they dwell?"

"Haven't they suffered enough?" the woman said. "Why do you want to find them?"

"I have some business with the caretakers."

"It's not fair to charge tribute if the atorium's gone. Orgos charges enough as it is."

"You mistake my intentions. I'm no tax collector."

"Then why are you looking for the atorium's caretakers so discreetly? You can't trick me. I'm not dumb. If your intentions aren't evil, why the secrecy?"

Kael exchanged a quick glance with Sariah. "You're right, madam. I best tell you the truth." He paused contritely. "I've come for help for my brother here." He patted Sariah's back as if petting a dog. "He's lame and mute and now he's turning deaf and dumb as well."

Deaf and dumb?

"The poor thing's not fit for a decent life, you see. I'm his only kin but I can't care for him the way my mother did. She passed away and I thought perhaps, if there's a place—"

"A terrible thing to have to deal with such a dreadful matter," the woman said. "And your poor mother dead. I had a sister once, born not so good of the head. Took care of her for fifteen years. That's a long time, isn't it?"

"Hard work. I'm sure you did the best you could."

"We didn't have atoriums back then." The woman was abruptly aware of the time. "You must go. Be off. You'll be caught."

"Caught?"

"A most dreadful matter." She dragged in the last bundle of flax and began to close the door. "Go back to your deck. Seal your doors and windows. Search tomorrow."

The door bounced off Kael's foot. "And the atorium?"

"Oh, that. The seventh level, right tower. But look tomorrow." The door slammed shut.

"Seventh level it is." Kael hurried to the nearest ladder.

"Deaf and dumb?"

He chuckled. "It's not so far from the truth."

"I really ought to kick your rear." Sariah halted in her tracks. "What's that?"

A monstrous sound overtook Alabara, a rumbling crescendo. A guttural belch resonated through the pile of decks. *Croakeee.* The sound grew to a gruesome chorus. Sariah thought it was the wood breaking, the beams screeching as they split, the impending groan of the settlement's destruction. Something cold brushed her shoulder on its way to the floor, followed by more of the same, raining from the upper stories.

Kael caught something between his hands. "I've seen these in the Goodlands, although never gathered in such great numbers." A huge green-lipped orange frog spanned the full cup of Kael's palms, staring at Sariah with red eyes that matched its long-toed feet. *Croakeee.* It belched. *Croakeee.*

Sariah was surprised to see three or four smaller frogs piled on top of the bigger frog. She looked around. Thousands of likewise loaded frogs claimed the ladders and roofs around them. They hopped on the decks and perched on the railings, coating every surface with the viscous substance oozing from their bodies.

"Now we know why people here wanted to go home in a hurry." Sariah shook a frog from her foot. "Are they poisonous?"

"I don't think so." Kael swiped a dollop of slime and held it up against the light of a torch. "I think some of these are hatchlings in the slime." Before their eyes, tiny tadpoles popped out from the membrane like pebbles from a slingshot.

Kael tried to step around the critters, but since the floors were piled with frogs of all sizes, it was impossible. "We should hurry. The footholds will be slippery in no time."

Sariah overcame her revulsion to follow Kael up the ladders. The monstrous croaking was unbearable and the repugnant slime dangled from ceilings and railings like spit from some slobbering creature.

"It's like a plague."

"A plague? Maybe. But there are species whose natural habits favor congregation for reproduction. What if this is natural behavior? We wouldn't know, would we? Because there haven't been frogs of this kind in the Domain for generations."

"You're thinking it's all linked. The fish, the red hawk, this."

"I'm not sure what to think, but something's changing, and I can't tell what it means for the Domain."

The seventh level on the right tower was the most decrepit part of Alabara. The floorboards were slanted to one side at an alarming angle. The few railings still standing were broken and unreliable, and the entire level swayed when the breeze blew. Sariah broke out into a sweat as she balanced over a wobbly ladder hung in lieu of a bridge to cross to the tower. An incipient fear of heights bloomed in her mind.

Despite the frogs' spectral serenade, the sounds of the atorium's refugees guided them to their quarters. The moans, cries and even the shrill laughter drifting from behind the closed door carried the identifiable mark of madness. Sariah's knuckles had begun to ache by the time the door finally opened.

"We're not taking any more," a weary woman said. In the shadows behind her, bodies sprawled on the floor and piled in close quarters, not unlike the frogs outside.

"We've come to inquire after one of your boarders," Kael said. "We'll settle his account while we're here."

"A paying boarder for a change." The woman allowed them entrance. "Come in at your own discretion. Nights like these, anything can happen."

The room brimmed with anguish and irrational fear. Sariah could feel it in the air, in the boarders' repressed whispers, in the quiet wails that escaped the bound, the catatonic and the ailing.

A frog dropped from the rafters onto a crowded pallet. A single scream spread through the room like simmering fire. The caretakers knocked the screamers senseless with wooden bats, until the outburst of communal panic was broken by the forced silence.

Sariah's throat was too dry to swallow.

"Don't blame the caretakers," the woman said. "After the attack and the journey here, it's been hard on them. Boarders don't take good to change, and this place is not good for the sick or the sane. They hate it here."

That was easy to see.

"You said you came to inquire about a boarder? What's your relation?"

"I'm a friend of the family," Kael said. "His daughters asked me to look in on their father and to bring back news of his condition. They said they paid good coin for his keeping and if their father is well, they're willing to pay some more."

"Aye, well, it's been a rough year," the caretaker said. "I'm sure you know we were attacked. Attacked. Since when is a poor atorium a target for thieves and murderers?"

"Did you lose many during the attack?"

"We lost a few, but not as many as we feared at first."

Sariah kept her hopes up.

"We lost more on the journey here than in the raid," the care-taker said. "On account of the fiery fever."

Damn the fiery fever.

"What's the boarder's name?" the caretaker asked. "When did he start with us?"

"Six, maybe seven months ago," Kael said. "His name is Leandro, originally from Nafa."

"Leandro?" She thought for a moment. "You mean the wild one? His daughters paid good, I remember. Lizard's gills, it had to be one of *them*."

"One of them?"

"And you with coin and everything."

Sariah had to steady her voice before she spoke. "Was Leandro one of the ones killed?"

Kael hushed her with a warning glower.

"Killed?" the woman scratched her armpit. "I'm not sure."

"What is it?" Kael said. "Is Leandro dead or alive?"

"They took a few," the caretaker said. "Leandro was one of them."

In that moment, Sariah's hopes of deciphering the mystery of the pure crashed. All the time traveling to Alabara had been wasted, misspent following a worthless lead. Sariah wanted to hit something or someone, preferably someone who deserved it, but a door or a wall would be fine as well.

"Who took him?" Kael asked.

"Who else? The Shield."

"Why?"

"How am I supposed to know why they took Leandro?" the caretaker said. "The wall's broken. The whole world has gone crazy. The land is like a huge atorium."

Perfect. Not only was Leandro not at Alabara, but he was lost to them, and they didn't even know why. Sariah's search was as wrecked as the atorium.

"What will you tell his daughters?" the caretaker asked. "They can't expect retribution on a madman, can they? I can't be blamed for this tragedy."

"I'm not sure what I can do," Kael said.

"Wait." The woman scurried to a small chest in the corner. "There might be a way."

Kael exchanged a glance with Sariah. There was nothing more to do here. It had been a worthless errand and now the best thing to do was leave Alabara quickly.

The caretaker pulled out a tiny sack from the chest. It was marked with Leandro's name in large crude letters. "His gaming set. I was going to keep it for fees. Perhaps the daughters will be appeased by their father's belongings? Will you take it to them?"

"I suppose it's the least I can do." Kael accepted the little sack. "We'll be leaving now."

They had not taken more than three steps toward the door when a boarder, an old woman, blocked their way, pointing at the sack with a filthy finger. "That's not yours."

"It's all right," the caretaker said. "I gave it to them."

With amazing speed for someone her age, the old crone lunged to snatch the sack from Kael. She missed, but her jagged fingernails caught on the sack's cord, ripping it open. A cascade of little snakes and scorpions spilled on the dirty floor.

"That's not very nice," the caretaker said.

Kael scooped a handful of gaming pieces from the floor and returned them to the sack. Sariah picked up a tiny scorpion and held it on the palm of her hand. It was a perfect diminutive replica of a live scorpion. It had a sleek, elongated body, endowed with four pairs of legs and a set of impressive claws. A segmented, artfully carved tail curled high in the air and ended in a sharp stinger. It was masterfully sculpted from very fine stone, some type of deeply veined orange-yellow rock imbued with sparkling, iridescent crystal. It must have been Leandro's very own little treasure. No wonder the caretaker had wanted to keep it.

A strange sensation tickled her palm, and for a moment Sariah thought the scorpion's fanged tail had stung her hand. She recognized the feeling. Could it be? She pressed the piece to her palm. Meliahs help her. It was wised!

The old woman dropped to her knees besides her. "Will you take me with you? Please, I beg you, take me with you."

"I'm sorry, I can't."

Was there a tale in the game piece? Could it hold a viable trance? Sariah tapped the scorpion's base. A face flashed in her mind, Leandro's stubbly profile. Excitement blazed through her veins. Had the man imprinted his tale in these stones? Was the trail of the pure still fresh in the game pieces? If only she could wise these right now. Would each piece hold a different tale? Or would each piece hold a part of the same tale?

"We need all forty-eight pieces." Sariah scrambled on all fours, scouring the floor for snakes and scorpions, trying to shake off the boarder. But the pleading crone was stronger than the bones sticking from under her rags suggested. She clung to Sariah's leg with determined zeal.

"Take me with you," she pleaded. "The cold demons. They're coming."

"Hush," Sariah said. "You'll wake up your friends."

Other boarders began to stir, a murmur of dark draped shapes rising in the shadows. The old crone got a hold of Sariah's veil and wouldn't let go.

"He said someone would come," she whispered. "For my soul. For yours."

"Who?" Sariah asked. "Who told you I would come?"

"Madam, please." Kael had come to help. "Let go."

"She knows something."

Unexpectedly, the old crone dodged Kael and fell on Sariah, an assault of coarse blankets and flinging arms, a flash of wild eyes and sharp claws. "You've brought doom to us."

A blood-curdling scream issued from the woman's toothless mouth, a high-pitched, sinister shriek that pierced Sariah's eardrum and blasted her face with a rush of fetid breath. An invisible gate toppled. The madness in the room spilled into pandemonium. A man sprang from the floor and began to trot in pointless circles. A woman sat on her haunches, shouting a song without melody. A number of bodies contorted on the floor or climbed over each other, howling. A man dangled from the rafters bellowing obscenities.

The door crashed open. Men poured into the room. Frogs spurted in by the thousands. Hysteria took over the boarders. The caretakers swung their bats without pause. Kael was struggling to rid Sariah of the mad woman's clutch.

"Beware of the one who always wins." The crone's slobbering mouth pressed hard against Sariah's ear. "Beware of the one who plays the stone and not the game. His tales are your demise."

There was a sequence of muted thumps. Blood spurted from the crone's nose, spraying Sariah's face. The old woman's head caved in on one side. A clump of white hair sunk in a puddle of blood. Something struck Sariah hard. The room spun like a wobbling wheel. Croaks and shrieks deafened her senses.

The next blow, to her forearm, shattered her inconspicuous cast. Her bracelet's red glow spilled through the cracks. She looked up to see Kael above her, still wrestling. She heard the sickening crack of wood against bone and watched helplessly as his face tensed and then went slack. The last thing she remembered were his closed eyes and a trail of blood trickling fluidly over his forehead.

Fourteen

"Look who's awake," Alfred said. "Welcome, Sariah, isn't that your name? Welcome to the house of Orgos." The man's camel lips flapped with his version of a smile, and whatever haze still shrouded Sariah's mind evaporated with the chilling show of fangs.

She remembered the commotion at the atorium, the old crone, Leandro's wised gaming pieces. Wised! She remembered the caretakers, knocking people's heads with their bats. Many more had come. One had obviously carved a knot on her head—

Kael. Where was Kael? She craned her neck to look around, testing the ropes binding her wrists and ankles. They were sturdy enough. She found Kael lying face down next to her on the floor, trussed like hunted fowl. The side of his face was crusted with dry blood and his eyes were closed, but thank Meliahs, his respiration seemed steady and strong.

"I have to say, you both have iron balls showing up here," Alfred said. "You must be Stonewiser Sariah. The banished vanished. The Domainer who doesn't belong in the Domain. The lad who is not a lad. Yes, I looked in all the places I shouldn't, and confirmed all of it."

"So you can tell gals from guys?" Sariah said. "How impressive."

Alfred's boot collided with her stomach and left her wriggling like a stomped maggot.

"Watch your mouth, you little trollop. There're a couple of nasty posses clamoring for you outside the gates. I'd be happy to feed them pieces of you."

Breathe. If she curled around her knees, the pain throbbing in her middle became bearable. *Breathe.* Never show fear to a growling dog.

"The mob?" she rasped.

"They're waiting," Alfred said, "and I have no doubt that as soon as Orgos returns, you'll find your end at their hands."

That explained why they hadn't been killed yet. Orgos wasn't currently in Alabara and Alfred was waiting for his boss to return. He wouldn't move without Orgos's approval. Damn, her middle hurt. Perhaps he had broken a rib or ruptured her bowels. How long did they have before Orgos returned?

"You can tell the bastard that Alabarians don't forgive fire and blade." Alfred toed Kael's inert body with the tip of his boot. "I might have missed him if we hadn't been warned. This time he won't get off so easy."

So Alfred hadn't recognized Kael after all. Who had warned Alfred and why? Choice or duty, Sariah regretted Kael's presence in Alabara. If only he hadn't been so stubborn.

"You knew, didn't you?" Sariah wheezed. "About me. That I was coming here?"

"Wouldn't you like to know?"

Someone was tracking her and closely. Could it be the same man who had spoken to the forester? Or was it the burly mob leader? Was it Arron's or Grimly's agent? Perhaps it was another executioner sent after Delis? They had to find their way out of Alabara. What about Mia, Malord and Delis? Had they been caught?

No. If little Mia felt threatened and unleashed her power in Alabara, the whole settlement would know it. They must be hiding. There were more crannies and nooks in the watery basement of Alabara than in Meliahs' maze.

"Don't think I didn't find the stones in your braid," Alfred said. "We heard about those. They're deep in the rot flow, mind you."

She shook her head and found her plait undone. The stones were truly gone. Whoever was tracking her must have seen her attempt to use the stone at the executioners' nets. The loss, however, was not as poignant as she first thought. The bursting stones she carried were too powerful to help them in Alabara. The settlement's structure was too frail to withstand an explosion. It could cause parts of the settlement to collapse, killing them as well as a whole lot of other people. She made a mental note to consider this problem later. If they survived.

She had to get them out. Perhaps she could get a message to Delis. She looked over her shoulder to Kael. Like hers, his weapons belt was missing and so was Leandro's game. She couldn't leave without it. Leandro wouldn't have gone through the trouble of imprinting those little stones unless he had something important to say, hopefully about the pure. What had Alfred done with their possessions?

One of Alfred's men barged into the room. "Trouble at the gates. Will you come?"

"I want these two guarded at all times," Alfred said. "They're very dangerous. Orgos will be happy to profit from the woman's fate, but he will be even more delighted to see his old flame. Maybe this time, Orgos will get his price."

Old flame?

The door closed, leaving Sariah in a darkness tinted red from her bracelet's glow. Outside, the hasp fit over the staple and the padlock clicked in place with horrifying finality. Sariah sat against the wall and found it solid. They weren't in the flimsy part of Alabara, but rather in the second or third level, where the floor boards were two stones thick and the walls and ceilings were built of petrified wood. The weather had turned steamy again. The tiny room had no windows, no vents, no openings of any kind. It was as if they were in a locked box. *Box.*

The memories crushed her like a rockslide. She remembered her knees jammed under her nose, bruised and scratched from hitting the wood; the darkness, bearing down on her child's mind like a hammer's blow; the growl of her empty stomach almost as loud as her cries before her voice had eroded into hoarse wails; the acrid taste of blood trickling in the desert of her mouth. She had been what? Maybe five years old?

"Kael." She whispered against his ear. "Wake up. Kaelin?" She leaned against his shoulder and shook him. "Please. Get up."

She didn't know she was crying until Kael stirred. With a grunt and a heave, he turned on his back and sat up groggily. "Sariah?

Are you crying?" He pressed his face against her cheek. "What is it? Are you hurt?"

Where had these tears come from? "I'm fine, I swear. And you? Is your head badly wounded?"

Against the tinted darkness, she spied his head's slow motion as he leaned it carefully against the wall. "It's aching some but I think I'll live. Are you sure you're all right?"

She was fine if she didn't mind her heart. It was pounding against her breastbone, a deserter trying to jump out of her throat.

"We have to get out of here."

"It's this place," he said. "You can't stand the tight space. Try not to remember. It's not that bad. I've been in worse places. And with your bracelet's glow, I can even see some of you."

"Don't make light of this," Sariah said. "You're a wanted man in Alabara."

"But yours is the only light I need."

He said it factually, naturally, as if she were his sword, or his sling, or his lamp, and yet the words were like a bandage to a ruptured stitch. Sariah laid her head on his shoulder. Orgos's cell was not so bad. It was small and hot, but she could move and breathe and he was right, her bracelet's glow helped her to make out her surroundings.

"Do you recall the fray?" Kael asked.

"I think those were Alfred and his men who broke down the door."

"Aye, perhaps the caretaker sent word to him."

"Leandro's gaming pieces are wised. I have to have them. And the crazy old crone, she knew something too."

"I seem to recall she's dead. She can't help us now."

"The mob's out there. Alfred was here, gloating." She told him about her conversation with the thug.

"I wonder when Orgos is expected," Kael said. "Turn on your side, let me see if I can work on your ties."

"Alfred said something strange. Something about you being Orgos's old flame?"

Kael's fingers faltered on the knots, but then resumed the work.

"He said this time Orgos will get his price."

"Over my rotted carcass," he muttered. "Damn these ropes."

"What is it that he wants?"

"Something he's not getting."

"He wants you. Doesn't he?"

"Me? No. He wants my arse. Or, more to the point, he wants the hole in between."

Meliahs help them all.

The door crashed open, but it wasn't Meliahs. Alfred entered the room, grabbed Sariah by the back of her weave, and dragged her out.

"Where are you taking her?" Kael said.

Alfred delivered a mind-numbing kick to Kael's head. "You won't care now."

□ ■ □

Alabara's marcher was more or less what Sariah expected. If Alfred was a camel, Orgos was a bull, a red bull with broad hips and a long coarse beard which dangled as a single clump from his chin. He wore his hair long, to hide the absence of his earlobe perhaps. But the brutality of his appearance was misleading. Sariah would not make the mistake of underestimating Orgos's intelligence. Practical wit brimmed in his hazel and gray eyes.

"So you're the banished stonewiser everybody is talking about?" Orgos leaned back in his chair and slammed his boots on the table. "Not a lot to look at presently. They say you're dangerous. But you don't look so dangerous to me."

"What a difference a strand of rope makes," Sariah said. "From where I stand, Orgos, you look the part of quite fearful."

The man's impressive belly quaked with laughter. "They said you wield a sharp tongue. They're right. I've made a deal with your little mob out there. They're waiting for you. Aren't you going to beg for your life?"

"Beg? If you'll spare me, I'll gladly beg, but I have a feeling such begging will be worthless, so I had more a mind to use persuasion in the bargain."

"It's the mob that needs to be persuaded. Care to try?"

"I'd much rather take my chances with you."

"Now, sweetheart, you're confusing my good humor for mercy. You're as dead out there as you are in here, but your death is more profitable and less problematic to me if they kill you."

"You may be right, but only in the short term." Sariah was thinking on her feet. "Let's see. What have they offered you? I know. They offered not to tell the executioners that I was here, so you don't have to pay the huge fine incurred for having this conversation with me."

Orgos didn't admit to it, but neither did he deny it.

"But a man with a keen business sense such as yourself wouldn't settle for erasing fines. No. They offered you more. A cut of my death ransom, I think."

The man's smile was his only gloating admission.

"A large cut, more generous than the offer you received from the one who came to warn you about me." Sariah paused. "Or could it be that you favored the mob because the other alliance was too dangerous even for the likes of you? Who was it, Orgos? Was it someone from the Guild?"

"You're clever," Orgos said. "But that hardly counts for anything with me."

"This might be a good opportunity for you," Sariah said. "But it's not a secure venture. After all, they have to take my dead body back to the executioners before they can charge their mob's earnings. Then, they'd have to return to Alabara to bring your share. I hope they come back, because you might have the brawn to control Alabara, but beyond that, no other marcher in the Domain would take up your cause. How will you collect your share then?"

Orgos slammed his fist on the table. "I mind my business well enough. Did I ask for your advice? You're going to the mob."

On the shelves behind Orgos's chair, standing among the flashy ornaments adorning his quarters—mostly copper and bronze trinkets and the occasional gold-plated forgery—Sariah spied their weapons belts, Kael's purse, and Leandro's game sack. It was a small consolation. At least she knew where the game was. If she could only devise a way of getting out of Orgos's lair alive. She had to think like the Guild wiser she had once been. What could she trade Orgos in exchange for their lives? The blurry outline of a plan began to take shape in her mind.

"I've been thinking." Sariah strained to make her voice sound calm. "What if my life could profit you greater than my death?"

Orgos flashed a smug smile. "You have nothing of value to me. I don't like stones and I don't care about wising tales. You have no coin. We all know you live on Ars's charity. What could you possibly offer me?"

"You have a problem, a big problem, one you don't know you have. I'm the only one who can help you."

"Lizard's gills. You're good. I almost believe you."

"You should, if you want your little kingdom to prosper."

"It won't do you any good regardless, but spit it out, you little viper."

"The channel's arch stone, the one that holds the passage to Alabara. When was the last time it was wised?"

"Why do you ask?"

"I'd say about twenty years since the last wising? The lifespan of a good deck, wouldn't you agree?"

Orgos tapped his beefy fingers on the table. "I'm bored."

"The wising is spent. The stone is weak. You've excavated it to a fragile thinness in your quest for red dye. Soon, it will no longer protect you from the rot flow."

The man's eyes preyed on her face. "Liar. There's nothing wrong with Alabara's stone."

"Haven't you noticed the new cracks fracturing the stone midway through the channel? Didn't you have to post a deep dead water warning by the gate where the bottom gave way? What's causing the palisade to tilt at odd angles in several places?"

"Stone cracks and shifts all the time."

"Not as fast as it's happening here. Not as severely, either. Any day now, the channel bridge will collapse and the ridges will crumble. Alabara comes after that, and with it, the end to your rule. Heed my wiser's sworn warning."

That caught Orgos's attention. His head snapped up and his eyes were on her again. Sariah withstood his glowering. In reality,

Alabara needed an extended visit from a Hall of Masons' stone-wiser. Trained in the geology of sacred stones and experienced with quarries, a wiser from the Hall of Masons would have been much more helpful to Alabara. To be truthful, Sariah didn't know exactly how long Alabara's wising would last. It could be a day, a year, a century, but she could swear with certainty that the wising was weak. Sooner or later, Alabara would fall to the rot.

"Let me guess," Orgos said. "You can fix the wising?"

"I can. In exchange for a few favors."

"Wisers always want favors."

"A deck, a bit of red dye for the road, our possessions returned, safe passage from the mob, our weapons, and our lives. No sense in working for free."

The man threw his head back and roared a string of booming hacks. "The daring." More laughter. "I can pay a wiser to come to Alabara. Why grant you all those favors?"

"Wisers aren't so common in the Domain. They're busy and far from here. It would take a lot of persuasion on your part to entice one here. Depending on your methods, you may not get the wiser to do as you wish."

"Whereas you, coincidence of coincidences, are conveniently here."

Sariah opted for silence. If she could convince Orgos of the need to wise the stones, she was as good as on her way. With her hands freed and a bit of stone, she could defeat the guards, fetch Delis, rescue Kael from the cell, get the game, meet the others, and get out of Alabara. It was not perfect, but it was a plan.

"It would take a long time for a wiser to come." Orgos pulled at his beard thoughtfully. "But if what you say is true, and the stones are too weak to hold..."

Sariah held her breath and prayed to Meliahs that Orgos saw the need for her services.

"I tell you what, wiser. You've got yourself a deal. Wise Alabara's stones and you'll get your deck, enough red dye to help finance your wanderings, weapons, possessions, safe passage from the mob, and your life, as you asked. I swear it on my marcher's oath."

Sariah thanked Meliahs from the bottom of her soul. Then she realized Orgos had omitted something important from her list.

"You forget Kael."

"Forget? No. Him, I'll keep."

"My offer is all or nothing."

"Don't be so quick. Consider your options carefully. I get Kael. You get safe passage from the mob. It's a fair trade."

"Fair? How?"

"Will it change your mind if I told you I don't intend to kill him?"

"Oh? Why do you want him then?"

"The lad has a special place in my heart."

The air flowed out of Sariah's lungs and didn't return.

"So, have we come to an agreement?"

Why was Orgos willing to negotiate with her when he had what he wanted most anyway? It didn't make sense. It was more like a bribe than a negotiation. He was almost rewarding her to go away and leave Kael behind. Unless Orgos wanted something only his deal with Sariah could achieve. Realization dawned on her. She resisted the terrible notion.

"You understand what I want from you, don't you?" Orgos said. "You are not dumb."

Curse Meliahs and all her boulders. She had been playing Orgos's game all along. If Orgos killed Sariah, if he delivered her to the mob, he would lose whatever advantage he had over Kael. But if Kael thought Sariah would go free, Orgos believed Kael would submit to him. It was a cold, calculated game, and given the present circumstances, it was one Orgos could very well win.

Sariah set out to destroy Orgos's notions right away. "What makes you think Kael will yield to you on my account? I'm nothing but a stonewiser to him."

"You lie again. You don't do it very well. I've wondered about you. There were rumors, talk he'd fallen prey to your witchcraft, that he'd left Ars for you, that he'd bled on the quartering block and almost died, all for you."

The pain in her chest kept her silent.

"I wondered what unearthly power could do this to a man like Kael. Is it some sort of stonewiser trick? Is it sorcery? It has to be. Some say he took you by the ways of the blanket. That's where your value to me lies. You see, you'll bring Kael to me in the only way I couldn't have done it on my own—willingly."

Fifteen

SARIAH HAD A vision of Kael's body strung on the quartering block. No. It wasn't going to happen again. She swallowed the fear weakening her throat. When she spoke, her voice was strong, calm and clear. "You give me too much credit, Orgos. But I'm willing to try it your way if you'd like, as long as you stand by your oath to me."

Surprise flashed in Orgos's eyes. Perhaps he had expected she would argue and plead. Perhaps he thought she would refuse his offer upfront. He had been ready to force her into his game a moment ago. Now he was shocked and not a little bit disconcerted.

"The man has been a good tool to my endeavors," Sariah said. "But you must understand, nothing can stand in the way of the stone truth."

"You wily bitch," Orgos said with a hint of admiration. "What won't you do for your stones?"

Honesty was easy. "There's nothing I wouldn't do for the stones."

"Is it true then, that he'll do whatever is necessary to save your life?"

It pained her to admit it.

Orgos's blunt features came alive with his emotions. She saw the hunger on his face, immense and insatiable, fixated on the one man his power couldn't grant him. Wistful hope flashed in his eyes as he beheld his fantasies coming true. Then the deep lines on his ruddy face set like dried mud. This was Kael they were talking about. She knew what Orgos was thinking.

"See this?" Orgos yanked a fistful of red hair out of the way to display the side of his head where his ear's intricate canal sunk into his head without the lobe's protection. "I asked for so little then, just a lick of the lobe to warm my loins."

Sariah had to keep her mouth closed. A tear escaped Orgos's eyes. That Orgos had feelings was discovery enough; that his feelings for Kael were as strong as they seemed was unbelievable. It mattered little to Orgos that Kael had killed his men and burned his quarters. What mattered to him was that Kael had denied him his price and spurned his advances. For that, Kael had to pay him back, and not with his life.

"He won't bend the knee to any man," Orgos said. "He's too proud to submit."

It struck Sariah that Orgos knew Kael well, that he had spent many hours thinking about the man he coveted. Orgos's conclusion, right as it might be, could mean only one thing for Kael—immediate death. Sariah couldn't allow that. She loathed the idea of fostering Orgos's fantasies, but she needed time. Could she risk losing Kael in a trade to ensure his life? Did she even have a choice?

"For a man who likes to win his battles, your pessimism is noteworthy," she said. "It won't be easy, but I can deliver Kael to your bed, of his own accord, as you wish."

Orgos was on her in two steps. He shook her so hard her eyes rattled in her sockets. "Are you mocking me? Do you think that I'm a smitten weakling who can be led by the nose?"

"No, nay, no. I understand your need. I do."

"Then explain it to me because I don't." Orgos released her abruptly.

Sariah tried to find her balance, but the room was still quaking to her shaken senses.

"Well?"

"You want to own him," she stammered, "of body and mind, of soul and will."

"Why?"

She had to think straight. She thought of all those years growing up at the keep, forced to please the absolute will of her masters and mistresses. What had they wanted from her? And most importantly, why?

Because power is absolute when you command the object of your darkest desire, she wanted to say. But this wasn't a moment for truth. Instead she said the words that would have pleased her Guild masters and mistresses. "Because you know what's best for him, even if he doesn't know it himself. Because without you, he'll never become what he's meant to be. Because only his complete acceptance of your rule will satisfy the depths of your passions and... his needs."

She saw hope rekindled in Orgos's eyes, and then she saw it flicker. "You're right, of course you are. But he's rash. He'll make me kill him right away."

"Not if you do this properly." Sariah found herself in the appalling position of having to encourage Orgos's perversions. But if Kael was going to survive the day, she didn't see any other choice. "You don't want Kael's death, you want his faithful service, remember? You want his trust. This deal, it has to guarantee his life."

Orgos smirked. "Do I detect a note of caring in your voice?"

Sariah flashed her coldest smile. "Care isn't the same as convenience. You want Kael alive and docile to serve your purposes. I need him alive for my own protection."

"How's that?"

"Must I explain everything to you? What happens if I abandon Kael here to die in your hands and go on my merry way? What will his brothers think? What will Ars and the rest of the Domain think? I can't afford for people to think I'm a traitor. I'm not exactly welcomed in the Goodlands. I have to be able to survive in the Domain. Whatever agreement you and I reach today must secure Kael's life, at least until I'm done with my business here."

"I see." Orgos leaned back in his chair and fingered the stringy beard on his chin. "You'll tell him. You'll beg him to do this for you."

The horror glutting at her throat was hard to suppress, but she knew she had to function if she was going to succeed. "You'll need to gain his trust. You'll have to show him some kindness. You'll have to give him some assurances of your good faith. Like allowing me to wise the stones before you require your due. He'll be more accepting of his fate. When he sees I've returned safely, he'll trust you."

Sariah didn't intend to return safely from her wising. She intended to come back with help, firm escape in progress.

"A night. We'll start with a night," Orgos said. "You'll tell him that I'll let you both go the next morning if he complies. But what happens after that? How am I supposed to keep him here, alive, serving me?"

There was no way out but forward. She had to make it all come together. "Do you think so little of yourself to ask that question? I'll be gone, by your oath, won't I?"

"Yes?"

"How will he feel when he realizes that I'm gone, that I've left him behind?"

"He'll be angry?"

"He'll be beyond angry."

"He'll be crushed when he learns himself betrayed," Orgos realized. "But I'll be here. I'll keep him from doing anything foolish, for his own good."

"And then?"

A spark of comprehension ignited in Orgos's eyes. "I'll console and comfort him. I'll seduce him. It may take time, but he'll learn to like me. Won't he?"

Sariah doubted it. "How can he not?"

Orgos stared at her with a hint of respect. "Aye. This might just work. Kael's servitude in exchange for your life."

"You won't kill him, Orgos. You'll face my wrath if you do. I can come back any time and wise Alabara's stones to dust."

"You've got my marcher's oath," Orgos said. "I think I like you, wiser. You're as cruel as they come. If he's as smitten with you as they say, he'll be broken worse than turned soil and pulverized stone when you leave him. Yes, after you desert him, he'll be ripe for me, all right."

□ ■ □

"You want me to do... what?" Kael's smoldering stare shifted from Sariah to Orgos and back to Sariah.

She knew what she would wise from him at this moment—rage, disbelief, suspicion—the wild emotions of a caught beast. Something inside of her was breaking. Her soul, her heart, her spirit, whatever they called it, it was being wrenched from her being.

A chain tethered Kael to the wall post. He stood rigidly before Orgos, hands fastened behind his back, feet restrained by the irons around his ankles. Orgos had learned from Kael's last stay in Alabara. He was taking no chances this time. He was no fool. He had refused to allow Sariah to speak to Kael in private. Instead, Orgos forced her to stand beside him as he explained to Kael the advantages of his proposal.

The whole setup was the doings of an ailing mind. Before he sent for Kael, Orgos had taken pains with his appearance. He had combed out his long hair, making sure to place a few strands over the balding middle. His cheeks were freshly shaven and his scrawny beard had been braided into a plait that dangled beneath his jowls like a turkey's wattle. A whiff of overly sweet perfume scented the air in the chamber.

The table was set with a selection of meat, cheeses and dry fruit. Leandro's tiny snakes and scorpions lined up on their checkered cloth, as if Orgos intended a game or two. A flagon of wine stood on a table by the bed, flanked by two pewter cups. For some reason, the sight of those cups struck Sariah like a fist to the gut.

Even though Kael's hands and feet were bound, Orgos approached Kael cautiously, measuring the rage in the other man with a keen attention to self-preservation. Kael just stood there with his feet planted apart, his matted hair sticking up, and his bruised face caked in dry blood, enduring Orgos's scrutiny.

"One night," Orgos said. "In exchange, she gets safe passage from the mob. It's not such an outrageous request. All I ask is that you don't fight me. Tomorrow you leave with your woman safely."

For all his stoicism, Kael flinched when Orgos's hand landed on his shoulder and slithered over his bicep. It moved slowly, as if testing the reality of the man before him. Kael's hands fisted, his body went still as stone, and his face turned blank. Sariah thought she would break. Her resolution was crumbling to dust. Was the promise of Leandro's game worth the risks? She couldn't leave Kael to this man, could she? Not even for a moment. Did she really have the courage to walk away and leave him behind?

"Take the woman to do her wising," Orgos commanded Alfred.

"No," Kael said. "I'll have her safe and away before we conclude this transaction."

"No, nay, no." Sariah tried to conceal her alarm. "It's all right, Kael. It's all arranged. I'm going to do the wising and only when I return will you... it... happen. We'll be going tomorrow morning. Together." She hoped he caught the hint.

"I want her out of the settlement before the sun settles," Kael said without looking at her. Was he trying to wreck her plan?

"You need not worry about me," she said. "Orgos and I have made very thorough arrangements. Everything's fine."

"Everything's *not* fine." Kael glared at Orgos. "I don't trust you or your oaths. I make my own deals. If you want my—me," he gulped dryly, "you'll deal with me."

"Kael?"

"Shut up, Sariah, I know Orgos better than you do. He doesn't intend to fulfill his oaths. Any of them. What is it going to be, marcher?"

"You'll come to my bed willingly?" Orgos said. "And you'll stand whatever I say?"

"Provided you'll give her whatever she asked you," Kael said. "Let her go. Now. No delays. I must have proof that she's safely away."

No. That's not what needed to happen. Sariah launched another warning look in Kael's direction, but he wasn't meeting her eyes. She tried to keep desperation from her voice. "I must wise Alabara's stones. The settlement is in danger. Orgos is being fair here, there's no need to—"

"There's need." Kael cut her off. "Great need. What say you, Orgos? The stones or me?"

Orgos's greedy eyes were fast on Kael. By the changes in Orgos's expression, Sariah could see her carefully negotiated agreement disintegrating before her very eyes. Kael was recklessly undoing her precious gains. She was furious, desperate, terrified.

"Orgos, those stones must be wised," she said. "You are a marcher. You can't put yourself above duty."

"I can't, can't I?" Orgos turned to Kael. "I can't send her through the front gates, but she'll be gone, believe me. She can wait for you out in the flats. Nobody wants the wench gone from Alabara worse than I do. Trust me on that, my boy."

Kael winced at the nickname. "She has to go. Now. And I have to know. Else, you take me dead."

"You're being difficult," Orgos said. "But I suppose I like that best about you. It's the challenge, I think. I'm going to enjoy it."

Sariah fought a suicidal impulse to rip Orgos's suggestive smirk off his face. "It's not necessary to change our agreement—"

"A witness," Orgos said, ignoring Sariah. "Pick any witness you like."

Kael sneered. "I don't know the honest people of Alabara."

"I'm told you know a couple," Orgos said. "The caretaker? The weaver?"

Sariah didn't need any witnesses. The smaller her escort, the better. "Really, Kael—"

"The weaver," Kael decided, mostly because they believed the caretaker had betrayed them to Alfred. "You also allow my deck and my friends to go free. Right now. I know you keep them under vigilance."

Orgos couldn't conceal his surprise and neither could Sariah. How did Kael know that?

"You know where they are, although you haven't seized them yet. Set them free." Kael must have been talking to his guards while Sariah had been negotiating with Orgos. At the very least, he had been doing some good listening.

"Throw them out kindly," Kael said. "Tell them I command them to go. I won't be willing if any of my friends are harmed."

"That's a lot to ask for one night," Orgos said. "Next you'll be asking for my marcher's right."

"It's my last condition."

"Why should I agree to it? I can do as I please with you *and* your friends."

"That you can. But not with my leave."

Kael's acceptance, his submission, his compliance, those were Orgos's deepest cravings.

"And if I let them go?" Orgos asked.

"I'm sure you'll require fair trade for that too, perhaps later?"

Sariah blinked twice. Had she just seen Kael... flirting with Orgos? The slight tilt of his head, the shy tug at the corner of his mouth, the faint shrug offering a quick show of the clavicle and the base of the strong neck, they were not imagined. Orgos had seen them too. His tongue ran over his lips. By the rot. What was Kael doing?

Ensuring her life. And the others' too. Making sure she got out of Alabara with Leandro's game in hand. Doing everything in his power to help secure the tale that would safeguard Ars. She knew what he was thinking. He would see to himself later, if there was a later for him and if there was a way. But all those ifs were making Sariah sick. Because he was also spoiling Sariah's chances of getting him out of Alabara unscathed.

"Throw them out," Orgos said to Alfred. "Don't harm them."

"They're close to the gates, my lord. It won't be but a moment." Alfred went to issue Orgos's commands.

Sariah's pulse was pummeling her ears. She wished she could talk some sense into Kael. But he was still avoiding her eyes, staring straight at Orgos, provoking him with the sheer intensity of his presence.

Orgos fiddled with a lever on the wall. To Sariah's astonishment, part of the wall rolled aside to show a narrow balcony overlooking Alabara's gates. As a precaution, Orgos clutched the lead chain around Kael's neck. Both Kael and Sariah took a step forward and looked down.

Within a few moments, their deck floated into view, pulled by Delis and escorted by a number of Alfred's guards. Mia was not in sight, thank Meliahs. Malord was arguing with the guards to no avail. When the deck reached the gates, the guards halted and turned toward the balcony.

Orgos caressed the length of Kael's back. "Will you wear the chains for me, my boy? It would please me so."

Every muscle on Kael's body contracted in a communal clench. "*If* you let them go."

Orgos signaled. The gates opened. The two men watched in silence as the deck advanced down the channel and into the Barren Flats' vastness. Then Kael and Orgos turned as one and a colorful quad of ferocious eyes fell on her, black and green, hazel and gray.

"Give her things back to her," Kael said.

Orgos gestured with his head. Alfred, who had just returned, dumped their possessions into a basket.

"The game set too."

Alfred scooped the snakes and scorpions into their little sack and added it to the basket.

"Satisfied, my boy?" Orgos asked.

"When the witness returns," Kael said. "Get her out of here."

Sariah tried to keep her bluff together. It was hard. Alfred seized her arm. Sariah stood her ground. "This is not what we agreed to do, Orgos."

"I'd say this is better for you, unless of course you'd been planning on betraying me the entire time?"

Had Orgos known? Had she been playing his game all along? She had been a fool to believe his oaths. She might be getting out of Alabara alive and with Leandro's set, but her game was over, and it was Orgos who had won the day.

She made a last, desperate plea. "Kael, please. Some things aren't worth the price."

"And some are." He looked out the window. "Go."

□ ■ □

"Your deck, your weave, your red dye, your weapons, your game, everything you asked for is right here." Alfred tossed the basket in the deck's shelter. "Now be nice and go."

Sariah felt her mind unraveling, overwhelmed by a sequence of events that had gone terribly wrong. She had a vision of Kael

as she had seen him last, darkly outlined against the sunset with
Orgos's arms around his shoulders. Meliahs help him. She couldn't
leave without Kael. Could she? She needed to stay in Alabara. She
donned the weave slowly. She couldn't bring herself to clip on the
deck's ropes and start pulling.

"I can't very well go out the front gate." Sariah tried to stall.
"The mob's waiting for me."

"Never mind that." Alfred pulled the deck forward. "Come."

Walking alongside Alfred and his men, Sariah recognized
Katrina the weaver. She flashed Sariah a crooked sneer. "Deaf and
dumb, eh? What a load of dung that was."

Kael's damn witness. When Katrina returned and reported
Sariah's departure, Orgos's fun would begin. If she could only
drown the woman with her glare.

"We don't really need a witness, do we?" Sariah said.

"A witness is what Orgos needs the most," Alfred said. "He'll
be waiting for Katrina, raring to go like a high-strung bull."

Sariah choked on her bile. She swallowed an acid gulp and
forced a suggestive smile to her lips. "Alfred, we don't need all
these people to escort us. You are more than sufficient."

He snorted. "You little whore, strutting your stuff, trying to
get me in trouble with Orgos? I wouldn't mind trying, on account
of your fine tits and your round ass, but I bet that every part of you
is cold and hard like the stones."

So much for her clumsy attempts at seduction. She forced
herself to place one foot in front of the other. She pulled slowly
through the settlement's tortuous basement, trying to gain some
time to think. She had hoped her deal with Orgos would give her
a little leeway in Alabara, enough to elude the watch and enlist
Delis to mount a quick raid on Orgos's quarters. Instead, the fool
had shredded her plans to pieces. Sure, she had Leandro's game,
but without the excuse of wising the stones and with Delis gone,
Sariah had little chance to raid anything, let alone Orgos's well-
guarded rooms. She was a wiser, for Meliahs' sake, not a runner.
Worse, if she were ejected from Alabara, how would she get back
into the settlement?

"This is where we part company," Alfred said when their little group arrived at an isolated place by the settlement's back palisade. Sariah saw no evidence of a gate there, but to her surprise, Alfred unlocked a box in the ground and fumbled with a lever. Just as it had happened in Orgos's room, an unmarked portion of the palisade rolled out of the way.

The sound started all at once. The frogs' thunderous croaks overtook the night. They seemed to rain from the sky, landing on the deck in droves, thickly coated with their pungent slime.

"Hurry up." Katrina pulled her weave over her head and stomped on the frogs. "I hate them. I can't stand them."

"Misbegotten freaks." Alfred cursed. "They're early tonight."

Sariah's attention strayed from the frogs. She saw nothing but a river of rot flowing in front of her. There was no channel or bridge to cross here, only the boiling corruption bubbling up as it surged, the frequent hiss of poison vents popping, and the occasional glow of a freshly ignited flow.

"This is not what I had in mind when I traded with Orgos."

"Safe passage from the mob, that's what he offered," Alfred said. "Orgos is as good as his word. I guarantee that no one from the mob is around here."

"How am I supposed to cross the rot flow?"

"That's your problem, isn't it? Count yourself lucky. Most folks we let out this way don't even have a deck. Orgos, he insisted you have your due, just as he agreed with Kael. He doesn't want to give the fellow any reason to forsake his oath. The witness here, she'll tell Kael you had your deck, but I assure you, she won't tell him it lasted three minutes or less before it began to dissolve in the rot. We won't let Katrina here see you die, so she can be truthful to her tale. And that's all fine with Orgos and me."

There was no time for questions or protests. Alfred seized Sariah. His guards hurled the deck down the embankment. It fell flat on the rot flow, igniting a cloud of sparks that shot up toward the sky. Sariah was still kicking when Alfred pitched her in the general direction in which the deck was drifting. She overshot the edge and slid across the deck over a slippery coat of frogs and slime. Her fingernails screeched as she dug her fingers in between the deck's logs and stopped herself from going overboard. She looked up to find Alfred's smile wide on his camel lips.

"She's free, Katrina. Say it's so." Alfred patted the weaver's wide rump.

"I say so, lovey." She planted a quick nip on his cheek. "Let's go tell Orgos that he can inaugurate his new boy."

Sixteen

THE HEAT BURNED through the deck's shuddering logs. A hiss of steam obscured Sariah's view. She grabbed for the pole. She had three minutes to find the dead waters, maybe less. Use the pole, ride the flow, aim for the outer edge. Or die. The pole withered as she planted it in the rot flow. It glowed like a fired iron when she took it out. She figured she had three pushes out of it before it dissolved entirely.

The air was toxic with the rot's breath. Her eyes burned with the vapors. Sweat drenched her body and made her grip slippery. The deck caught in an eddy and tipped to one side. Sariah plunged the pole and pushed. The deck hesitated, heaved, and moved forward, free of the eddy but still caught in the deadly flow.

Sariah squinted, trying to see the edge of the rot flow despite her stinging eyes. She spied a change in color to one side, a line of low flames, a possible indication of rot meeting dead water. Suddenly, a poison vent hissed beneath the deck. The deck lurched. Sariah thrashed in the air and almost went over the edge. Hanging on to the pole, she shoved her other hand under the twine and stuck with the roiling deck like a rider on a wild beast. She flattened herself on the logs just in time. A rush of scalding heat brushed her back and barely missed her. Around her, the frogs stuck to the deck with stubborn resolve. Sariah wished she too had tiny suckers on her fingers to hold on tighter.

A splash of rot crashed over the deck. Rot droplets blistered Sariah's cheeks, but the bulk of the wave landed on the frogs at the front of the deck. Sariah expected to see only smoke and bones left when the rot drained, but to her surprise, the frogs were there, intact and unperturbed. She didn't have time to think about it. The logs were hot to her body. The twine was smoldering. The deck was coming apart.

Sariah rose to her knees, planted the pole and pushed with all her strength. The deck responded, gaining speed and drifting towards the edge. Then it rattled and bounced down a series of drops where the rot had eaten through rock. Ahead of her, the rot flow divided into a fork. The remnant of an old boulder stood in the center. The rot flowed at increasing speeds on both sides, but to the left of the boulder, Sariah thought she saw the lighter hue of the rot dissolving into the dead water. It would take a monumental effort.

Sariah clutched her pole. Burnt and broken, it was half its original size. The deck shrieked. An entire log ripped off from the side and burst into flames. The boulder came at her quickly. She aimed, planted the pole and prayed.

□ ■ □

Sariah lay among the frogs, her own breathing as harsh as their croaks. The tattered deck was hot, broken and scorched, but she had made it through the rot flow. Her face stung. A splash of rot must have seeped under her weave, because something burned fiercely under her arm. The stars reflected on the flats' placid cradle. Exhaustion weighted her down, oppressive like the night's heat. She took a deep breath and ended up hacking instead. Her lungs were in no condition for deep breathing at the moment.

She closed her eyes and had a vision of Orgos's hand riding the lean muscles of Kael's thigh. She saw the marcher's tongue curled over Kael's nipple, sliding across his chest, leaving a trail of saliva as it searched for the matching treat. She could almost hear the marcher's delighted gasps at his discoveries; the smack of his mouth, nibbling at the site of the nipple's absent twin; the rustles of his tongue flickering over the fine scars that edged Kael's ribs.

She sat straight up. She wasn't going to dwell on that just now. She had always relied on her wits. Those wits better deliver right now because she needed to find an alternative to her defunct plan. She couldn't summon help. She was clear on the other side of

Alabara's main gates and even if she made it there, if she somehow managed to elude the mob, she had no way of entering the heavily guarded gate until morning. Morning would be too late.

A fat frog landed on her lap, unafraid and oblivious. Preoccupied with her thoughts, Sariah toyed with the critter, nudging the consorts on its back. It was a strapping beast, she noted vaguely, and not a drop of the rot had harmed the frog or its passengers. Why?

Sariah examined the frog. How had these animals survived traveling through the inhospitable territories of the Domain? They didn't have wings, and in as much as it looked like they rained from the sky when they appeared, they were nowhere to be found during the day. Where did they hide?

It had to be in the dead waters. They must have developed some sort of protection against the rot and its brew, and at the very least, that protection was enabled during their reproductive cycles. It was worth the risk.

She smeared the animal's slime over her weaved hand. She leaned over the deck and reached out to the rot flow's nearest tentacle. She was crazy and she knew it, but better crazy than untrue. She dipped her hand in the rot, a quick in and out. A distant sensation of heat, a little vapor, but her weave, and most importantly, her hand, was unharmed.

Hope. Sariah grabbed the deck and ran in the dead water, pulling upstream, parallel to the rot flow. Her lungs ached with the effort. She was intent on the palisade on the other side of the flow. There had been a torch atop the place. Meliahs, please let her find the torch.

A trace of the torch's smoke was all that remained, but it was all she needed. She pulled the deck further up-flow and estimated the distance. Thirty spans maybe? The width of a healthy river. She ran into the deck shelter. Rope. A decent deck had to have good long rope. She found two, and knotted them together, before stringing an end to one of Kael's arrows. Archery was not her strength, but she figured she had a very large target on the palisade. Once the arrow was embedded in the wood, she would use the rope to pull herself across. Not ideal, but it would have to do.

Next, she stripped the deck from its shelter, untying ropes, dismantling the two sections that made the thatched roof and folding the walls. A bit of thatch got caught on her bracelet. Ironically, she plucked it out of Shrewdness's link, the one engraved with the knotted rope. Domainers were indeed clever, crafty, diligent and practical. She had learned much from them during her year at Ars. Now it was her turn to be shrewd. She worked fast, mindful of the time, talking to an absent Kael.

"If you mind your arse, you better dillydally, you stubborn ox," she rambled like a crazy woman. "I'm working as fast as I can."

She undid the twine holding the deck's logs together, split the deck in two, and then reknotted the ropes. She had to replace some of the burnt twine and reallocate the intact ones. When she was done, she had two decks, one much narrower than the other, but both still stable enough to float. She piled the makings of the shelter on the bigger deck, along with the supplies Orgos had provided, and dropped the claws to anchor it safely away from the rot flow. Then she turned her attention to the other deck.

The width of five logs comprised the smaller platform she had created. It was longer than she needed, and a bit unwieldy, but she had neither the time nor the tools to shorten it.

"Here's to nothing." She lifted a frog to the sky in solitary toast.

She wiped the deck with the frog as if it were a sponge and she was a new Guild pledge assigned to mopping the floors. With small, circular movements, she smeared the logs with frog slime. Even though the frogs seemed to produce the slime on demand, she took turns using different animals. She didn't want to hurt the helpful critters. She worked diligently until the entire surface was covered with the pungent secretions. She turned the deck over and did the same with the scorched underside, smearing the frog slime over her weave and on the ropes as well.

"Sorry, mate." Sariah caught another frog. "I hate to do this to you, but the ride is free if you want to go back in there."

The frog belched irately.

"I know," Sariah said. "I feel the same way."

□ ■ □

Sariah hooked her leg over the railing and willed her lungs to accept the air she was desperately sucking in. She dangled from the balcony of Orgos's quarters like a tangled bat. Her arms and legs quivered with the strain. She heaved herself up painfully, coming nose to nose with a loaded frog. The animal hopped clear to the next level.

"Showoff," Sariah muttered.

She flung herself over the railing and landed against the sliding door. The frogs had provided her with many advantages this night, including keeping Alabara's residents indoors. But as she pressed her ear to the wood, their infernal croaks smothered the sounds inside Orgos's quarters. Sariah inserted her fingers along the window's clever frame, palpating blindly until she found the wheels which moved the panel out of the way. They were locked in place. With a bit of prodding, she pushed the pin sideways and opened the window just enough to slide inside.

Fine wax candles imbued the room with a pleasant scent that tricked the nose into normalcy. The candles' golden gleam numbed the eye to the crass and the vulgar. The mellow glow softened everything in the room—Orgos's trinkets, his coarse furnishings, the shock of Kael's nude body sprawled on the bed, the brutality of the chains that bound him by his wrists and ankles to the massive bed's spiraling posts.

She took quick stock of his condition. His face was pale, maybe a bit pasty. His eyes were closed. His mouth struck her as unnaturally red. His limbs were tense from the reflexive fight against the bonds and his white-knuckled fingers gripped the chains as if in just retribution. She knew he was alive and awake because his breathing was fast and shallow. Was Orgos hurting him? She loaded her sling and aimed, cursing the tremors shaking her hands.

The muted sound he made delayed her shot. More than a moan, it was a muffled grunt she recognized. For a moment, she stopped looking at him in order to take in the totality of the situation. It was only an instant or two, a stumble in the disciplined progression of time, but it played in her mind excruciatingly slowly, as if time had taken a break to show her the moment in vivid detail.

She saw Orgos for the first time. She had known he was there all along, a large menacing shadow looming over Kael, sitting next to him on the bed, weighing down the mattress with his bulk. In the candlelight, Orgos's nakedness was suffused by a red nimbus of coarse hair that outlined his body. His belly's bulge was trapped between heavy pectorals and sprawling thighs. He leaned over to kiss Kael, not harshly, as Sariah expected, but rather gently, taking his time, savoring the inert lips, prying, probing, plunging, until his tongue had excavated the well of Kael's reluctant mouth and settled there to drink from his throat.

But it wasn't Orgos's kiss arching Kael's body and convulsing his limbs. It was the firm grasp Orgos had on Kael's erection, a harrowing clutch the marcher was mirroring on his own sex, a rhythmic, relentless stroking up and down both larded shafts. Kael's sex was engorged to imposing proportions. His cheek pressed hard against the pillow. He was biting down on the pillowcase, grinding on the fabric with the force of his clench. It was Orgos who roared first. His body shuddered. Bursts of clotted semen rained over Kael's taut belly in a sudden irrigation of his groin.

"My boy," Orgos rasped. "My beautiful boy."

He reached out to tousle Kael's hair. He thumbed the cusp of Kael's eyebrow where the scar broke it in two and then slid his fingers over the raised outline of his well-defined mouth. There was something intrinsically intimate about the gesture, something that sparked Sariah's proprietary outrage and left her struggling to suppress the growl gathering in her throat.

"You promised you wouldn't fight me. Remember?" Orgos rubbed his face against Kael's groin, like a big red tomcat, marking its territory. "Come, my boy. Your turn. I want to see you do this just for me."

Sweat streamed down Kael's face and pooled above his lips. His body was slick with perspiration, stretched to extreme tautness, a fitting continuation of his erection. His skin was a geography of prickling goose bumps. His blood rushed in a maddening race to fill every vein to bulge. Betrayal loomed in every part of his body.

"No?" Orgos's smile was a grimace of pure lust. "Then I have something special planned for you. Not even you can stand this."

Unexpectedly, Orgos dumped a beaker of thick oil over Kael's groin and rubbed it in. Then, in one great gulp, Orgos took Kael's sex in his mouth and swallowed it to the balls.

Kael roared.

Without further hesitation, Sariah took aim and shot.

Seventeen

SHE MUST HAVE made a small noise, a squeak, a rustle, or perhaps the growl she had been repressing simply escaped her senses' guard, because Orgos lifted his head at the last moment, mouth drooling with tinted saliva, eyes wide with surprise. Sariah had known she had only one chance. The stone hit him in the center of the forehead, sinking into the bone with a satisfying crunch. The man toppled backwards and crashed on the floor. He lay there, obscene and inert, like the waterlogged wreck of a massive swept-off timber.

Sariah rushed to Kael's side. "Where is the key?"

Kael's eyes were dull and unfocused, red-rimmed and unclear, squinting to see through a haze that wasn't there.

"Are you all right?" She took his face in her hands. "Are you hurt?"

"Who?"

"It's me, Sariah. Kael, what has he done to you?"

She looked him over quickly. He was slippery with a combination of sweat, fragrant oils, and Orgos's emissions, but she couldn't find any major wounds on him. She tried to unravel the chains from the bedposts, but it was useless. If she was going to get him out, she needed to find the key to the manacles. It was a small key, she could tell by the lock, slim and blunt at the ends.

"Kael, make an effort. Tell me. Where is the key? The key for the irons."

His brows knotted in concentration. "The key?"

What was wrong with him? Sariah examined his face again, the rolling eyes, the ashen pallor, the mouth, bright red. "Rotting pits. Did he give you something? What did he give you? Kael, listen to me. I need to know what he gave you."

His words slurred, but he gestured to one side with his head, indicating some level of comprehension. Sariah looked at the table beside the bed, and gasped, horrified.

Hepa. She recognized the nuts littering the table, shaped like her fist, hard like a rock, deeply grooved and coated with coarse curly fibers. There was a jug of strongly brewed canundro on the table as well, and a cup reeking with the scent of the hepa's treacherous milk. The canundro had turned red, the same deep color staining Kael's lips. There were several cracked shells on the table and floor, far too many. The bastard had fed Kael hepa.

Sariah fought the panic overtaking her. Delusions, disorientation, confusion, weakness, extreme sensitivity, these were the side effects of ingesting hepa. How was she going to get a hepa-stricken Kael out of Alabara?

One problem at a time. The chains. She had to get him free and off the bed. She searched around the room, on the pegs by the door, in trunks and drawers, and through Orgos's discarded clothing. Nothing.

"Kael, I understand Orgos fed you hepa." Sariah pressed a cup of water to his lips. "I need you to listen to me. I know it's a great effort right now, but I need your help to get us out of here. Where's the key?"

He couldn't keep his quivering pupils steady on her, but his brows were knotted again and his mouth was trying to speak. "Ate... it."

"He ate the key?"

What kind of vile beast swallowed the key to his prisoner's manacles? The kind that intended to consume his prey alive and on site. The type that began by destroying hope from the start. The kind that indulged his horrid fantasies from beginning to end.

"Meliahs curse you, Orgos, you miserable dung of a polecat."

No key. The realization hit Sariah like an icy gust. She had a vision of herself kneeling by Orgos's gutted carcass, arms dripping to her elbows with gore and blood as she rummaged through the mangled mess of his entrails looking for the key. What were the chances such a search would yield it?

Wait. She could pick the locks. She had done it at the keep

many times. She could do it again. With what? She looked around the room. A stylus? Too thick. A needle? Too weak. A tooth from Orgos's ivory comb? Long, slick, sturdy. It might work. She broke the tooth from the comb, climbed on the bed and tackled the left hand manacle.

"Let go." She tried to peel Kael's four-fingered clutch from the chain, but he wasn't budging. She worked around it. The lock was shallow but sturdy, a little slippery inside. Or was that her hand, shaking? There, she found the bolt. A twist, a jiggle, a push at the right time. *Click.*

The hand was free, bruised but intact. She didn't think that Kael could completely understand what was happening, but he brought the hand to his chest and flexed his fingers, staring at them groggily as if they were separate from his body and unexpected. Sariah fed him more water. She thought he looked a bit more alert.

Next. Left foot. Same procedure. Hurry. She dared a quick look at the door. It was barred from the inside and safe for the moment. For how long? Damn this iron, it had decided to be difficult.

Hepa. It was a secret of the wealthy and the powerful. Sariah knew about it because of an incident at the keep years before, when she witnessed Ilian, the worst of her mistresses, experimenting with the drug over the course of a few weeks. It had been particularly trying on Sariah. The results had been disastrous. By the time she recovered, her mistress had been close to expulsion from the Guild.

The hepa milk was the most insidious and potent of all stimulants, the drug of choice for those seeking experiences well beyond the ordinary. Combined with canundro, it was even more formidable. It played havoc with the mind and destroyed the stomach and bowels. It was highly addictive. It was also the most powerful aphrodisiac known to the generations, no doubt the main reason why Orgos had resorted to it.

Done. The left foot was free. She fed Kael more water, two cups, one after the other. She splashed his face with the water as well, and poured a few ladlefuls over his neck, chest and belly as much to refresh him as to rinse off Orgos's filth.

His eyes seemed to focus briefly. "Sariah?"

"Present and accounted for."

"You came?"

"Of course."

"Orgos said..." The black and green gaze wandered away again.

"And you believed him?"

He blinked, closed one eye, and gazed at her with the green eye only. "Nay. I knew. If you could."

"Hold on to those senses, can you?" Sariah placed the cup of water in his trembling hand. "We're going to need them to get out of here."

No time to waste. On to the right foot. The right ankle was bleeding a bit. Kael had been pulling at it hard. "We have to hurry. If Orgos's men find us here—"

Kael squinted. "Dead?"

Sariah didn't want to look at the man. "I think so. And we'll die too, if I can't get these chains off you."

"Won't come. He. Told. Them." His eyes drifted lazily to the back of his head.

"Orgos told his men what?"

"Who?"

"Orgos, the man who put you here, remember him? What did he tell his men?"

A spark of forced lucidity flashed in his gaze. "Don't bother. Him. It could be... days."

Sariah could have kicked Orgos's corpse to pieces.

"The room's spinning," Kael murmured.

"No, it's not. It's the hepa."

"The red juice?"

"The red juice."

"I can't... think."

"You're thinking now, at least some, but yes, that's why you can't think very clearly." Damn. The bolt was stuck. The ivory tooth cracked. She shook the broken fragments out of the lock and broke another tooth from the comb.

"Who are you?"

Meliahs grant her patience. "Sariah. Remember?"

"Sariah. Yes." He spilled the water all over himself. "I think I love you."

"Oh, yes you do. Try not to forget that."

"Can't see you very well." He squinted, cross-eyed. "Why did you come?"

"To save your arse. Literally."

The lock clicked and the right foot was free. She rubbed the maimed foot, restoring circulation to the limb. He bent and stretched the leg several times before bringing his knees closer to his chest and leaning his head in the crook of his chained arm's elbow. He looked somewhat more comfortable. He closed his eyes. Sariah thought he was asleep.

"It wasn't going to work," he mumbled. "Your plan."

"Well, it was better than yours, and it didn't entail chains. Meliahs help us, Kael, what have you done to your hand?" The cuff had dug to the bone and was encrusted in his flesh.

"I was getting it loose."

"Loose? You were planning to leave your hand behind to escape Orgos?"

"Just a bit of it."

"Hold tight, this is going to hurt." Sariah jiggled the lock as gently as she could, but the chain shifted against the wound all the same.

"One hand." He wiggled his fingers weakly. "To kill him."

He wasn't boasting, not even in his present state. He was sharing the plan he'd had in his head all along.

"I needed you gone. And the others. Are there others?" Confusion brimmed in his eyes.

"Delis, Malord, Mia."

"Pile of dung." That was the old Kael speaking. "He kills. You. Them."

Click. Sariah slid the cuff off his wrist carefully, but still a spurt of fresh blood stained the bed linens. She ripped a pillowcase and wrapped it as a makeshift bandage around his wrist and over his thumb. She fed him more water and helped him to sit up on the bed.

His bones creaked like rusted hinges. His face went suddenly white. "I'm going to—"

Sariah caught most of the vomit in one of Orgos's fake gold basins. "It's quite normal. You'll be doing a lot of that in the next few days."

He wiped his mouth with the fouled bed sheet. "Is it... normal too?"

He stared at his groin, looking very young and vulnerable. The startled expression on his face was almost comical, until Sariah saw the object of his concern.

Dear Meliahs. It hadn't eased. She had been too busy to notice, a good measure of her single-minded focus, because his erection was simply impossible to miss. His red-streaked sex stood out like a bloodied horn, longer, thicker and harder than any Sariah had seen.

"Are you doing this?" He eyed her with deep suspicion.

"Me? No, nay, no, not me. It's you. I mean, your body. The hepa."

"He was doing this." It was an outright accusation.

"Aye, but he stopped. He's gone, you see?"

"But *it* is not gone."

Obviously.

"Shall we try some water?" Sariah poured several cups of water on his lap, directing the flow to wash the tincture away. Kael growled like a snarling beast. It was as if some exotic reptile was cornered at his groin, a frill-necked lizard unfurled in full threat, ill-tempered, and ready to strike.

Sariah dared a whiff at the tincture's beaker. Hepa, this time mixed with some sort of aromatic oil. Her problems, like his, were growing rapidly.

"Are you he?" He was hallucinating. His pupils contracted and expanded in quick succession. His eyelids had gone stiff. He wasn't seeing her, but rather Orgos, and who knows what else.

"The hepa is doing this to you," Sariah explained. "Do you remember?"

He struck without warning. An avalanche of muscle and bone launched from the bed and flattened her on the ground. The weight of his body squashed her against the floor. His hand landed on her neck, a block of cold marble. Her throat's fragile cartilage crumpled under the clawed fingers, but his grip was slippery and fumbling. Time seemed to slow down to match the tiny dribble of air trickling into her lungs. She had the presence of mind to manage a sarcastic thought or two.

Perfect. She was going to die from his hepa-induced delirium, strangled, smothered, or worse, bludgeoned to death or punctured through the gut by the force of his godless erection. She tried to talk to him, but his knuckles cracked around her neck and her larynx buckled. The chamber dimmed. Black dots speckled her vision.

"Ka—Ka-el—lin. No!"

"Sariah?"

He was looking down on her as if *she* was attacking *him*!

The pressure was suddenly gone. The air was flowing. The weight was off her. Kael was gasping beside her as loudly as she was. Spraddled on the floor like a trampled toad, Sariah breathed great quantities of air. She thought for sure every bone in her body was crushed, but she managed to sit up. They had to get out of Alabara. It was the only coherent thought sticking in her mind. She managed to grasp the table and heaved herself up. He looked lost, sitting dejectedly on the floor with his swollen sex curling toward his belly like a deadly blade.

"Did I... hurt you?"

Sariah's hand went to the bruises on her neck. "No, nay, no." She fumbled for his clothes, and found them by the bed. "Let's get you dressed. We have a long night ahead."

He snatched the shirt from her. "Don't touch me."

Oh, please. Not again.

"You make it worse."

"Me?"

"Go away."

Damn. They were not getting out of Alabara, not alive, not with Kael like this. She considered the man at her feet. He had been aroused for hours and she gathered he had managed to hold back all that time, despite Orgos's tortuous efforts. It was just like

Kael, defiant in submission, compliant of his oath yet utterly disobedient. He had found his own way to fight the unequal battle, to triumph over Orgos, even in defeat.

The persistent state of arousal would only get worse, because the hepa caused not only delusion and confusion, but intense arousal and sensitivity so keen that she had seen a grown woman cry from the agony caused by the casual brush of linen against her nipples. Sariah realized he wasn't going to be able to escape in such conditions. What to do?

The only thing she could.

She hoped with all her heart that Kael had heard right and the guards had heeded Orgos's orders to stay away. She was about to borrow the marcher's quarters for her own unholy purposes. She stripped her weave and her leggings, but kept her boots on, just in case she had to run. When she looked up again, Kael had backed himself into a corner. With his muscles corded and the veins of his neck bulging like rising magma, every part of him seemed primed for destruction.

"I don't want to hurt you," he said. "I may."

The genuine, non-delusional statement made Sariah smile. That was him speaking, not the hepa. "You won't hurt me, but we have to solve your problem. Will you let me help you?"

He was as edgy as a spooked stallion. "I don't think I can stand you. Not you. I won't stop. Not with you."

"That's precisely the point. You don't need to stop with me. I don't want you to. I can't say these are the best of conditions, but I can be practical about this, if you can be quick."

"Practical?" Hepa induced or not, his bewilderment was about to kill him.

Sariah untied her tunic and parted it to brandish her breasts. She shook off modesty for the sake of expedience. Not that she liked being naked and vulnerable in such circumstances, but her breasts had always had a good effect on Kael. How had it come to this? She was baiting a hepa-stricken man. Did she have a death wish or had she gone stone mad?

It was taking too long.

"Please, Kaelin?" She placed his hand on her breast. "Please?"

A groan erupted from his throat, shaking Sariah's fortitude. Then all semblance of control was gone from his face and he fell on her like a rabid wolf. In a flash, she was on her hands and knees, lanced and skewered by his brutal rigidity, smarting from the battering and quaking with the force of his strokes. Bursts of hot breath gushed over her neck. Primal grunts matched his blows. Her back strained under his weight and her hips ached from his fingers' ruthless clutch. But if she had managed to endure her Guild masters and mistresses, she should be able to withstand Kael for just a little longer. She would help him through this, even if her bones were clattering like a nest of rattlesnakes.

Just when Sariah thought he was going to finish, curse her luck, he stopped. He turned her over and forced her to face him.

He frowned. "I've never used you like this? Have I?"

"Nay," she said. "Not like this."

"Is it really you?"

Sariah understood. He feared she was another one of his delusions, that his mind, feeble and clouded as it was, was failing him. He dreaded the possibility that in the haze, he was yielding to Orgos. It was more than dread, fear of the one defeat he couldn't endure. She didn't hesitate. She embraced him, pressing her palms against his back, infusing him with a flood of her affection.

"It is you." The dullness in his eyes lifted, and the smile birthing on his lips took to his bloodshot eyes as well. He caressed her face, brushing the spot on her jaw where the rot drops had blistered her, softly outlining the raised redness burning under her arm. "Are you hurting?"

"It's nothing. Shall we finish this?"

"It won't go away?"

She couldn't give him any hope. "We really have to go."

Draping her legs over his thighs, he brought her close to him, pressed his hand on her lower back, and entered her, struggling to suppress his urgency. The intensity of his strain was evident in his labored breath, in the blustery hisses that blew so close to her ear. She didn't know why he reached up to the table and swiped his finger in the beaker, but she noticed acutely when his thumb anointed her with the slightest touch of the red tincture.

A rush of need shot through her, igniting her body into pure lust. "Meliahs help us," she gasped. "What have you done?"

The intensity was extraordinary, the need overwhelming, and this was only one drop of hepa, nothing compared to what he suffered. Sariah had never felt so alive. She fathomed she could feel his every shift, his every change with exquisite detail. Her flesh had transformed into a finely tuned collector of even the tiniest sensations. This time, when he moved, there was no enduring the malady. She understood why people would risk life and health to feel like this. Then, she stopped understanding, because she couldn't think anymore.

They lasted nothing, a mere three or four strokes, and yet the sensations were overpowering, the pleasure incomparable. Their eyes met, mirrors upon mirrors where each other's reflections continued forever. That's how they came, in the grips of the infinite shared, in the tortured trust of each other's arms.

Eighteen

SARIAH DUMPED THE contents of Leandro's little game sack on the floor. She counted a complete set, forty-eight snakes and scorpions slightly iridescent against the colorful blanket. On the pallet beside her, Kael stirred and groaned in his sleep. "Hush," she whispered. "You're safe." She petted his tousled hair and wiped the sweat off his forehead with a wet cloth. Then, pressing her palm against his temple, she infused him with a trickle of solace and a deep sense of slumber. He needed the rest. And she had work to do.

Wising Leandro's game pieces had been the first thing she had done after escaping from Alabara and pulling the divided decks into the safety of the Barren Flats' expanse. True, she'd had to pause several times to reassemble the deck and to tend to Kael's urgent needs. But the good news was that she had managed to wise all the game pieces already. On the other hand, tracking Leandro and going to Alabara had taken too long. Worse, she had recently discovered her bracelet had a very accurate if mysterious way of tracking that precious commodity they didn't have—time.

Indeed, they had left Ars over one-and-a-half months ago. Incredibly, a shimmering opacity had crept over the first of the bracelet's crystals, a silvery glow which didn't preclude the bracelet's radiance but made it different from the other crystals. The opaque glaze was pouring into the next crystal over, streaming from its center to fill it up about halfway, a slow spiraling silver trail marking the all-too-quick passage of time.

She stirred the blue ink mixture in the inkwell she had improvised. The pebbles she had dumped in the ink-filled cup rattled pleasantly. She had carved tiny holes in the middle of the pebbles before imprinting them. She really hoped her work would pay off.

She turned her attention back to Leandro's game. She selected her favorite game piece, a tiny scorpion that was different from all the others. It had a blunt tail and a missing claw. She pressed it to her palm. She groped for the little trance, which felt like the faintest tug of the thinnest thread pulling through a wide-eyed needle. The image of Leandro formed in her mind, a thin, tall, stubbly-faced man, never too tidy or well-kept even before his madness.

He sat by a wood burning fire, repeating the same cryptic words. "The truth keepers. The pure's guardians. Every game trumps well before the end is played. Victory is a tale and trail."

It wasn't a straightforward corroboration of their existence, but at least there was a mention of the pure in Leandro's muddled riddle. It was very odd. When she pressed the little stones, in all forty-eight pieces, she hit a strange blankness at the end of the wising. It wasn't something she had encountered before, but today she had a new plan to address the strange occurrence.

She dropped the little scorpion in the pot of dead water boiling over her blazing brazier. She watched it sink, buffeted by the roiling bubbles, clinking a muted protest against the copper bottom. Meliahs would have to forgive her. She had never tortured a stone so. But she had heard that the Hall of Masons often used such methods to coax a stone to yield a stubborn tale. A stone grew tender as it remembered its fiery birth, the masons taught. With wisdom, care, and barring its destruction, the use of the elemental forces that shaped stones—heat, erosion, corrosion—could sometimes soften access to the tightest links. Sariah waited until the sulfuric stench matched the vehemence of the brew's steam to fish out the little scorpion.

It hissed when she dunked it in a cup of fresh water. It was still hot when she pressed it against her palm. Leandro's simple tale flowed like a steady downpour in her mind. But she wanted more than Leandro. She grabbed on to the ragged edges she had detected beneath Leandro's imprint and lunged for the mysterious link unraveling from the plane of his tale. Before her mind's eye, Leandro's face transformed, overtaken by another face. The image of a portly, toad-faced, balding man emerged, frayed and none too stable, but clear enough. He spoke the same words Leandro had recited. Fascinating. An original imprint lurked under Leandro's newer imprint, as if one tale had been imprinted to mask the other.

A shadow wising. It had to be. It was a little known technique by which a new wising was imprinted on top of an older, more established wising. It was sometimes done to reuse wised stones. She didn't think that was the case now. She probed deeper. Leandro's imprinting skills were not as good as the other man's, whoever he was. She concentrated on his tale. The scent of a very sophisticated wising rose in the back of her throat. The acrid taste grated on her tongue and flavored her mouth with the primeval taste of an ancient wising. She reached out to the old tale and pressed it gently. The darkness that flashed in her mind was so sudden and terrifying that she cried out. How by the rot could anyone wise an obstruction as absolute as this one?

She tried to get beyond it. She tried boiling several other snakes and scorpions in the caustic brew of dead water, all for naught. With the links softened, the old wiser delivered his message every time, steadily, reliably, and unchanged. But nothing else.

Curse her luck. Sariah had expected more from Leandro's game, a clue about her final destination, a set of directives, something more than just an opaque riddle. She had to get a jump start while she figured out the game. Leandro had said he had encountered the pure while roaming, so she decided to set a course toward the closest crossing into the Goodlands. She had to go slowly at the moment, because Kael wasn't well enough to pull yet and she couldn't leave Mia behind. She had to wait for the child to catch up to her using her sense for Sariah, or risk harming Mia fatally. *Hurry up, child.* She had the stones. She had to find the pure.

☐ ◼ ☐

Kael shot up from his pallet all of a sudden, startling Sariah from her work. He scurried to the bucket on his hands and knees. His belly heaved compulsively. He gagged an awful croak, but somehow, he squelched his stomach's uproar and kept his breakfast, thank Meliahs.

He stood there, on all fours, taking small shallow breaths.

"Wicked goddess," he rasped. "Will I ever feel right again? I wake up craving the accursed thing. My stomach, as revolted as it is, wants to be hot with it. How long can I last like this? How long can *you* last?"

"I'm hearty and properly made for the job and you're getting better." Sariah reached out to knead his shoulder's knotted muscles. "It hasn't been so many times today."

He shook her off. "Say it. I'm a wretched beast. You ought to stone me out of my misery. I take it you've seen this before?"

"She got well, if that's what you want to know, and she was on hepa for weeks rather than hours. Water?"

His hand was shaking when he took the ladle Sariah offered and drank in small sips. He dragged himself back to the pallet and collapsed with his customary lack of modesty, although these days, his nakedness was more of a practical choice.

"Are you sure I'm thinking clearly?"

Delusion. Confusion. Disorientation. The loss of the self. Those were Kael's worst fears.

"You're thinking well enough."

"So all these crazy things I remember—Are they true?"

"Like what?"

"At Orgos's quarters, I fainted after the... mess, but you got me dressed and managed to drag me to the rope."

"You did your part."

"We climbed down. From a high level, I think."

"Third."

"We waded in the dark. Alabara's basement? All I wanted to do was... well, you know. "

"I know."

"You stole poles from other decks as we went. You needed them, to guide the deck across the rot flow. The deck. The slime. The frogs. Was all of that true?" His eyes swept the space beyond the threshold.

"They're gone. They didn't come back last night. Remember?" Sariah was glad she had managed to milk and store a good measure of frog slime before the creatures disappeared. One never knew when one might need a little extra protection from the rot.

"You crossed the rot flow," he said. "Thrice. Meliahs strike me. You're unbelievable."

"Can you remember what we did yesterday?" She tested his short-term memory.

"You've been busy, reassembling the deck and wising your stones. I've been little help, sleeping off the hepa and bedding you like a rutting beast. Mind you, just thinking about it makes me hard."

"Stand strong, my mighty stallion, a little restraint helps you overcome the cravings. You're doing just fine."

"Great news. I can spare a toe and a finger here and there, but I don't think I want to live like a witless idiot. What are these for?" He stirred the pebbles soaking in the cup.

"These are the smallest stones I've been able to imprint. Are you well enough to get them out of the cup for me? If you are, set them to dry on that old cloth over there, please."

His hands were not as steady as usual, but Kael resisted his compulsive cravings and forced himself to focus. He acted almost grateful for the distraction. He picked up a strand of similarly colored beads already strung on a leather string. "And these?"

"Let me show you." She weaved the string through her plait. "What do you think?"

"You look like those Sadonian women who decorate their hair with strung beads."

"That's exactly how they should look, a harmless trinket to indulge my vanity."

"But they aren't harmless, are they? And by your pout, I'm guessing you're not happy about it either."

Kael got up, a little wobbly on his legs, but made it fine to the bucket. A creak and a clack sounded behind Sariah as he opened the lid. The strong spurt of his water struck the bottom with healthy force. The acerbic scent of hepa mixed with concentrated ammonia rose from the bucket and drifted through the small shelter, the familiar whiff of the last few days.

"Are you still passing hepa?"

"It's blood red, if that's what you're asking." He finished, shut the bucket's lid and returned to sit next to her. "So you've made these little pebbles helpful?"

"I don't like making abominations. But I need to be better prepared."

"I thought you did rather well."

"Did I?"

Silence. He didn't want to talk about it. Knowing Kael, he would never mention the matter again. Well, it was his right. Sariah didn't need long explanations to know how he felt. The anguish, the despair, the helpless rage, they were as familiar to her as the stones, courtesy of a heartless Guild. She knew the pain that hurt beyond the body's soreness, beyond the day's wounds. The human body was built to take the abuse, Mistress Ilian used to say. But what about the human mind?

Her heart ached for him, but pity would only destroy him. Courage. She fingered the crossed swords etched on the bracelet's link. She knew Kael had plenty of it. What she needed was Faith. She turned the bracelet and spotted the link's winged birds in flight. She had to trust Kael to heal himself.

"I wonder," he said all of a sudden. "Which emotion did you use to make bursting stones out of these very nicely colored pebbles?"

"Never mind." Sariah plucked one of the small scorpions from the neat rows of Leandro's game set. "Who would have thought about hiding a wising in a game?"

"You've got to admit. There's brilliance to the notion. But I'm curious, Sariah. Which emotion did you use? It has to be a rather violent one, for these pebbles are tiny, and they must burst very hard if they are to work."

His mind was far from wallowing or idling. In fact, he was responding very much as only Kael would. His mind was moving and on the prowl, much to her disadvantage.

"Well?"

He wasn't going to let up.

"It wasn't anger or frustration, you wouldn't mind talking about those—" His expression transformed from puzzlement to surprise. "Jealousy?"

"No, nay, no."

Indignation flared in his eyes. "Of him?"

"No, not him, of course not."

"Who then?" His mind was sprinting free of the hepa and unstoppable. His eyes lit up with the sudden knowledge. "The forester? Did Eda go after you?"

If only he knew how.

"You don't think I—?"

He had a right to his silence and she had a right to hers. "Pay attention, Kael. The riddle."

"Did the wench tell you she had rights over me?"

"*Every game triumphs well before the end is played.*"

"She did tell you, didn't she?"

"*Victory is a tale and trail.*"

"And you believed her?"

"Somehow, winning the game should give us something."

"Granted, I took the hepa," he said. "But you're the one acting strange."

"A map maybe?"

"Don't pretend this doesn't bother you. You wouldn't be avoiding me if it didn't."

"A map would be Meliahs' best gift. But I've been playing this game at every opportunity I get and nothing happens."

"Do you think something happened between Eda and me?"

There it was. Stated bluntly and earnestly as only Kael could. Her heart was pounding like a dozen sets of hooves. She didn't think she could muster the courage to say it, but she had to.

She took a deep breath. "Why would you choose me when you could have her?"

He stared at her for the longest moment. "That doesn't even merit a response."

"She would be the perfect mother for those children you want."

He opened his mouth and closed it. "You want me to have children with the forester?"

What could she say to that?

"Because you think she would be a better mother to my children?"

Infinitely better than a soulless orphan raised by a heartless Guild.

"And you?"

She shrugged.

"Ah." The infuriating sound announced he had reached his own conclusions and now understood whatever he thought he understood. "You two wenches talked about this?"

Sariah had made an oath, so she focused on Leandro's game. "Do you want to give it a try?"

"Not particularly."

"Well, I have to keep at it, so if you don't mind—"

"I do mind. What I really want to do is thrash you right now and I don't think that's the hepa talking."

The hair on the back of Sariah's neck stood on end when she met his glower. He looked poised to thrash her indeed. Instead, he landed a furious, lip-numbing kiss on her mouth.

"The hepa again?"

"Sorry," he whispered between clenched teeth.

"Hush," Sariah said. "I never want you to be sorry for making love to me."

□ ■ □

Malord, Mia, and Delis arrived the next day, together with a swift change in the weather.

"Cursed winds, I'm freezing." Malord stomped his hands together. "We would've been here yesterday, but we had to lose the mob."

"They know you travel with us?" Sariah asked.

"No, they wanted us to join with them."

"Did they recognize Delis?"

"We didn't let them get that close, my donnis. Are you well? Have you been eating enough? You're a bit short of flesh in the rear, I see—"

"Delis," Kael said, "keep your eyes off Sariah's rear. I'm asking you nicely. Aye?"

Delis rolled her eyes. "I've brought you a present, my donnis, something I think you'll like." She retrieved a jar from her shoulder bag and opened the lid. The fragrance of pure honey filled Sariah's senses. Delis swiped her finger in the jar and offered a taste. "I traded it. It's from Ars's own apiaries. They say it's the finest in the world."

Sariah suckled the honey with the greatest appreciation. The sweet flowery taste draped her lips, coated her mouth and flowed in a slow caress down her throat. When she opened her eyes, Kael and Delis were staring at her wide-eyed.

"I didn't know you like honey so much," Kael said sullenly.

"It's delicious. Taste it."

"No thanks. I've had enough exhilaration lately."

"And you?" She offered Delis.

"No, my donnis. It's for you."

Sariah realized with a start that Delis had been holding her breath with the expectation of pleasing her.

"I've been very anxious about your safety," Delis said, "but the child assured me that you lived."

Mia admired Leandro's gaming pieces, neatly set up for the next game. "They're beautiful. Can I play?"

"Try your Uncle Kael. He's easy to beat."

"Your auntie is gloating again."

"The pieces are wised."

"Wised?" Malord scooted to the board faster than a rolling wagon.

"I have news, my donnis. From Alabara."

"You didn't go back in there after we sent you off, did you?"

"No need, my donnis, I heard the stories wherever we went."

"You mean about Orgos's death?"

"Death? No, my donnis. Orgos isn't dead. He's alive, although his forehead is said to bear a hole deeper than a sunken cave. Orgos is alive and pissed. He's looking for you."

"He nearly killed us for no good reason."

"The channel's stones gave way a few days after we left," Delis said. "Alabara is dying and Orgos says it's your fault."

Nineteen

PLAYING SNAKES AND scorpions with Malord was futile. The old man always won. The repetitive defeat was an exercise in wiser discipline to Sariah, intended to shed light on the riddle's mysterious words: *Every game triumphs well before the end is played.*

"You are unbeatable," Sariah said, after losing again. "Was there a point in this game when you knew you had won even before you won?"

"It was a struggle to the end," Malord said. "At every play, you could have thwarted my victory."

"Not a compliment to my brilliancy. I thought I had lost long ago."

A burst of wind howled outside and rattled the deck on its claws.

"I can't sleep." Mia's tremulous voice came from under her blankets.

"Come sit with us, Mianina. It's just a bit of rough weather."

"But those people, yesterday, they said that doom was coming to the Domain."

"They were just a bunch of babbling idiots making a run for the wall."

"What about the blood-drinking rot monsters they talked about?"

"Overactive imaginations, if you get what I mean." Sariah twirled a finger around her ear and was gratified by the little girl's grin. "Don't worry, Mianina. There are no monsters about."

Well, maybe there were monsters around, not the kind Mia feared but rather the ones Sariah dreaded. Where were Kael and Delis? When would they return? What if they didn't return?

She had to stop thinking like that. Neither Kael nor Delis

had stayed on the decks that night. In rare agreement, armed and weaved from head to toe, they had slipped into the dead waters earlier and lost themselves in the night. They had gone to investigate a cluster of suspicious decks they had spotted earlier in the day. They had been gone a long time.

"Blood," Mia said. "You're bleeding from your bracelet."

"Oh." Sariah stopped twirling the bracelet and blotted the bloody scrapes. "It's nothing."

"Does the bracelet hurt?"

Only in her heart. "Not really."

Malord finished resetting the game. "Your move."

Sariah threw the dice and considered her options. "This is giving me a headache."

"My mommy gives me persimmon water with honey when my head hurts."

"Sounds delicious. We have no persimmon but I happen to have very good honey."

"Not again." Mia giggled. "You're going to go wide at the hips, that's what my mommy would say. And you're going to lose to Malord if you don't pay attention to your game."

Malord winked. "She's going to lose to old Malord even if she pays attention."

"Are you that good?" Mia asked.

"I'm unbeatable."

"I bet you Thaddeus could beat you."

"You mean that scoundrel brother of yours? Never."

"Oh, yes, he could. With his lucky dice. A double three, a three and five, a four and three, a double five, and a double two. Ten plays and he can't lose."

"Surely good Thaddeus doesn't cheat?" Sariah said. "Your mother would never allow him to have a pair of loaded dice."

"Mamma doesn't know. I'm the only one who knows. He always beats me. I told him I'd tell Mamma. That's how I got his secret winning numbers."

Something fluttered in the back of Sariah's mind. *Beware of the one who always wins*, the old crone had said in Alabara.

"The secret winning numbers? Do you know about this, Malord?"

"Never heard of it, but then I'm not a seventeen-year-old apprentice trying to force my luck for the sake of coin."

"You won't tell Mamma, will you?"

"Of course not," Sariah said. "Tell me again. If you throw those numbers, do you always win?"

"If you follow the right order, you'll win no matter what."

Beware of the one who always wins. And *every game triumphs well before the end is played.* The fluttering feeling coalesced into a concrete thought. Could it be?

"Put it back." Sariah repositioned her scorpions quickly. "Put it all back."

"What?" Malord asked. "Why?"

"Humor me." She played a double three. "Does it matter what the other person plays, Mia?"

"For you to win, Malord's got to play the reverse."

"That would be a double two, right?" Malord moved his snakes.

"Now me," Sariah said. "Three and five."

"This can't possibly work." Malord played the double five. "It doesn't make any sense. How can a person ensure the dice will throw the right numbers?"

Mia leaned over to Malord and whispered. "That's the cheating part."

"You must use loaded dice," Sariah said. Maybe even wised dice?

It all began to make sense. Wised dice would assure the required throws. Did Leandro know this? Sariah doubted it. He would have been a much richer man if he had owned wised dice. And he would have needed a prohibitive amount of coin to procure something as rare and forbidden. Just to make sure, Sariah pressed the dice against her palm. They weren't wised. They weren't even a loaded set.

"Four and three for both of us," Sariah said. "Is it possible, Malord? Do you see a trend? Something?"

Dark brows clashed above Malord's sharp nose. "It's very strange. Since we started playing these numbers, the board has become blocked, eliminating any choices to the moves. To play the numbers, the pieces can only move into certain spaces. Remarkable."

"Auntie's gonna win!"

"Five and five." Sariah moved. "Three and five, you. Can any kid figure this out?"

"This is the scam of a brilliant mind," Malord said, "a mathematician perhaps, one who I've never met in the Domain."

It struck Sariah like a hammer to the knee. "Someone from the Hall of Numbers spent a lot of time figuring this out."

Malord gaped.

"Who else?" Only the Guild, and only a wiser trained in the Hall of Numbers could manage a feat of this kind. "The secret numbers may be out in the back alleys among betting players, but the original maker of this scam belonged to the Guild."

But something else was bothering Sariah. "Even if Leandro had wised dice—which I doubt—how did he, or any other cheating player who knew the winning numbers for that matter, manage to win the game without triggering whatever trick was wised into these snakes and scorpions?"

"A fair question," Malord said. "Whoever went through the intricate process of creating this game would have safeguarded the trick from the casual player."

"And that safeguard must be something else, something not available to the typical player, something that only a stonewiser would have and readily recognize as rare and valuable."

Malord frowned. "Are you thinking about the missing wised dice?"

"I'm thinking about what the missing wised dice *represent* once the winning numbers are known."

They both said it at the same time. "Wised stone."

Sariah fumbled through her pockets and took out a handful of stones. "Any wised stone?"

"Not a memory stone," Malord said. "Those would have been all too common, at least among Domainers."

"What then?" She thumbed through the stones. "A bursting stone? Too risky. A festival tale stone? Too diluted."

"An ancient tale," Malord said. "The oldest tale you have in your collection."

"Maybe even a forbidden tale?" She held out the stone where she had imprinted the tale of her wising of the seven stones.

Malord grinned. "Ideal."

Sariah placed her stone on the middle of the checkered cloth board, on a square which had always puzzled her because it was the only one painted black among the red and white ones. Hers wasn't an original stone, but it was worth a try.

She played a double two. "Your turn."

A tremor betrayed Malord's hand as he played a double three and moved the last of his snakes into place.

Nothing happened.

"You win!" Mia jumped up and down, hugging Sariah. "Auntie, you finally beat Malord."

Sariah wasn't thrilled. Beating Malord had become decidedly unimportant in the great scheme of things. "Maybe we need the wised dice after all. Maybe we didn't do it right."

Malord was no less disappointed than she was. "Do you want to try it again?"

"Wait. Do you hear that?"

Pop. Pop. Blast. She knew those sounds. Somewhere out in the night, Kael was using his bursting stones, small and large. Sariah ran out to the deck. The night was dark and the wind was ferocious, but if she had doubts, a burst of fire in the distance revealed the dire extent of their trouble.

A deck went up in flames not half a league away. The flames shed light on the surrounding cluster. The wind carried the sounds of the fray—grunts, cries, the clang of weapons—a terrifying racket.

Sariah twisted the bracelet around her wrist. "Do you think they need our help?"

"Kael and Delis didn't take on those decks without good reason," Malord said. "They're not mad."

Sariah wondered.

"Is that a shooting star?" Mia asked.

Sariah turned just in time to watch a blinding streak slash the sky with unfathomable speed. It was like a shooting star, only bigger, and lower, and brighter, and... It was coming directly toward their deck. A muted rumbled stirred the flats' dead waters into a quivering tide. The deck rattled and sloshed under Sariah's feet. A strange hum grew in intensity. It strummed her eardrums into unbearable vibration.

Mia covered her ears. "What's happening?"

The impact shook the deck and sent Sariah and the others crashing to the floor. The scent of smoke and burnt thatch filled the air. Ashes and cinders flew everywhere. Green smoke poured through the deck's open door and out of the busted windows. Sariah ran to the door.

"The rot take me."

The beam had burned through the scorched thatch roof and landed squarely on Leandro's game, igniting each piece into glowing embers. A pulse of energy brightened the glow every few moments, accompanied by the throbbing hum.

She tracked the strange beam. "North by northwest."

Malord stammered. "Is it—?"

"Pointing the way? I think so."

"It looks like Ars's bridges," Mia said. "Only bigger."

"I guess it's sort of a bridge, leading us." But where?

The hum was so loud that they didn't hear Kael and Delis until they thundered onto the deck, panting like racing mastiffs.

"What's that?" Kael's face wrap was torn. Sweat streamed down his face. His weaved hands were dripping blood. Delis didn't look any better.

"It's not a map," Sariah said. "It's like a guide, a pointer."

"Whatever it is, turn it off." Kael clipped his harness to the ropes.

"We just got it to work. I can't just turn it off!"

"Turn it off, cut it out, smother it down, whatever it takes."

"And hurry." Delis was already pulling the other deck.

Shouts rang in the night. Voices cried out in the dark coming from where the decks were burning and nearing fast.

"We just got it to work. We don't know if we can—"

"I got the stars," Malord said.

"Me too," Kael said. "Turn it off or we die."

Sariah ran into the shelter and halted before the beam. The

deck was already going at a good clip but the light didn't waver, fixed stubbornly on the game set. How on earth could she stop the beam from shining on the snakes and scorpions?

She exposed her fingertips to the throbbing beam and found out quickly that it was hot. She wrapped her hand in a spare weave and groped at the cloth that served as game board. After a few scorching tries, she managed to grab the corner and pull. The little pieces toppled and scattered. The hum boomed inauspiciously. The beam retreated through the smoking hole and drew back to wherever it came from, the very place Sariah needed to find.

Twenty

WITH A RENEWED sense of urgency, they pulled for a fortnight straight and without pause. Sariah didn't dare set up the game again, afraid the beam would reveal their location to their pursuers. To keep the risk to a minimum, they had decided to call the beam only after they arrived at a safe location in the Goodlands. At least they had a clear sense of direction. They had hitched their two decks together and took turns to pull the augmented load day and night, trekking steadily towards the nearest breach in the wall. Two of them were always pulling while the third rested. Malord and Mia served as lookouts. The prime pulling team was Kael and Delis, but Sariah strained herself to match their punishing pace.

It was during one of those interminable pulling sessions, and only after Sariah had asked a hundred times, that Kael reluctantly explained some of what had happened the night the beam struck the deck.

"We were quiet," he said. "You know how we do that."

She knew. She had never met creatures as lethally quiet as Ars's runners.

"Given the lights and the sounds, the decks were easy to find. We settled to watch."

"What did you find out?"

"As we suspected, it was Josfan and the mob. Alfred and some of Orgos's men travel with them. Still, it's a smaller mob than before. Either they broke up into smaller groups to cover the ways out of the flats, or part of it gave up. The executioners were there too, two decks of them. Delis thought she recognized a couple of her fellow assassins."

"What happened then?"

"Delis walked onto the executioners' deck as if she was taking a leisurely stroll through the Crags. She asked them to leave."

"Crazy."

"One of the executioners asked Delis why she hadn't killed you yet."

"What did she say?"

"Delis said you were her donnis and she would protect you with her life."

Unbelievable. Sariah craned her neck to find Delis. She was on the deck, talking to Mia, hunched over a steaming pot. Delis, who wanted her as a pet, had declared herself against her people for her sake? She didn't understand the woman or the notion. Perhaps she never would.

"Delis was swift with the executioners, impressive really."

Was Kael praising Delis? This was a rare day indeed.

"The others heard the commotion and joined the fray. I thought the odds were poor for Delis, so I lent a hand. Then that damn comet or light beam, or whatever you want to call it, shot overhead and stunned us all. The rest you know."

"I don't understand. If I'm supposed to be her donnis, why does she mind me instead?"

Kael gave her an odd look. "Do wisers have pets?"

"Some do. Cats. Dogs. Mice. Lizards. The occasional goat. Ashmid had a pet fish once."

"In my experience, people who have pets are of two minds: those who love to master their pets and those who love to pamper them instead."

"And you think that Delis is of the latter inclination? I guess it's the better choice. If I was someone's donnis, which I'm not."

Kael's pressed lips quivered slightly.

"Does that mean you like Delis better now?"

"Like her?" He looked perplexed. "No. Do you?"

"It almost sounds like you would."

"She pulls well, and she minds your safety, I like that. But look at her. How could I like her?"

Sariah stole another glance at the woman. Delis waved from her place by the cauldron.

"She looks harmless to me."

"Do you know what's in that pot of hers?"

"Boiled turnips?" she hoped fervently.

"Friends turned foes," Kael said. "Her executioner friends' ears and noses, her little war trophies."

□ ■ □

Sariah and Kael climbed atop a tall boulder, one of many gigantic slabs which had been ejected during the wall's destruction. The grueling ascent, notably stingy of hand and foot holds, took the better part of two hours. Once on top, they settled on their bellies against the rock, further hidden by the dark weaves they flung over their backs to blend with the granite. They waited through most of the afternoon.

The heat of the stone was Meliahs' gift on Sariah's sore thighs. She pressed her cheek against the hard surface, inhaling its bland metallic scent, the distant whiff of ardent volcanoes, the pure promise of the earth's raw core. She could have stayed there forever, hugging the coarse-grained beauty, riding the compacted links, listening for creation's primeval wising with her eager palms. But she had already wised these stones the day of the wall's breaking, and she had climbed this boulder today for a different purpose.

The climb had been worth it. The boulder offered the best view of the area and it allowed them to see both sides of the ruined wall while remaining concealed. She saw the ruins of a guard tower scattered at the base of the crack, and noticed how quickly the green and brown vines had overtaken it on the other side. The shock of seeing the broken wall again squeezed both her throat and her heart.

"You didn't want to do it," Kael said. "Remember? It was Zeminaya who overtook your power and tried to destroy the wall for her own purposes. If anything, you saved what remains intact. She almost killed you that day."

It was little consolation when faced with such destruction. Zeminaya, who had built the wall at the time of the execration, believed that the wall's destruction was the only way to bring the

Bloods together. For this purpose, she had wised Zemi, a powerful intrusion of herself into the twin stones tales. Through Sariah, she had achieved her goal and broken the wall, but her dreams of unity had not been realized. The irony wasn't lost to Sariah. Zemi had bequeathed the legacy, but it was the executioners who had forced Sariah to carry it out by imposing a deadline on her life.

Was there a person in the Domain or the Goodlands who had not heard of the day Sariah broke the wall? Many different versions circulated about that day, many ill-disposed toward Sariah. The Guild's version in particular was one to mind. But there was no time to dwell on the past now. The future. That's what they had come to fetch.

"Do you see them?" she asked.

Kael scanned the woods with one of his most prized possessions, a looking glass he had purchased during his last roaming. "Huddled by the wall."

The large group of men, women and children were massing by one of the wall's huge cracks. The Domainers had been hiding all day, waiting for the darkness's protection. Now they were stirring like bats wakening at dusk.

"Is the Shield gone?"

"They're in the woods. Waiting."

With her eyes accustomed to the twilight's blue darkness, Sariah saw the Domainers crawling through the wall's crack, following each other like docile sheep.

"They're too many and too slow," Kael whispered. "I told them it wasn't safe."

"You risked your own life and went to talk to them. You warned them not to cross here. Nothing you can do if they chose to disregard your warning."

"Crossing here is madness," Kael said. "The place is crawling with Shield. The Shield has this break well covered, just like the other two spots we scouted yesterday."

Sariah glanced at her bracelet. Already three of the nine red crystals had grown opaque with the silver haze. Worse, a trace of it was beginning to trickle into a fourth crystal with the inevitability of sand pouring into an hourglass. "Can we go a different way?"

"Aye, but we have Malord and Mia to consider, and you're not going to like it."

"You don't think they'll be able to handle it?"

"I'm not sure. I don't particularly want to go that way, let alone bring all of you along, but I gather from my conversations with other Domainer travelers that the mob and Alfred are no more than a day or two behind us. And the Shield, as you can see, is still very much minding the wall. I don't think we ought to get ourselves stuck between enemies—"

The first arrow struck the woman in the lead between the shoulder blades. It was fired from such a close distance that it burst through her chest like a morbid medallion. What ensued was a massacre. What the arrows didn't kill, the pikes and swords did. The Shield emerged from the woods like rampaging locust. All Sariah and Kael could do was watch in angry but helpless frustration as the hopes of these Domainers died along with them and their children.

□ ■ □

Sariah and the others followed Kael over the rocky promontory, dodging the fumaroles' sudden eruptions and the boiling orange puddles, taking care not to slip in the warm mud, picking their footing carefully over a span of jagged limestone.

"Watch it, rot spawn," Malord said, when Delis slipped and sent him joggling inside the basket where she carried him on her back.

"Hold on and shut up, half-man," Delis said. "I'm not your mule."

"Quiet." Kael crouched behind a low ridge. "Hide yourselves and be still."

Sariah and Mia knelt beside him. He watched a sliver of trampled mud at the edge of the rocks. He took in every detail, seemingly oblivious to the slow passing of time. Sariah wasn't so patient. She had hoped to be in the Goodlands by now, following Leandro's beam and much closer to her final destination.

Mia started to play with the tiny crabs crawling on the rocks. The armored eight-legged fellows had quick claws that nipped at Mia's harassing fingers. Crying gulls flew overhead, landing occasionally to dig out the krill marooned in the mud or to steal the eggs of a flock of long-legged cranes nesting on the muddy beach. Life in the Domain never ceased to amaze Sariah. The rot and its bitter brew had taken over and yet, like the Domainers, life still endured, resisting all attempts at extinction. Sariah watched the riotous gulls and the black-beaked cranes for a while. Then, bored and a little curious, she pressed her palm against the rocks. A vision of coral polyps, algae and kelp entered her mind, a sense of deep blue depths, undulating with the sun's sparkling refraction. A whiff of salt and seaweed slammed her like a wave to the face.

"What was that?" Mia, always mimicking Sariah's action, had just experienced the same.

"It's a sense of the sea."

"What's a sea?"

"A very vast pool of water, not dead water like the Domain's, but salt water, full of life. They say it used to be everywhere before the rot came. Now it's only on the other side of the Goodlands."

"I'd like to see the sea someday," Mia said. "Can you wise these rocks?"

"Most of the time all you can wise from it is what you just saw. These types of rocks are not very good at holding tales. There was too much life in the sea, little animals darting everywhere and flower-like plants. I saw a tale of it once in a Guild stone."

"It's all that life," Mia said. "It doesn't like giving up its tale. It wants to go on and on."

Mia's observation struck a chord with Sariah. The best stones for wising were rich with the earth's core matter. Comparatively, these stones had very little of it and lots of animal and plant remains. Mia was right—life never relinquished its tale easily.

Kael motioned for everyone to be silent.

The water by the muddy beach stirred. Two straight steles aimed towards the rocks. Something popped from the dead water, two jiggling globes wrapped in some kind of wrinkled tissue, mounted on long stalks just now emerging to the surface.

The glimmering base supporting the stalks surfaced like a budding island. It approached the beach as if looking for berth. A slow bovine movement brought a squirming cluster of tentacles out of the water. One of the globes on the stalk swiveled her way. Sariah realized with a start that she was staring at a dark, gleaming eye.

"What by the rot is that?"

"A rot monster?" Mia whimpered.

"No, not a monster." Kael said. "An animal. She's an empress snail."

"Snails are little," Mia said. "And they have shells. I play with them all the time at Ars."

"This one's big. Her shell is far from here. She and her kind are the biggest of all the snails."

"You mean there are more of these?"

"Several more that I know of."

"I heard rumors," Delis whispered.

"I never thought them true," Malord said.

"I've seen her before," Kael said. "She's got a crooked left eyestalk, the poor old thing, and a missing tentacle in front. She probably lost it fighting some contentious pretender. She's an old gal. She likely dates to the execration itself. She's a horrible beauty."

It was a very accurate description for the gigantic beast. It crawled through the water slowly. A black muscular body skirted by a single massive flat foot rose from the water. Painfully, almost languorously, it launched itself forward. A huge, loose-lipped mouth landed on the beach's mud to suck birds, eggs, krill, and whatever else laid there, in one enormous slurp. There was little to say as the giant contracted back into the dead water and disappeared gradually—eyestalks last—leaving the mud streaked with feathers and cracked eggshells.

Malord broke the silence. "She's huge."

"She spans almost a league," Kael said.

"Where has she gone?" Mia asked.

"She's around. She dines in the Domain but she excretes in the Goodlands."

"You mean she's so large that her head is on this side of the wall and her tail is on the other side?" Delis asked.

"Precisely."

The pit of Sariah's stomach flooded with dread. "Kael, Kaelin. Please tell me. How are we going to cross the wall into the Goodlands?"

He didn't smile. "We're going *through* her."

Twenty-one

"I won't go." Mia stomped a stubborn foot in the mud. "You can't make me go." She turned from Kael and collapsed in Sariah's arms, sobbing. "Auntie, please, don't make me go."

Sariah couldn't blame the child. She felt like weeping too. If it wasn't because she really had to get to the Goodlands right now, she would do what any coherent person in their right mind would do—run away.

As it was, they had no choice. A quick glance at her bracelet showed that the fourth crystal was filling up. Word among the Domainers they had encountered in the last two weeks was that the Shield had mounted a new offensive on the wall's cracks and refugees were dying by the hundreds. Word also was that Alfred and the mob were but a half-day behind them. Malord and Delis's ashen faces told of the same dread she felt.

"Perhaps you don't have to go, Mianina." Sariah patted the girl's soft curls. "Perhaps you can stay on this side with Malord and Delis."

Relief made a subtle appearance on her companions' faces, but Malord shattered the reprieve. "You know she has to be with you. She can stand a little time and distance without you, but Meliahs knows, you may have to travel long and far into the Goodlands to reach the beam's source. Until we figure out a way to unhinge Mia's mind from yours, we can't risk the separation. And I pledged my work to you. I'm going."

"So will I, my donnis. I'll come. By whatever deranged way."

Sariah's gaze shifted from Delis, to Malord, to Kael, and back to Mia. She didn't want the heavy burden of their lives on her soul. "If something were to happen to any of you—"

"We make our own decisions," Kael said. "We have three

choices: We try our luck with the Shield, go this way, or we turn around and return to Ars."

"Ruin Ars?" Malord scoffed. "That would be a great gift."

"Only to have my donnis killed?"

"So we go." Kael pulled out three oversized weaved sacks from his pack. "We don't have a lot of time to prepare. I've told you what to expect."

"But I don't want to go." Mia's hands trickled drops of black flow. "I won't go."

The flicker on Kael's clenched jaw signaled his impatience. They had no time for Mia's tantrum.

"Go get ready," Sariah said to him. "Let me talk to her."

The others might have a real choice, but Kael was forgetting that Mia didn't. She was stuck in a decidedly adult and unpredictable world. To make matters worse, the child was somehow linked to her, a rogue stonewiser whose lousy odds for survival trended from bad to worse. No wonder the child hesitated.

Slim and small for her age, at twelve Mia was barely emerging from a protected childhood in her family's happy home. Despite her courage, her trials as a new wiser and her unwonted presence at Sariah's breaking of the wall, Mia was frightened. It made perfect sense. Sariah was afraid too, terrified, horrified. What they were about to do called for no lesser emotions. She hated herself for endangering the child. She made a silent vow to find the connection between Mia and her, and shatter it to oblivion. Mia would be better off for it.

She spoke very softly, looking into the girl's tearful green and blue eyes. "I know you're scared, Mianina. So am I. But sometimes we have to be brave and do things we wouldn't do otherwise."

Mia stuck out a defying chin. "My mommy's gonna poke your eyes out if I get hurt. She said so."

It was no idle threat. If something happened to Mia, Torana would do more than poke Sariah's eyes out. She would rip out her beating heart, chop it to pieces and feed it to the goats. Sariah had learned the hard way that motherly rage fueled the fires burning in Meliahs' rot pit.

"I'd do anything to avoid harm coming to you," Sariah said.

"But I can't lie to you. This is dangerous. We do it only because it has to be done."

The pout on Mia's face didn't waver.

"How about if I infuse you with a little sleep? That way, you won't be afraid. You'll dream nice dreams through the worst part, and when you wake up, you'll be fine on the other side of the wall." Or so she hoped.

"Can you do that?" Mia asked. "Will it be all right?"

"You won't be afraid."

"What if we die?"

If they granted children coins for good questions, Mia would be rich. Sariah wracked her brain for a remotely good answer. "Do you remember when old Matty died back in Ars a few months ago?"

Mia nodded.

"She died having dinner on her deck, remember? She was slurping her gruel one moment and next she was gone."

"To Meliahs' gardens," Mia said.

"My point is we can all die suddenly and without cause. It's the nature of our lives. Some of us get to die snug in our pallets. Some of us get to die in the rot's fire."

"Or in a worm."

"Technically, it's a snail." Sariah smiled. "I happen to think if we die trying to do something good, something that will help our kin and make life easier for those who come after us, we die better than if we passed from choking on pits while stuffing our faces with cherries."

She was beginning to sound like Kael. How by the fiery rot had she gotten stuck with explaining something she didn't understand?

"I like cherries," Mia said.

"What?"

"I said I like cherries. But you want me to be brave."

"I wish you didn't have to be." Sariah took Mia's hands in hers. "I *need* you to be brave."

"I'm sorry. I'm not very brave, Auntie." Mia wiped her nose with her sleeve. "Put me to sleep. I'll see you on the other side."

□ ■ □

"Let me tie that knot," Kael said, after kissing her hard on the mouth.

"Who's going to tie yours?" Sariah asked.

"I'll do it from the inside. Remember everything I told you. Every word. Understand?"

Sariah hugged the sleeping girl against her body. The weaved sack's opening narrowed, until she could see only Kael's black and green eyes, fast on hers.

"Be there," he said as he closed the gap.

□ ■ □

The wait was nerve-racking. She couldn't remember if the snail had made a sound when it came. Very little light made it through the weave. The luminescent glow of her bracelet cast macabre shadows inside the sack. It reminded her of... No. She wouldn't think of the box. Instead, she thought it was a very good thing her legs were folded at either side of Mia. She didn't think she could stand if she tried.

Sariah tugged on the little sack that held Leandro's game. It was fastened securely around her neck. The things she had to do for the stones. She caressed Mia's hair. She too would have preferred to make this journey insensible. Mia wasn't very safe with her, but Delis was taking Malord, and Kael was bringing the bulk of their gear, gear they would need on the other side *if* they survived the crossing.

"Poor little girl," she whispered. "You're stuck with me."

Balled around Mia, Sariah reviewed Kael's instructions once more. He said he had done this twice before. Crazy. She tested the deep-cockled shell over Mia's face. It was fastened to her head by a flexible leather twine. All she had to do was put it over her weaved face at the last possible moment while donning hers at the same time. She was practicing just such a maneuver when the moment came.

The darkness and the stench arrived suddenly and together. Sariah took a last breath of fetid air and pressed the shells over their mouths and noses. She felt herself aspired. Bagged in the protective weave, she and Mia tumbled in a channel along with other things, some of them maybe even her friends.

They bounced on a prickly surface, the snail's radula perhaps, the tongue-like muscle covered with bristled teeth. She had been worried about snails having teeth. Kael had said the snail's soft denticles didn't concern him as much as the parts coming after the teethed tongue. Great.

The weave was getting heavy, no doubt coated with mud and saliva. It was holding, though, and barring a snag, it should hold fine. The air in the shell was warm with her breath. Sariah had a sense of tumbling down the beast's narrowing gullet. The throat tightened over them as the snail swallowed. They fell into a large space, the snail's crop, the pouch formed by the gullet's widening, where things, according to Kael, could get complicated.

Ideally, momentum would drive them through the crop and up the digestive canal towards the snails' mantle cavity. Instead, they plummeted like stones and landed at the bottom of a sloshing pile. Not good. Time to act. Kick. Wriggle. Rolling down and up was good. The reverse was decidedly bad. It meant a return to the mouth and the risk of becoming snail vomit or overly masticated cud. Lovely thoughts. She dug her heels in the crop's floor. By now, they needed to be rolling up.

The snail gagged, a deep expulsion of air and slosh which sucked Sariah backwards. All her fears of double-mastication proved to be in vain. Instead, she got stuck in the narrow opening leading to the crop, where the muscles of a very active throat churned over her like a gigantic stone grinder.

They were already late in the journey, taking a pounding, and worst of all, they weren't moving. The air in her shell was hot and rancid. Damn if they were going to die as a snail's choking hazard. She wasn't going to let Mia down. She stretched out between compressions. At once, she felt the pressure of the snail's muscles ease. She slid back down to the crop and up into the digestive canal, this time swiftly.

The canal seemed to stretch for hours. She tumbled up an incline, a remarkable feat of gravity. She was traveling up towards the mantle cavity, the hump tucked under the shell in the snail's back. She only knew about the snail's anatomy because Kael had drawn it in the mud while he described in detail his previous journeys. He had also shared the knowledge he had gained during the dissection of a dead giant snail he and his father had found many years before. Knowledge was the key to a successful snail crossing, Kael had explained. Meliahs help them.

Mia started to wheeze in her sleep. Sariah followed promptly. How long had it been since they had begun the perilous journey? Kael had explained that these giant snails had *precipitated* digestions, fast-paced processes to convert great quantities of food into energy adapted to the beast's continuous feeding practices. The journey had already taken much more than the three minutes the average crossing took. She was sure of it. How long was the snail's damn digestive canal?

Longer than the Royal Way? Longer than the wall? Long enough to lose consciousness, she realized. Twice. Long enough that she wanted to rip the shell off her face and breathe whatever foul substances were traveling with her. She fought the impulse. The stomach had to be close now. Wait. What had Kael said? The stomach was the most dangerous place of all.

On cue, they dropped feet-first into in a broiling sack. Tumbling in a viscous pond, Sariah fought for some kind of purchase or footing, difficult since the stomach walls felt more like rubbery nets under her feet. She seemed to be bouncing against those writhing walls, engaged in an aimless back and forth, sloshing in a dizzying, angry churn. Despite the weave and the shell, the vapors set her lungs and stomach on fire. She started to heave from the stink. She forced herself to swallow her own vomit.

The red dye. She groped for the rope she had tied to her wrist and pulled. The rope released the contents of the dye bag attached outside of the sack. She prayed it worked fast. The weave had kept the brunt of the gastric acids out of the protective sack, but a bit of the thinner liquids, saliva, slime, and now some fizzling foam, were filtering through the top. The hot air in the shell was no longer breathable. She was drowning in her own breath.

Abruptly, the snail's stomach went into spasms. A huge gurgle exploded around Sariah, a giant, awful croak that reverberated through her bones. Sariah was ejected with the force of a catapulted stone. She hit her head against something hard. The space around her constricted gradually, until she was being smothered again, torn to pieces by a spastic gut, asphyxiated by the glut compacting around her. She realized what was happening. She was dying an ignominious death, squashed senseless in the snail's turbid excrement.

Twenty-two

PEACE. FRESH AIR. Meliahs' gardens. It had to be.

"Sariah?" Kael's voice spilled over her body like a swift caress, blessed relief pampering both mind and aching flesh. She wanted to keep the dream going, but she forced her eyes to open for the same reason she always went on—she had to.

The sky was as blue as Mia's sparkling eye, which along with her green eye, looked down on her with glistening humor.

"We were pooped by the snail." She giggled. "In-as-snail-bait-out-as-snail-dung."

Sariah started to laugh but hacked instead and had to turn to wretch profusely. Her bile floated away in the river's efficient current. For a moment, she thought she was floating away as well. She fumbled and dug her knees in the gravel, only to find Kael sitting on a rock behind her, holding her fast between his legs.

"Hello there." She held on to his calves and dove underwater. The current stretched the length of her hair with a playful, steady tug. She kept herself under for as long as her lungs lasted, then came up for breath. "I'm never traveling by snail again."

Kael was laughing as she went under once more.

The river bottom was a treasure of polished pebbles and stones, black, brown, gray, yellow, all glimmering with the sun's reflection under the sparkling water. She eyed the stones with a wiser's lust. She had to slip a few in her pocket. A pale fish darted by. The water was clear and delicious, flowing nicely over her skin and clothing.

She came up to swallow great gulps of clean air. Water was streaming down her face like a translucent drape. "Did they—?"

Kael pointed to the nearby bank. She wiped the water from her eyes. Malord was rinsing his weave in the river and Delis was sprawled on top of a rock, swinging her big feet in the current. "You should see the pile, Auntie. We came out of the side of the thing, right next to its huge shell."

"I think I'd rather not see it."

"We were covered in—"

"Mia, don't you remember?" Kael said. "We weren't going to tell Auntie about that."

And she didn't want to know. "Which way are we going?"

North and west was somewhere upriver, between a tall cypress and a coral-tree blazing with blooms.

"We'll have to scout the area," Kael said, "before we call the beam."

"We have until nightfall," Sariah said. "I doubt the beam will be visible during the day."

The sight of the forest around them, the damp leaves' lush scent, the river's gurgle, even the woodpeckers' hammering threatened to overwhelm Sariah's dulled senses. No wonder they called it the Goodlands. No wonder Malord and Delis stared in shocked fascination and Mia splashed in the shallow river. She realized she had missed trees, water and good soil under her feet. Meliahs be blessed. They had made it to the Goodlands.

The quails' rancorous call announced a covey in the brush. Her belly grumbled a pathetic growl. "Is that dinner? I'm famished."

"Is that so? I suppose we ought to do something about it." Kael picked her up halfway out of the water and locked his arms around her waist, keeping her face to his eye level. He was thoroughly wet too. Clear water drops clung to his thick eyelashes and sparkled on his face like a host of tiny stars. "You took a long time."

"But I came."

"I can't forgive the anguish."

"Wandering a snail's innards is not exactly anxiety free."

His mouth quivered. "I was beginning to think of ways of buggering a damn snail."

Sariah kept her face perfectly straight. "Sinful vice or virtuous search?"

His laughter echoed in the clearing and startled the quails into a tumult of clucking and wing batting.

"Are you going to kiss Auntie now?" Mia said.

"Do you really think I should?"

"My daddy says it's your job to kiss her lots."

"I'll do it," Kael said. "But only 'cause it's my job."

To Mia's delight, he smacked Sariah loudly on the lips.

Then he kissed her softly below the ear. "Don't be late next time."

□ ■ □

Sariah swallowed the last bite of roasted quail leg with a moan of delight. She licked the bone until no flesh, marrow, or flavor remained, before she tossed it into the fragrant wood fire. She leaned back, laying her head on Kael's lap and rubbing her full belly.

"Satisfied?" he asked.

"Very." She licked the last of the delicious grease from her fingertips. "I'm clean and full. What else could a woman want?"

Kael's brow rose suggestively.

"I know," Sariah said. "A spoonful of honey?"

"You've all but turned into a honeybee." Kael groped through her pack and handed her the jar. "It's about done."

"I'll find you more, my donnis," Delis said from her perch by the stream. She pointed to the water in awe. "It keeps coming, and it's not the same as before."

Malord mumbled through a mouthful of berries. "It's a river, you twerp. I already told you. You can throw in as many branches as you want, but they're not coming back."

"What do you think, Auntie?" Fingers dripping with paint and etching knife in hand, Mia stuck her latest work in front of Sariah's nose.

The scene was remarkably vivid. A lush forest stood in the river's background, rich with the aspen's golds and the birch's peeling red-brown bark. The silvery water captured the sun's waning light to perfection. She could see all of them there, sitting around the campfire as they had been just moments ago.

"It's beautiful." Sariah pleased Mia into a satisfied blush. "Your grandmother Aya would be proud of you. Do you feel a little better now?"

"Much better. Like a warm kettle without the steam, as my mommy likes to say."

They all laughed. Sariah was relieved. Mia's art was as much expression as it was compulsion, and holding back her dark flows was hard enough for the little girl. Until she met Mia and learned about Aya, Sariah had believed what the Guild taught—that sight copyists were extinct and that their translation had been an aberrant remnant of the Old World, of the times before the rot when parchment and paper had kept the tales well enough and art mixed easily with wising.

Now she knew better. The sight copyist blood endured in the old line of Ars. Aya, Kael's mother and Mia's grandmother, had been a stonewiser of that translation. Sariah struggled to lead Mia through her sight-copyist apprenticeship blindly, but she was sure of one thing—the child was happiest when she unleashed her power to engrave her work on parchment. Mia's latest masterpiece still smelled of fire and smoke. Sariah was about to comment on the beauty of the engraving's foreground when the screams began.

Kael's head snapped up. He was on his feet and running instantly, followed by a hatchet-wielding Delis. Sariah ran after them, but not before directing Mia and Malord to put out the fire and hide. She had her sling loaded by the time she caught up with the other two. They stretched on their bellies at the top of a shallow ravine overlooking a muddy lane. She crawled quietly to join them and stole a look at the scene on the road.

The gray shields were unmistakable. About fifteen or twenty well-armed guards outfitted with the wood, copper and hide shields surrounded an upturned cart. The screams were coming from two young girls twisting in the soldiers' grips. An older woman knelt on the ground amidst her cart's spills, clutching a bunch of corn ears to her breast.

"It's the Shield's right to requisition your cart and its contents," the man in charge was saying. "It's the law."

"It must be another one of your new laws," the woman said. "My grandchildren are hungry and I didn't take my savings and travel all the way to Ellensburg to feed you stinking pests."

The swipe of the man's pike struck the woman in the back

with a dreadful thump. She flung forward and fell on the corn, hacking from the blow. She was stout and small but she braced herself on arms strong as oaks and faced the brute over her. "Is this how your master intends to rule?" she said. "Through brawn and pike?"

"We'll teach you to respect the Shield." He turned to his men. "Take the cart. And take them. All three of them."

The guards wavered. One of them said, "They're but an old woman and two little girls—"

"Shut up, Kenzy. That one must be at least thirteen. They're three wombs. You know the drill."

By then Kael had motioned Delis up the road and had an arrow notched in his bow. To see him wielding the traditional Goodlander bow was rare. Kael usually preferred his Domainer sling. But Sariah had seen Kael fight enough times to know he always chose purposively from the impressive array of weapons he carried on his belt. The arrows would throw the Shield off for a moment or two and Kael would profit from the confusion.

He stood up and shot. The same deadly arrow punched through his target's neck, killing the man instantly, and then went on to efficiently skewer another man's calf, disabling the second soldier. Sariah aimed her sling and shot. She winced when she heard the stone clang against one of the men's helmets. *Pop.* The stone burst on command, and the man fell to the ground, clutching his head through the half-melted helmet.

Her next stone was aimed at the guard who held the smaller of the girls. It bounced on his neck and dribbled down into his shield. The man smiled, thinking she had missed. How she hated using the stones for harm.

She gave him a last chance. "Give me the child."

The warrior charged her, clutching the crying child in one hand and his pike in the other. *Pop.* He stumbled midway and looked down in surprise. Dark blood poured down his legs and pooled at his feet. Only his shield kept his guts' gore from spilling on the ground. His eyes rolled to the back of his head. He keeled over. Sariah picked up the screeching girl and set her on her hip, all the while searching for her next target.

She shouted a warning at the same time she shot at Kael's attacker. Kael hit the ground. The stone struck his opponent in the tiny strip of skin exposed between the back of the helmet and the neck guard. *Pop.* Meliahs forgive her. The brain would shoot upwards into the helmet.

Kael tucked away his bow and unsheathed his twin swords. They clashed against three of the shield's pikes. The woman who held the other girl was putting up a good fight but she let go when Kael sliced open her shins. Sariah grabbed the girl, dodged a pike, and then ran with the two children to the edge of the road.

"That way." She pointed the older girl in the direction of the woods. "Take your sister. Hide. Don't come out until I call you."

A shadow loomed behind Sariah. She whirled just in time to see Delis's hatchet coming down on her attacker's back.

"Thanks," she said hoarsely.

"Don't mention it, my donnis."

Sariah's next shot was not lethal, but it would hurt like the rot. It struck under the shield of a man beating the older woman by the cart. *Pop.* He wouldn't be sitting comfortably for a long time. She helped the woman to her feet.

"Meliahs be blessed, who are you?"

"Don't thank us yet." Sariah pushed the woman out of a pike's way. "It's not over."

The surviving Shield regrouped and faced them. They stuck together like hares on a string, holding their barbed pikes ahead of them, advancing in step like a bristling porcupine. Sariah dug in the depths of her weapons belt to find a stronger stone. Kael was already rolling one of his on the ground. *Bam.* The advancing line broke at its center. Three more men lay in a heap of arms and broken shields. At their commander's behest, the two remaining sides closed the gap and became a line again.

The sound of hooves behind them did not dissuade the Shield from their attack, but the unexpected collision that broke their weakened line did. Malord rode down the lane mounted on a wide-hoofed draft horse and crashed against the back of the Shield's line. He wielded his hefty mace with enormous force, banging on the attackers' helmets with powerful blows. The early afternoon was filled with the clang of wood on metal and the grunts of Kael and Delis's last efforts.

When the fray was over, Kael came to Sariah. "Are you all right?"

"Not a scratch. Kael, may I present—what's your name?"

"Mara." The woman tucked a strand of long white hair back in her bun with great dignity. "Mara of Targamon Farm."

She was short of stature but strong of body, equally rounded at the hips and at the bosom. Besides her smart blue eyes, the most prominent feature on her face was her nose, a fleshy knob with a flat dent at the top of the upturned tip.

"This is Kael," Sariah said. "He's my mate—"

"Your mate?" Incomprehension clouded Mara's eyes. "Animals mate."

"He is my..." What was it that Goodlanders called it? "He's my husband."

"Your husband, eh? A Domainer?" She looked at Sariah's face, noting her matching eyes, and then stared at Kael's black and green eyes with a hint of suspicion. Her pinched face relaxed and her hand shot up to shake Kael's. "I guess we get them husbands from wherever we can. Domainer or not, it's only fair that I thank you for your help. You could have walked on blind to all of this."

"No, madam," Kael said. "I couldn't."

He crossed to the other side of the road where Delis kept watch over the wounded. Sariah and Mara followed. He dropped a skin on a young man's lap. Sariah recognized one of his blue fringed arrows in the lad's calf. Kael crouched before the young man and examined the wound.

"Why are you here?" He snapped the shaft, taking off the point and the feathering.

The lad was shaking with fear and shock.

"I won't ask again. What's your mission?" With a quick thrust, Kael pulled the shortened shaft through the wound.

The man flinched. "We're to requisition foodstuffs and supplies for the wall's guard."

"Your commander said something about wombs and drills. What was that about?"

"Why should I tell you anything? You're going to kill me anyway."

"If I were going to kill you, why would I bother treating your wound, you rotting excuse for a brain?"

The young man stared agape as Kael tied a tourniquet below the knee and cleansed his wound. "It's the mandate," he blurted out. "To seed the pure folk of the Goodlands with the Shield's excellent stock. To save the Goodlands from takeover by the rot's vermin."

"Ah." The young man wilted under Kael's terrible glare. "Who commands you?"

"The Main Shield," the lad said. "Stonewiser Master Arron."

□ ■ □

Arron. The name set Sariah's belly to ice. He was the Main Shield now? The last time she had seen Arron, the day of the breaking of the wall, he had been fighting against Mistress Grimly for control of the Guild. The mistress had taken over the Shield after the Main Shield, Horatio Maliver, quit his command. Arron had probably prevailed in that battle or shortly thereafter. And at the very least, in a stunning reversal of roles, he had managed to wrest command of the Shield from Mistress Grimly. He must have named himself Main Shield after that.

It made sense. Arron wouldn't care if Goodlanders died of famine as long as his purposes were served. His *mandate* seemed utterly plausible, in character, and not so far removed from the Guild's lesser known notions. Was he close by? Sariah shivered.

Kael knotted the young man's bandage. "Arron. I should have known."

"That arse-licking mongrel is bleeding us dry," Mara said.

"Why?" the lad asked, perplexed. "Why won't you kill me?"

Kael's eyes fell on the young soldier's face. "Because you, Kenzy, right? You asked the right question when hearing a bad command. Perhaps in time, you'll learn to act beyond questions, but for now, that little bit of hesitation in your voice when your commander ordered you to hurt the woman and the girls saved your life."

"My grandchildren?" Mara asked anxiously.

"Here comes one." Sariah smiled at the sight of Malord on the old horse with the smaller one of the two girls riding abreast. "This is Malord," she decided for simplicity.

"Mounted on Rodney?"

Sariah couldn't help but notice that Mara took in the entire sight of Malord, as absent of wholeness as it was.

"How valorous of you," Mara said, "to come like that in our defense. I'm in your debt."

"Not at all." Malord hid his face's furious flush by helping the girl down from the horse.

"You're a Domainer too?" Mara asked.

"As mismatched of eyes as they come," Malord said.

"Where are Mia and the other girl?" Sariah asked.

"Here they come."

The girls emerged from the forest hand in hand.

"Come here, Roxana. Are you hurt? Clara?" Mara embraced her granddaughters. "That was close, my girls, very close. If these good people hadn't come..."

"We'll need every hand to right the cart and reload it," Kael said. "Let's hurry."

Between all of them, they righted the cart. The girls joined Delis and Kael picking up the spilled groceries. Malord hesitated before quitting the beast. Clearly, he was enjoying his newly ac-quired heights.

"You'll be needing your horse, I suppose."

"Oh, no, sir, Malord," Mara said. "Rodney does so much better with a mounted lead and I so dislike straddling the beast. I think you should ride him, I mean, Rodney, over to the farm. Regardless of whatever drives you to travel this forsaken road, you must allow me to thank all of you with my hospitality, at least for tonight."

A roof. A bed. A dry blanket. It was tempting.

"Thanks for your offer," Sariah said, "but we're in a hurry and we—"

"Can I talk to you for a moment?" Kael pulled Sariah aside. "We have a new problem—Kenzy and his surviving friends.

They're our prisoners now. If we let them go, they'll go straight to the Shield and tell them about us. They might even lead them back here."

"Are you suggesting we—"

"I have a different idea. I'll stay behind in the forest, guarding the prisoners for a day or two. If all goes well, I might even be able to play around with the Shield to deflect any attention from you. You go on to this Targamon place. As soon as it's safe, call the beam. If you're successful, we'll meet in three days near the confluence of the twin rivers. You can't miss it. If you can't call the beam, we'll meet at Targamon instead."

Sariah saw the plan's logic. "Delis can stay."

"No, Delis must go with you to protect you and the stones. We can't leave her in my place because she's never been here before, whereas I'm a roamer and I know my way around the Goodlands. I don't think these three know where Mara is from, but I think that given enough time I can persuade them from telling their bosses about us."

"How?"

"How will they feel when they have to tell their superiors their whole unit was wiped out by an old woman and her poor family? Such defeat would surely involve some hefty punishment, not to mention humiliation. Wouldn't they look a lot better, like heroes, if their explanation entailed a more impressive opponent?"

"And you're going to feed them that story?"

"A good battle story, about Domainer runners in the hundreds and Goodlander rebels. Anything that will throw the Shield off our trail. It's worth a try. In the worse case, we'll have a few hours' advantage. In a day or two, I can haul these three to town and arrange it so they can't get loose for another day or so. I might even fit in a bit of business in Ellensburg."

"Business?"

He shot her a glance askance. "We're not idiots, Sariah. Since the time before the execration, Ars has had investments in the Goodlands. The children of Ars have been prudent enough to augment those reserves. There's more business between the Goodlands and the Domain than you can imagine."

"Is that how you're financing our little expedition?"

"Partly. There are some assets that must be turned into coin and some goods that need to find good buyers. It's part of my roamer's duties."

"I'm going to be the ruin of you." She said it factually, like the coin-based Guild wiser she had once been.

He took her hand. "Some women like jewels, others like trinkets, and others prefer gowns or shoes. You like stones, and the stone truth, and I happen to be after that too."

"I won't have you and your kin ruined on account of my stones."

"You're right. You won't let it happen and neither will I. So let me do my job and you worry about yours."

"But I don't want to leave you behind."

"It's not like that, Sariah. And the alternative is—Well, you know what it is."

Sariah surveyed the surviving Shield. Under all that wood, leather and copper, she saw fear in the young anxious faces. She didn't like it. But did they have any other choice besides murder?

Kael turned to Mara. "Your hospitality would be very much welcomed. If your offer still stands, these folks will be spending the night with you."

"What did you say your name was, my dear?" Mara asked.

"Oh, forgive my oversight. I'm Sariah."

The woman's brow wrinkled like well-used parchment. "Sariah of the Hall of Scribes' sixty-sixth folio, formerly of the Guild?"

There went the roof, the bed and the dry blankets.

"Aye," she said reluctantly. "That's me."

Twenty-three

FROM THE TOP of the hill, Sariah could see that Targamon Farm had once been an extensive enterprise. Furrowed fields extended as far as the eye could see around the distant shape of an old two-story house. It was the kind of place Kael would have loved—serene, private, unspoiled, and charmingly quaint. The idyllic setting would have made the perfect background for his dreams. By Meliahs, he had been gone from her sight for less than a couple of hours, and she was already missing him fiercely.

But on closer inspection, Targamon lost some of its appeal. The once fertile vale seemed deserted of crops and people. Other than the house's produce garden and a couple of failed wheat fields, nothing grew in the undulating countryside.

"What happened here?" Sariah asked Mara, who walked beside her by the tumbling cart.

Mara's round face broke into a grimace of pain. "Misery. That's what. It started a year ago. A sickness came and took my daughter-in-law and two of her babies, leaving my son, the two girls and me untouched. My son kept trying to grow the grain. We had orders from the Shield coming due and they were already suspect of us because we hadn't welcomed them to our lands. The weather turned queer, cold like the chill some days, hot like a blaze some others. How can a farm endure with weather like that?"

Up ahead, Delis scouted the road while Malord rode the hitched horse, leading the cart through the muddy lane. The three girls, Mia, Roxana and Clara were sitting on the cart's front bench, jabbering happily. Sariah listened to Mara, but she kept an eye on Delis.

"A few months ago we discovered the reason for our misfortunes." Mara glanced at the nearing house. "The rot came. What the sickness hadn't done, the rot did in three days. Targamon's tenants fled, abandoning their houses. With no hands to work the fields and the orders due, we were ruined. My son, sick with grief, fell on his own scythe. The girls and I remain. What else can we do? This cart is the whole of our stock to pass the chill. It's coming, and people say it will be a long one. That's why I risked the trip to Ellensburg."

"I'm sorry for your troubles. You've had a hard burden to carry, all by yourself."

"It's Meliahs' will, I suppose. I'm not sure what will happen to us. In compensation for the failed orders, the Shield took all of our seed. If we can't deliver next year, we'll lose our right of autonomy."

"What's that?"

"It's the Guild's permit, the sanction that allows us to hire independent laborers to work the farm and harbor them under our protection. If we lose our right of autonomy, I fear we'll lose our land and they'll evict us shortly after that."

Plague, the rot and the Shield. Mara's story was a nightmare come true.

"Do you want to take a look?" Mara asked.

"At what?"

"Why, at the rot, of course. It's just yonder, on the other side of the fence. It won't take but a moment."

"But the girls, the wagon—"

Skirts hiked to her knees, Mara was already climbing over the stone fence.

Sariah sighed. "Wait here," she said to Delis and Malord. "Keep an eye out for the Shield. I'll be right back."

She followed Mara through a small meadow where the red-capped robins' song cheered the land.

"I've heard Domainers are very good with the rot." Mara puffed up the slight incline. "Very good indeed."

Sariah kept her mouth shut. She was surprised to see so many birds, flowers, trees and bushes. Even the weeds were suspect to her eyes. The rot usually destroyed those first.

"Where is it that you and your folk are going?" Mara asked.

"We're following a trail. North of here."

"There's nothing north of here, only the mountains. The Bastions, they call them. They can't be crossed. It's the end of the Goodlands, the end of the world, some say. Other than wild beasts, I can't imagine what you think you may find there."

"How far away are these mountains?"

"Seven days' hard walk, maybe six in good weather."

"That's closer than I thought."

"Not far enough if you ask me. You have no business going there."

"Be that as it seems, they appear to be in the general direction in which we're going."

"What a shame," Mara said. "I kind of like you folks. People tend to die or disappear over there. Do you know the hounds that Meliahs fashioned to nip at Menodor's heels? Well. That's where they dwell."

"Isn't that more like a legend?" Sariah asked politely.

"Not when you've seen the dead and the injured as I have. I'm telling you. It's an evil place. Don't go there."

Sariah tended to scorn superstition, but the cold shiver that ran the length of her spine filled her with an eerie sense of foreboding. Maybe when she set up Leandro's game again, the beam would point in a different direction.

"I can't help but wonder why you'd want to go there," Mara said. "I hope it's not foolishness on your part. I know your kind. I've seen them come and go in my time."

Her kind? Perhaps the old woman was a little off-kilter.

"Don't play dumb with me." Mara stopped in her tracks and pulled something out of her pocket. "I know who you are."

The folded parchment in Mara's hand fluttered in the afternoon breeze for a few moments before Sariah took it. She gave it a cursory reading. By the rot. That's why the woman had known her name.

"Where did you get this?"

"There were several of those going around town." Mara took the parchment back. "Are you going to tell me you don't know what this is?"

"I know what it is."

"And does this journey to the Bastions have anything to do with it?"

"I'm not sure. Maybe."

"This is no time for maybes, stonewiser. An awful lot is at stake. You don't intend to leave it at this, I hope?" Mara waved the accursed parchment in the air.

The woman's smallish blue eyes probed her like a hard poke to the shoulder. Sariah couldn't quite understand. Who had devoted the time and effort to do this? And why? Who stood to benefit from it? And why should Sariah care about what Mara thought? Mara was a stranger, a passing acquaintance, one of many whose lives and livelihoods depended on... what? The unity of the Bloods? Stone truth? Her?

Of course not. There were millions like Mara in the Goodlands, in the Domain. She couldn't mind each one of them. Not with the stones calling as they were, not with her service requiring the whole of her life. Mara and her grandchildren were just a pebble on the road, a quick goodbye in a string of fast farewells.

"Here we are," Mara said. "And there it is. By the bushes."

By the bushes? The rot typically killed those quickly. She was only a step or two from a large cluster of chokeberry when she finally got a whiff of the rot. Following her nose, she pushed the bushes aside, shaking a few red purple berries from the low branches. The bush was still making fruit?

The rot was on the other side, not the enormous black sores she was used to seeing in the Domain, but rather a cluster of six or seven tiny lesions spread over a small area, gurgling quietly beneath the weakening sun. The poison in it was a tea-colored brown, in marked contrast to the dark rot she knew. Sariah was no land healer, but she had been with Kael long enough to have learned a few things.

She twisted the bracelet around her wrist until it hurt. Generosity's link landed on top. She gritted her teeth. She was in a hurry. She didn't have the time or the resources. This was just one of a thousand rot cases, small, unimportant, isolated. A tiny stumble in the long journey. That's all Targamon Farm could be to her. It struck her forcefully and rather unfair that she had come here. Because standing there before this mild interpretation of the land killer, she realized that Targamon Farm could be saved from the rot.

"Ugly plague, isn't it?" Mara's blue eyes were intent on Sariah's face. "Do you reckon there's something you could do about it?"

Sariah looked away. "I doubt it."

□ ■ □

They were almost to Targamon's main gates when Sariah noticed Delis, ambling towards the side of the road and then disappearing into the brush. Without missing a step, Sariah scooped her sling out of her weapons belt and tucked her hand in her pocket, grasping a good-sized stone. It was but a moment before the first floundering figure hit the road head-first at Rodney's hoofs. A second screeching shape was flung from the trees and came to rest on top of the other. A third addition to the tangle of arms and legs followed, this one delivered directly onto the heap by Delis's indelicate paws.

"Three," she said. "Spying on us. Following along."

Sariah stared at the pile. Two men and a woman dressed in rags looked up from the mud, a combination of angry, affronted and mismatched looks. Domainers. Young ones at that.

"Who are you?" Sariah asked. "Why do you follow us?"

"They do that all the time," Roxana said. "They're always looking, circling like buzzards to steal our stuff."

"That's not true." A young man bolted to his feet. "We don't want your stuff."

"You want to destroy us and take our land."

Fists clenched, the lad started towards Roxana. "You blabbering little witch—"

Malord reached from atop the horse and caught him by the scruff of the neck. "We don't hit people in the Domain. Not even when they deserve it."

"Roxana, dear, where did you hear such lies?" Mara asked.

"The widow told me. They bring plague. And rot. It's in their spit."

"I'm a Domainer," Mia said. "You said you liked me."

"Use your head, child," Mara said. "Don't you remember? The plague and the rot came before these people arrived. Say nothing more. You're embarrassing yourself."

From his perch on the horse, Malord released his grasp on the kid and glared at the Domainer trio. "What are you doing here?"

"Same thing you're doing here," the young man said.

"I'm the Domain's gathering wiser." Malord's mismatched eyes, his title, and perhaps most importantly, his tone of voice, granted him irrefutable authority over the chastened rascals.

"We were guarding the road," the lad said, "looking out for the Shield."

"You're far from Panadan."

"How do you know we hail from Panadan?"

"Panadanians like to use onyx for memory stones."

The young man clutched the stone on his neck.

"Orm of Panadan would have a fit if he knew you were here," Malord said. "Does he even know? Did you ask permission to come to the Goodlands?"

"We're not going back."

"How many of you are there?" Sariah asked.

"Many."

"Ten, twenty, a hundred?"

The kid kept his stubborn silence.

"I reckon they're about eighteen," Mara said. "They're squatters at the Siguird Farm."

"We're not squatters!" The young woman shot to her feet. "We're under the widow's protection. We bought a parcel of land from her a week back. We paid good coin for it."

"Is that so?" Sariah said. "A parcel of land? Did she give you a stone or a parchment saying so?"

The three exchanged puzzled looks.

"I didn't think so. How are you going to manage with your coin gone and the chill coming?"

The young man's chest swelled like a puffing hen. "We're Domainers. We'll manage."

"You're as clumsy as hobbled oxen," Delis said, "as easy to catch as stunned cockroaches."

Sariah took in the shabby trio, the tattered rags they wore for mantles, the dirty faces, the bony limbs. Somewhere in Panadan a mother wept for this frail-looking young woman and a father agonized over the fate of his sons. Sariah fathomed she could hear the trio's empty stomachs grumbling. Or was it her stomach growling?

"What are your names?"

The girl spoke up. "I'm Ginia. These are Rig and Harsten."

Somewhat regretfully, Sariah handed the girl four shaggy hares they had caught along the way. "Take these."

The trio stared at the hares on the string.

"For dinner," Sariah said. "You roast them. Like fowl. In the fire?"

"Oh, yes, we know how to do that."

"You said you were keeping watch for the Shield," Sariah said. "Why?"

"The widow likes to know when they come," Rig said. "And we don't trust the Shield."

"That's wise of you. Did you see any?"

"Several Shield patrols have been on the road today. The last one we saw no less than an hour ago, setting a night camp over by the crossroads."

Curse her luck. She couldn't call the beam tonight if there was a Shield patrol camping so close. They would be on Targamon as soon as they spotted the beam. She hated to waste the time, but Kael was right, she had to wait until it was safe to call the beam. They couldn't find the tale if they were all dead.

Mia climbed down from the cart and neared Rig, a reedy lad of perhaps fourteen, a gangly assembly of long limbs and curly black hair.

"Your leg. It's bleeding." She pressed her scarf against the boy's knobby knee. "I'll make it better."

Rig blushed like a roseroot.

How she hated to abandon these Domainer youths to their scant devices. How many Domainers were in the Goodlands now? How many would perish from starvation this chill? Lacking knowledge and experience, how many would be tricked, abused, misled, persecuted and outright killed?

Well, if she couldn't call the beam tonight, she might as well do something else, something fruitful preferably. "Where is this farm? It's nearby, yes? I'll need to speak to the widow. If it's true that you paid her coin for land, I'll make you a stone of property."

The trio's eyes widened.

"But if I find out you didn't pay the widow for land, if you're squatting, stealing, or harassing her, then you will return to Panadan. Your kin must be worried sick. I expect you to be men and women of the oath."

The three heads bobbed in unison.

"Now let's see. We have, what? Three more hours of light? Malord, won't you take the girls to the farmhouse? Delis, you can keep watch. Can you two boys run fast? I thought so. Stay with Delis. Bring word to us if you spot trouble. Ginia, come with me. Mara, I wonder, will it be too much to ask for an introduction to the Siguird widow?"

"Not at all. You saved our lives."

"Do you really think a stone of property will make a difference?" Malord asked.

"I don't know," Sariah said. "The Third Covenant prohibits Domainers in the Goodlands, so I don't know that the Guild's justice applies to Domainers. But we have to start somewhere."

"What do you mean, *start*?"

"This is probably happening all along the wall. Only bloodshed can stop it now. I fear Arron will try that well enough. Meanwhile, we have to build a record of justice for those who come to settle here."

"A record of justice?"

She took a deep breath. "One day, it may be all Domainers have to defend themselves in the Goodlands."

Twenty-four

THE SIGUIRD WIDOW was a strong, lively woman with striking black eyes that shone like polished onyx. She wore her lustrous black hair loose over her shoulders and her dress tightly cinched around her body's prominent curves, demonstrating with the swing of her hips that she was very much still in contention. She manifested great pleasure in receiving Sariah once she understood that she was a Guild stonewiser. Sariah didn't contest the small detail about her Guild membership.

"I'm honored to receive you in my house." The widow's gaze scoured Sariah from head to toe. "Although, I must confess, I've never seen a stonewiser without the brooch and black robe."

"I've been traveling a lot. I find comfort in these clothes."

"They're strange." She ran her hands over her long and proper Goodlander skirt. "But to each its own. Besides, no man or woman I know would want to pass themselves for a stonewiser—" She tittered. "Not that there's anything wrong with stonewiser blood, of course, that's not what I meant—"

"Of course not." Sariah knew all she risked by coming to see the widow. Granted, she couldn't call the beam right away, but she wondered, not for the first time, why the plight of people she didn't know kept sidetracking her.

The widow served Sariah and Mara tea in her front parlor, but she left the Domainer kids standing by the open front door under a drizzle of rain. Sariah counted twelve boys and four girls wearing rags for mantles and mud for boots. Some of them showed cuts and bruises, and a few of them had some kind of rash around their mouths, on their necks and hands. They were a pathetic sight, thin, ragged, and huddling together under the rain like a pack of mangy mongrels waiting for scraps.

"What brings a Guild wiser to our humble parts?" the widow asked when she finished tinkering with her prized tea set.

"I understand there's a matter of property at stake," Sariah said. "In deference to the Guild laws, I seek to formalize the agreement."

"I'm not sure I follow, stonewiser. What did you say your name was?"

"I didn't."

"Oh." The widow cleared her throat. "My husband has been dead a year now. The business of succession has been resolved to my name."

"These Domainers told me they purchased a parcel of land from you not a week ago."

Sariah had been to the so-called parcel of land before coming to see the widow, a steep, muddy hill by the river's sharp embankment where the youngsters had built a number of fragile lean-tos that threatened to slide down with the first hard rain. Sariah was no expert, but even she could see that the hill would flash flood easily and that not even a simple garden would grow in the thick mud.

"You're here about the vermin's younglings?" The woman didn't bother hiding her surprise. "I didn't think the Guild cared about stuff like that."

"The law says that any trade should be documented by parchment, or preferably, by stone."

"A widow like me doesn't have the means to afford your services."

"Never mind. My services are offered without charge."

"Without charge?" The woman's mouth pursed in a perfect circle. "Forgive my trepidation. I've never met a Guild stonewiser who worked for free."

Neither had Sariah.

"Well, you see, the thing is—" The woman squirmed. "I don't need your services after all."

"What do you mean? Didn't these youngsters pay you for the parcel?"

"I don't want to get the poor bastards in trouble." The widow lowered her voice. "I'm just letting them stay here out of the goodness of my heart."

"Out of the goodness of your heart?" Sariah repeated the words aloud. "So these youngsters are squatters in your land?"

"We're not squatters." Ginia stepped into the parlor. "We paid her all of our coin and more. That parcel is ours!"

"Get out of my house, you snotty vermin. You're tracking mud on my floor."

"Ginia, stand back," Sariah said. "You don't want to owe penalties to this woman." She turned to the widow. "So these Domainers didn't pay to settle on your farm?"

"Most decidedly not."

A gasp of indignation rose from the group outside. Even Mara, who had concentrated on her cup of tea to this point, flashed the widow a doubtful look. Sariah got up from her stool.

"What about this collection of Domainer weaves you have here?" She fingered a pile of weaves stacked on the corner table. "Are they not part of the youngsters' price?"

"I've been collecting those for years. I keep them for the Shield. They have a standing order to confiscate all Domainer weaves. They think they provide some sort of protection against this or that."

"Those were our traveling weaves," Ginia said. "If you look, they're marked with Panadan's weavers' seal."

"Enough," the widow said. "A Guild stonewiser won't take your word over mine."

The widow was right.

"What about this coin?" Sariah picked up a single hexagonal copper she had spied half-sticking from under the widow's colorful rug.

"Coin? I don't have any coin. Where did that come from?"

"From the Domain, I'd say. It's minted with the coiled eel at the center. I can't help but wonder if there are other Domainer coppers about."

The widow didn't bat an eye. "There are a lot of Domainers wandering the border these days. They're always coming to the farm, asking for handouts. Maybe one of them children dropped a copper in my house."

"So these youngsters don't own any of your land?"

"Not a lick."

Sariah whirled on the group. "You are all squatters. You're trespassing on the widow's land. You must leave."

"I'm not so uncharitable as to boot out this little herd on the spot." The widow smiled sweetly. "The roads are dangerous. I don't mind if they stay under my protection for a while."

What did the witch want from the youngsters? Perhaps the Shield had offered a reward on Domainer heads. Perhaps she intended to use them as slaves on her farm. Whatever her purposes, Sariah had to extricate them from the widow's claws before it was too late. But why did she feel so strongly that she needed to help these wretched souls?

Because they were Domainers and she had lived among their kind and benefited from their kindness? Maybe. But there was more. The stone truth meant nothing if not justice for the Blood. She wanted to help these kids for the same reason she had wanted to help Mara and her grandchildren on the road—because just as she served the stone truth, the stones were meant to serve these people and therefore, so was she.

"Abetting Domainer refugees is a breach of the law." Sariah wasn't sure, since no Domainer refugees wandered the Goodlands during her time at the keep, but she tried it anyway.

"*Abetting* is a strong word," the widow said. "In Meliahs' spirit, I don't mind using my right of autonomy to protect these kids. Can we leave the poor souls to wander the Goodlands unaided?"

"Why can't we stay if she says we can?" Ginia asked.

Her guileless innocence seemed too much like stupidity at the moment. Would these hardy sons and daughters of the Domain relinquish their lives so easily?

"Squatting is prohibited in the Goodlands," Sariah said with a tone that barred all protests. "Get your stuff and meet me at the gate. Now."

"I can't understand your part in this, stonewiser," the widow said. "You've come to my house for no profit, spewing the law like Meliahs' prophetess and yet I wonder, why? You don't dress like any stonewiser I've seen and you don't act like any Guild wiser I know. Why must you interfere with my affairs when the Guild has no stake in this?"

The woman was no fool. She was polite, but there was a calculated threat in her voice. Sariah knew she was treading in dead water, but she wasn't walking out of the farm without the Domainers. She had to prevail over the widow fast and conclusively. Her gaze returned to the youngsters' faces. She saw them anew. What if...?

"That's exquisite lace at your neck." Sariah admired the woman's collar. "The best I've seen in a long time."

The observation surprised the widow, but the vain woman was delighted that Sariah noticed. "Imported from the sea people. Expensive too." She lifted her hair from her shoulders so that Sariah could better appreciate the lace.

And there it was. The key to the Panadanians' freedom. And the main reason why the widow wanted to keep the Domainer children around. Sariah kicked herself for not seeing it before. At least her mind had made sense of it before it was too late.

"The squatters are coming with me," she said. "It's the best I can do for you."

"For me?" The woman's limp hand came to rest on her chest.

"Don't make me bring charges against you."

She blinked stupidly. "Charges? Against me?"

"The penalties are very harsh for those who break the Guild's tidiness laws," Sariah said. "You'll return the weaves to the Domainers. They're marked with Panadan's weavers' seal."

"I'll report you to the Shield."

"And I'll report you to the Guild. Expect confinement. Ruination. Death. For spreading disease."

The woman's porcelain face froze in horror.

"What disease?" Ginia asked.

"The rash on her neck," Sariah said. "It's a sign of a common ailment among a certain kind of woman in the Goodlands. But I've never seen it in the Domain. It first appeared a few years ago among the Shield ranks. The Guild had to act and the Healer's Hall was hard-pressed to deliver a cure."

"I'm a reputable widow!" the woman said.

"Who obviously cavorts with Shield soldiers," Sariah said. "Look, Ginia. Some of your older friends have it on their faces and necks." She grabbed the young woman's hand. "You have it on your arm. Do you know what causes this itchy rash on your skin?" Sariah pointed a straight finger at the widow. "She does."

□ ■ □

"You look tired," Malord said. "Perhaps we ought to finish this tomorrow."

"No, nay, now. We'll do it tonight."

Even if she couldn't call the beam tonight, Sariah meant to make good use of her time. She was determined to free Mia from the mysterious connection that plagued her. True, more than anything else, she wanted the child safe and back in Ars, freed from the bond that tied her to Sariah's dubious fate. But she also needed to expedite her search and accelerate her journey. If she was going to find the pure and the tale she sought, if she was going to save Ars from the executioners' greed and save her own life before her time ran out, she was going to have to be faster, sharper, shrewder. Aye, Mia would be much safer back in Ars.

She didn't look at her changing bracelet. She set aside the problem of the Panadanian youngsters camping out for the night in Mara's empty barn. She tried to forget the widow's blatant abuses and the rot lesions bubbling in Targamon's front field. She refused to think about Kael and the Shield. One problem at a time. One solution to find.

"Mia." Sariah called down the stairs. "Where is she?"

"I bet you she's with the young Panadanian," Malord said. "She's been following Rig like his shadow."

"I'm surprised he hasn't booted her heinie out of the way. That's boys for you at that age."

"This one seems fascinated by our little wiser."

Mia trotted up the stairs. "Did you call me, Auntie?"

"Several times. Where were you?"

"Playing cards with Rig in the kitchen."

"Isn't he kind of old to be playing with little girls?"

"He's only fourteen and I'm not a little girl anymore. I'm

almost thirteen." She spoke rather firmly, in a tone completely new to Sariah. "He doesn't mind that I'm going to be a stonewiser. He's my friend. I need a friend."

"I don't mind if Rig is your friend. But you've only known him for—"

"Did you call me for a reason, Auntie?"

Was that irritation in the little girl's voice? "I told you we would have to wise tonight. Remember?"

"I'm ready. Could we please do it quickly? I'm winning."

Mia, Malord and Sariah sat cross-legged on the floor of the bedroom Mara had offered to Sariah, a comfortable space furnished with a small fireplace that illuminated Mia and Malord's expectant faces. The three stones Sariah had painstakingly prepared for the occasion came from the river's bottom. They were light-colored, tight-linked granite, perfectly sized to fit in their palms, tumbled and polished to comfortable smoothness by the river flow's persuasive caress.

Sariah laid the stones on the ground between the three of them. She had never tried this before, but during her time at the keep she had wised a couple of forbidden Guild stones that discussed the notion of amplifying stones. She just hoped she had remembered to imbue her river stones with all the necessary details. Otherwise, the exercise would be a waste of time.

"These stones will help us look within ourselves," Sariah said. "They're like a bright candle, like a magnifying glass. We want to take a thorough look at Mia's wiser mind and then travel my links to look at my mind. Be thorough and take your time."

Holding a stone in each hand, Sariah rested her hands on her knees, palms up. Mia's left hand and Malord's right one came to rest on top of Sariah's hands with the stones in between. Mia and Malord were similarly linked. They formed a perfect wising triangle, something the Guild forbade. The prohibition itself, combined with Sariah's experiences, led her to believe the triangle would increase their combined wising power.

Sariah took a deep breath, closed her eyes, clasped the other wisers' hands, and pressed the stones against her palms. They had tried looking into her and Mia's wiser cores several times before without success. Would the stones she had prepared make any difference?

The amplifying stones' effects were astounding. Her own wiser mind glowed like a sparkling mirror under the sun. The thickness of her links at the roots stunned Sariah, and the spiraling lengths of some of those links struck her as endlessly complex. The blackened stumps that stood lifeless and scorched between swaying filaments of light saddened her. The reckless mistakes she had made, the feebleness, the damage she had suffered wising the seven twin stones, Zeminaya's crippling blows—they had left terrible scars. They were the true measure of her losses, the final score of her service to the stones.

Beside her, the little girl stirred. "I'm done."

"It's too soon, Mianina." Sariah didn't bother releasing her trance. "Look carefully."

"But I'm done."

"I asked you to look into my links too."

"But I did. I even looked into Malord's. Didn't you feel me?"

Now that she thought about it, Sariah did remember feeling a swift shadow running through her mind, like a quick stir of the summer breeze. "That was too fast. Do it again."

"But—"

"I said do it again. A wiser's work is hard and tedious sometimes, but it must be done even if you want to go back and play cards with Rig."

Sariah returned to her wiser's mind. Almost immediately, she felt the shadow cross over her mind, the wind, this time blustery, blowing through. With a sigh, Sariah dropped her trance and opened her eyes.

"If you don't want to do it, just tell—"

"Auntie. I'm telling you. I already did it."

"You examined your links, and Malord's, and mine in such little time?"

"Thrice."

"It's not possible." Malord too had dropped his trance and was staring at Mia.

A preview of adolescent rebellion flashed in Mia's blue and green eyes. "Maybe you're just slow."

"All right, let's say, for the sake of discussion, that you did review your links and ours," Sariah said. "What did you find?"

"My mind is much prettier than yours," Mia said without a trace of modesty. "Newer is better, I think. I worked a little on my blemishes. I don't like the way they look."

Wiser vanity and little blemishes? Sariah's stomach pitched when she remembered making the bulk of those *little* blemishes during Mia's breaking. They had not been easy to make, or small for that matter. And Mia had said that she had *worked* on those blemishes. A wiser couldn't repair sliced links and truncated connections. Could she?

"Malord, some of your links look worse than Lou Ella's pox-marked face," Mia said. "And Auntie, one would think bursting stones struck your links judging from the craters in there. You two ought to spend some time sprucing up." Her tone was unmistakably maternal, as if she were her mother telling Thaddeus to wash behind his ears.

Malord was choking on his spit and Sariah was not doing any better at getting the words unstuck from her throat. "Uh. Mia? Can you heal the blemishes in your links?"

"Of course. You can't?"

The child never ceased to amaze her.

"I can't heal all of them, not all of the time," Mia said. "And it makes me very tired, so I don't bother with everything."

"Everything?"

"You know, the stuff you get when you're trying new tricks."

New tricks. Mia was experimenting on her own and there was nothing Sariah could do to stop that. But then again, if the child was healing herself, why should she be stopped?

"Can you heal others?" Malord asked.

"I healed Auntie once. When she was fighting Zemi."

"That was you?"

"I thought you knew."

"Can I—we—watch you?" Malord stammered. "Healing?"

"Sure. What do you want me to heal?"

"Pick whatever you want."

Mia closed her eyes. Sariah grabbed the trance and followed her links through to Malord's mind. Her vision was enhanced by the amplifying stones. Malord wiser's mind was actually in good condition compared to others she had seen at the keep, but watching Mia's pristine links at the same time, she could see why the child would find Malord's mind—and hers, for that matter—lacking. The luminosity of Mia's links was blinding. The power coursing through those links was immense.

Sariah witnessed as a filament of Mia's power reached through the stones and palpated over crusted links and broken connections. Mia picked at the most grievous-looking of all injuries, a ragged hole close to the center of Malord's core. Her healing filament coiled over the frayed remains of the link segment. Her links pulsed with a willful concentration of power. To Sariah's disbelief, right before her eyes, the edges of Malord's torn link grew even and joined to create a healthy stub, a usable shiny knob.

Malord gasped. "The pain. In my legs. It's gone."

Sariah looked from Malord's stunned face to Mia, unable to believe what her wiser senses were telling her.

"I can't regrow links if they're gone," Mia apologized. "At least I don't think I can. But I can heal them as long as there's something to heal."

Was Mia's healing power specific to her unique nature? Was it the result of her unusual breaking? Were some wisers able to heal and not others? Or was it a gift of all stonewisers, a skill suppressed long ago, a lost art, a learnable trait? Could she heal her wiser self? Sariah had never tried. Could she heal other wisers if it were necessary? She had no answers for all her questions, only a terrible thirst to know.

"Mianina, you're the most gifted stonewiser I've ever met."

"Then you believe me? You believe me when I tell you I did look in your mind?"

"Meliahs help me. I do."

"Can I keep this?" The girl twirled an amplifying stone in the air. "It makes it all easier."

"Of course you can."

"And did you see it?"

Sariah thought she had seen enough for a lifetime. "What?"

"The seal we bear. At the bottom of our cores?"

Sariah's heart skipped a beat and for moment, she thought it would never beat again. She fumbled for hands and stones and grabbed at the trance like a drowning woman. She went to her mind first, to the core from whence all her links were born. The mysterious pink organ was tucked in the deepest recesses of her convoluted brain. It pulsed there like a second heart, feeding on the frenzy of her stonewiser's tainted blood. She maneuvered to pull apart the bulbous roots growing from it in a tangled mass, until she found the pink corrugated tissue where the wavering brown lines had scorched the familiar seal. It pulsed to the beat of her heart.

Sariah darted to Mia's mind, riding the girl's links and accessing the bottom of her smooth core. And there it was. Small and almost invisible, the tiny translucent brand was imprinted clearly, a little oval with an even smaller triangle inside.

Zemi. It took Sariah all but a moment to realize that the same brand the intrusion had forced upon her had also imprinted itself on Mia's mind. Mia had unwittingly participated in Sariah's fight against the intrusion. The girl's extraordinary power had saved Sariah from death at Zemi's hands. Mia had been present when Zemi bestowed the legacy on Sariah. They had been sealed together. The seal had turned into an indelible connection. And now the connection had to be destroyed.

"Mianina, can you try to wipe the seal off your core?"

"Why?" Mia said. "It's pretty. I kind of like it."

"I think the seal is the source of the odd connection between us," Sariah said. "I'm afraid the connection is dangerous. It could hurt you."

"Hurt me? How?"

"You know, like when you lost control and burned your father's deck? Then you had to brave Alabara and the snail, just so you could be with me. It would be better if we could break the connection."

"I kind of like being near you."

"Could you please try?"

Mia sighed. "Fine. If you really want me to try, I'll try."

Both Sariah and Malord rode Mia's links and watched her try

to heal the seal off her pulsing core. She wielded her links skill-fully, but she flinched every time her links made contact with the seal.

"It hurts," Mia said. "A lot."

Sariah's core was hurting too.

"Try it again," Malord said. "One more time. We'll mimic your links and try to add our power to yours."

Malord and Sariah introduced their own links into Mia's mind, following Mia's lead. Approaching the seal cautiously, they hovered above it until Mia was ready. They aligned in tranquil flows of light. Together, they descended on the seal like a trio of peaceful doves.

The spark that flared at the contact blinded Sariah. The force that hit her was like a punch to the nose. She heard Mia cry out. A painful darkness swirled around her like a spinning top. When she finally managed to see again, Mia was crumpled on the floor clear on the other side of the room and Malord was writhing on the ground, hacking and bleeding from his nose.

Sariah wiped the blood dripping from her own nose. "Mia. Malord. Are you all right?" She crept to Mia's side. "Mianina. Are you hurt?"

Mia sat up, blinking in confusion. "I think I'm fine." She looked down on herself. "Aye, Auntie. I'm not hurting anymore."

"Malord?"

"I'll live." The old wiser was regaining his composure. "But I don't want to do that again."

"What happened, Auntie?"

Sariah rubbed her aching head. "If I had to take a guess, I'd say we've hit a dead end."

"The seal is permanent," Malord said. "It can't be removed. At least not that way."

"The rot take me," Sariah said. "How are we going to end the connection then?"

"It's not so bad," Mia said.

She looked much recovered, unlike Sariah, who was feeling the aftereffects deep in her bones. By Malord's gray face, she could tell that so was he.

"The strange thing is that before the blast, I was feeling some of Mia's pain."

"You think the connection goes both ways?" Malord asked.

"Maybe," Sariah said. "I don't feel Mia as she feels me. But that pain we shared."

"Why don't you try stretching your links and reaching out for Mia's links?" Malord suggested.

Sariah focused, but even with the amplifying stone in hand, her links remained rooted to her mind. "Do you want to try, Mia?"

Mia's face wrinkled in concentration. But after several attempts, she gave up. "Nothing there, Auntie. It appears I can only sense you when we're far away. There's no real linkage when we are near."

"Perhaps we've been going about this all wrong," Malord said.

"You're right," Sariah said. "Instead of trying to remove the seal, perhaps we ought to try to find a way for Mia to master the connection."

"So I could keep sensing Auntie without losing control over my power?"

"Exactly."

"I'd like that better," Mia said.

"I could devise a series of tests to see if anything helps," Malord said.

"We don't have a lot of time," Sariah said. "We'll have to do it on the run."

"But in the meanwhile, I could stay with you. Right?"

"Right." Mia was unfazed by the dangers Sariah faced.

Sariah stared at the little girl, at the tangled beauty of her blond curls, at the brilliant blue and green eyes, at the freckled face. Was this face the legacy's future?

Mia yawned. "Are we done? Can I go now?"

Twenty-five

THE NIGHT WAS cold and Sariah was warm tucked beneath the blankets, but as inviting as the bed was, it felt vast and lonely without Kael. Sleep eluded her. She was uneasy. She draped a blanket over her shoulders and tiptoed out the hallway to the room next door where Mia shared a bed with Mara's granddaughters. The Panadanians were on guard duty tonight, but Delis, sleeping on a pallet at the foot of the bed, woke up, hatchet in hand. Sariah gestured for Delis to go back to sleep. She only needed a glance at Mia's peaceful face to know she was fine.

It was frustrating. She hadn't been able to call the beam and though she had found the source of the strange connection between Mia and her, she was at a stalemate. She hadn't figured out how to break the dangerous link or if there was a way in which they could ascertain control over it. The location of Mia's seal made any attempts at removing it dangerous and ultimately useless. A wiser's source was precious and untouchable. Tampering with the delicate core was akin to wrenching a beating heart from the flesh. It was now up to Malord and his methodical but slow tests.

Perhaps Malord was awake too. Maybe they could narrow down the scope of his approach. She found his door open and his bed deserted. She figured he would be downstairs in the kitchen, heating the oil he used to massage his maimed limbs. How wonderful that after many years of phantom aches, Mia had been able to alleviate some of Malord's chronic pain. Her stomach grumbled. Perhaps she could also find a taste of something sweet in Mara's pantry.

She heard the hushed voices before she reached the bottom of the stairs. She peeked into the parlor. Mara sat by the fireplace talking with Malord, who reclined next to her in a comfortable chair. She had never seen Malord like that, sitting like a whole man in a cushioned chair, conversing amicably with someone his age. His swarthy features looked softer when relaxed, and a shy smile Sariah had seldom seen flashed on his face at regular intervals.

"You think you're done," Mara was saying, "finished with the duties of raising a family and making a living, old, battered and decrepit. Then life puts you in play again, and you've got to find some spark to get the old hide moving."

Malord took a sip from his cup. "You wonder why you live when the ones who should be living are dead."

"You had a family once?" Mara asked. "A wife? A child?"

"I don't think of it often. It's like my legs. What use do I have for that which I no longer have?"

Sariah was stunned. She had spent long hours working with Malord, learning from him, traveling with him. Yet she had never truly known him, the person who had once had a wife and child and a pair of sound legs, the friend who had lost so much and yet continued on regardless.

"I know what you mean," Mara said. "You resent it must be you who fights the day again, yet part of you is selfishly thankful to have a reason to live."

There was a strained pause and then they both burst into quiet, hysterical laughter, a young sound which had nothing to do with their bodies or their age, a peaceful, contagious hilarity.

"And you, you had a good man?"

"What a question you ask. Is there such a thing? He was good sometimes and very bad too. I hated him most of the time, but I must have liked him well enough some nights, 'cause I bore his children and now care for his grandchildren. He was mine, that's what I remember most, and now he's gone."

"Do you miss him?"

"Like you miss your legs, I suppose."

They were looking at each other, giggling like naughty children. Sariah had to wonder what was in those cups they held. She surprised herself wishing for a taste.

Mara lifted her cup in the air. "To your wife, to your child, to your legs."

"To your man." Malord touched his cup to hers. "However fair or not he was."

They sipped their drinks in comfortable silence. Mara reached for Malord's calloused hand. He hesitated, then plaited his long fingers through her short stubby ones, tracing the thickened veins that ran between the dark spots on her hands. Mara's smile creased the skin around her mouth and eyes into radiant clusters.

Sariah retraced her steps in complete silence and returned to her bed to consider the many choices she needed to make, alone, because Malord and Mara deserved the rarity of the uninterrupted moment.

□ ■ □

The Shield arrived in the morning.

After a sleepless night and a long deliberation, Sariah had just begun to tell Mara and Malord about her plan when Delis burst into the kitchen, followed by Ginia, Rig and Mia.

"A regular patrol," Rig panted. "We were standing guard by the river when I saw them go over the hill and take the turn to the Siguird Farm."

Sariah whirled on Mia. "I told you to stay close by the house. What were you doing by the river?"

"Auntie, please."

"I was keeping watch on the roof when I spotted a cloud of dust," Delis said. "It has to be those beasts they like to ride. Then I saw these three running as if the belch was after them."

"They'll be here in an hour," Rig said. "Half an hour, if the widow tells them about us."

"She most surely will," Mara said.

"She'll tell them about the strange stonewiser who came to her house," Malord said. "Once Arron learns of it, he'll come for you like an eel lusting for blood."

"What are we going to do?" Panic rattled Ginia's voice.

The blood in Sariah's veins turned cool as fresh water. "We'll do what we have to do. Delis, get our gear, wipe all traces of our presence here."

"Yes, my donnis."

"Ginia, watch the road. Rig, go tell the others to hide Mara's chill supplies. Make sure that even if they look, the Shield won't find them."

Ginia took her place by the window. Rig darted out the door with Mia at his heels. Sariah propped her foot on the stool by the table and began to tighten her boot laces with quick tugs.

"Are you leaving?" Mara asked.

Sariah had known Mara for less than a day. Other than witnessing the woman's fortitude when facing the Shield, and her generosity afterward, she really didn't know Mara. She had made a decision based on dire need. She prayed her sense of the woman was right.

"If the Shield finds me here when they arrive, we'll all die," Sariah said. "I don't want to leave, but I must. What do you say, Mara? Are you willing?"

"You want me to take these Panadanian youngsters into my employment and grant them room and board in exchange for labor?"

"If you employ them on your farm, they'll be well protected under your right of autonomy. The Shield can't eject them from your land, or massacre them at random. And you have the room. Targamon tenants' houses sit empty."

Sariah finished knotting her laces and looked up. A very stern-faced Mara stood over her, clutching a massive kitchen knife. Sariah couldn't breathe. Had she misjudged the woman's character that badly?

"Cut yourself a wedge." Mara dropped the knife on the table, followed by a wheel of cheese. She handed Malord an old sack and threw open the cupboard's doors. She pulled out some biscuits and handed them to Malord, who packed them swiftly. Sariah breathed again.

"What am I supposed to tell the Shield when they come?" Mara asked.

"Allow the Shield to search your house and barns. Give them no reason to hurt you. Tell them that you took in the youngsters cheaply after I drove them out of the Siguird Farm."

"But I have barely enough food to feed three for the chill. How will I feed all of them?"

The cheese was hard. The time was short. But Mara needed answers and Sariah needed Mara. "When Kael returns, he'll have coin and credit. He'll give you both. Purchase what you need to pass the chill and some seed for the new planting. Teach the Domainers to grow grain. What say you, Ginia?"

From her post at the kitchen window, Ginia's eyes didn't waver from the road. "We can do this. You'll find us to be hard workers. You won't regret this day."

"You forget a small detail." Mara grabbed a sausage from the rafters. "The rot. The farm's dead."

"About that," Sariah said. "You have a bit of rot in the back-fields, but it can be contained. These young ones can do the work necessary to stop the rot from overtaking Targamon Farm."

Mara halted in the middle of the kitchen. "When were you going to tell me this?"

"I wasn't going to tell you at all."

"Why tell me now?"

"It's complicated."

"I see." Mara hacked the sausage in two and dropped a half in the sack. "Do these children know how to fight the rot?"

"Not yet. But Kael will teach them. He's the best land-healer in the Domain. When he's done, you'll have laborers for the farm and rot fighters at Targamon."

"Your man won't stay in Targamon if you're gone."

"She has a point," Malord said.

"He won't be pleased, but if I give you my stonewiser's oath, he'll honor it. He'll train the Panadanians and they in turn can train any other Domainers who come your way in both rot fighting and crop growing. With so many Domainers about, you can revive Targamon and make it as large of an enterprise as you wish."

"What will you do?" Mara asked.

"I'll make for the mountains and set Leandro's game in three nights. The mountains aren't so far away, so Mia will be able to stand the distance. I'll leave her with you, so she can help Kael find me."

Mara grabbed the funnel and put it to the ale barrel, refilling Sariah's skin. "I wouldn't want to be the one who tells him that." "You won't be." Sariah's eyes fell on Malord. "You're leaving me behind? Again?" "Not exactly, not behind. I'm leaving you here so you can help Mara fight the rot and offer good counsel to the Domainer refugees who come through these parts." "But—" "Hear me out, Malord. We're running out of time. The wall's broken. Nothing can stem the flood of change coming. The best we can do is to try to route it as we can. Mara will need you here, at least for a time, to wise the stones that will contain the rot and to help her direct the flow of Domainers coming into the Goodlands. And I need you to help Mia through those tests we talked about. She's bright. If you teach her, she'll know what to do." "But you need me too." "I do. Very much. To help start the legacy. Not in the future. Not when we find the tale. Right now." "There." Mara knotted the sack. "That should last you for a few days. I might be able to hide Mia among the Panadanian youngsters, but how will I hide Malord?" "That's easy," Malord said. "I'll pretend to be a cripple. It works well. Nobody expects wisdom or wits from a disabled old man. I'll put on a blindfold to hide my mismatched eyes. We'll pretend I'm your kin, maimed and blind from a farm accident." "We're ready." Delis stood by the kitchen door with their packed bags. "The Shield will find no trace of you here." "I know I ask a lot," Sariah said. "You have a choice, Mara." "And turn you in to the Shield? Get all those youngsters killed? You didn't walk by us when we needed your help. I won't walk by you either." Mara took the wrinkled parchment out of her pocket and laid it on the table. "Targamon Farm lives when it was dead. Let it be the beginning of this legacy you talk about." Sariah cringed. "Burn that. The Shield will kill you for less." "I'll burn the parchment, but I won't forget it," Mara said. "Let it be known that Targamon was first to come when the stones called."

Twenty-six

THE ESCAPE FROM Targamon Farm didn't go exactly as planned. By the end of the third day, when she was supposed to call the beam, the Shield was too close on Sariah's heels. Shielded warriors flooded the forest like ants fleeing ahead of a fire. Sariah could barely keep up with Delis's unrelenting pace. She hadn't had much sleep, and the constant running was sapping her strength. They burst into a small clearing. She tripped on the roots of a massive tree and stumbled against the trunk, gasping for breath.

They heard the warriors before they saw them. The clang of shields and the march of booted feet came from all directions, converging on the clearing. The sound of men and horses crashing through the brush alerted Sariah to their considerable numbers.

Delis's knuckles tightened on her hatchet's hilt. "We're going to have to fight them."

Was Delis mad? They couldn't fight that many and win. Sariah whispered a prayer and looked around for options. An enormous spreading chestnut towered above her. It was as confused by the weather as the rest of the forest was, thick with green leaves and lush with white flowering spikes despite the approaching chill.

"This way." Sariah grappled up the trunk. Delis boosted her to the lower branches and followed as Sariah struggled to reach the higher branches. She was no graceful climber, but it didn't matter. They were climbing for their lives.

The first of the shielded warriors broke through the clearing, hollering for the others to follow. Sariah froze on a branch half-way up, hoping they couldn't be seen through the tree's expansive canopy.

"We make camp here," one of the men announced. "Prepare for the night patrols."

Here? At this very clearing?

With an efficiency that matched their reputation for ruthlessness, the warriors began setting up camp. The forest was alive with men and women digging fire pits and latrines, collecting firewood, setting up neat rows of four-man tents, gathering water and heaving great cauldrons onto the fire pits. The camp sprouted before Sariah's eyes as if by magic.

A commotion ensued at the far end of the clearing where the warriors halted their duties to salute the newest addition to the camp, a high ranking, heavily bulked commander riding a red stallion. Sariah recognized the face wedged between shield and helmet, the full lips, the wide nose underscored with long narrow nostrils which flared as he sniffed the air. The brown eyes unknowingly brushed over Sariah as he scoured the clearing.

Arron. A heavy chill settled in her bones. Hundreds of men poured into the clearing behind him, spreading out into the camp and around the chestnut like the full moon's tide.

Sariah considered putting a bursting stone to her sling. If she aimed well, he could be gone in a moment. But there was the small matter of his hundreds of followers. No stone she carried could tackle all of them. If she killed Arron, she would also kill Delis and herself. Worse, she would be surrendering everything she was set on saving, Ars, the legacy, the stones. Later then. She would kill him later.

"The bracelet," Delis mouthed.

Sariah realized with a start that the sun was setting and the bracelet was beginning to issue its telltale glow. Carefully, she pulled her latest creation from her pocket. She wrapped her wrist with the triply folded weave she had stitched together. She had treated each layer with frog slime to prevent the bracelet from burning through the fabric. It should last her for a few days.

The smell of ham and pea soup drifted through the clearing, an invitation to her hunger. Under a cold drizzle, the men and women of the Shield lined up before the bubbling cauldrons. Sariah's stomach rumbled. Mara's supplies had dwindled to nothing. When was the last time they had eaten?

"Can't you see it's raining?" Arron's powerful voice boomed

in the clearing. "Move my tent. Over there, you idiot. Set it under the spreading chestnut."

Arron's tent ended up right beneath Sariah's feet, complete with a sentinel posted at each of the tent's four corners. She fingered the stones in her pocket, cursing her reluctance to kill with them. She knew better. She had a stone that might work, one that would most likely wipe out the tent. Gone would be Arron's bloody rule over the Goodlands' borders, her main obstacle to reach the Bastions, the man she feared. Would Arron's death bring unity to the land?

A new group on horseback entered the clearing and was ushered to Arron's tent. Despite the drizzle, Sariah recognized the woman who dismounted from the lead horse. Short brown hair, brown eyes, arched eyebrows not unlike her own. *Ilian.* Sariah's stomach churned with acid. Ilian was Arron's loyalist. She had also been Sariah's first mistress, the stonewiser responsible for Sariah's brutal breaking. She held no fond memories of Ilian.

Sariah recognized the other black-robed stonewisers who followed Ilian. Uma. Lorian. Olden. Half of the Guild's Council was present at Arron's tent. They didn't look happy to be here. In spite of Delis's disapproving glare, Sariah climbed down a few branches.

"Where are Nestore and Altara?" Arron asked.

"They refused to come," Ilian said.

"We're not fools enough to come together when you call," Lorian said. "Death is the fastest way to turn over a Council seat. Isn't it?"

The shadow of Arron's arm on the tent's canvas held up a goblet. "To my trusting peers and friends." He drank the whole cup in one swallow.

"You better have a good reason to call us here," Lorian said. "The Goodlands aren't safe for riding these days."

"I take it you're still at the keep, living under Mistress Grimly's roof. It would be such a bloody affair if she found out you're here."

"Your threats don't scare me," Lorian said. "You have seconds to tell me what you want. After that, I'll be gone."

"I wanted you to see Grimly's scam with your own two eyes."

"We saw little that mattered," Lorian said. "Nothing capable of thought or reason."

"I took them as you commanded," Ilian said. "But they weren't satisfied."

"It's hardly the proof you promised," Uma said.

Arron's voice rose a notch. "Grimly's behind it. You refuse to see it."

"Refuse to see what?" Lorian said. "What you want us to see? A broken, stuttering fool?"

Who were they talking about? Had they caught Kael? No, it wasn't possible. Kael was no fool and he was too cunning to get caught. He was far from here and hopefully safe. And he wasn't proof of anything. Malord? She didn't think so either. His disguise was solid. The Council knew nothing about him. He wouldn't figure in any of Grimly's scams. No, Arron's unfortunate prisoner wasn't one of her friends. Who was he then?

"How do I know this is not all your creation?" Lorian demanded.

"Have you thrown your lot with Grimly then?" Arron said.

Lorian's irritation was audible in her voice."So this is what this meeting's about. Headcount? I have thrown my lot with the Guild. You, on the other hand, seem to have forgotten the stones we serve."

"Have you at least found the missing wiser?" Olden asked. "The appearance of order is important. As long as she's out there—"

"We're close," Arron said. "I can almost smell the bitch."

"You have the entire Shield at your command," Lorian said, "yet you can't find a single runaway stonewiser? That's not very impressive. Your failure doesn't bode well for your ambition."

"Are you suddenly feeling fit to do the dirty job yourself?" Arron said. "Or do you think that whining is somehow a desirable trait for a Prime Hand?"

"We're not here to fight each other," Ilian said. "We're here to discuss Grimly. Is she fit to be the Guild's Prime Hand? And what can we do if she isn't?"

"You can't trust the witch," Arron said. "Tell them, Ilian. Tell them what we know."

"Grimly has ruled the Guild for forty years," Lorian said. "She was doing a fine job of it until you decided to throw the gauntlet on the whim of a bad lease. I need more than your word, Arron. Don't expect me to take sides without good reason." She stomped out of the tent.

"Don't call on me again unless you have a solution to this mess." Uma followed Lorian.

"I'll try to talk some sense into them," Olden promised, before mounting his horse.

As swiftly as the Council members had arrived, they departed with their respective escorts.

The Council was cracking under the strain of the divide. Distrust was rampant, even among the highest of the high. Loyalty was dead. Who was Arron's mysterious prisoner and why had he failed to impress the other Council members?

"Can you believe those fools?" Arron said. "How could they think that Grimly is innocent of plotting for her own purposes?"

"She's a crafty old fox," Ilian said. "We have another problem." The shadow of Ilian showing Arron a sheaf of parchment played on the tent's roof.

"Another one? Where did you find this one?"

"I bought it from a peddler. They're selling like hot buns."

"I don't understand. How can it be everywhere when we know there's only one original?"

"Someone wants it out there."

"Grimly?"

"Or you."

"I don't have it," Arron said. "Besides, how is this any advantage to me or her?"

"I don't know," Ilian said. "But I better stick to Uma for now. Otherwise, she and Olden might ride straight back to the keep and into Grimly's welcoming arms. You know Lorian is halfway there already."

Ilian took her leave. Sariah couldn't see through the tent's canvas, but she thought she knew what Arron and Ilian were talking about. Arron was right. How was it beneficial to him or to Grimly? She fingered the stone in her hand. Arron was within her reach. He would be dead in an instant. She stretched out her arm. All she had to do was drop the stone.

The fire came from nowhere. Whistles preceded the solid thud of the arrows piercing the tent like glowing needles. The flames flared, consuming the canvas, reaching out to singe the chestnut's lower branches, sending Sariah and Delis clambering high in the tree.

"Over there." Delis's gaze was fixed on the opposite side of the clearing.

Sariah heard Arron screeching and cursing inside the blazing tent. If she hadn't had to use both hands to climb away from the scorching heat, she might have overlooked all caution and added her stone to the attack. But by the time she made it to the treetop's safety, Arron had bolted out of his burning tent and the camp was in full alert.

"You idiots." Arron slapped his confused sentinels. "It's her! She wants to burn me again. Get the bitch." He stumbled after his men barking orders, leaving a few of his minions to smother his tent's fiery remains.

It struck Sariah strange that Arron would think her powerful enough to orchestrate an attack on his camp when she was as good as shipwrecked in a sea of Shield, marooned in the besieged chestnut and drowning in a plume of heated smoke. She spent another sleepless night stranded in the tree, pondering what she had heard this night and wondering who had attacked Arron. She watched as he rallied his men and commanded his patrols, so close and yet so far away from her stone's reach.

□ ■ □

On the tenth night after her escape from Targamon Farm, Sariah still hadn't called the beam. It wasn't that they hadn't made enough progress. On the contrary, using her new strategy, she and Delis had followed Arron and his warriors and arrived at the mountains' foothills right behind them. Instead of trying to outrun the Shield, she had decided to trail it closely. It was safer that way, because Arron was concentrating on the forest ahead of him, combing it to the last bush and pine needle. It also allowed her to keep good tabs on the Shield without sacrificing her pace.

The problem was that she couldn't call the beam to verify her destination without giving away her position. The Shield was too close. She could wait until they reached the mountains before she set up the game, but after that, she would be wasting time she didn't have.

Sariah spotted a growth of thick brackens. She shook them to scare away the critters and then flattened the concealed undergrowth towards the middle to make a bed. She stretched her wet blanket over the fronds and lay down. She was likely to die from exhaustion.

"Not bad, my donnis." Delis laid her blanket next to hers. "A little wet, but at least the rain has stopped. Here's the last of Mara's corn biscuits for your dinner."

She had really liked Mara's biscuits hot from the oven. Now she gnawed on a hard, dry mockery of those biscuits, watching the clouds chasing each other in the dark sky above and wondering how Mara and Malord had fared with the Shield. It must have gone well enough. She hadn't spotted fire or smoke coming from Targamon's direction and the Shield had moved on too fast after her to account for an attack on the farm.

She wondered how Kael was doing. He would be mad at her, but she had no doubt that he would understand her reasoning and do as she swore. She closed her eyes and tried to sleep. He would be worried. Somewhere in Targamon Farm he waited for the sight of a beam that wasn't going to glow tonight either.

The slightest touch traced her lips in the darkness. Delis. Her fingertips were light on her skin, outlining the shape of her face with barely a contact. Sariah didn't move. She kept her breathing steady and her eyes closed. Hadn't she endured much more than an unwanted caress from people as fickle and selfish as her Guild masters and mistresses?

The rich scent of clove-spiced molasses dwarfed the humid frond's lush smell. A slight brush of cheeks announced the nearness of Delis's face, the slow, hovering approach of plush lips. Just when she expected the inexorable landing, something happened.

Delis shook Sariah. When she opened her eyes, Delis crouched beside her, hatchet in hand.

"What is it?"

"Something's coming this way."

Sariah thanked Meliahs for the Domainers' blessed hearing. They were the keenest creatures in the world. She waited among the ferns, stone in hand. She didn't see anything at first. Then, the tall sinister shape of an animal she didn't recognize lumbered from the woods.

Something landed unexpectedly between Sariah and Delis, a stinking leg as wide as Meliahs' pillars, standing on a paw the size of her head. Long claws brushed the bushes as the tall beast passed, unleashing a rain of shredded leaves on Sariah's face. Leandro's clawed terrors had arrived.

□ ■ □

Sariah would have screamed if Delis's hand hadn't landed over her mouth. She would have crawled and scurried out of the woods like a scared possum if Delis hadn't held her in place.

The shadow looming over her moved on, matching the pace of its companions at either side. Those animals were hunting together, Sariah realized, like a pack of wolves, only they were most definitively not wolves. They were hunting humans. They were going after the Shield.

"Shouldn't we run?" she whispered.

"We stay put," Delis murmured. "More. All around us."

A horrendous howl overtook the night. Vicious growling echoed from the Shield's camp. Voices shouting commands combined with the terrifying screams of those facing the beasts. Sariah had never seen Delis shaking like this.

"Meliahs' hounds," Delis whispered. "Mara told me they dwelt here."

"That's just—"

"Legend?" Delis peered into the forest in the direction of the Shield's camp. "Those things kill, my donnis. They're no legend."

"There must be an explanation—"

"They're coming back."

They huddled together, watching in terrified silence as the beasts retraced their steps. The brackens shook under heavy paws. Sariah stole a quick glance up and saw a crumpled man skewered on a set of brutal claws. With a vicious swing, the creature strung the victim's guts on a gnarled oak. A broken rib cage, still pink with flesh, landed next to the brackens. Sariah swallowed a scream.

The beast licked the blood off a cracked skull. It savored the dark flow for a moment, before dropping the mangled head and uttering a hair-raising howl. Howls answered from all directions, enlivening the night. Then, as quietly as they had come, the beasts lumbered away and disappeared into the woods.

□ ■ □

On the twentieth night after their escape from Targamon Farm, Sariah and Delis ventured around the Shield's camp and up the escarpment that led to the Bastions.

"What if those things come back?" Delis asked.

"Let's just pray they don't," Sariah said.

The beasts' attack had rattled the Shield, but Arron didn't give up. In fact, after the beasts' first attack, it had gotten more dangerous for Sariah and Delis. The Shield had increased their daily patrols and strengthened their night watches. Twice in the last few days, Sariah and Delis had come close to discovery by patrols in the woods. Once, they had stumbled upon the bloodied remains of a massacred Shield patrol. They had no doubts as to what had caused the carnage.

The forest's varieties, pines, firs, cedars, tamaracks and leafless aspens stopped abruptly at an invisible line. The steep escarpment at the foot of the Bastions was dotted sparsely with juniper, spiny sagebrush and slippery rocks. The going was slow. In the darkness, Sariah walked carefully, mindful of twisting an ankle or breaking a foot. It was Delis who tripped. *Crunch.* Something tumbled and shattered against a rock.

"Are you all right?"

"I'm fine," Delis whispered, rubbing her bruised shin. "What was that?"

Sariah crouched on the ground and lifted her wrist wrap to add her bracelet's glow to the tenuous light of a faint crescent moon hiding behind a bank of clouds. She picked up a piece of the remains of an earthenware vessel.

"It was a clay jar of some sort," she said. "It was decorated with some kind of dotted design. There's script on it. The old language, I think. It's a shame Kael isn't here. He could tell us what it says."

"Here's another." Delis limped a few feet. "And another."

The moonlight broke through the clouds. For an instant, Sariah spotted the sinuous shapes of thousands of vessels standing around an open-mouthed Delis. The vessels were under the trees, in between the rocks, all along the escarpment's slope. Some were small and some were large, some were squat and round, others were fluted or narrow-necked. Some were heavily decorated while others were simple and unadorned. Then the moonlight was gone again, leaving Sariah clutching the cold pottery shards in her hand.

"Maybe it's an offering," Delis whispered. "To Meliahs' hounds. To keep them away."

"There are no people around here. We haven't seen houses since we entered the forest." Sariah picked through the broken pieces on the ground and cupped a fistful of tiny white pebbles in her hand. "Maybe these are food stores of some kind?"

Under the tenuous light, Delis examined the pebbles in Sariah's hand. "I don't think so, my donnis. Unless you think of humans as food, little children at that."

The hair at the back of Sariah's neck stood on end. The little teeth were but speckles of bones and yet they burned her palm. She suppressed an urge to drop them. Instead, she returned them to the broken vessel as carefully as she could manage and wiped her hands.

"Let's not break any more of these."

Delis crouched. "Fresh tracks. Here."

"Are they people's footprints?"

"They might be." Delis looked closely. "This one isn't."

The beasts. They had tracked this way, not too long ago. Sariah could barely swallow. She wouldn't be dissuaded from her duty by a pack of... what? She was having a hard time with the notion and yet when she recalled the beasts, the idea of the goddess's hounds wasn't as hard to accept as she had first thought.

Sariah and Delis advanced up the escarpment and through the trees, mindful of the prolific vessels. The crescent moon came out again, illuminating the deeply grooved, copper-streaked rhyolite cliffs that rose above them like an impenetrable fortress. Sariah had to stop, despite her trepidation, to admire the earth's extraordinary creation.

The massive stone mountains had been birthed in the earth's core, fused, compacted, crystallized, heated and cooled in chaotic progressions. Expelled from those turbulent depths, they had escaped en masse through a stubborn crustal rift in a slow but catastrophic transformation of the landscape, only to be further tortured by the elements, sculpted by ice, eroded by wind, transformed into a stunning monument to the earth's power.

"The Bastions," Sariah said. "The drop of three thousand spans. Possibly more."

Delis eyed the cliffs. "Do you want to climb this?"

"We can't call the beam from the forest. The Shield would be on us in a snap. Those beasts, too. But if we find a way up the cliffs, we can call the beam from the top. It would take the Shield a long time to follow us."

"No offense, my donnis, but it will take us a long time too. It will be a difficult climb. And if the Shield spots us on the rock face, we'll be practice targets to their arrows."

"I have to make it up there. I can't keep wasting time. I have to call the beam."

"All right. For you, I'll try it. How about over there? There appears to be a long groove on the rock face, a vertical crevice. It's partly sheltered from sight and wind." Delis reached out to examine the cracks on the cliff face.

A flash of light flared against her hand. As if hurled by the goddess's own hand, Delis flew backwards, tumbled down the escarpment and crashed back-first against a thorn bush.

Sariah skidded down the hill. "Are you wounded?"

Delis wrestled with the bush. "More like pinched and pricked, right about now. Sorry, my donnis. It's just not my night. What happened?"

"I'm not sure. Let's get you out of here." Sariah helped Delis untangle her weave from the thorns. After she was back on her feet and Sariah was satisfied that she wasn't hurt, they returned to examine the cliffs.

"Don't touch it," Delis whispered.

Sariah reached out with her palms to sense the wising, a muted buzz that tickled her eardrums. She recognized a command in that vibrant layer. She braced her mind to absorb the shock and pushed her hand through the invisible layer and directly against the striated rhyolite.

Repel. Reject. Refuse. The commands were unbearable shrieks to her mind. Vivid and extraordinarily shrill, they converted will into sound and sound into force, generating the physical repulsion of flesh. Sariah was stunned. She had experienced the will of the Domainers' gifted imprinters on the stones they used to contain the rot, as well as the wall's powerful wising, but she had never encountered anything like this. Only her mind's readiness to absorb the wising kept her from harm. She didn't know how long she could stand the assault on her senses, or if she could even manage an ascent on those cliffs while taming the powerful wising. Who had wised these magnificent stones?

The howl startled her out of her thoughts. The replying chorus left her trembling with dread. The pack was out this night and, judging from the howls, in more numbers than before. Fire burst from the direction of the Shield's camp. A battle was ensuing.

Now. The Shield was engaged. The beasts were hunting the Shield down by the camp. She wouldn't find a better moment to call the beam without having to climb the forbidding cliffs. She knew she risked attracting both Arron and the beasts. But she also knew this was her only chance.

She fetched Leandro's game from her bag.

"My donnis, what are you doing?"

Sariah set the cloth board on the ground, placed her stone on the black space and lined up the little snakes and scorpions at their starting places.

"Now? You're going to call the beam now?"

She moved the pieces as fast as she could manage.

"Those beasts, they'll come, my donnis. The Shield, too."

Sariah was completely focused.

"My donnis, are you sure?"

"If you want a running start, go ahead." What was next? Pair of threes. It was done.

The rumble started much sooner this time. The whole of the Bastions growled. Loose dirt and gravel rolled downhill. The hum echoed through the escarpment and charged down the cliffs. The beam followed, plummeting toward her. She pulled back from the light at the last moment.

The beam landed on Leandro's set and ignited the pieces to little flames. It seemed to feed on them, to nudge them into sparkling, pulsing brilliance. Sariah pushed herself from the ground and stepped back to get a better view. All she could see was the beam rising from somewhere behind the Bastions and the light diving along the cliffs to land on the game.

"The rot take me." They'd have to find a way up those wised cliffs regardless. The call of the beam had shed little light on her direction. The sounds of battle had quieted in the Shield's camp. She knew she had very little time. She snatched the cloth board, toppling the pieces, sending the beam into retreat. The snakes and scorpions were hot to the touch as she scooped them back in the bag.

"My donnis?"

"Almost done."

A little scorpion slid a few paces down the hill. Sariah scooted on her hands and feet after it. The tiny piece came to a halt at the drop's edge. It clunked faintly against the curved claw of the enormous paw planted firmly on the ground.

□ ■ □

The beast that looked down on Sariah belonged to another world, where evil gods and goddesses engaged Meliahs in a fierce battle to destroy her Blood. Huge black eyes stared from a desquamated skull. A heavily fanged snout dribbled with bloody slobber.

Colossal horns coiled about the massive head. Sariah would have groveled in fear if it hadn't been for her body's paralysis. Her heart had stopped beating and her knees were rooted to the gravel. Seized by some suicidal spell that eviscerated all sense for self-preservation, she couldn't take her eyes off the hideous creature. She was thinking when she should be running. Thinking! The beast exceeded all expectations of evil ugliness. As the long claws began a slow arch toward her throat, she realized with a start that it was an all too perfect incarnation of mankind's worst nightmares.

□ ■ □

"Are you Stonewiser Sariah of the Hall of Scribes' sixty-sixth folio, formerly of the Guild?" the creature spoke, in a neatly accented speech, no less. The long claws came to rest beneath her chin, tilting her face up. Her mouth snapped shut at the cold lifeless touch.

Another beast stepped down from its lumbering heights, leaving a pair of enormous legs standing on their own. "Are these yours?"

He clutched a rumpled parchment in one clawed hand and a crystalline scorpion in the other. Sariah couldn't help it. She laughed. She cackled, uncontrollably, like a mad woman, like the sickest of the atorium's boarders. She laughed until her belly hurt, despite Delis, who stood pale and wide-eyed, flanked by more of the beasts, despite the icy stare of the horrid creatures gathering around her. The last thing she remembered were the beast's claws, aligning fatefully, and the side of a fisted paw coming at her face.

Twenty-seven

SARIAH WOKE UP groggily. She had a faint recollection of a fast ascent, of dark stones rushing by, an endless plain streaked with coppery veins. For a moment, she thought perhaps she lay at the bottom of the Bastions, but then her vision cleared and she saw the tall dome above her, an array of richly carved panels adorned with elaborate dotted designs. The dots came together to form a colorful mural, a collection of stylized images that showed a hoard of ragged people traveling a spiral path across the dome, from a walled city, through streams and mountains, to kneel around the cupola's opening. Remarkable. Where had she seen similar designs before?

Sunlight streaked in through the dome's hollow middle, warming her skin. Her shoulder bag lay beside her. She pushed herself to her feet. She was in the middle of a round dais that stood at the chamber's center. It wasn't very large, maybe twenty spans across. She took a tentative step. Light came through the empty cracks between the boards. A sudden sense of vertigo struck her. She forced the dizzying sensation out of her mind and inched toward the edge.

A tall, single pillar supported the dais where she stood. Beneath the boards, several posts and dowels extended at different angles, supporting the platform like sturdy branches. Above her, a ledge rimmed the lower part of the dome like a rail-less balcony. But it was useless. A wide moat surrounded the platform on all sides. She couldn't jump the distance if she tried. She looked down.

An army of barbed spikes covered the moat's floor. A few decomposing bodies were impaled on the spikes, one or two recently killed, judging by the stench of blood and feces, the rest desiccated or rotting. Rats scurried between the spikes. Bones lay scattered about. Perfect. Whatever she had gotten herself into was no benign or harmless venture.

A movement on the ledge above caught her eye. A tall figure, dark against the dome's lighter hue, stood flanked by the frozen outline of one of the human beasts she had seen before.

"Who are you?" Her own voice echoed painfully in her head.

"Today's keeper," the man said. "I was waiting for you to wake." He wore a straight garment, a bright, colorful wrap which covered him from armpit to knee, exposing bony, narrow shoulders and long sculpted calves. A thin crust of short, tight curls topped his narrow face. Even though he stood a ways away, Sariah noticed the impressive curve of his nasal bone and his matching brown eyes. But it was the macabre row of horizontal scars on his forearms that caught her attention.

"Why am I here?" Sariah asked. "And why are those people dead in the moat?"

The man spoke stiffly, formally, as if his lips were not used to putting thoughts into words. "Those are your predecessors. That last one, he died the day before yesterday."

"Why did you kill him?"

"He killed himself. From ignorance. We found him quite interesting."

"Then I'll strive to be boring."

"You'll be anything but boring."

"How do you know?"

"He told us."

Sariah glanced at the dead man in the moat. He had landed on his back. The spikes had skewered him through the ribs, the abdomen and a leg. A slow death then. Death's rigor had preserved the pain on his face's expression. The wide nose, the scrabbling beard, she had seen that face before.

Josfan. The dead man in the moat was the shooter who had tried to kill her at the nets, the ruthless mob leader who had destroyed their deck at Nafa. Had he been the one who had always been a step ahead of her? The one who had warned Alabara's marcher of her coming and contracted out her capture with the forester? Had he been Arron or Grimly's agent? She would never know now.

"The sages will come," the keeper said. "They will speak through the Wisdom and only through the Wisdom. Your questions shall be answered. And so will theirs."

A set of beastly claws burst from the keeper's fist. Without flinching, he ran a single blade against his skin, slicing another notch above the crook of his arm. Blood trickled from the wound. Sariah's horror turned to revulsion. The man lapped at his own blood like a famished bat.

Before she could make sense out of the keeper's actions, the human beast beside him came to life and blew a long horn that stood on a gilded stand. A single note issued from the horn, a powerful blast that filled the chamber.

In the dome, the row of panels above the keeper's ledge opened. People began to emerge from those openings. Sariah counted fourteen men and women, some old, some of average age, some barely children, all dressed in the same colorful garb the keeper wore. They stood on small ledges in front of their respective openings, looking down on her.

"This is Sariah," the keeper announced. "Daughter of the Hall of Scribes, quitter of the Guild, wiser of the seven twin stones, breaker of the wall, banished of the Domain, wanted of the Goodlands, procured of the Hounds."

Sariah forced herself to breathe. She didn't know who these people were. In turn, they knew exactly who she was.

"*You shall fetch and drag the impostors before you,*" the keeper said. "*And they shall die in horror for their falsehood until truth prevails to the Wisdom's satisfaction.* First decree of the Lawman, Vargas."

Why was the keeper speaking as if in quotes? Who by the rot pit was the Lawman Vargas? And why had she been brought here in the first place? Could this odd assortment of people on the ledges, young, old, matching eyes and not, comprise the people she sought? She looked up at the reliefs on the dome. Was the answer there? Had she finally found the pure?

The sages intoned a communal prayer. "*Hollow are the impostors' claims, dark is the truth's journey. Grant us wisdom, merciful goddess, to redeem the worthy and forsake the frail, to lead your restoration or perish.*"

Raised in the ways of the Guild, Sariah recognized ritual easily. She sensed a certain familiarity in the strangers' words. No, not in the words—Sariah was sure she had not heard the prayer before—the familiarity stemmed from the tone. She had heard the same fervor in the Domainers' sacred oaths and in the Guild's mandates. She had seen the same determination that gleamed in these people's eyes, in the Domainers' mismatched stares and in the Guild members' steely glares. These strangers shared in the Blood's zealousness, an emotion she respected as much as she feared. However far removed from their kin, they were of the Blood.

With great ceremony, the keeper lifted a huge lever embedded between a set of evenly notched posts. With a loud thump, the lever dropped to the higher notch. A rattle of chain and pins clattered beneath the boards. The scaffolding under Sariah's feet quaked. A good span of the dais's fringe uncoiled from the rest and fell away before her very eyes.

"Your time will be done when the pedestal is no more," the keeper said. "May the goddess bless you with her wisdom."

How much time did she have? A minute? An hour? Sariah didn't have the slightest idea. She stole another look at the moat. Those corpses down there had failed at whatever ordeal these people proposed. Would she end her days impaled in the rat-infested moat?

Sages. They couldn't be too different from the Guild's masters and mistresses. She cleared her throat and called on her best pledge's manners. "Respected sages, why am I here?"

A little boy with slanted eyes stepped forward on his ledge. "*In falseness, many will come. In truth, one will become it. The Seer, Tirsis.*"

Did these people always speak in riddles? What had the keeper said? *They will speak through the Wisdom and only through the Wisdom.* Were they following an ancient protocol? Were they speaking words they had been taught, perhaps quoting from a communal source? Aye, Sariah decided, on both counts. A child of the Guild was trained to recognize tradition and authority.

An old man spoke. "*A sunless dawn. A branded beast. The life taste of the waiting dead. They are Meliahs' sacred tools and Hounds will wield them in her stead. The Dreamer, Poe.*"

How was she supposed to make sense out of that? Delis. First of all, Delis.

"Where's my companion? Is she hurt?"

A tall woman stepped forward in her ledge. "*Why shall the wise converse with the sinful? Why shall the pious reach out to the ignorant?* The Teacher, Eneis."

She took that as a your-Delis-is-fine-thank-you, but with a bit of skepticism. They didn't give a lick about Delis. She did. "Were those monsters in the forest your warriors?"

"*The beasts shall rise to defend the truth*," a young woman said. "*The hearts of warriors shall beat with the strength of the fiercest Hounds.* The Lawman, Vargas."

Meliahs' Hounds. No wonder they were legendary. That's what they called their brutes. Whoever bloody Vargas was, he would have been utterly satisfied to see the monsters he commanded. Tirsis, Poe, Eneis, Vargas. Seer, dreamer, teacher and lawman. Their sayings seemed to comprise what the keeper had called *the Wisdom.* The sages didn't speak for themselves. The Wisdom spoke through them or better yet, they spoke through the words of... who? Their rulers? Wisers? Long dead soothsayers?

The thud of the lever dropping to the next notch startled her. The boards rumbled beneath her feet. A new portion of the platform's rim disappeared. How many notches on the beams? Time. Sariah remembered she didn't have it to spare.

She went for the basics. "Who are you?"

A young woman stepped forward. "*Who are we but the witnesses of treason, the heresy's spurners, Meliahs' faithful followers? Who are we but the fist that waits in the shadows to unleash the blow?*"

At least they saw themselves as Meliahs' own. "I too worship Meliahs. I was seized while pursuing the stone truth. I must continue her work."

The young woman shook her head. "*Many are those who claim the goddess's service. Few will serve her faithfully.*"

They were as suspect as they should be. "Look, I don't know what you want from me—"

"*You shall not be deterred*," a tall woman said. "*Just as

strength is rewarded with life, weakness can only be cured with death."

In the Guild, they beat you to get your attention. These sages slapped you equally hard, but with their verses. "Are you the people called the pure?"

The sages exchanged odd looks. A moment passed before the boy stepped forward and said, "*What's pure but stone? What's impure if not all but stone?*"

Her hopes that she had found the pure collapsed. This place wasn't it. But if she hadn't found the pure, could she at least find confirmation that she was on the right path?

"Are you the keepers of the truth?"

There was general laughter and a burst of applause. Sariah gathered she had gotten the answer to her question right. Yet she despaired at the cryptic exchange. What could she tell these people that might prevent her death? What did they know about the Guild and the stones, about everything that had happened in the last few years? Would they believe anything she said?

As if reading her thoughts, the old man spoke again. "*I saw lies in the stones, tales fashioned to proclaim the false and promote the wicked. I saw death and obscurity for the endless aftertime.*"

However far removed from the rest of the world, these people were thoroughly informed. The sequence of ominous noises began again. The lever's thump, the chain's whine, the quaking rumble, they all conspired to distract Sariah. This time, she didn't stop to watch the next chunk of platform fall away.

"Did you come here as a result of the execration? Were you punished for some trespass, like the people of the Domain, and condemned to live here?"

"*Behold, Meliahs saw the future's ruins,*" one of the sages said. "*She dreamed a warning in the fairest minds, that her children would be separated, hunted and killed. She saw the land broken, the suffering weeping, the stones betrayed. Her tears fell on the souls of the righteous and we were born one thieving people out of the wretched divide.*"

Fascinating. Was this the tale that Leandro's wising promised? Surely, it had to be. These people had retreated to the Bastions' isolation in the times before the execration. But what did they mean by *thieving* people? Perhaps they were Zeminaya's doing too. Perhaps Zeminaya's powerful wisings extended to the Bastions.

"Do you know of an ancient stonewiser called Zeminaya?"

The old woman hissed. *"Curse the sinners' names, for they carry the dead on their souls."*

Sariah gathered Zeminaya was not a safe topic to discuss with these people. This time, when the lever dropped and the boards quaked, she had to step away from the crumbling edge. The dais was disappearing from under her feet. They wanted her tale, a reason to spare her life or end it. She wasn't sure how much to tell them, but the combination of the shrinking pedestal and the deadly moat were enough to compel some truth from her.

"I follow a beam of light."

"Welcome is the brilliance that leads us." The girl smiled. *"Noble are those who follow, for they have earned a chance at the truth."*

"That's very encouraging," Sariah said, "but it doesn't tell me what you want from me."

"*A sunless dawn*," the same old man repeated. "*A branded beast. The life taste of the waiting dead.*"

With a crashing boom, the lever dropped another notch. Sariah bolted from the crumpling section. The pedestal was less than a third of its original size and the lever seemed to be falling faster each time, making it more likely that Sariah's question-and-answer session would end earlier than expected. *Calm.* She summoned the difficult emotion. One problem at a time.

A sunless dawn, the old man had said. *I follow a beam*, Sariah had said. *Welcome is the brilliance that leads us.* Of course. Had she been rendered deaf and blind?

She moved fast and purposefully, trying to outrace the lever. She fetched Leandro's game from her shoulder bag. The cracks between the boards presented a new problem, but she didn't allow it to slow her down. She spread her tattered mantle on the center of the diminished pedestal. The sages watched her intently. She didn't speak as she set up the board. Words, she knew, were of no consequence to these people.

With the game set, she ran the plays in her mind, moving the snakes and scorpions faster than she had ever done before. Done. She stepped aside and waited for the arrival of the only sunless dawn she could summon of her own accord.

□ ■ □

The hum preceded the light, but when it arrived, the beam fit through the dome's opening exactly. Stunned, Sariah realized it had been built for that very purpose. It landed on the game and fired the little pieces to sparkling brilliance. The sages' gasps and prayers rose above the hum. The boy was crying. The old woman knelt on her ledge.

"*Joyous is the day of the light*," someone cried. "*The promise has arrived.*"

Despite the beam, the lever boomed. The wood whined. The boards trembled. The rim collapsed again, leaving only a few paces of space beyond the beam's searing light. Sariah feared that Leandro's snakes and scorpions would spill over, but the beam held them fast in place.

The beam was welcomed but it was not enough. What had the man said? *A sunless dawn, a branded beast?* The only beast she could find in the chamber was the warrior standing by the lever. She didn't think he had anything to do with this. What about the brand? There were no branded animals in the chamber, nor depicted on the dome's expansive decorations. A brand. A beast. A mark. A seal. Her seal?

She stared at her hands with trepidation. These were not scars she liked to show anyone, let alone these strangers who disliked Zeminaya. How would they feel about her seal? Could it stand for something or someone other than the old intrusion?

The boards trembled beneath her feet. Concentrated on her thoughts, she had missed the lever's loud drop. The chunks of planks were falling faster now. The marks on her palms were the only brand she had at hand. No alternative.

She lifted her hands and displayed the scars, turning slowly for all the sages to see the seal the twin stones had bestowed on her, the triangle within the oval stamped on her palms.

"*The future's glimpse,*" the tall woman said. "*Meliahs' herald, come to collect the tribute of our lives.*"

Cold dread iced Sariah's belly. She was no herald, no tribute collector, no future to these people. She only needed to live to do her duty. Now if they would only stop the lever—

They didn't. The sages weren't content with the beam and the seal. They still wanted something else from her. What was the other thing the old man had said? *The life taste of the waiting dead?*

Light and seal she had managed to put forth. But a *life taste?* What was that supposed to mean? Sariah wanted to scream. *Life taste.* Unafraid to spill their... *Blood?* She groped for her little blade. "Do you want my blood? Yes? Have it then."

She cut her palm below the thumb and turned it down to bleed on the boards. She looked up hopefully at the sages. No response. That wasn't what they wanted either. What was she supposed to do?

The keeper landed before Sariah without a sound. The rope he had ridden across the moat hung limply to one side. He stood on the opposite side of the beam, like darkness born out of the light. He was much taller than Sariah had surmised and younger too. The beastly claws protruded from his fisted hands, sharply honed blades sprouting between his clasped fingers. The scaffolding quaked, this time much harder. The keeper edged the light beam. She crept in the opposite direction, avoiding him.

He beckoned her with a quick curl of his claws. "Come."

Damn the keeper. She couldn't possibly defeat those blades. Wait. Was it *his* blood that the sages wanted? Not that she wanted to engage him in a fight, but she remembered she had some weapons she could use. Think. Breathe. Act.

The keeper's claws swiped at her head. Sariah stepped back, ripped a handful of beads from her plait, and hurled them at him.

Pop, pop, pop. It was a satisfying sequence, like bubbles gurgling in a boiling pot. The small stones stung the keeper, leaving bloody punctures on his throat. Surprised, he stumbled backwards and retreated to the other side of the beam. He was rattled but not dissuaded. He considered her through lidded eyes. The sages watched in silence.

A quick glance at the dead corpses in the moat strengthened Sariah's resolve. The keeper was fast. She sidestepped his new attack, managing to drop more beads under his dress. This time, he was prepared. He shook with the impact, but he was no longer surprised. Instead, he stood his ground and lunged. His claws scoured through Sariah's weave and raked her arm. Simultaneously, the other set of claws severed the remaining string in her braid. Her wised beads spilled on the floor and dropped down into the moat.

Now what? She faked a blow to the left and went for the larger stone in her pocket. The keeper's claws ripped through her wrist, screeching against her banishment bracelet. It felt like a scuff to the head, like a bloody scrape directly to the brain. She stumbled and almost fell off the ledge. Her wrist bled with a deep slash, but the wretched bracelet had saved her hand.

The keeper stalked her around the beam. He didn't wear his fellow Hounds' terrifying garb, but he was no less fearsome. He sneered. She could tell he thought she was weak and unworthy, a sad combination of trinkets and tricks. Perhaps he was right. She kept to the opposite side of the beam.

The scaffolding rattled. One by one the remaining boards began to fall away. Sariah ran away from the void but towards the keeper's inevitable claws. Without stones she had no weapons. Or did she?

She called on her fear, on the massive reservoir of frustration and anger stored in her soul. At that moment, she hated the keeper, the sages, their maddening Wisdom; this useless, endless search, which had taken her away from Kael, from the little she had. At that moment she wanted to live when she knew she was going to die.

It was an act of desperation. The boards where she stood caved in as she launched across the beam. The beam's dry heat scorched her back even as she kneed the gaming pieces off the cloth board. With the pieces scattered, the beam quit and with it went the burning on her back. Her hands landed on the keeper's legs. Her fingers contracted around his calves. Her palms pressed against his skin like thirsty leeches. She struck. *Stone Wrath.*

The keeper howled like a gutted man. He flopped on the quaking floor like a dying fish. Sariah grabbed him by the ankle an instant before he fell into the moat. She was as astounded by her attack's strength as the sages were. Out of desperation, she had created a new weapon. Had she been too late?

The lever began to fall again, this time towards the last notch, despite all her efforts. It happened too fast. The keeper clutched the back of her neck. His fingers breached her mouth with extraordinary force, bruising her lips, scouring her teeth, smearing her tongue with his blood. Sariah gagged. Fresh blood. *The life taste of the waiting dead.* It trickled inevitably down her throat to her sickened stomach. She tried to bite him. He didn't budge. Bloody saliva dribbled out of the corners of her mouth. She had to swallow.

"*What you are to me, I am to you,*" the keeper said.

The sages lifted their hands as one. The impassive warrior wedged his spear across the lever. The lever bounced on the Hound's spear, and stopped. The boards beneath Sariah's feet held. The acrid taste of the keeper's blood was ablaze in her mouth.

Twenty-eight

SARIAH CRINGED WITH the vinegar's sting.

"*Welcome is suffering, for it shall not be wasted,*" the woman cleansing the wound on her arm said. "*Wise are those who suffer in the flesh, for they are strengthening their souls.*"

"Don't tell me." Sariah winced. "Tirsis, the Seer."

The woman beamed.

They were in a small airy room on the top floor of a mud brick house. Jars and bottles lined the shelves while dry flowers and desiccated leaves dangled from the ceiling's rafters. The kind woman had scoured Sariah clean of blood and filth and was now stitching the slice above her wrist.

Sariah looked out the windows. The house was nestled within a sprawling settlement of two- and three-story buildings. They had walked over a maze of rooftops to navigate the streetless place. Twin domes rose in opposite corners of the city. The sheer size of the settlement and the number of people who lived there astounded her.

The keeper stumbled down the ladder like a teetering toddler.

"Are you still feeling the jolt in your legs?"

He took a chair by the window and, ignoring her question, arranged his skirt on his lap. "*The goddess's greetings, for she is just and fair to all her children—*"

Sariah couldn't stand it any longer. "I know you don't have to speak to me in the Wisdom. You talked to me at the dome."

"*Wise is he who speaks what has been wisely spoken before him, for his wisdom cannot be doubted.*"

"That's Tirsis again."

"*Who needs the burden of a voice when all has been properly said?*"

"The teacher, Eneis. He asks questions all the time. But I don't want to speak to the sages. I want to speak to you."

The man made a big effort, as if his mind had forgotten how to translate independent thought into word. His mouth curled in disgust, but he finally spoke his own words. "Why speak to me when you can speak to the sages?"

"Because the sages are gone and dead. Because they can't tell me what I need to know. Don't you want to speak for yourself?"

"*There is no wisdom greater than the Wisdom.*"

"I don't have time for this."

The man's claws popped out of his right hand.

"What are you doing?"

The blade froze against the keeper's forearm. "Do you want me to speak without the Wisdom? Fine. I do. I trespass. I cut myself."

"No, nay, no." Sariah was horrified. "I want neither your pain nor your blood."

"You want my words but not my blood?" He stared at her as if she was both crazy and dumb.

"You. Your people. Do you cut yourselves every time you don't speak the Wisdom?"

He nodded.

"Meliahs spare us. I just want to speak to you. Without bloodshed. Can you do that?"

The man's Adam's apple bobbed helplessly up and down his throat. "Only if you command me to do so."

"You would heed my command?"

"I'm your keeper now."

"Oh, no." She wasn't falling for it again. "I'm not your pet or anything like it. And you're not mine."

"Pet?" The man considered her dubiously. "Of course you're not my pet or I yours. But you can command me as you wish."

Strange. One moment she had been fighting the man on the bloody pedestal and now he wanted to obey her? "I really don't want to command you. I just want to talk to you."

"Now that the sages have found you true, you can do as you want."

"And you won't cut yourself?"

"It's a strange command to follow, but if you want, I won't cut myself when I speak to you."

"And you won't make me drink your blood again?"

His eyes flashed with fury. "Do you find my blood unworthy?"

There was much more to the blood drinking than she knew. "I just don't like blood."

"You don't *like* blood?" His brows clashed in complete incredulity.

Was that so hard to believe?

"Perhaps you find my blood unimpressive."

"Unimpressive?" Sariah was lost. "You don't need to impress me. Your claws did that."

"You won the fight."

"Oh, that. It only happened because I thought I was going to die. Otherwise, I'm sort of clumsy with the blade."

"I thought so." A flash of teeth broke right beneath his nose's audacious septum. "But you didn't have to tell me. You're unexpectedly unassuming."

"Sorry to disappoint, but I'm in a hurry. I need answers and I need to rejoin my friends."

"They've made such a ruckus at the cliffs."

A measure of relief washed over Sariah. If Kael and the others were able to make a ruckus at the cliffs, then they were alive and in good condition. Just to make sure, she asked.

"You haven't hurt them, have you?"

"Not much."

"I must see to them." Sariah shook off the woman's attentions and stood up.

"*The body's healing precedes the mind's peace,*" the woman said.

"*Meek shall be the dragon at the foot of the stone,*" the keeper replied.

"*Fierceness in all things,*" the woman spat. "*Killing AND caring—*"

These two were fighting. With the Wisdom's words. Incredible.

Sariah spoke to the woman. "Thank you, but I don't need your services anymore."

The woman glowered at the keeper before she left the room.

"I want to see my friends," Sariah said.

"You can't leave," the keeper said.

"Am I your prisoner?"

The man's eyes widened in surprise. "Of course not, but there's much you must yet see."

"I've got a people to find. I've got a beam to follow, and very little time. And I won't abandon my friends to the Shield or to your monsters down there." It all came out a bit more blustery than she meant.

"Peace, stonewiser. Perhaps I can help."

"How?"

"Given the circumstances, I can try to persuade the sages to admit your friends into our lands without a lien of conversion."

"A lien of conversion? What is that?"

"It's the customary way of admitting outsiders. A way must exist to turn treason into faith if one of Meliahs' defectors is brought up the cliffs."

"Are we talking about Goodlanders who want to come here?"

"Defectors never seek the truth on their own."

"Let me see if I understand this lien of conversion. You abduct people from the Goodlands, bring them up here against their will and make them your slaves?"

"Only until they have learned and accepted the Wisdom."

No wonder people were scared of Meliahs' Hounds. "And what happens if one of these defectors wants to return to the Goodlands? What happens if they're just dumb and cannot learn a lick of the Wisdom?"

"We kill them, of course. There's no value to a life without the Wisdom. But don't worry. Their souls are not forfeited. We drink their blood, even if it's bitter, and we commit their remains on hallowed land as is proper and fitting."

Mara's terrifying abduction tales made perfect sense to Sariah now. So did the thousands of earthenware vessels she and Delis had seen at the foot of the Bastions.

"Why do you bring these defectors up the Bastions in the first place?"

"In obedience to the Wisdom. *Be fruitful and multiply,* commands Vargas, *for we must be prepared to inflict the blow with honed claws for every hand. We must turn the soul to flesh and the flesh to stone until they're one and the same.*"

This was a culture of war, blood, violence, zealousness. "This conversion lien, does it apply to me?"

"Of course not."

"But I don't know the Wisdom. Am I a defector too?"

"You survived the dome. The Wisdom is in your heart."

"Can you assure me that my friends won't be submitted to a lien of conversion or anything like it?"

"Not unless you wish it."

"Why would I wish it?"

"For a friend who's perhaps not such a good friend?" The keeper smiled. "I'll help with your friends."

"Why would you do that?"

"I'm your keeper. It's my job."

"I don't need a keeper."

"You do."

"Is this a trick? I don't like tricks. Will there be another keeper tomorrow?"

"For someone else, perhaps, but for you, it will be me tomorrow, and the day after tomorrow."

"Do you have a name?"

"I'm Jol."

"Why you, Jol?"

"It was me the day you came and it was my blood you licked."

She gagged. She could almost taste it in her mouth.

"You'll need to set off the beam again."

She was instantly suspicious. "Why?"

"Only you can do it."

"What do you mean only I can do it?"

"You've been dreamed," the keeper said. "*The beam shall only answer to the call of the branded beast.*"

Sariah felt as if she had been smacked on the face. It wasn't

the stone she placed on the checkered cloth board which acted as
a safeguard to trigger the wising in Leandro's game. It was she,
or more to the point, the brand stamped on her hands and on her
core that released the game to call the beam. She had been shallow
in her appraisal, overly confident and yes, even cocky. A complex
wising required complex answers, not cheap wising tricks.

Sariah scolded herself. Mistakes were dangerous. Mistakes
cost lives. To think she had felt accomplished when she thought
she had cracked the wising in Leandro's game. Instead, the wising
had cracked her. The snakes and scorpions were wised to somehow recognize Zeminaya's seal. That's why she was able to call the
beam. That's why no one else who played the game—wittingly or
unwittingly—could trigger the wising.

"That's why you are important," the keeper said. "Besides, how
else will you know where the beam leads you unless you call it?"

The man was right. Sariah had to overcome her bewilderment
and think clearly. She wouldn't underestimate the stones again.
She had to get her new bearings, and as long as these people went
along, it would be safer to do it from behind the Bastions' protection. At least now she had a new bargaining tool. She was the only
one here who could call the beam.

"Fetch my friends and I'll call the beam."

"I'll go meet with the sages now and return with news." He
stopped at the bottom of the ladder. "Be at ease, wiser. It will all
happen as foretold."

"Foretold?"

The keeper was gone and she was alone with her questions.

□ ■ □

Decisions were made slowly in the land of Meliahs' Hounds.
That's how Sariah had begun to think of the people who lived beyond the Bastions, fierce in resolve and stubborn by nature. They
shared that notable trait with their Domainer cousins. Although
they had split from the whole of the Blood before the execration,
they also shared something else with the Domainers—the intensity
of a fateful purpose.

She understood the Domainers' oath, the pledge to return to

the stone through building new land. But despite the abundance of blustery and readily available Wisdom, the Hounds' purpose was still a mystery to her.

The keeper arrived as he had done every afternoon, bowing before her reverently, offering a greeting and a smile but no news. Again.

Sariah prayed for patience. She feared if she called the beam without securing her friends first, she would be putting their lives at risk. On the other hand, every day that passed was wasted time. She felt like screaming at the keeper. Instead, she spoke calmly.

"It has been a fortnight since I arrived. Why can't we fetch my friends today?"

"We must have the sages' approval." The keeper made a sweeping gesture toward the ladder. "*Walking is like dreaming*, Poe says. *It calms the soul and quiets the heart's protests.*"

Sariah didn't think she could appease the urgency in her soul, but she got her mantle and followed the keeper up the ladder. She had been doing a lot of pacing in the confines of her small apartment. She might as well catch some fresh air while she was at it.

The sting in the air reminded her that the chill had arrived. The sheer number of people going about the settlement amazed her. The rooftops were even more crowded this afternoon. Perhaps it was market day. Open fires and countless tents stood beyond the mud brick walls and steady caravans of newcomers peopled the roads. Never before had she seen so many assembled in one place.

Sariah pointed to a slow-moving line of shackled men carrying bundles on their backs. "Are they...?"

"Defectors."

As long as it dwelt deep in the human heart, slavery had a way of working itself into every culture.

The sun rode weak and low on the horizon, on account of the newly arrived chill. The sight of the yellow orb flaming between the settlement's tall domes took Sariah's breath away.

"Beautiful, yes?" the keeper said. "*Three domes dazzle the eyes at the waiting—one for the coming, one for the going and one to signal the end of the time.*"

"Poe?"

"Very good."

"It's a good thing, then. Only two domes stand."

"*What's good but what we know? What's evil but what we don't know?*"

"Eneis." Sariah faced the keeper. "I'm not here to learn the Wisdom."

"Are you not happy among us? Is your bed not firm enough? Is your food not plentiful and your fire hot?"

She was comfortable, as comfortable as she had been in months, no, in her entire life. She had food, warmth and comforts aplenty. She was safe from the Shield and the Guild, surrounded by people who treated her with kindness and deference akin to devotion. She had her own set of rooms with a crackling hearth that burned day and night, a huge luxury when compared to her life at the Guild, her journey's hardships, or even her Domainer deck. She had servants, for Meliahs' sake. Servants. People who tended to her every need with single-minded determination despite her vociferous protests.

No one in their right mind would deny themselves the reprieve and resign from such comforts. Except her, of course. She had good reasons. Not only were her dearest friends cold and hungry, exposed to the Shield's dangers in the forest, but she had a people to find and her stone pledge to fulfill.

"I'm not fated for comfort, keeper. I have very little time to do as I must. I need my friends and my freedom."

"You need much more," the keeper said. "I've been trying every day."

"Yet nothing happens."

"*Double the domes and triple the sages shall grant the approval—*"

"Don't speak to me in decrees. You've been to the dome every day. You even said that you gained the sages' approval yesterday and the day before yesterday."

"I've made the same argument to different domes of sages."

"The sages are different every day?"

"*What is wisdom but clarity of thought and continuity of purpose?*"

"Where do you find different sages every day?"

"*Everyone shall know the Wisdom and everyone shall serve to speak it—*"

"You mean every citizen serves as a sage in the dome?"

"Everyone serves. In both domes."

Sariah reeled. If she understood correctly, the keeper had to persuade three different groups of sages in each dome to obtain approval. She looked at the faces around her—carpenters, traders, smiths, herders, farmers, weavers, artists, people of unlimited occupations. There were young and old, cultured and uncouth, smart and in some cases obtuse. The keeper had to find consensus amidst such differences. No wonder it was taking so long.

She clasped the keeper's rugged hands. "I wish I had the time to know you, to learn your ways, to understand your purpose. But I must go, with or without the sages' approval. Do you understand?"

"*The meek will be called to be strong. The unworthy will be redeemed from their fate.* I go again to the domes and won't rest until you are on your way." The keeper turned and disappeared into the multitudes.

Sariah watched him go. She took in the sights around her and let out a slow breath. To think that just a few days ago Mara had thought that the Bastions, guarded by Meliahs' Hounds, marked the end of the world.

The Hounds she had found, all right, but Mara had been wrong about the rest. The world didn't end at the Bastions. It went on for as far as the eye could see, like a promise in progress, like a wild tale unraveling before its maker. For reasons she couldn't quite understand, Sariah was loath to let go of the legend.

□ ■ □

Sariah donned her clean blue breeches and tunic, politely declining the robes that the nameless woman who called herself the servant had laid out for her. Sariah didn't like the notion of having a servant, but in the absence of a name, what else could she do but call the woman as she asked?

Her sense of comfort was enhanced by the luxurious bath she

had just taken. After a long soak in hot rose water, a thorough scrubbing of lavender soap and perfumed sand, and a delicious eucalyptus oil rub, she felt cleansed beyond clean, warm and soothed beyond promise. She thanked the servant profusely, the gifted author of such wonderfully wicked delight. If only her soul was so easily appeased.

She accepted the brand new boots that the servant insisted on lacing for her, but only because it was cold and she had mended her old boots beyond repair. She also wore the mantle she offered, a warm fur cloak that tied at the neck and matched her boots. She drew a few coins from her purse and tried to pay the woman for her troubles, but she wouldn't have it.

"What's kindness but generosity in all things?"

"The teacher," Sariah said. "Eneis."

"In caring, all things bloom, including the soul."

"The dreamer?"

"Tirsis."

"Ah, yes, sweet, sweet Tirsis."

The woman smiled. Her soft hand landed on Sariah's belly. *"May the seed grow in the fields. May the goddess protect both, field and harvest."*

It was a simple prayer and yet it left Sariah sucking for breath, as if the woman had punched her in the gut. She snatched her tunic out of the way and stared. Her belly *had* changed. She cupped the incipient curve. It felt hard, and perhaps a little round? She had noticed the snugness in her clothes but she had also been eating like a famished bear.

"Are you saying I'm—"

A gentle swell rippled against her palm, a faint reply to her firmer touch.

The teacher spoke through the servant. *"What are we but Meliahs' vessels of life?"*

Twenty-nine

SARIAH WALKED BESIDE the keeper lost in her own thoughts. Could it be true? She had no warning, no signs, other than her monstrous appetite and her craving for honey. She had been so sure Mistress Grimly's potion hadn't worked.

Exhilaration. Worry. Terror. The emotions took quick turns dominating her mood. She didn't know what to think. Timing. What dismal timing. Considering the strain of the last few months, it was a wonder that anything but bile could thrive in her body. Sariah caught herself stroking her belly, searching for a sign of the life that had taken root in her, longing for a repeat of that extraordinary moment when the child had rippled through her body like a wave through the sea.

Poor baby. It must have happened right after Alabara, because Alfred's vicious kick would have surely destroyed any life in her. The hepa might have had something to do with it. If nothing else, the frequency must have raised the odds.

She twisted the bracelet around her wrist. The opaque crystals reminded her that her troubles had begun a good five months ago. Alabara had happened—when? Three and a half months ago? Her baby was most likely that far along.

A sense of wonder overcame the fear. She wasn't barren. She was more than her craft, more than a servant to the stones. This is what Kael wanted. He would know what do to next, how to protect it... Him? Her? How would she manage a pregnancy in the middle of her dangerous search?

Well, there was no way she could favor one over the other, not with so much at stake. She would just have to manage both. Surely, Kael had arrived at the Bastions by now. She anticipated the look on his face when she told him. Her lips quivered with a repressed smile. She craved his arms more than honey.

"Watch your step," the keeper said. "It's foul smelling."

The stink of manure recalled her to the trail. Under the moonlight, silvery vapors rose from fresh piles of dung. In the cold, clear night, thousands of huge beasts grazed on the gently rising fields for as far as Sariah could see.

"Meliahs' gift," the keeper said. "Coiled-horned ox, of the musk variety."

It all made sense now, the warriors' terrifying disguises, the sprawling prosperous town, the populous world beyond the Bastions. Meat, milk, wool, leather, horn, bone, manure. Who knows what other life-giving treats the massive beasts yielded? The land was plentiful above the Bastions, a wide, fertile plateau contained between precipitous cliffs. These people were safe here, away from the Goodlands' bloodshed, protected by lethal warriors outfitted with the Hounds' horrible disguise.

"Why do you go down there?" Sariah asked. "Why do you put yourselves in danger when you are safe here?"

"*Who will listen and watch if not the Hounds?*" the keeper said. "Who will fetch the likes of you?"

"Had you been looking for me?"

"*Wise are those who mind Meliahs' business beyond their own boundaries, for they shall hear the call.* We've been following your progress, wondering if you could be the one. We even sent Hounds into the Domain to fetch you."

Hounds in the Domain? No wonder those rumors about monsters had spread like the belch through the Barren Flats. During these times of fear and doom, what else could a Domainer see in a Hound but a monster?

Movement ahead diverted Sariah's attention. Sets of huge wheel-and-pulley contraptions emerged beneath the last rise. They were powered by teams of oxen pulling around horizontal wheels. She realized the contraptions' purpose. They served to pull the lifts that transported people and, presumably, things up and down the cliffs.

A group of no fewer than fifteen Hounds came up on a wood platform holding on to rope railings strung above them. Frankly, the lift looked rickety and a bit unsafe, but it worked. At long last and thank Meliahs, Kael was coming.

Two by two, the Hounds stepped onto the stairs carved in the rock, murmuring a prayer of thanks for their safe return to the Bastions. Delis was among them.

"My donnis, finally, I find you." To Sariah's mortification, Delis knelt at her feet, kissing her boots, her knees, her hands. "These beasts tried to keep me away." She glowered at the warriors.

Sariah was looking behind Delis, sorting through the faces stepping down from the next lift. He wasn't there. Or in the next lift over. Had something happened to him? She drew Delis to her feet.

"Where is Kael? Where is Mia?"

"Don't be alarmed, my donnis, but they haven't come. I'm sure there's a good reason. The forest down there has been a maze of death since you left."

It wasn't like Kael to stay behind or cause delay. Either something very important had detained him or something terrible had happened. It all bode badly for him, for her, for her hopes of holding him in her arms tonight and in the near future. The disappointment must have been evident on her face.

"Don't worry, my donnis. I'm sure he's just being careful."

Meliahs help and protect him. It was the only favor she asked of the goddess. Sariah had to believe he was alive and well. How else could she find the strength to go on?

"I was rather vocal demanding to see you," Delis admitted. "But your friend helped much."

"My friend?"

"He insisted on coming up with me."

The latest load of warriors stepped out of the hoisted lift. A wall of Hounds parted to let their ward pass. Sariah blinked, once, twice, three times. Surely it was a trick of her eyes. She had not expected to see him again. Ever. The reality of his presence struck her like the chill's cold wind. For reasons she couldn't begin to fathom, Horatio Maliver had found her again.

□ ■ □

"Why are you here?" Sariah broke the silence of the small-ish chamber where they waited for her audience with the sages. She didn't disguise the hostility in her voice. She didn't need to. Horatio Maliver knew very well how she felt about him.

"He said he had to find you." Delis circled the man like a fam-ished raptor. "He said he had to warn you, that finding you would save great hardship and much blood."

"I can assure you, whatever reason brings him here isn't re-lated to my welfare." Sariah met Horatio Maliver's cold gray eyes, as empty of life as always. The stubble on his square jaw hinted at a day or two without shaving, a major break in his compul-sive neatness. He remained lean and strong, with a full head of curls meticulously oiled away from his face. He wasn't wearing the Shield's uniform, but that was to be expected—he was a deposed Main Shield now. As to his soul, it had been in frank putrefac-tion a long time before they met. She didn't think the damage was reversible.

"Still cynical, my little wiser?" Horatio Maliver said. "You don't believe I'm a changed man?"

Nothing was capable of melting the iron encasing his heart.

"Tell me why you came," she said. "Answer my question or I'll have you returned to the Goodlands, without the lift's assistance."

"So you have gained a little authority up here," he said. "I haven't found him yet."

His son. He was still looking for the boy he had fathered years ago by raping Kael's blind sister, Alista. To find the boy, he had deserted his post as Main Shield during the breaking of the wall. That was after he hunted Sariah and Kael throughout the Goodlands and the Domain; after he tried to kill Kael on the quartering block, and after he forced Sariah to trade more than just information with him in order to save Kael's life.

"I know nothing about your son," Sariah said.

"But that mate of yours does."

"As you can see, he's nowhere near here."

"As if the hand could stay away from the arm."

It was a cruel jest from a man who excelled at quartering.

"Even if he knew," Sariah said, "he wouldn't tell you. You've wasted your time coming here."

"I don't think so." He flashed his mirthless smile. "I intend to stick to you like the stitch to the weave. I'll follow wherever you go. I'm prepared to stalk you until the last crumb of land succumbs to the rot if necessary."

As if she needed more of that. It had started with the executioners, with Delis herself, with the mob and Josfan, Arron, Grimly, Orgos of Alabara, and maybe even others she didn't know about. Was she destined to be hunted and hounded for the rest of her life?

"Do you want me to kill him?" Delis looked as if she was about to do so regardless.

"Another classy acquaintance, I see," Horatio said. "In what wretched pit do you find your dogs and bitches, wiser?"

Delis's hatchet was at his neck.

"She won't let you kill me," he said. "She has a weak belly for blood, and I wouldn't have come here without some assurances. You see, I have something your wiser here wants. She's likely to be curious."

Sariah didn't bite.

"I was hoping you'd remember the gilded mirror for the sights it reflected more than for the valuables it contained?"

She hated Horatio Maliver.

"I removed them," he said to Delis. "The stones. Only I know where to find them. That's why your wiser here won't kill me. I have a cache of rare stones she has always wanted."

That was true. But right now, she was considering killing him anyway.

The door opened and the keeper beckoned. "We're ready." Jol's black eyes fell on Horatio Maliver. "What shall we do with him?"

Right now, Sariah had to concentrate on facing the sages and finding the pure. She didn't have a lot of time to consider Horatio Maliver's shocking arrival, but knowing him, she was sure that neither his appearance nor its timing was coincidental. He might be looking for his son, but he hadn't come just to exchange information or to tempt her with rare stones. He was here for a different reason, a devious purpose which could mean nothing but grief and danger to Sariah and her friends. She would have to figure it all out later.

"Do you have a jail?" Sariah asked the keeper. "Can you lock him up for now?"

"We can gift him to Meliahs' defectors," the keeper said. "Or kill him, whichever you prefer."

"But gifting him to Meliahs' defectors is a lifelong sentence, isn't it?"

"Once given, the life can't be retrieved but by the Wisdom's miracle."

"So it's either slavery or death," Sariah said. "Nothing in between?"

"*Wise is she who destroys the weed before it stakes its roots, for she will have no enemies.*"

It was a notion as absolute as the Hounds, as uncompromising as the Wisdom itself. And it was rather tempting. But gifting Horatio to the defectors would make him permanently inaccessible. His purposes would remain a mystery, a dangerous pitfall stalking Sariah's every step. And there was the small matter of justice. Could she condemn a man to death or slavery without proof of his crime?

She was stuck. She couldn't get rid of Horatio Maliver just yet. In fact, by the expression on the keeper's face, she'd better keep Horatio close by or risk losing him to the Hounds' much swifter sense of justice. Horatio's calm expression gave credit to his courage. Perhaps his willingness to face such grim fates related to his mission's importance. Perhaps it was a measure of his desperation. Most likely, it was the sure bet of a cunning, calculating man who believed that Sariah had neither the will nor the guts to kill him.

She was very tempted to show him otherwise.

Instead, she faced the man who had come to muddle the present with the past.

"I think I'll keep you with me. For now. But don't get too

comfortable, Horatio. Delis here is the best executioner of her generation, and when she's busy, some of my Hound friends will be keeping you in very close company."

"We can do that," the keeper said. "For now."

□ ■ □

From top to bottom, the Dome of the Coming was crawling with people. Small ledges extended from the thousands of square panels that formed the dome, crowded with three and four people per ledge. Horatio and Delis couldn't help but stare. The dome was swarming like a hornets' nest. Looking up, Sariah felt like a wretched midge.

A lavishly carved bridge spanned the moat to reach the restored pedestal. The keeper gestured and Sariah crossed without glancing down. The sages' decisions had been a close thing. She still feared an untimely death in that moat.

The dome settled into an expectant silence. Sariah sensed they wanted to hear something from her, but she didn't know what to say. Instead, she knelt down and set up the game. She didn't bother with the stone. She knew now that it didn't matter. She went through the motions quickly. Within moments she was done playing Leandro's game.

The roar from the people standing outside the dome preceded the beam. Then, as the light made its way through the dome's opening, the roar extended to the ledges above her, drowning even the beam's powerful hum. It was fascinating to see it glowing in the dome, as if it belonged there, as if the goddess's divine finger had pointed at this precise time and place to favor her children with her light. A sob caught in Sariah's throat. Her tears' refraction only enhanced the beam's brilliancy.

"This way," the keeper said.

"Where are we going?"

The keeper led Sariah over another bridge, to an outside balcony. Here again, people spilled from the dome, from other balconies, from windows and doors and rooftops. Sariah stood on the balcony surrounded by today's sages, the ones who had granted the last necessary sanction to fetch her friends and call the beam. Sariah followed the path of light ascending high above the dome, only to find that it descended precipitously in a tight arch onto the opposing dome.

It was there, what she sought, the reason for her long, exhausting journey, the object of Leandro's game.

□ ■ □

They made their way over the rooftops from one dome to the other, pushing through the tides of people surging around Sariah and the Hounds escorting her. Flushed faces interrupted Sariah's sight, competing for her attention. Eyes cried, mouths moved, frantic hands reached from the crowd. By far, the worst offerings were those extended limbs proffering blood. Arms, hands, fingers, all dripping with blood, aimed for Sariah's lips.

"Gross," Horatio Maliver had the gall to mutter. "What's wrong with these people?"

Sariah didn't want to think about it. She feared she would falter if she did. She feared she would run away and never look back if she thought too much about what was happening.

"Saba, have we done right?" a woman cried.

"Saba, will we die by our own claws?"

"Why are they calling you that, my donnis?"

As if she wanted to know. Sariah's heart was beating too fast. She was breathless with anticipation. It was a cold day, yet sweat drenched her brow as they made it through the Dome of the Going's gates.

Today's sages were already on their ledges. Although the cupola in this dome was plain and unadorned, as in the previous one, it teemed with people. Faces peered through open panels. Ledges strained under the weight of too many. The air was thick with the stink of perspiration, the warmth of thousands of breaths and the beam's pervasive heat.

The beam. It was coming through the dome's opening and landing on a pedestal not unlike the one where she had stood at the Dome of the Coming. But this pedestal didn't hold anything similar to Leandro's game. Instead, the light fell on four life-size statues.

Sariah forgot the people around her. She forgot the crowds waiting outside, the panic pounding in her chest. Mesmerized by the sight before her, she walked across the bridge and circled the statues.

The beam landed in the center of the four statues, where a stone-sculpted chest stood unassumingly. The light bounced off the chest's polished surface and reflected on the sculptures' faces. The chest was vividly carved to look like wood and leather, but it was the keyhole carved on the rounded lid that caught Sariah's attention. She stared at it for a few moments before she decided what to do.

"Bring me Leandro's game."

Delis darted over the bridge and out the gate. Sariah returned her attention to the statues. A name was carved on the low platform beneath the stone figure of each of the sages.

Eneis would have been hard on his pupils' eyes. Bold, short, squat and portly, his girth almost exceeded his height. Sariah gasped. She recognized the man. She had seen him before. He was the plump toad-faced man who had originally wised Leandro's snakes and scorpions!

Sariah rushed to examine the rest of the statues. She didn't recognize the other faces. Poe had been a tall, reed-thin man with small, slanted eyes lost on a face wrinkled with age. Tirsis had been a stately woman whose full lips somehow echoed the elegance of her tall figure and the sinuous curves of her breasts and hips. Vargas, the biggest surprise, had been a small woman loaded with a good measure of excess flesh around the middle and an impish smile.

The statues were carved in the red coppery stone of the Bastions' cliffs. They were not painted, except for the eyes. Eneis, Poe and Tirsis's eyes had not matched. Vargas's had. These had been the Hounds' first sages, the Wisdom's eminent makers.

Sariah was struck by their ordinary poses. Eneis held between his hands what Sariah realized was probably a book, sculpted faithfully in its original tattered state. Tirsis held a small chisel. Poe, whose expression seemed a little deranged on second thought, clutched a small indistinguishable object. Vargas, the bloody law lady, wielded a pitchfork, a *broken* pitchfork. Sariah repressed a chuckle. The crowd's ominous silence reminded her of the solemnity of the occasion.

Abruptly, the beam receded from the statues. The crowd stirred, murmuring uneasily. Delis had succeeded at her task. The conclusion of Leandro's game was nearing and Sariah was about to find out the whereabouts of the pure. She had to wait for Delis's return. She was curious. The Bastions were protected by a powerful wising. The beam was fueled by similar powers. Had the original sages been able to wise stone?

She laid her palm against Tirsis's stone body, looking up at the ancient sage's striking face. Her pupils had been black and green, like Kael's. The trance overtaking her mind was gradual and kind. A mellow voice spoke without words. "The goddess's greeting, for Meliahs is just and fair to all her children."

Despite their people's singular devotion to the Wisdom's oral traditions, the original sages had taken precautions to protect the Wisdom. It endured in these statues, not unlike a sense of their spirits, committed to eternity in the care of wised stone. One after the other, Sariah tested the sculptures and found each buzzing with the precepts of its respective sage. She marveled at the clarity of purpose which supported the original sages' existence. She wished she had years to translate the Wisdom into fitting engrossments. She couldn't help but wish that the sages were alive in this time of terrible trouble.

"My donnis." Delis offered her the bag with Leandro's game.

Sariah sifted through the bag, looking for a particular game piece. She needed a scorpion, the botched one, the one missing one of its front claws. Her hand was trembling as she clasped the critter. She hesitated.

She couldn't know the nature of the wising she faced, but by her estimation, it couldn't be an easy one. She had to consider the dangers. She didn't think she had the option of refusing or delaying it. The tale had to be found and the Hounds weren't about to let her walk away from this wising without licking her spilled blood from the floor. On the other hand, she owed the little soul she sheltered in her body a chance at life, an oath of protection as binding as her stone oaths.

The keeper nudged her. "Wiser?"

"A moment." She closed her eyes and grabbed the amplifying stone she carried in her pocket. She entered the trance and weaved a protective sack around her womb, a strong encasement of luminous links. It was a skill she had learned from Malord. If it had worked to trap a powerful intrusion once, then it should serve to protect the baby.

"Be brave," she whispered.

She was ready. She stepped up between the sculptures and inserted the botched scorpion in the stone chest's keyhole. It fit. She turned it. It clicked. The light spilled through the keyhole first and then from the sides of the lid. Sariah opened the chest.

A stone glimmered in the chest's center, a fiery dawn, a rounded geode with a hollow middle, crammed with globules and spikes of yellow quartz druses. It was a large stone, one she wouldn't be able to lift on her own. It was gorgeous. A wiser could lose herself in the wondrous world of its shimmering charm.

"*Sacred is the sight of the guide*," the keeper murmured, "*for it shall lead us home.*"

Sariah's emotions surged with the light. The call of the stone taunted her senses. She was almost afraid to touch it. She looked at Tirsis's sculpted face, at the crowded dome, at the expectant sages. She closed her eyes and dreamed for a moment, as Poe may have done. She dreamed of peace, of Kael, of a search, done. Then she opened her eyes and studied the stone, knowing in her heart that it was likely to offer anything but the peace she sought.

Thirty

THE STONE THAT lay in the coffer between the sages' four statues was not a common wised stone. The strength of its call revealed it was of the highest potency. Ignoring the crowd's anxious oversight, and despite the light's brilliancy, Sariah took her time examining it.

It was a fiery stone by birth, twined with large quantities of slowly cooled crystal, blossoms of yellow and orange streaks that overshadowed the stone's other components. She didn't recognize them. Were they traces of wulfenite? Mimetite? Perhaps orpiment? A wiser from the Hall of Masons might know. She was sure of one thing, though—Leandro's little snakes and scorpions were made of the same dazzling combination.

Sariah dared a gentle tap on the stone. She was prepared to fight a violent trance. Instead, a pleasant murmur coursed through her mind, a joyful invitation to play. Sariah obliged.

The stone whispered a melody exclusive to her mind. "*Wise me, wiser, tenderly, bring me to my tale. Don't you know me, child of hers, don't you know my name?*"

The stone's voice was a lullaby to her senses. The song was an exquisite caress to her mind. She could have stayed in that trance for a long time. She could have leaned on the gentle melody and rested for years on end.

The dome. She had to get back to the dome. Sariah released the trance's peace reluctantly, regretfully. It had been an extraordinary experience. There had been no stern command, no mandate like that which permeated the Domainers' protective stones, no violent tale like the ones contained in the seven twin stones and no lurking intrusion waiting to wrestle her powers.

Don't you know me, child of hers, don't you know my name?

There had been something familiar, something soothing and intimate about her link to this stone, a sense of belonging, like the safety of Kael's embrace.

She returned her attention to the stone. It had a smooth, egg-shaped underside, but it was broken on top. It seemed to have been split open like an overripe pumpkin, revealing the crystal druses inside the geode's hollow, a ghoulish yellowish grin.

She noticed the small gaps that stood at regular intervals between the hollow's crystals. Regularity wasn't common to the natural world. She counted them. Just as she thought. Forty-eight. There was a pattern to those gaps. They started at the edge and spiraled towards the hollow's middle. She knew what she had to do. She strengthened the baby's protective weave and eyed the crowded chamber.

"I'm not sure what will happen," she said to the keeper. "It could be dangerous. It could be deadly."

"We couldn't make them go if we wanted to," the keeper said. "It's their right to live or die by the domes. Do as you must. So will we."

Damn the Hounds' rights. They shouldn't be there. But Sariah knew of no way to persuade them to leave, and a cursory glance at her bracelet reminded her she didn't have time to waste. Courage's link was at the top, as if the goddess's sister was urging her on. She picked up a game piece from the bag. Carefully, she set a little snake, bottom first, into the outermost gap. It fit perfectly.

The coiled snake sparkled to life. It fused to the geode seamlessly, as if it had always belonged there. One by one, with deliberate care, she fit all the pieces in place. Something nipped at her mind each time. She could feel the energy gathering in the stone, the void reaching out to draw from her strength. She had a sense of loss, knowing that with each snake and scorpion she yielded, she was forsaking the stones that had led her to the Bastions.

At last all the gaming pieces but one were in place. She had to chuckle at the stone's eerie grin. A mouthful of snakes and scorpions. Who by the rot pits thought of that?

The botched scorpion was the last one. Only one slot remained at the hollow center. Sariah noticed something strange then, something that had been concealed by the light's refraction on the surrounding crystal. There was a portion missing. She didn't think it was nature's work. It was a clean, straight-edged extraction. Precision was a human trait. Would the wising work with a piece of the stone missing? Was it a provision or an omission?

Nothing to do but try. The light gained brilliancy as she pressed the botched scorpion into place.

□ ■ □

The geode's core ignited, hot as simmering fire. A fist of hot air blasted Sariah and pinned her against Tirsis's statue. A short beam uncoiled from the stone and broke apart into four columns of humming light. The columns pierced the statues' colored eyes. The stone sages glowed. Their arms lifted. They clasped each other's hands, trapping Sariah in an indomitable circle of energy.

Poe's lips moved. "Behold. We have returned as it was foretold to redeem our theft and ourselves. Our dreams turn to tale. Our tale turns to blood."

Sariah's mind refused to accept what she was seeing. A thousand wild thoughts interfered with her reason. Stone. She needed to commit this moment to stone. She fumbled for the little memory stone she wore around her neck and pushed her memories out of the way. She would be incapable of remembering every detail. If she lived through this. If she survived.

She looked up to see that Tirsis's face was liquid on her stone façade. Her laughter filled the dome, brisk, joyful and sweet.

"Fear not, my beloved," Tirsis said. "You're ready. The goddess blesses your path. The stone leads you to its lair."

"Why must we perish to thrive when we thrive without perishing?" Eneis said.

"Because we're pledged to Meliahs," Vargas said. "Because we were born and bred to die. Of the stone we were created. With the stone we'll be avenged."

Sariah could only hope that her simultaneous inscription was working and that she would live long enough to understand the sages' words, because every word they said triggered a hundred questions and every one of her questions had a thousand possible answers. Tirsis's eyes settled on her, and even though she knew that the woman had been dead for hundreds of years, she couldn't help but gape at the sage's vitality, at the beauty of her broad face, at the wisdom burning in her stare.

"Our ways are most likely primitive to you," Tirsis said. "But it was all we had."

Primitive? If only Tirsis knew. The Guild's prohibitions had weakened stonewising, forcing the craft to revert to its simplest and earliest stages. Only Zeminaya's wisings matched the complexity of these sages' wising and even then, her work had been buried and suppressed.

Questions. Sariah had questions. Was the sages' extraordinary wising capable of interaction? There was so much she wanted to know, about the Hounds' origins, about the Guild and the sages, about the Wisdom, about the amazing stone powering their revival. Where to start? The tale. She had to focus on her search.

Sariah's voice was raw to her own ears. "Where can I find the bane of the pure, the tale that can unite the Bloods?"

"See with your eyes," Tirsis said. "Feel with your heart. What you seek is beyond proof. It's reality."

"What's pure but stone?" Eneis asked. "What's more credible than proof, more credible than action and moment, but substance itself?"

"The dream dreamed us thieves for a purpose," Poe said.

Sariah's hand was numb from clenching her stone. Her knees were weak from the effort. She slid down and sat against Tirsis's legs. Her own strength was being sapped to power the sages at a time when she needed it most to make sense out of chaos.

"I don't understand."

"Stonewiser," Tirsis said patiently. "You've found the bane of the pure."

"I have?"

"*This* is the pure." Tirsis's ethereal hands cupped the brilliant stone at the center. "And we, my beloved child, *we* are its bane."

☐ ■ ☐

Meliahs help her. All that time looking for a people called the pure, when she was instead looking for the stone these sages called the pure! She wanted to kick herself for her ignorance. Yet she had wised this stone already, and the tale it had sung to her had been sweet and peaceful, but it wasn't the tale she was looking for. Where was the tale that would bring unity to the Blood? Where was the one tale that was going to satisfy the justice gathering, the executioners, and both Domainers and Goodlanders?

Vargas eyes flared. "Can you sense it? She's sealed. She's Zeminaya's spawn!"

"One of Zeminaya's?" Poe said. "Just as I dreamed it."

Tirsis's crystal clear laughter filled the dome again. "She tried and she triumphed, Meliahs bless her skillful hands."

"She should be destroyed," Vargas spat.

"But aren't there different climbs to the same summit?" Eneis asked. "And who's the thief? She or we? Who shall prevail in the end?"

"As if we could know the end to any beginning," Tirsis said. "We have no choice but faith alone. Time's done. Our blessings and our apologies, stonewiser."

"For what?"

"For what has been, is, will be. For the legacy unleashed, for the burdens bestowed."

"What burdens?" Sariah asked, but the sages were no longer listening to her. They raised their linked hands towards the dome.

"I grant you leave to live my dreams," Poe said.

"I add my questions to yours," Eneis said.

"To you I entrust my Hounds." Vargas glared. "You'd best be faithful to my beasts."

"Wait. Wait. I don't want—"

"The waiting's over," Tirsis said. "The scent is the spark of a reckless life. What thrives in the light yields only to its own darkness. What restores the whole destroys the parts. I give you a warning: two fortnights. That's all the beam will last, or else the darkness of generations."

The light changed, pouring into the statues at an accelerated pace, igniting them crimson. The heated draft of the noiseless explosion rendered Sariah flat on her back. The entire dome shook and seemed to expand with the blast. The earth quaked. For a few, long moments, she couldn't breathe the scalding air singeing her lungs. Words burst from her mind. Voices settled on the surfaces of her wiser's core and then sank into her consciousness. The Wisdom. She could hear it all at once, a chorus imprinting itself on her soul.

Her eyelids fluttered open just in time to see the statues shattered. Tirsis and her fellow stonewisers no longer stood. If she had only known, if she had sensed the trigger in the wising, she might have been able to prevent the statues' destruction. She had talked to the sages and in doing so she had almost touched the goddess's hand.

She rubbed her eyes in disbelief. A cloud of the statues' debris whirled just above the intact stone in the chest. Before her, before the bewildered crowd, the debris transformed from pulverized rock into dots of brilliantly colored lights. The lights floated up towards the dome, like cotton blooms surfing the air. They landed languidly against the cupola, forming four distinct clusters of highly stylized script.

Sariah gasped with the crowd. An enormous, glorious engrossment was born out of the statues' destruction. The four sages' Wisdom had survived their makers, not just in Sariah's mind, but also on the Dome of the Going. Colorful images began to form around the dome's open apex. Curls blowing in the wind, a wisp of a woman led a procession, trailed in turn by a long spiraling line of Hounds.

She had no time to consider the image.

Light gushed up from the geode stone, punching through the dome's opening like a steaming geyser, escaping out of sight. People forsook their places at the dome in droves, racing outside. Another beam. Sariah felt her knees give way. She was exhausted.

"My donnis?" Delis's strong arms held her.

Sariah slipped her hand in her pocket and clutched the amplifying stone to check on the baby's protective weave. It was sound and undamaged, perfect, like the life it held in trust.

Sariah could hardly speak. Somehow, the keeper convinced Delis to follow him. Soon, Sariah stood on the Dome of the Going's balcony propped up between Delis and the keeper like a rag doll. The light streamed out of the dome, over the Bastions, and sank into the distant horizon.

Some things began to make sense to Sariah, not what these people had stolen or why, but rather, from where. "Is that—?"

"Aye," Horatio said. "The right direction."

Sariah tore her eyes from the beam to look at the crowd gathered around the dome. The high plain was covered with people for as far as she could see. They had gathered here from all over the Bastions just to see the beam. How many? Thousands? Millions? More?

A chilling howl echoed in the plain. At once, the people turned into armed Hounds. All the people. The rotting skulls claimed the faces of old and young, and a rhythmic cry resonated throughout the Bastions. Sariah could barely make out the words.

"We pledged to come," they chanted. "We pledge to go."

"What do they mean?"

"They're ready," the keeper said. "They'll follow you."

"Me?" Horror was glutting at her throat.

"By the domes, you're the saba."

"The saba?"

"In the old language. The guide."

"The guide to what?"

"*Wise are those who recognize the signs, for they will be the people of the going, the hands of Meliahs' restoration. Look.*"

The beam's luminous path formed a third dome in the sky, an identical reproduction of the other two domes' distinct outlines. What was it that Tirsis had said? *Our apologies. For the legacy unleashed, for the burdens bestowed.*

Sariah wiped the sweat from her brow. Great. Just perfect. Damn sages. The joke was on her.

□ ■ □

"As I see it, you've got no choice," Horatio Maliver said, even though she hadn't asked for his advice. "You've gained yourself a few new followers, wiser. I don't know when or why these people came to the Bastions, but I tell you, they're going back to the Goodlands now, and with a thirst for blood. The Goodlands are history. The Guild's screwed."

Sariah flashed him a look that should have burned him to cinders. Didn't he understand? She didn't want this. Any of it. She didn't want Vargas's damn Hounds, and she didn't need Eneis's questions adding to her own. She didn't want Poe's dreams either. She had her own nightmares, thank you.

Wasn't there enough violence as it was? And what about these zealous people, these lethal, blood-licking fighters who had created a new and rich existence for themselves high in the Bastions' isolation? Did they deserve annihilation just because of blind piety and old pledges?

"Face it," Horatio said. "Their entire existence has been devoted to preparations. The idle wait they called it, but have you seen their weapons? Over the years, they have accumulated a wealth of destruction. Catapults, pikes, spears, rams, claws. Their weapon-making furnaces are lit day and night. Every toddler knows how to use claws. They have been ready for generations."

"There's no real threat to the Goodlands." Sariah pretended a measure of calm she didn't feel. "They can't lower all of their weapons in those rickety lifts. It's just not possible."

Horatio had no qualms about thrashing her hope. "They're ready, I tell you. They've made every necessary provision to transport themselves and their equipment down those cliffs. Trust me. I've commanded many armies before. They have plans to bring everything with them—families, cattle, possessions. Everything."

It would be a disaster for them, for the Goodlands, for the Domain, for all the Blood. Was she the only sane person who could see that?

"They're making arrangements as we speak," Horatio said. "Do you know they're organized in waves of warriors? I heard them talking. Devastating. I have to give it to you, wiser. You've done well. You've gotten yourself an army to shred Arron and Grimly to the rot pits."

An army? For Meliahs' sake, she was a stonewiser. Horatio Maliver couldn't begin to understand her horror.

"We could leave, my donnis," Delis said. "They're too busy with their celebrations to notice if we escape."

It made all the sense in the world. Run away, escape, finish what she had set out to do, abandon these blood-lapping mad people to their communal hysteria. Then, if they went, if they lost their lives tumbling down the cliffs or fighting the Shield in the Goodlands, their deaths would be on them, not on her. Aye. Leave. Quietly. Unseen. Undetected. That was the option that appealed to Sariah best.

"What about the stone?" Horatio asked. "Don't you need it to prove your innocence?"

Sariah had been thinking a lot about the stone. Leandro's game, useful as it had been, was now lost to her. It had become part of the stone. The stone itself contributed no helpful tale. The wising had only given her a new direction. The beam would shine for two fortnights, twenty-eight nights, and if she was right, it would lead her to the one place where it had all started, the very place she dreaded.

That's where the sages had sent her. That's where she was going. Alone.

□ ■ □

"Stop arguing with me," Sariah whispered. "Delis, you'll travel to Targamon and then to the Domain, and that's final."

"I won't leave you alone, my donnis. I can't."

"Of course you can." Sariah turned to Horatio. "And you, you're not coming with me."

Horatio flashed his infuriating smile. "Think of me as your newest pet."

"I warn you. Be gone. I don't want you with me."

"I'm coming," Horatio said. "And right now, you're in no position to prevent it. If you try to leave me behind, I'll shout so loud that every Hound within ten leagues will know you're trying to escape their adoration."

"Carcasses don't shout," Delis rumbled.

"A peep from you, Horatio, and I'll turn you over to the Hounds. They'll enjoy teaching you the Wisdom."

Horatio had the grace to pale a little. He too had seen the treatment that defectors received. Sariah was fairly sure Horatio had had no dealings with the Hounds until the day he came up the lift. That he had braved the Hounds and the lifts to come after her was a true measure of his urgency. He had risked much. But even if she bought the notion of his desperation, she didn't believe him.

Sariah crept down the trail towards the next cluster of trees, thankful for the darkness's protection. The night was cold. Snow crunched under her feet. They were close to the cliffs. She could hear people talking just over the hill, and the quiet sound of the ox teams' muffled hoofs, pounding the ground at a steady pace. Followed by Delis and Horatio, she skulked toward an abandoned stone wheel and halted there to put on the heavy Hound suits they hauled.

Horatio wrinkled his nose. "The stench."

"The better part of fear," Sariah said. "Stay then. Don't forsake your nose's sensibility for the likes of me."

"There's only one way down," Horatio said.

"I can make it faster for you," Delis offered.

The stolen cape was too big, the skull was too heavy, the damn claws burst open every time Sariah touched them, threatening to cut off her fingers or nose.

"Where are you going?" The keeper's voice froze Sariah's clumsy attempt at Hound-dressing. "You're not leaving, are you?"

The panic in the man's voice threatened to undo Sariah's resolutions. "No, nay, no. There are... arrangements that must be made. There are things I must do before—"

"We can help," the keeper said. "We're ready. We can scout, infiltrate, attack. We can do anything you need."

"Heed me, keeper, the time is not right yet—"

"But the dome, the sages, the signs. They're all there. We're worthy. Let us show you."

The misery stamped on the man's face was too much for Sariah to bear. It was not just the keeper who would feel this way. Her desertion would affect all of the Hounds. She didn't want to use them for her own purposes and yet here they were, at her feet, begging to be used.

She hurt for them, but a descent from the safety of those cliffs meant more useless destruction. She didn't want them dead or annihilated. She had to keep them here. It took her by surprise. When had she begun to care for Vargas's blood-licking Hounds?

"Listen to me, keeper. You're right. The signs have been given but it is I who must decide the time of the going. There's much work to do before your people can come down from the Bastions."

"I understand. It's foretold. The guide will know the when and the how."

At least the damn prophecy gave her a little working room. "Your people must stay here for the moment. First and foremost, you must protect the stone at the Dome of the Going. Do you understand?"

"The stone will be protected, on the Wisdom we swear."

"The Hounds, they must continue to do whatever it is that they do. No changes."

"No changes." The keeper nodded. "The defectors won't suspect us."

To the Hounds, the defectors included everybody in the Goodlands. What a mess.

"What else will you have us do?" the keeper asked.

Sariah was thinking fast. "There will be need for food and supplies, so the harvests must be kept and the herds must be tended to. There will be some who will recklessly want to follow me to the Goodlands. They must be kept back."

"Done. Do you wish for us to deepen our recognizance of the Goodlands?"

"Recognizance?" Dear Meliahs. "No changes, remember?"

"But we have always patrolled the foot of the Bastions."

An idea occurred to her. "If you must continue your patrols, then strive to make friends."

"Friends?"

"We'll need all the allies we can find when the time comes. We must seed goodwill among all we encounter."

"Even the armed ones?"

"I'll be the first to admit that making friends with the Shield is not easy," Sariah said. "Keep them away as you must, but try to refrain from slaughter."

The keeper scratched his head. "I thought our mandate was to spill their blood."

"Not at the moment."

"Strategy, aye. We understand it."

"You must learn from friends and enemies. Learn about their customs, their beliefs, their concerns."

"What else?" the keeper said. "What else can we do for the guide?"

"That's a lot, keeper."

"We're capable of more."

"I know, but—"

"Targamon." Delis interrupted. "Send messengers there."

Meliahs grant her patience. "I said *you* should go, Delis."

The keeper jumped at the chance. "We can be your envoys. Nobody will run swifter or surer than us."

"My donnis, the Hounds can run your messages and I can stay with you. They can journey to Targamon. They can report back to you faster than I ever could. They can also take your message to Metelaus."

Metelaus. Meliahs only knew what he would make of her message. But what else could she do? How long had it been since Kael had purchased her atonement from the executioners? Over five months. The journey had been grueling, the end wasn't yet in sight, and less than three months remained before the deadline. Who knew how much farther she would have to go? What guarantees did she have that she could return to face the executioners in time?

"It's the right decision, my donnis. The Hounds can be trusted with your messages and I can come with you. You won't have to travel alone and unarmed."

"Alone and unarmed?" the keeper croaked. "Not the guide. Never. We'll carry your messages and escort you wherever you go. How many do you require? Ten thousand perhaps?"

Ten thousand?

Horatio Maliver was snorting like the damn pig he was. Why didn't she just leave him behind? She didn't need him and he wasn't telling the truth, that much she knew. He was probably lying about the stones he claimed he had. Then why was she considering

letting him come? Was it because putrid as his soul was, he had
helped them escape the Guild once? Was it because after wising
his life's tale she pitied him? Because she wanted to know if he had
changed? Maybe. But she had other reasons as well.

*Safer is the rabid wolf tied to your leash than the faithful mas-
tiff stalking you freely in the bushes.* Vargas's notoriously fierce
Wisdom surfaced spontaneously from the depths of her mind. She
didn't like having Horatio close by, but there was no better way of
watching him than through her own two eyes. She had reasons to
suspect his every action, his every thought.

He had come here, risked his life, for an important purpose.
Sariah needed to discover what it was, because ignorance was the
lure of tragedy, and even the slightest glimpse of deceit was an
omen for destruction down the road. He was most likely a deadly
trap. Without knowing why Horatio Maliver needed her, Sariah
risked walking into that trap in the worst possible way—without
warning or recourse.

"We could provide ten times ten thousand if you'd like," the
keeper was saying. "We could flood the Goodlands with Hounds
if you wish it so."

"I travel in secrecy," Sariah said. "My inquiries are discreet.
I don't need a hundred thousand Hounds to terrify everybody in
sight."

"Then you need a fast team, quiet and fierce. Twenty pairs of
claws can massacre a hundred Shield. We did it at—"

"I really don't want to know." A headache was beginning to
gather behind Sariah's eyes.

"It's a good idea, my donnis. We can manage, if they dress like
proper Goodlanders. We can pretend we're merchants, like when
we went to Alabara."

"Remember the trouble that got us into?"

"I'm just saying, my donnis. I welcome a fist and a blade if it
makes you safe."

"Fine. If it gets us off these cliffs and on our way, let's have
them and be done with it." Damn if they didn't gang up against
her with the slightest ease.

The keeper was already giving orders and sending messages

to the domes. It was as if they had always been packed and ready. In less than an hour, a group of fully equipped men and women without their Hound disguises materialized at the cliffs. The keeper took his gear from one of them and strapped his pack on his back.

"You?" Sariah was surprised. "But what about your family?"

"They'll be proud that I go with you. Some come with me." He slapped the man standing next to him on the shoulder. "My brother, Torkel."

"*The goddess's greetings*," Torkel said. "*For you we die.*"

She flashed Torkel a tremulous smile and followed Jol, who was painstakingly reviewing the others in his outfit. "Listen, keeper. I don't want you or your brother to die."

"*To die for the guide will be the greatest honor.*"

"You'll hate this trip. You'll hate me. I'll be bossy. There won't be any Wisdom allowed, no blood licking or self-mutilation. You'll have to do what I say."

"*What's obedience but faithfulness to the truth?*" the keeper said. "*What is faithfulness but loyal following?* Do you forget, wiser? You drank my blood. I'm your keeper. I must come. Because if you die, who but me will drink your blood?"

Thirty-one

THE DISTANT HOWLING stopped at the night's darkest hour. Wedged between Delis and Horatio, Sariah sat up on her blanket and waited anxiously for the keeper's return. She figured she had a good hour before he came back. It was amazing how the Hounds managed to communicate using their ferocious howling. The terrible sound carried for great distances. Messenger teams established relay positions across extended territories, conveying important if abbreviated news faster than any runner. That's how she kept abreast of her messengers' progress. A fortnight had passed since she left the Bastions. Despite the awful weather and the Shield, the messengers had to be very close to Targamon.

The communication system had its drawbacks. No details could be properly conveyed, and the howling, as brief as possible, couldn't take place near their camp for fear of attracting attention and revealing their location. She had tried to go with the keeper, but he wouldn't have it and neither would Delis. Inasmuch as they accepted her authority on most everything, when it came to her safety, those two stuck together like love bugs.

Sariah lay back down on her blanket, but she was listening for the keeper's return. What news would he bring tonight? She didn't know what she feared worse—knowing or not knowing Kael's fate. And poor little Mia. Had she found a way to cope with the legacy's separation effects? Sariah dared to hope, mostly because the thought of her inadvertently hurting the child made her ill. They were putting more leagues between her and the farm every day. Sariah looked up at the beam streaking the sky like an omen. She had no choice. Although she was fairly sure of her destination, she couldn't chance making a mistake.

Delis got up and walked to the nearby woods. Almost immediately, Horatio Maliver rolled over to her blankets. His warm breath tickled Sariah's ear.

"My little wiser can't sleep?"

"I'm not your little wiser, and my sleep is my business."

"Cranky, aren't we?" Horatio snuggled closer. "I don't blame you. It's damn cold. Arron's Shield is everywhere we go. People in the Goodlands are in a state of panic. That so-called road is nothing more than a neck-breaking deer track."

"Stop whining and go to sleep." She didn't want to have an argument with him. Neither Delis nor the Hounds purported a liking for Horatio Maliver. One of these days his antics were going to get him killed before she could learn his true purpose.

"Do you ever regret us?" he asked.

"There was never an us."

"Do you regret it?"

"Every time I see your face."

That would have sent any dog yelping with its tail between its legs. Not Horatio Maliver. She almost screamed when she felt his hand on her thigh.

"Take. Your. Hand. Off me."

Horatio whispered. "Are you sure?"

"Very."

"I don't regret it." He deliberately ignored her warning. "The road is long, the night is cold. Loneliness is a sad condition, my little wiser, easy to cure, even now." His hand froze on her belly. "The rot burn me. Are you pregnant?"

In one swift movement she had him flat on his back with her knife at his throat. "Don't you dare touch me again. Ever."

"You *are* pregnant."

Rage was easy to call on Horatio Maliver. All it took was a palm to his throat and a quick, short stone wrath strike. It left him gagging, whimpering and slobbering like a dog choking on a bone.

She hissed in his ear. "If you say a word to anybody, I swear I'll kill you."

Delis was just returning from the woods when Sariah stomped by her.

"My donnis, what happened?"

Sariah walked away, ignoring Horatio's strangulated squeals and the scent of urine rising from his blankets. She took some consolation from Delis's delighted chortles.

□ ■ □

"As you suspected, there was trouble at Targamon Farm," the keeper reported.

"What kind of trouble?" Sariah asked. "The Shield? The rot?"

"Sickness."

"Sickness?" Sariah's belly went to ice. "What kind of sickness?"

"I can't tell from the howls. Many died."

Her throat bunged like a knotted rope.

"But not the man you asked about. Or the girl. They live."

Thank Meliahs. She had met the keeper just outside their camp, on a slight rise overlooking the forest. Sariah's hands were cold as ice blocks. She had dreaded the news. At least they were alive. The sickness must have been bad to delay Kael for so many weeks.

"Is he coming?"

The keeper shrugged. "The howls request assistance from the Bastions."

"What kind of assistance?"

"Supplies. Medicines. The usual."

"Will you help them?"

"You did say we must make friends, didn't you?"

Sariah nodded because she couldn't speak. Kael, Mia, Malord, her friends, the people she cared about most were trapped in disease-ravaged Targamon and she wasn't there to help them.

"If they can't get out to get their own supplies—"

"A quarantine is in place."

A quarantine. Of course. That's what was keeping Kael away and without choice. It was only then that the thought occurred to her. "Is he sick?"

"Who?"

"The man from Ars, Kael. The one I sent for."

"The howls didn't say."

Sariah squeezed her head between her hands. Now what? Another fortnight left to follow the beam or do as her heart was telling her and run like a madwoman to Targamon? She didn't care that thousands of Arron's Shield warriors were between here and there, or that a quarantine was in place. She would find a way to get through. But what about her search? She didn't think she could afford the time or the leagues that a return to Targamon required. The beam wouldn't last forever. The executioners wouldn't hesitate to take over Ars. The bracelet wouldn't wait to kill her. And what about the baby? Could the disease ravaging the farm hurt the baby too?

"Are you feeling unwell?"

Aye. She was feeling very unwell at the moment, bad enough to want to howl at the top of her lungs like the Hounds, sad enough to crawl into a hole and cry. "I'm fine."

"Do you want some of my blood?"

"No, nay, no. Thank you, but no. I need to think. Go. You've had a hard night. There's some stone-heated tea I made for you and your men. Get some rest."

"Won't you come with us?"

"I need to think." She dreaded the prospect of imposing logic on her ragged emotions. "You can watch me from the camp. I'm not thirty steps from the lot of you."

The keeper conceded. Sariah sat on a rock and forced herself to take long, even breaths. *Quarantine.* The word scared her worse than the rot. At least the Shield would leave Targamon alone for the moment. They wouldn't risk contagion. But if a quarantine was in place, there was nothing she could do for Kael and her friends. If she went, and insisted on gaining entry, she would be endangering the child she carried and imperiling her search.

What would Kael do?

No way out but forward. Get it done, protect the baby, find the tale, finish it, that's what he would say. It wasn't as if she was being reckless. On the contrary, she wasn't alone. She had Delis and the Hounds to assist her, a fierce, tidy outfit, capable of handling most contingencies. With the baby growing, now more than ever she had to think beyond the stones and to the future. She glanced down at her bracelet. The outline of the fisted hand caught her eye. Strength's link had landed on top. She had to be strong. And fast. Time was passing too quickly.

Going to Targamon made as much sense as diving headfirst into a rot pit. If she wanted to be with Kael and her friends, if she wanted to bring her child safely into a kinder world, she had to end this dangerous search once and for all. Along with the journey's hardships, fueling the baby's protective weave tested her strength. The more the baby grew, the harder it would be to keep up such protection. It was best if she moved on swiftly to finish her business.

She was in dire need of a plan. They would be waiting for her. They would be ready. How would she gain access to the place chosen by the beam when everybody else knew too? She wagered that the sages in all their wisdom didn't think of that small detail. Or had they?

She rummaged through her pocket looking for the memory stone where she had imprinted the tale of her latest wising. Perhaps she had missed something, a clue that would better her chances. She pulled the memory stone from her pocket, together with the amplifying stone she always carried and the larger bursting stones she kept there just in case. She spied another stone among the others, a small white pebble she didn't recall putting there.

It wasn't one of hers, she was sure. She tapped the stone and sensed a peculiar wising, a unique, almost imperceptible vibration that came at equal intervals. What by Meliahs' rot pits was this stone doing in her pocket?

Horatio Maliver. His amorous advances had had a double purpose, to test her resolve and, most importantly, to put a tracer stone on her. She had heard about those. The Guild councilors used it to track their leases when they went on wising-trading missions away from the keep. Only they knew how to make tracking stones. That narrowed her field of suspects. Who was Horatio Maliver working for?

She tossed the little stone in the air and caught it on the way down. She had been right to suspect Horatio's reappearance. The man was a walking justification for murder. Was the tracking stone's wising somehow anchored to Horatio Maliver? Probably. She was suddenly very glad she had decided to keep Horatio with her. Horatio himself was most likely being tracked by whoever tracked her. His tracking stone could be anywhere, hidden among his belongings, sown into his clothing, even lodged in his body, smuggled in his food or forced down his gullet with or without his notice. Horatio's abrupt disappearance or a sudden separation from Sariah's path would tip off her stalker. Even now, when she knew all that, it wasn't time to get rid of him. He was an advantage she wasn't willing to relinquish just yet.

Her coin was on Grimly. He had to be working for the Prime Hand. Horatio couldn't be bought with promises for coin or power. That's all Arron had to offer. Mistress Grimly, on the other hand, knew how to make a hard bargain. A shrewd and experienced player, she knew people bent at complex angles. She had the skills to figure out Horatio's needs and use them as leverage to obtain her own ends. Besides, the past couldn't be ignored. Horatio and Grimly had been allies before the breaking of the wall. They had worked well together. They had made a formidable foe.

Sariah considered the little white stone in her hand. It was newly chiseled. The gouges were fresh and the ridges were sharp. She sighed. She needed to know. She took a quick lick, a touch of tongue to stone. Salt. Pepper. Cumin. Mustard. She smiled. The stone had been recently harvested from the keep's underground stores, a group of caves used to store valuable spices, a place she knew well from her errands as a Guild pledge. With the Guild split and Arron locked out of the keep, only Mistress Grimly had access to those stores.

Sariah returned the white stone to her pocket. Whoever was set on finding her would do so—at her convenience. If Horatio Maliver was working for Grimly, he was more than a traitor, more than a lying, cold bastard. He had become her best opportunity.

□ ■ □

The wind that chilled Sariah was ice's purest breath. It cut through her mantle as if she wasn't wearing every garment she owned at the moment. Even her eyeballs felt frozen. For as long as Sariah could remember, the chill had never punished the Goodlands with cold as bitter and unrelenting as this.

She was happy to step away from the wind and into the protection of the spacious cave the Hounds had found to make camp this night. Exposure was likely to kill anybody who braved the weather tonight. A quick foray beyond the mouth of the cave confirmed that the beam continued to lead them in the same direction it had glowed the night before. Part of her was glad for the consistency. The other part was terrified.

She made her way down the dark passage. For an instant, a ripple of movement tripped her balance. Pebbles and dirt trickled from the ceiling. She hunkered against the wall, just in case, but it was only a mild earth tremor, nothing like yesterday's bone-rattling quake. Regardless, the ground was too restless since they left the Bastions. Sariah prayed it had nothing to do with the rot.

A plan was beginning to take shape in her mind, dangerous by all accounts, but viable. She wished, not for the first time, that Kael was with her. She missed his mind's brilliant strategic eye as much as she missed his body's warmth next to her every night. He wouldn't be such a fool as to undertake a journey on a night like this. Would he?

The campfire's orange glow burned in the cave's safe depths. Sariah smiled to the sentinel and halted just beyond the light's reach. Her Hounds loitered around the fire. Some of the warriors were sharpening their claws, some were sleeping, some were sipping hot cups of the thick brew they favored, listening to Torkel, who sang verses from the Wisdom in a mesmerizing raspy bass.

Horatio, Delis and the keeper were engaged in quiet conversation apart from the others.

"I don't understand," Horatio Maliver was saying. "At least she gave me something once. But you two, you follow her like tame pups after a full teat. You're not so deluded you think she may let you suckle, are you?"

"*What I am to her, she is to me*," the keeper said. "*Quiet strength and subtle beauty is always simple and done.*"

"The Wisdom." Horatio Maliver sneered. "And what do you get for your troubles? Not what your blood-licking fellows get for theirs, that's for sure."

"*She who comes from the night must learn to enjoy the sun's glare.*"

"And you're a very understanding chap." Horatio laughed.

Had the keeper ever had any expectations from her? Had he waited patiently for her to realize those expectations?

Horatio Maliver shifted targets. "And you, rot spawn, why would you choose her as your donnis?"

Delis didn't answer.

"I've watched you. You have a weakness for a sound pair of teats and a round arse."

"*The heart's reasons are for the goddess's ears alone,*" Jol said.

"Is she really your pet?" Horatio asked. "Or are you her fetching mongrel instead?"

"What would a mangy dog like you know of the donnis honor?" Delis spat. "You're not even worthy of a rotting leper."

"I wouldn't speak too loudly, if I were you. You stink worse than a leper to Sariah's very fine nose."

"*Wise is he who refrains from judging the unknown. Understanding will favor him.*"

"Poor blood-licking keeper." Horatio pouted mockingly. "What is it that you keep? A vigil? A pathetic, slobbering wait for what? A taste of her blood?"

The color rose in the keeper's cheeks. Delis's hands fisted by her sides. What sick pleasure did Horatio Maliver derive from taunting her friends?

"Can't you see?" Horatio said. "She despises your blood-licking ways. She abhors your executioner's blood. She has already chosen her beast. He's no better than you, but she doesn't care. She flaunts her indulgence before you like the carter waves the carrot in the asses' noses. She's like a splinter: The more you scratch the itch, the deeper she sinks into your soul."

Sariah was furious with Horatio Maliver, for mocking her friends, for stirring matters that were best left alone. Too late. She saw the provocation in Delis's blue and violet eyes, the hurt in the keeper's frown. Horatio had stabbed them in the gut and left the wounds open to fester. Furious, she twisted the bracelet around her wrist. The sight of the coupled rings adorning Loyalty's link enraged her even more.

Sariah couldn't explain the need that fueled her actions. Was it outrage against Horatio Maliver or a loyal defense of her friends? Was it an act of revenge or an act of justice? Was it a sudden settlement between her oaths and her obligations or a spontaneous release of her own dark cravings?

In three steps, she knelt between Delis and the keeper and laid a hand on each of their shoulders. She closed her eyes and summoned all the gratefulness that dwelt in her being, the devotion she felt for those who had extended to her even the strangest forms of friendship, the passion she had for their lives.

It came out in the form of affection, the emotion she was most used to conveying. And even as it poured from her palms, it flared with new and unique furor. There was something self-indulgent about the act, a tenuous flirt with sedition to the oaths she had made to Kael, to the stones. But this moment was due. It was fair and necessary to cure the wounds Horatio Maliver had inflicted, to enable her friends to heal themselves, to free herself from every instance of neglect and regret. It felt right.

Delis and the keeper gasped in unison. Their bodies tensed and trembled beneath her hands. *Affection. Passion. Elation.* She allowed the bulk of her emotions to pour out, until the keeper's eyes bulged and Delis's throat issued a whimpering moan. In the end, Delis's unfocused eyes and the keeper's white-lipped release proved Horatio Maliver's taunting right and wrong. It didn't, however, prove her friends' loyalty lacking or her own trust misplaced.

□ ■ □

The explosion cracked in the air like the strike of a whip.

"What was that?" Sariah asked.

"Over here." The keeper was already sprinting towards the

source, veering off the trail and into the wintering forest. Steam was issuing from a tiny fracture on the ground next to an old oak tree. A bit of bluish liquid bubbled from the ground, a smallish fountain that froze on contact with the frigid air.

"I've never seen anything like it," Delis said.

Horatio Maliver shook his head. "Maybe lightning struck here?"

Sariah put a fistful of frozen dirt to her nose. She didn't recognize the scent. It was irritating and sulfurous, like the rot, but it was also saltier, like brine. The little fountain sputtered, fizzled, and died.

"I guess that's all there is to see here." Delis followed the keeper back to Torkel and the Hounds guarding the trail.

Sariah was about to do the same when the ground swelled under her feet. Within seconds, she had risen four or five spans on a thin bubble of frozen earth. A gurgle resonated from within the ground. A jet of blue gas shot from the expanding hole in the bubble's middle.

The oak groaned and tilted to one side. Half its branches snapped in the air. Sariah grabbed on to a root. It broke. She dropped into the swelling's deep crease. For a moment, she lost sight of the sky, buried in the shifting crust. Smothered, she recalled the snail's spastic gut, the box's oppressing darkness. She tried to scream but inhaled a mouthful of frigid dirt instead.

The earth rose beneath her back, shooting her upwards. The sky. She struggled to reach the surface. A face. She groped for a handhold. Horatio Maliver? A stern pull of her hair. Pain. The stink of ozone. Light again.

"Hold on!"

They tumbled down the side of the swell and hit the icy ground hard. Clinging to each other, they scurried away from the thing. It had grown as tall as a tower and as wide as a pond, and it gargled loudly like a full-throated pelican.

Horatio groaned. She realized she had landed on top of him, entrenched between his arms. His heart was beating wildly against her own.

Delis came running from the trail. "My donnis, are you all right?"

"I think so," Sariah rasped.

Sariah pushed herself to her feet and shook the dirt from her mantle. Horatio was slower getting up. She offered a hand.

"For a skinny thing, you've got some weight to your bones." He took her hand and gave her a sober gray stare. "I thought you were gone, wiser."

"Me too." She helped him up.

Horatio stared at the pulsing boil. "What by the rot is it?"

Sariah was looking at him. "By the rot, I have no idea."

□ ■ □

Sariah had to give the Hounds credit for bringing her from the Bastions to her destination in twenty-seven nights. It was a great distance to cover, particularly when avoiding the main roads and dodging Arron's Shield. The keeper was a quiet, efficient leader. Every member of the outfit was fit, smart and brave, especially the keeper's pride, his brother Torkel, who fueled his fellow Hounds' courage with songs of the Wisdom and single-minded intensity.

From afar, the place looked like a slumbering giant sprawled on a trash heap. The sparkle of the wall's black and white granite competed with the new snow's shimmer. The dirty town huddling around the walls contrasted with the keep's pristine beauty. But beauty and order were not equal to truth and devotion. Sariah had never wanted to see this place again. Yet here she was, staring at her past and future through a gentle screen of falling snow.

The beam landed squarely between those dreaded walls.

□ ■ □

It was time to put her plan into action. The light was beginning to wane. The weather was worsening, promising a fitting night for her errand.

"Any brilliant ideas on how to get in there?" Sariah asked.

"Nary a one," Horatio said. "But I can't wait to hear yours."

Her voice's own softness surprised her. "Do you think Grimly has your son? Is that why you agreed to trail me?"

"What are you talking about?"

"Who did you try to bribe to find me? The forester? Alabara? I know Josfan followed me all along, but you're the better tracker."

Even as Delis and the Hounds surrounded Horatio Maliver, he kept to his gamble. His gray eyes revealed nothing.

"Don't you trust me, Sariah? Don't you remember that you were my prisoner once and I treated you well? That we played snakes and scorpions every day? That our one night together, I did well by you?"

"You did well for yourself, Horatio. There's a big difference."

"I saved your life the other day."

"And I had to wonder why."

"Do you really think I could betray you?"

He seemed so eager, so earnest that Sariah hesitated. It wasn't often she wanted to believe that however flawed, people could change; that friendship could offer a welcomed reprieve. It only happened on days like today, when her little belly weighted down her spine and her feet buckled from her lonely path; when fear lodged in her throat and danger, real and immediate, iced her every breath.

"Horatio," Sariah said. "You found me only to betray me."

Delis struck. With her executioner's efficiency, Horatio Maliver was out of his senses in an instant. Sariah had brought him as far as she could. She had given him every opportunity for redemption. He could have chosen to do right, to tell the truth. Meliahs knew, the journey had been long enough and he had had plenty of chances. Instead, he had chosen to undermine her before her friends and to continue with his deception. Even when he acted rightly, he did it for the wrong reasons. Sariah was sure he had saved her life because he had already sold it to Grimly.

He had been a calculated risk all along, but now she couldn't afford the danger of having him with her anymore. The Hounds retrieved their newest defector from the ground and secured him with knotted ropes. For the time being, Horatio Maliver would remain under guard at this very spot, screening Sariah's movements with his stillness. Soon thereafter, he would be on his way to spend the rest of his life serving the Hounds and learning the Wisdom's intricacies. Sariah couldn't help a sense of disappointed sadness. It was a better fate than the alternative. Or was it?

□ ■ □

"Are you sure you want to do this?" Sariah asked.

"*For a drop of your blood,*" the keeper said.

"*For a lick of your life,*" Torkel added.

Meliahs wouldn't be so kind as to grant her a break today. "How about you?"

"I go where you go, my donnis."

"It's nowhere nice, I can assure you," Sariah said.

"A trophy garden of noses and ears."

Were they really going to do this?

She handed out the small pouches she had carefully prepared. "Do you all remember what to do?"

Everyone nodded.

"Timing is very important."

What did you say to men and women you were sending to die?

"*May you die well,*" the keeper said.

Thirty-two

SARIAH FOUND THE well shack almost solely by its scent, a squat, dilapidated hut made of mud and rotting wood, leaning crookedly against the keep's wall. It was no bigger than a Domainer deck. She had made a calculated guess about its location outside the wall. She could have saved herself the trouble. Her nose alone would have guided her true.

The night was late. The business had been closed for hours. Sariah wasn't surprised when she spotted the watchmen. The Hounds neutralized them easily. Bound and senseless, they wouldn't be found until the next day at the earliest. Of course, the lowly watchmen didn't warrant a key for the well house, so the Hounds went to work on the padlock.

"This is a well house?" Delis whispered while the Hounds wrestled with the lock. "I wouldn't drink a drop in this town if it came from here."

"Dead water would be the safer choice." Sariah followed the keeper into the well shack and secured the door behind them. In the darkness, Torkel and his Hounds bent over the next set of bolts locking the well's wooden enclosure. Sariah uncovered her banishment bracelet and held her arm over the locks to give them light. It took the Hounds but a moment to pry open the trap door. A reeking cloud of methane burst from the well.

Delis pinched her nose. "It stinks worse than the rot."

"That's why I insisted we all bring Domainer weaves." Sariah stripped her mantle and set it aside. She was already wearing the weave beneath. She took a moment to fasten the scarf over her face. The others followed suit.

They climbed down the iron steps anchored into the well's walls. The descent was not difficult, but the rising fumes were unbearable. Sariah had to master the revulsion that threatened to undo her. She tapped on the stones tentatively, scattering the millions of cockroaches crawling on the wall. Her suspicions were confirmed. The keep's powerful wall wising didn't extend this far out. It made sense. The Guild's arrogance at work. No Guild wiser in their right mind would conceive tampering with, let alone voluntarily come close to, the stinking well.

She arrived at the last step on the ladder. She put in her foot, her ankle, her knee. Curse her luck. It was pretty full. She found bottom when the muck reached her waist. Talk about nasty wading. She started up the gradual incline of the dark and narrow channel which fed the well. At times, she had to turn on her side to fit. The others followed in single line.

"My donnis," Delis whispered. "Is this what I think it is? A shit hole?"

"The biggest around."

"Why would the Guild want to collect their shit in this hole?"

"The dung trade. It's quite profitable."

"The Guild sells their muck to these impoverished townspeople?" the keeper asked.

"By the pound of slush."

"But, my donnis, don't these people shit on their own?"

Sariah had to chuckle.

"For the crops, isn't it?" the keeper said.

"Aye, to produce the Guild's required yields, the land around here needs the help."

"You'd think the people should be weary of taking the Guild's crap," Delis grumbled. "And now you tell me they pay for the Guild's shit too? They deserve the stink."

"Shit is coin and the Guild likes coin."

"*What is coin but contempt's truest measure?*" Torkel murmured from down the line.

"How come you know so much about this, my donnis?"

"Pledge duty. Privy pipes."

Sariah had a memory of herself as a child, dangling from a rope strung through the privy seat, scouring the foul walls after a brutal bout with Mistress Ilian.

"Don't even think about stepping away from the rope," Ilian had said. "The gutter is deadly, that is, if the rats and the roaches don't eat you first."

She had never forgotten Ilian's sneer as she lowered a terrified Sariah into the stinking pit. She had used those memories to come up with this plan. She hoped she remembered everything.

"I'm glad I'm an executioner," Delis was saying. "The only time I get to clean shit is when my charge's death spurt drips on my boots."

The Hounds chuckled. They really appreciated Delis's warped sense of humor. They sobered up quickly. Up ahead, the red glow of Sariah's bracelet illuminated a thick set of bars built into a narrow arch, dividing a rounded chamber from the channel where they stood. It was as she remembered. It wasn't customary, and it wasn't necessary to do the job, but Ilian, the cruel witch, had dropped her all the way down there to frighten her beyond terror. The stinking muck pool trickled fluidly between the bars.

"Now the real work begins," Sariah said.

"We'll need to pry those bars from the wall," Delis said.

"This arch sits beneath the powerfully wised keep's walls. Touch the stone that anchors these bars and you'll die."

"Will you use your bursting stones, my donnis?"

"Rattle the bars and you'll die as well. An explosion in this place will kill us all."

Torkel fumbled through his pack. "We'll use the goddess's breath."

"Fire isn't the best of ideas down here," Sariah said. "The gas here is as combustible as the belch, as prone to explosion as a rot pit. Give the Guild some credit, Torkel. They weren't risking the keep in the least when they conceded to this narrow gutter."

With his enthusiasm brutally curbed, Torkel had the grace to look chastened and offended at the same time.

The keeper began to ask, "Then how will we—"

"This is a matter for stone."

Sariah worked quickly, attaching the stones she had brought onto the bars with weaved twine soaked in frog slime. The grill was about two spans wide and consisted of four vertical bars crossed by a dozen or so horizontal bars. She was careful not to touch the stone wall, placing her eight stones at the innermost bars' crucible, opposite to each other and above the muck line. She worked them two at a time, pressing her palms against the amplifying stones she placed in between, seeking the stones' primal heat and stoking it with her mind.

She had done this once before, in the Shield's fortress. It had taken her days. Now she was better prepared. Not only had she selected the darkest basalts she had been able to find, but the addition of the amplifying stone served as a speeding catalyst. Within a few moments, the first set of bars began to glow as red as her bracelet. As soon as the bars gave way, Sariah folded the melted metal out of the way with her weaved hands, and moved down to the next pair.

Delis whistled. Even the Hounds were impressed.

She was a bit dizzy when she was done. "Careful now." She climbed over the lower bars and slid sideways through the narrow opening. She motioned for the others to follow. "Whatever you do, don't rattle the bars." She breathed again only after the last man passed through.

"Your turn, Jol." Sariah pointed to the shaft overhead. "It's straight, narrow and slippery."

"We'll get you up." The keeper whispered a curt set of orders. Torkel planted himself beneath the shaft. The others surprised Sariah by coiling some rope around her waist and lifting her onto Torkel's well-muscled shoulders.

"All you have to do is keep your balance," the keeper said.

Balance wouldn't be a problem. She took a peek up the shaft. It was too narrow to allow for a fall. That's why the Guild used children to scrub the walls. Sariah was full grown now. She worried about getting stuck in there. The methodology for going up became clear an instant later.

"I go next." Delis puffed and grappled.

Beneath Sariah's boots, Torkel's shoulders strained with effort.

Delis tapped her calves. "Shift your feet to my shoulders."

Sariah rose up the shaft by Delis's full height. The Hounds

were building height with their bodies, propelling her upwards by intercalating one man at a time on top of the base man, the only possible point of insertion. She felt sorry for Torkel, bearing the tower's full weight at the bottom of the pile. She was glad for his strength.

The ascent had its moments. They struggled to fit in the narrow shaft, the Hounds and Delis more than Sariah, on account of their larger build. The human lift progressed. Illuminating the way with her bracelet's glow, Sariah kept count of the side shafts as she passed. She was thankful for each unoccupied privy seat.

At last, she arrived to the last side shaft, where the main tunnel ended. A burst of fresh air hit her face. She leaned to one side and saw the dark shape of the round privy seat framing a hint of silver light. Someone had left the privy turret's window open. Now she had to figure out how to climb up the last few paces of the secondary shaft.

The howl startled her into action. It was the night's first signal. Somewhere, a Hound was unwrapping his ward and beginning his run. The side shaft was slippery. Despite Sariah's efforts, she kept on sliding backwards.

"Can you give me a boost somehow?"

A whispered discussion ensued below and quickly thereafter, a count of three. The entire human structure where she stood flexed like a copper spring, launching Sariah a few feet into the side shaft, enough that she could grasp the privy seat's wooden edge with both hands. She hung there for a moment, gathering her strength for the final push.

She hauled herself up through the seat's opening, first the coil of rope, then an arm and a shoulder, then her head, then the other shoulder, until she was finally half-out of the shaft. Crawling up the privy shafts. There had to be an easier way. She had just managed to twist her hips out when a strangulated gasp echoed in the tiny chamber. Her head snapped up. Standing by the open door, a dark-robed stonewiser stared at her, openmouthed.

She read it all in his darkening eyes. Surprise. Disbelief. Had she fallen into the privy? Denial. Suspicion. He opened his mouth to call the alarm. By then Sariah's knee was anchored on the privy

seat and her stone was loaded in her whirling sling. Her shot found
his temple just in time to mute his cry. He crumbled on the floor
like a fallen boulder.

She rushed to drag him into the privy turret and closed the
door. She snapped the bolt shut, just in case. Hurry now. Her plan
had been three seconds away from being foiled. She tied the knotted rope to the window bars and dropped it down the shaft. Despite
the recent fright, she was amused when Delis's head popped out of
the privy, followed, one by one, by the keeper, Torkel and a host of
full-grown Hounds. Stinking, scraped, but smiling, they huddled
in the small turret like mischievous pledges plotting a prank.

"Saba?" Torkel gestured at the man on the floor. "You?"

"Make sure they don't find him for a while." He would have a
bad headache tomorrow.

Now to the second part of her plan. She cracked the door open
and scoured the deserted hallway. With the others in tow, she tiptoed down the hall to the first door on the right. She listened. As
she expected, no one was in the dressing room. The black stonewiser robes were folded neatly, stacked on floor-to-ceiling shelves
and organized by sizes. It took them all but a few moments to
change. They tucked their dirty weaves at the bottom of the laun-
dry pile.

Sariah was shocked when she saw her reflection in the mirror.
Dressed in the black robe, the stonewiser that stared back at her
was not really her, but rather her old self, the foolishly naïve lease
she had once been. The only thing missing was her stonewiser's
brooch.

No, nay, no. She was a different person now. The stonewiser in
the mirror was tanned and toned, slightly wider at the waist, wary
and alert. The gaudy bracelet was glowing on her wrist. She also
sported long bangs and plaited hair. So did some of her companions. That would be a sure giveaway.

"Wear a hooded mantle." Sariah grabbed one from the shelves.
Guild wisers were issued the additional garment during the chill.
It was the best concealment that she had been able to think of and
it would have to do. She took care to cover her bracelet's glow as
well.

If she remembered correctly, they didn't have too far to go. She marched her little party down the hall and up a circular set of stairs. It felt strange to walk these halls. She had once belonged here. Now she was an intruder.

"Where are we?" the keeper asked.

"We're in the Hall of Stones' living quarters," Sariah whispered. "This next floor is bound to be more active."

Indeed, at the top of the stairs, a pair of armed guards blocked their way.

"Halt, stonewisers," one of the guards said. "What's your business here?"

Sariah managed to keep her voice steady. "We've been summoned to the Prime Hand's quarters."

"At this hour?"

"The Prime Hand never sleeps."

The guard's pinched expression relaxed. "You know her well. Go ahead."

Sariah walked on. She didn't look back when she heard the guards' muffled grunts. They had been dutiful young men. Now they were dead.

The doors to the Prime Hand's chambers were to her right, flanked by additional guards. Sariah turned left and up a smaller set of stairs to reach a smallish door leading to the darkened gallery. There would be no eager pledges crowding the private gallery this late, no little future stonewisers waiting nervously for the Prime Hand's weekly admonishment. The keeper closed the door behind the last man and bolted it from the inside. There was no turning back.

Protected by the gallery's pitch darkness, Sariah and her companions crawled to the balcony's edge. Her hands were shaking. Her sight was blurred. Her heart was beating too hard. The first time she had stood in this gallery as a child, she had been sent to the box. The last time she had seen Grimly, the Prime Hand had commanded her death. Sariah had a sudden urge to run away from the keep, from the Guild she had renounced, from Grimly. Instead, she braced herself on the rail and looked down into the Prime Hand's private bed chamber.

Thirty-three

THE PRIME HAND'S bedchamber was an expansive, luxurious realm, contrasting in all ways with the average stonewiser's ascetic cell at the keep. A huge bed stood as the chamber's centerpiece, adorned by an exquisitely carved headboard and a heavy set of silk and velvet curtains. A massive table stood at the foot of the bed, directly beneath the gallery. There, sitting on a high-back chair and surrounded by a host of lit and perfumed candles, was Mistress Grimly.

From where she was, Sariah could see the top of the Prime Hand's head, the even crown of bristling white hair bent over the map spread on the table. There were others in the room, but Sariah's eyes were glued to the small white stone that moved of its own accord along the section representing the keep's wall on the map.

"Tell them to set a trap at the south bend," Mistress Grimly was saying. "She'll be there in moments. We have her now. She'll never know how we knew."

The mistress was wrong. Sariah had figured out that the tracking stone Horatio had put in her pocket had a matching stone, following her progress along on the mistress's map. It had been a risk, to allow the Prime Hand to track her that closely, but Sariah had wagered that Grimly wouldn't send her guard out of the keep for fear of Arron's Shield. She had been right.

"What's this?" Grimly said. "The stone has stopped. Do we have her? Well?"

A man's voice came from the window. "The fire signals indicate that they're looking. Wait. There's a change. No one's there."

"What do you mean?" the mistress said. "She was there a moment ago. She has to be there!"

Sariah let out a slow breath. With luck, the Hound running that track had buried the stone he carried and made his getaway.

"Look," the other stonewiser said. "She's moving again." The tracking stone was now on the opposite side of the keep, moving swiftly through the orchards.

"Tell them," the mistress said. "Hurry. They can trap her at the presses."

The man at the window played with his flares, conveying a new direction.

"She's too fast." The other stonewiser leaned over the Prime Hand's shoulder. "Look at her go. She's running straight for the ponds. She has nowhere to go."

It was one of the riskier tracks Sariah had devised. She wondered if it would work. The second howl of the night sent a chill down her spine.

"What's that?" the mistress asked.

"Wolves, I think."

All of a sudden, Sariah recognized the man's voice. A quick peek over the railing confirmed her suspicions. Julean, who had been Horatio Maliver's second in command when Horatio was the Main Shield, was now working for Grimly. He had been forced by the Prime Hand to take over the Shield's command when Horatio had deserted his post and abandoned the Shield in the battle against Arron at the broken wall. Not only was the Guild divided, but the Shield also had been split by Arron and Grimly's fray. Julean must have suffered more than defeat at his first command, because the scars of a terrible burn deformed a large patch on his cheek.

"Wolves?" the Prime Hand asked. "So close? Are you sure?"

"Tracks have been found," Julean said, "and a dead sheep last night, outside of town."

The Hounds were thorough in all they did.

"We'll catch her soon," Julean said. "She'll be brought into the keep as she deserves. In chains."

The tracking stone stopped again.

"What's happening now?" the mistress said. "Where is she?"

Sariah prayed for the Hound she had sent into the icy ponds. *Hurry*, she urged the next man. As if he had been listening, the stone moved abruptly to the other side of the ponds and began a rapid run.

"How could she go that far, that fast?" the mistress said. "Did she swim? Is she riding?"

"We've no report of horses," Julean said from his post at the window.

"We're going to lose her. Julean, those fools of yours are useless. Forget the flares. Go to your men and lead them yourself."

The clatter of Julean's boots on the floor announced his obedient departure.

"Worthless bunch of buffoons," the Prime Hand muttered. "Nothing's right since the Guild split."

"And all because of a rogue wiser," the other stonewiser said. "All of this because of Sariah."

"Ilian, refrain from foaming at the mouth for the moment, won't you?" the Prime Hand said. "You're here for the night, to witness Sariah's capture, nothing else."

Ilian? Sariah's mind spun with the shock. She dared another look over the balcony. She had been so keen on the tracking stone that she had neglected to identify the other stonewiser in the chamber. What was Ilian doing here? Ilian was Arron's creature; she wouldn't cooperate with the Prime Hand unless... Did Arron want Ilian to work with Grimly?

"Now?" the keeper asked.

The prospect of facing the Prime Hand had been frightening. The prospect of facing both Grimly and Ilian was daunting. It was not too late. Her baby's safety increased in direct proportion to her distance from the keep. Forget the beam. Someone else could finish the job. She had wised the seven twin stones. She had wised Leandro's game and the sages' statues. Wasn't it enough?

Two fortnights or the darkness of generations.

Twenty-seven nights had passed.

Sariah fortified the protective weave about her womb and fisted her hands around the rope the keeper had tied to the rail. She swallowed a gulp of fear and mouthed "Now."

□ ■ □

As kidnappings go, this one went as well as planned.

It took the Hounds but a moment to secure the chamber and the two women. The days of planning, the fear and anxiety, they were all worth it to see the surprise on Grimly and Ilian's bewildered faces.

"Is this a trap?" Ilian whirled on the Prime Hand. "We had an agreement, safe conduct to witness Sariah's capture. Arron will have your head for this."

"No, it's not a trap." The Prime Hand kept her calm. "Our dear Sariah has come home."

Home? Sariah couldn't believe her ears. "Those claws at your back must be making you delusional."

"Didn't you get my messages recalling you?"

"I got your messages fine, the ones that put a price on my head, the ones that bribed a good many for my capture."

"I sent people to look for you, that's true, but I never wanted you hurt. I wanted you safely returned."

"You mean like Horatio Maliver? You told him you had his son and he believed you."

"Given the proper motivation, I knew that Horatio would find you. I wanted to help you."

"With help like yours, who needs hindrance?"

"Now child, I warned you about the dangers. I told you about the violence of the world outside the keep." The mistress took a step towards Sariah. A flash of claws stopped her in her tracks. She ran a single finger over one of the Hound's blades. "Very clever. I see that you have some new friends. What happened to your old friends? Are these, err, gentlemen from the land beyond the Bastions?"

"I'm not inclined to lengthy conversation," Sariah said. "I came for something and you're going to help me get it."

"The beam, yes, of course. I'll be happy to take you there. I'm most anxious to know what that's about."

"I wager you know more than you're saying." Sariah nodded to Delis, who stepped up to knot a leather string with a large stone around the Prime Hand's neck. "I can make it burst with a thought, even if it's my dying thought."

The mistress only paled a little.

Ilian, on the other hand, had to be held down while Delis secured another bursting stone to her neck. "You should have shared Sariah's whereabouts with us," she said. "Arron's Shield could have found her anywhere in the Goodlands. Now you've gotten both of us caught. She's here to kill us. Can't you see?"

"Why would Sariah kill us if we give her no cause?" Grimly said. "She knows my death would mean the collapse of order in the Goodlands, the Guild's destruction. She wouldn't do that. She's a stonewiser."

Sariah opened the door and indicated that the mistresses should walk ahead of her. "If any of the guards approach us, command them to stay away. Any of my people die, and you die."

The mistress strode down the hall. "How did you do it? How did you mislead us into thinking you were in one place, when you were in another?"

Sariah kept a stubborn silence.

"Did you copy the wising? Did you give the stone to someone else to run it for you? No. It was moving too fast." The mistress's knowing smile fractured her wrinkled face. "Of course. I see it. Clever. You broke the stone into smaller parts and somehow managed to retain the full wising. You must have packed the stones in what? Soil? Then you timed the relay runs, to make sure only one section at a time was sentient to my tracking stone. The runners must have buried their stones when their time as decoys was up. Marvelous. Simply marvelous."

The woman's amusement irked Sariah almost as much as her skillful guesses. The mistress was no fool. She knew her craft. She was capable beyond the others.

They walked down to the courtyard and out through the keep's gardens. Sariah had expected to see the beam landing on the Hall of Stones, possibly over the Sacred Vaults, where the oldest and rarest of stones were buried under prohibition. But as they made their way down the steep, icy stairs, she could see that the beam had landed far from the Hall of Stones, on the other side of the keep, an area forbidden to most stonewisers in the Guild.

They walked through the keep's dormant gardens, powdered

with a fine dusting of snow. Despite the weather, Julean and a hundred of his men were waiting for them in the courtyard in front of a large portal. The brilliant beam made a spectacular background for such an uneven encounter.

Julean stepped forward. "Is there something amiss, Prime Hand?"

"Don't interfere with stone matters," the mistress said. "Stand aside. Let us pass."

Julean's scar trembled with the force of his clench, but he stepped aside. The Prime Hand banged on the iron portal. When it opened, Sariah and the others followed her through a narrow patio and entered a squat, marble building. With no windows inside, the place was dim and murky, illuminated only by a few smoky torches. Somewhere below, a door opened and closed. The tap of quick steps broke the tense silence. Two figures emerged from the dark, hand in hand, identical in all details and yet opposite.

"Welcome, mistress," a woman said.

"To the Mating Hall," the other woman said.

"We're pleased you've come," the first woman said.

"How can we serve you?" the second woman asked.

Sariah willed her mouth to close. These two women shared the same round eyes and full-lipped mouths, the same curly hair cut short just above the ear, and a similar build of bodies, broad shoulders and narrow hips. But one was black as onyx while the other one was pasty white like the dead. Standing there, holding hands, offering the same dimpled smile, they looked like parodies of each other, complementing and contrasting at the same time, eerie and somehow wrong.

"Belana, Telana," the Prime Hand said. "We've come to see the beam."

"The curse of light?" dark Telana said.

"The bloodless scourge?" white Belana asked.

"Without delay."

The women turned as one and led them down a marble staircase, through a door. They covered their eyes with their hands as they entered an underground chamber. The beam's brilliance hurt Sariah's eyes and broke the darkness of a room constructed entirely of the blackest granite. The light had burned a hole through the courtyard above. It was hot. The scent of stale sweat clung to every corner. Sariah motioned her Hounds to secure the chamber and approached the beam.

Aye. There it was. Just as she had expected. Illuminated by the beam, it lay on a round black granite table. Sariah admired the lively yellow and orange tones flaring in the angular construction, the way the sculpted stone refracted and dispersed the light, a naturally occurring prism. There was no doubt in her mind. This stone was part of the stone in the Dome of the Going, just like Leandro's game pieces.

She had a vision of her hand, returning the part to the whole in blessed reunion. She hesitated. Was it her duty to steal what was already stolen? Or was it her task to rescue the stolen from the thieves? Would she be freeing or destroying the truth with her deed? Was the tale she sought the seed for a new beginning or the revival of an ancient evil?

The Wisdom had given her no clear answers. She couldn't, wouldn't know, until it was all done. She snatched the stone from its perch so quickly that only when the beam retreated did the others realize what she had done.

The dark sister gasped. "It's gone."

"It no longer hounds me," the other sister said.

"What does it mean?" the Prime Hand asked.

Too many questions. Legions upon legions of questions. Later. Step by step, thought after thought. "We're leaving."

The sisters tried to stand in her way, but the Hounds didn't allow it.

"You can't take it," Telana said. "It's ours."

Sariah couldn't stand to watch the pain on the strange women's faces. She tucked the stone in her pouch and started out of the Mating Hall, trailed by Delis, the Hounds and her prisoners. Wails rose from the building's bowels, screams of pain and anguish that stuck to Sariah like suckered tentacles and tore her heart to shreds.

"Are you all right, my donnis? Do you want me to carry that thing?"

Sariah realized she was crying. "I'm fine, Delis, but we have to get out of here."

Julean and his men were waiting outside, swords unsheathed.

"Tell him to step aside."

The Prime Hand gasped when, at Sariah's behest, the stone at her neck singed her skin. "Back away," she hastened to say.

They trotted down the keep's main lane. Julean and his men kept up, encasing them from the sides and rear. Frightened faces peered from cracked windows and doors as they passed. Sariah could feel the urgency in her soul, her luck running out with the night, and the accursed stone heavy as a boulder in her pouch.

"Open the gate."

"Idiots, didn't you hear her?" Ilian shouted. "Open the damn gate."

Sariah's eyes darted from Ilian's flushed face to the Prime Hand. What she saw there surprised her. A warning?

"Don't open the gate."

The guards froze by the gate's levers. Sariah mounted the stairs to the gate bridge and peered over the crenel. Her heart jolted to her throat. She understood Ilian's uncanny presence at the keep now. Just in case Grimly's clever plan failed, on the other side of the gate, Arron and his Shield massed like an eel rave, waiting for her.

Thirty-four

DESPITE THE FEAR, despite the stone in her pouch, Sariah forced herself to think. Julean and the keep guard were behind her. Arron and his Shield stood before her. Arron wouldn't care if she blew the Prime Hand to pieces. In fact, he might prefer it. Would Ilian be enough leverage to let them pass?

If she couldn't get them out of the keep, Delis and the Hounds were as good as dead. Both Arron and Grimly would see little value in their lives. She couldn't take them back through the privies. By now, Julean had figured out how they came into the keep and would have secured the well. It was a matter of time before he started to kill her escorts one by one, to test her resolve. She looked at the men and women who had brought her this far, at their sweat-streaked faces. They were Meliahs' true faithful. They didn't deserve to die.

Sariah had given her plan thorough thought. The keep's walls were wised with centuries of protective layers reinforced each year by the strongest of wisers. The wall's wising couldn't be erased. Tampering with it resulted in death. No matter how strong the inscription, her bursting stones couldn't dent those walls. It was wits over craft on this one.

She had considered every aspect of the keep's layout, every possible point of entry and exit. The keep had been impregnable when she lived there. But she had learned to think differently, to be resourceful and flexible while living with Kael and his kin. That's how she had come up with her escape alternatives. The trouble was, one option would work for Delis and her Hounds but not for her, and vice versa. It took her but a moment to decide what to do next.

"Up the ramparts. Quickly."

The north tower was her closest choice. It was no less intimidating than the rest of the keep's walls, but it had advantages. First, the land there rose in a slight hill, shortening the distance to the ground. It was still a high jump, but Delis and the Hounds were stronger than the average man. Second, with the town's encroachment, the tanning vats were located beneath the tower.

"How did you ever think of this?" Delis leaned over the tower's battlements to look at the vats below.

"There was once a man, a thief, long ago, when I was little. They said he jumped from the north tower into the tanning vats. They said he broke both legs but made it alive. We can do better." Sariah tried to smile with confidence. "Torkel, hang the longest rope we can string together to lessen the distance. Hang it over that one." She pointed at the grossest of the tubs. "Cured skins are soaking in water with just a little liquor in that vat. It's less toxic."

"How do you know that?" Delis asked.

"Ilian, over there, she liked to send me out to the tanning vats for penance."

"Perhaps we ought to drop her down head-first?"

"*A moment for every deed and a deed for every moment,*" Sariah said. "Climb down until you run out of rope. Watch your legs when you jump. Those vats are not as deep as they look."

"You first, my donnis."

"If you make it, I know I'll make it."

"And if I don't make it?"

"I promise I'll find a safer way."

Nothing else would have made Delis jump ahead of her. Eager to test the drop for Sariah, Delis climbed down the rope without a fight.

"Won't you go next, saba?" Torkel said.

"You go ahead. Only I can make the stones at their necks burst."

The keeper was the last one to go. Sariah handed him her pouch with the prism in it. "Take this to the Bastions. Make sure it's safe. Wait until I arrive."

"You must do it," he said.

"You promised to obey me."

"Are you afraid to jump?"

"No. I can't jump. Trust me. I have good reasons."

"You must let me stay with you then."

"*Meek shall be the dragon at the foot of the stone.*"

"You're quoting the Wisdom to me?"

"*There is no wisdom greater than the Wisdom.*"

"Why are you sending me away?"

"*Fierceness in all things. Killing AND caring.*"

"But—"

"We have to secure the stone at all cost."

"Don't make me do this," the keeper said between his teeth.

Apparently, she was going to have to. She unsheathed her knife and pricked her forearm above the wrist. "Drink." She offered her welling blood. "Drink!"

Ilian looked like she was about to vomit.

The keeper's tongue lapped slowly at first, but then his resignation turned to anger and his lips sealed on the wound and sucked hard, a small, painful vengeance.

"That's enough." She snatched her arm away.

He fastened her pouch to his belt and went to the rope tamely, defeated, dejected. Sariah felt his pain, the clash of duty and loyalty, friendship and obligation, pride and submission.

"May you die well, my friend," she said.

The steel returned to his eyes. "And you."

□ ■ □

"Are you really not going to jump?" Ilian gaped.

Grimly smiled. "Didn't you hear what she said? She can't."

"Why not?"

"It's none of your concern," Sariah said.

"Oh, but it is," Grimly said. "Do you forget who gave you the means to achieve your ends?"

Sariah willed the Prime Hand to keep her mouth shut. She wanted to seal her lips with the heat of the bursting stone. Yet she still needed the woman to get out of the keep.

"She's going to kill us," Ilian stuttered hysterically. "Why else would she stay behind?"

"Don't be silly," the mistress said. "She won't do anything of the sort. She needs us."

"For what? She kills us and she jumps."

"Are you really that blind, Ilian?"

"Is she afraid of breaking her legs?"

"No, not her legs," Grimly said. "She's afraid of breaking the baby in her."

□ ■ □

Hackles rose on the back of Sariah's neck. An inexplicable urge to tear out the mistress's throat with her own teeth left her shaking with fury. Instinctively, she reached for the amplifying stone in her pocket and strengthened the protective weave around her womb. For as long as no one knew, the babe had been safely hidden in her body. Now, the cunning witch knew.

The mistress smiled. "You carry small, I give you that. But you're showing."

"She's—?"

"Aye. Our dear Sariah is with child."

Ilian stared. "You mean *willingly*?"

"What are you?" Grimly said. "Maybe four months along?"

Meliahs help her. The mistress was fingering the stone on her neck, studying Sariah's body as if she were a foaling mare.

"Down the stairs and to the right." Sariah conveyed a spark of heat to the hostages' stones as added persuasion. Ilian gasped. Sariah caught a glimpse of Julean's guards retreating at the bend ahead of her. She picked up her pace.

Mistress Grimly spoke. "If you're thinking about escaping the same way you and your New Blood friends did the last time—"

"Be quiet." Sariah had no doubt that the underground passage had been found and blocked after her escape.

"Why are you so eager to leave?" the mistress said. "The keep is your home. The Guild is your kin. You're welcome to stay here and live in the safety you deserve. Aren't you tired?"

She was tired. Of the journey, of the intrigues, of the intricacy, of running away and seeking and planning and hurting and anticipating, of knowing and not knowing, of trusting and not trusting. She also knew that she had to get out of there. She turned into the

secondary corridors behind the kitchens. The mistresses were lost
in the maze of narrow servant passages, but because she had spent
hours on end doing penance in the kitchen, Sariah knew them by
heart.

"Even if you find a way out," the mistress said, "Arron will be
waiting for you on the other side."

"Then we'll see how much he values Ilian here."

Ilian croaked. She didn't know either.

"Understand, child," the Prime Hand said. "As things stand, I
can't protect you from Arron if you go outside the keep."

Sariah had no delusions that anyone would protect her here.
It was up to her now. Up ahead, she spotted her destination—the
beggars' vent. It was one of a set of four small, square openings
in the wall, typical of the keep's architecture, designed to circulate fresh air through the stifling back kitchens. Over the years,
overworked servants had sneaked in bundles of kindling into the
kitchens without having to maneuver the stairs and the long march
to the sheds. Under the cover of the encroaching town's back alleys,
beggars offered bark, dry sticks, cones, and the likes in exchange
for leftovers. As a child, Sariah had been a party to a few of those
exchanges.

Idle servants scattered like roaches when they saw the black
robes. Sariah had been right. Delis and the Hounds couldn't sneak
out this way. The wall's protective wising wouldn't allow a living
body to pass through the vents. But with a little work, she would.

She put a kitchen stool under the vent and placed the two small
stones she had prepared at either side of the window.

"You first," she said to Ilian, "and don't even think about fleeing when you get to the other side, because my mind can reach a
ways."

Ilian climbed on the stool reluctantly. "But the wising. It won't
let me pass—"

"Do as I say."

"You've wised those two stones to serve as a buffer, haven't'
you?" Grimly said. "They can't affect the wising in the stone, but
they can affect the empty space in between. They're triggered by

your wiser core. That's why you can get Ilian and yourself through, but not your friends. Marvelous. Well done."

As if Sariah needed the Prime Hand's praise. She climbed on the stool herself, gave Ilian a boost to make it through the vent, and watched as the woman cursed, slid headfirst down the wall and landed clumsily in the mud.

"You've learned so much since the last time we met," Grimly said. "You're a treasure, a wiser marvel."

"Not that it did me any good when I lived here." Sariah braced herself at either side of the vent. A little heave and she would be through.

"You must understand," the mistress said. "It's difficult for me. I can't let you go."

"You have no choice."

"But I do have a choice," the mistress said. "An easy one." She struck.

Pain burst from Sariah's ankle and shot up her spine, a bolt of stinging fire. She looked down to find the mistress's hand clutching her leg. Damn the witch, she had killed herself. Sariah commanded the stone to explode.

There was no explosion, no burst of stone and flesh. The only thing that happened was that the strength ebbed from her body, until her hands withered like dead flowers and her knees failed. Next she knew she was on the floor in Grimly's arms.

Why hadn't the stone burst? Sariah's eyes shifted from the mistress's wrinkled breast to the new faces appearing around her. Guards. The memory of the Prime Hand's long fingers toying with the stone at her neck flashed in her mind. The witch had disabled the stone's inscription. How?

"Don't struggle," the mistress said. "Try to relax. That was a very clever plan you had. But you made one small miscalculation, my dear. Do you know what it was?"

The world was spinning. Her spine was on fire.

The mistress smiled. "You forgot that you're not the only one capable of learning new tricks."

Thirty-five

FOR DAYS SARIAH sat in an isolated cell awaiting news of her fate. The guards had stripped her stones and weapons and manacled her to the wall, just in case she had devised a way to wise the lock away, she supposed. Unfortunately, she hadn't. Frustrated, she watched the silvery haze's advance on her bracelet's red crystals, cursing every precious hour wasted in her solitary confinement.

She had plenty of time to chide herself for her mistakes. Despite knowing that the Prime Hand was dangerous, she had fallen prey to the witch's cunning. Grimly had used the last year and a half wisely. How many of Sariah's wising discoveries had she mastered? What other new or ancient skills had she incorporated into her impressive capabilities?

She had been so close to making her escape. She had secured the prism, but she had to wise it, soon, before it was too late. What if the executioners learned she was trapped by the Guild? Worse, what if they assumed she was dead? She couldn't know for sure, but there was a high probability that the keep walls' formidable wising could prevent Mia from sensing Sariah at all. She had to find a way to get a message to Kael. She wasn't ready to surrender Ars and neither should he.

Why wasn't she dead? She should be. Her death would effectively end the threat to the Guild's rule and the search for stone truth. It made no sense that she lived on. And what about her baby? She had pledged to herself that if she was able to finish her business, she would find a way to sit out of danger and give the child a chance. Instead, in a moment of stupidity, she had forfeited both their lives.

A clatter of steps sounded outside. Finally, after all those days, a key turned in the lock and the door opened. Wordlessly, Julean and his guards flooded the cell. She was trussed, gagged, hooded and dragged down the steps to yet another room. She recognized the place when the hood came off. The black granite room. The Mating Hall. Word was that Guild wisers came here when ordered to procreate. She was already well on her way. Why had they brought her here?

The chamber was as warm as she remembered. The damage the beam had done in the ceiling had been repaired. Julean's guards forced her into an oversize stone chair, a strange contraption sporting an angular back and a wide seat with a hole in the middle. Fighting them only gained Sariah a cuff to the face. None too gently, they strapped her hands above her head and then roped her knees and calves to the chair's massive legs. Julean checked the bindings before he and his men marched out of the chamber. The two strange sisters stood to one side, holding hands, watching her with oddly rounded eyes.

"I'm afraid it's not very comfortable," the white sister said.

"A birthing chair is practical rather than comfortable," the dark sister said.

A birthing chair? Why was she strapped to a birthing chair? Her baby was hardly half-grown in her womb and she was nowhere near her term. Sweat trickled down Sariah's back. What were they going to do?

Grimly swept into the room like a queen entering her castle. "What a sight," she said, a little breathlessly. "The dream of a goddess. The gift of a lifetime. Hello, Sariah, welcome to the Mating Hall." With a twist and a tug, she ripped the gag out of Sariah's mouth.

Sariah moistened her parched lips. "Why have you brought me here?"

"Patience, child," Grimly said. "All will come to pass, as it must, in time. I thought perhaps you'd want to talk before we proceed. You might want to convince me that you're sorry. You could recant the bulk of your wisings. I could be fair, and you could be useful."

"Useful?" Sariah said. "How?"

"You could trust me," Grimly said. "You would, if only you knew how well I love you."

"Like a carter loves his mule?"

Grimly's stare fell on her with a cudgel's force. "Has it ever occurred to you that there's more at stake than just your puny little life? Have you ever considered that *my* investment in you must be saved? No. You have it easy. You go about making judgments from half-tales and half-truths. You take it upon yourself to criticize, without having the responsibility of rule. You speak of problems but you offer no solutions. You've seized the easy lot in life."

"Then why am I the one persecuted and about to be executed?"

"Do you think yourself infallible?"

"Infallible?" Sariah had to laugh. "More like constantly fallible, as my being here shows."

The mistress sighed. "Why won't you heed me?"

"Why would I?"

"To preserve your life. To protect your baby's life."

Now the bargaining started. Only Sariah wasn't willing to trade, not when she knew that the mistress's scale was always weighted to favor the Guild. Sariah didn't need a bargain. She needed a way to escape the keep, reach the Bastions and wise the prism's tale.

"Oh, don't tell me," the Prime Hand said. "You think your baby's better off dead than in the Guild's hands? Is that it?"

The words "baby" and "dead" were excruciating in the same sentence, but she didn't give the mistress the satisfaction of wincing. Life as a pawn in the Prime Hand's games was an insult to Meliahs and a betrayal to the stones. Death was a horrid fate for her child, but Guild-raising, a life at the keep, that was worse than death.

"I told the Council," the mistress said. "Execution would be a reward to the likes of you. A death by stoning, gruesome as it is, would be a vindication to you and yours. To be rid of you would be a great relief to them. But then, there's Arron and his little revolt to consider, and those silly people out there, and some of the others who have been disquieted by your adventures."

Others? Did she mean other stonewisers?

"But death doesn't always mean defeat," the mistress said.

"Meliahs knows what can come out of your execution. You're better off defused, like your bursting stone."

How had the mistress defused her bursting stone? She must have found a weakness in her wising. What was it? Sariah knew she had imprinted the stone correctly. She'd had plenty of anger. She'd had purpose as well. Where had she failed to lock her wising?

Her eyes widened with the realization. The weakness had not been in her wising. It had been in herself. She disliked killing with stones, and that hesitation must have translated into her wising as a small speck of doubt. Grimly must have grabbed on to that tiny break in her wiser's will and used it to defuse the stone. Sariah had built her own undoing into her most powerful weapon, and in doing so, she had sabotaged herself.

"So the pupil realizes, belatedly, that the mistress still has much to teach?" Grimly's smile held no warmth. "I've spent a lifetime serving the Guild. And in penance, Sariah, so will you."

□ ■ □

The mistress turned to the sisters. "Belana, Telana, do you like the treat I've brought you?"

The sisters looked down on Sariah as if she were their newest toy.

"She's pretty," Telana said.

Belana touched Sariah reverently. "And soft."

"But not harmless," Grimly said. "She must be curbed at once."

Belana admired Sariah's belly. "It's quite grown."

"I told you she's already breeding," the mistress said. "How far along?"

Belana's cold hands slid beneath Sariah's robe. It angered Sariah that anybody, let alone this creepy wench, would dare touch her and her baby without leave. It struck her like a mace to the teeth that, tied as she was, she could do nothing about it.

"I think she's about five months, maybe a little more." Belana sniffed along Sariah's pubis. "A boy, I think. Aye. Male spirit scent."

How could the wretch know that?

A boy. How happy Kael would be to have a son. Would she ever have the opportunity to tell him?

"She's of the best blood." Grimly unrolled a long parchment on a nearby desk. Sariah craned her neck, but she couldn't spot anything helpful beyond a myriad of lines and letters.

Belana traced the lines. "Oooooooooh."

"We couldn't have done better ourselves," Telana said.

"You see now how important this is?"

Telana scratched her head. "But how will we do it without—"

The mistress's eyes narrowed to slits. "Do you doubt me?"

"No, no, but—"

"Then put your trust in me and forget about the rest. How long will it take?"

How long would what take?

"Hard to say," Telana said.

"Very hard," Belana added. "A month, maybe?"

"That's too long."

"We'll do our best," Telana said.

"But not too much, too soon," Belana said.

"We've seen what can happen."

"It's terrible what can happen."

"I don't want any mistakes," the mistress said. "It's important. Do you understand?"

It annoyed Sariah that both women nodded exactly at the same time. The way they talked irritated her as well. Their high-pitched nasal voices reminded Sariah of little girls pretending to be adults. They talked in tandem; by Meliahs, they moved in tandem. It was very strange to watch them holding hands all the time, as if they drew confidence from each other's touch.

"Let me know when she's curbed and safe," the Prime Hand said.

"Do you wish her hands cut?" Telana asked.

Sariah had to swallow the strangled cry in her throat. Her hands. Cut?

"Perhaps later." The mistress's casual glance was a promise. "I might want to capitalize on her unique gifts." Grimly's lips were cold on Sariah's forehead. "Be nice, Sariah. Nice pays off down here. It saves hands. And lives."

□ ■ □

As soon as the door closed behind the Prime Hand, the two sisters turned to Sariah, grinning like cats on the prowl.

"She's gone," Telana whispered.

"That's good," Belana said.

"Say something." Belana sniffed Sariah's mouth. "She smells like sweet cream and warm cakes. Please, say something."

"Don't harm my baby."

The words came out so calm and clear that Sariah didn't realize she had said them until the sisters grabbed each other's hands reflexively.

"We swear, we don't want to."

"Harm your baby."

"We're sorry, little sister."

"We do as we must."

They spoke in relay, one after the other as if they knew what the other was thinking.

"Can you release me from my bonds?" Sariah asked.

Faces similarly stricken, both sisters shook their heads.

"We're sorry."

"It's not possible."

"We must do as we're told."

"We are what we are."

Telana turned her attention to a small side table in the corner. An extensive collection of instruments blanketed the table—knives, scalpels, scrapers, picks. Telana selected a pair of massive scissors and crouched between Sariah's knees.

Sariah's heart skipped wildly. "Wait. What are you doing? Stop."

Belana petted Sariah's hair and held her hand, just as Telana's creaking scissors emerged over her belly, ripping her robe into halves. *Now.* Sariah clutched Belana's pale hand. Now, or she would never get out of this rot pit alive. She struck. Stone wrath.

"What's that?" Telana's scissors froze in midair.

"Oooooooh." Belana's mouth was stuck uttering the modulated sound. With her eyes wide open and her pale lips puckered, she looked like a thick-lipped fish.

Why wasn't it working? Why wasn't the stone wrath searing Belana through and through?

"That's nice," Belana finally said. "Thank you."

"How do you do that?" Telana asked.

Sariah couldn't help but stare from one sister to the other. What had just happened? Could one sister experience what the other was feeling? She had issued her most vicious jolt of stone wrath and Belana hadn't dropped to the ground writhing like a starving maggot. On the contrary, she seemed... pleased by it?

Telana's black eyes hardened on Sariah. "I don't think she meant it nicely."

Sariah stared. "Who are you?"

"We are what we are," Telana said. "You, on the other hand, are trouble."

She removed the halves of Sariah's robe, exposing her body to the sisters' scrutiny. Her round belly emerged from concealment, framed by her full breasts and her pubis's tight curls. Sariah flushed with embarrassment, but the other women admired her, unabashed.

"Long legs," Telana said.

"Lovely flesh." Belana cupped her breasts.

"Get your hands off me."

Belana pouted. "Do you mean it, little sister? You don't want me to touch you?"

"I'm not your little sister." It was simply impossible to reconcile the sisters' apologies with their deeds.

To Sariah's surprise, Belana began to cry, a revolting vision of black ink spilling from her tear ducts. Sariah saw what she hadn't seen before. A milky film floated over the pale sister's pupils, matching the rest of her whiteness. Belana was blind.

"But I must touch you," Belana was saying. "Please. Let's be friends. Why won't you be my friend?"

It was Telana's fierce clutch on the scissors that convinced Sariah. She didn't want her baby ripped out from the womb by the avenging sister.

"Don't cry," Sariah said. "You're making your sister sad."
"You'll be my friend?"
Sariah buckled under Telana's black eyes. "I can try, but friends don't tie friends up and cut off their clothes."
"I'm sorry." Belana wiped black tears from her face.
"It must be," Telana said.
"But before and after, we can be friends."
"Before and after what?" Sariah asked.
Belana's eyes widened.

Thirty-six

THE SISTERS WORKED with ruthless efficiency. Sariah watched as clumps of her long brown hair joined her ripped robe on the floor. She was keenly aware of the dangerous blades the sisters wielded, of her complete vulnerability, of blind Belana shaving her head by touch only, and of Telana, shearing her pubis as if she was but a woolly lamb.

"Shiny like a silver spark," Belana said.

"Smooth like a kitten's belly," Telana said.

Sariah ground her teeth. The Guild's tidiness rules applied doubly at the mating hall and the sisters were joyful enforcers. They examined every inch of Sariah's body.

"What do you make of this?" Telana tugged on her banishment bracelet. "I can't get it off."

Sariah managed to suppress her gasps, but she flinched with every twist of Telana's savage pliers.

"You better stop." Belana fingered the bracelet. "It somehow hurts her. I'm not sure it's worth the trouble anyway. It takes more than it gives. It's not a source for her."

An exasperated Telana dumped the pliers on the table. "That's good, because it can't be unclasped." She seized Sariah's hands. "What about this?"

Belana ran the tips of her fingers over Sariah's palms. "Ooooooh." She admired the scars. "Powerful protection."

But not powerful enough to protect Sariah from the sisters' graters. They scraped the center of her palms, in the middle of the triangle within the oval scars. Sariah tried to resist, to fist her bloody hands and strike with stone wrath, but she discovered that the human hand was not very strong when bound palm-up at the wrist and that the sisters liked it when she tried to strike them with her stone wrath. They actually enjoyed it.

"You can do it again if you want," Belana said.

"Soon you won't be able to do it anymore." Telana inserted a small wised stone in the center of Sariah's whittled flesh.

A white flash jolted Sariah's body. Every nerve in her hand awoke to an excruciating burning and found a twin in her mind. Her fingers cramped. It was worse when Telana did the same to her other palm. A slow and gradual blankness descended on her wiser's core, as if her links had been severed.

A wave of panic crashed on Sariah. Without a sense of her wiser's core, her body didn't know how to function. She couldn't think. She couldn't breathe. If not for Belana's perfumed mouth covering hers and blowing hot air into her deflated lungs, she would have suffocated on the spot.

It must have taken her a while, but by the time Sariah learned how to breathe on her own again, Telana was strapping a strange contraption to her hands, a snug copper and leather encasing that pressed on the stones buried in her palms.

"A wiser's muzzle." Telana locked it with a tiny key and applied a blue flame to the keyhole, welding it shut. "It will keep you from trouble, which means we can preserve your hands for the moment."

Sariah didn't know such a contraption existed. The muzzle extended from the bend of her fingers' lower knuckles to the wrist. She was having trouble thinking. It was as if her palms were gone from her senses and her wiser's mind had been trapped behind solid walls, as if the ground had been kicked from under her feet and she was freefalling.

"She's properly curbed," Telana said. "Do we put her with the others?"

"I wish we could keep her with us," Belana said.

"She's the one who's created all the mess. We wouldn't want her talking to the others."

"What if we curb her voice?"

"That should keep her out of mischief."

The conversation didn't make any sense. How could they possibly curb her voice?

The sisters' palms pressed against Sariah's throat. A stone was lodged in between her skin and theirs. A quiet murmur. A rush of heat. A feeling of faintness. Sariah opened her mouth to protest. No sound made it through. Astounded, she tried again. Nothing. She wanted to scream, yet she couldn't even whimper. What had they done to her?

The sisters released her bonds and slipped a strange garment over Sariah's head. It was a short, thin, low-backed white cloth that fit her loosely. Translucent and without seams, it offered little warmth and no privacy. Then, the sisters supported her through a heavy pair of iron doors and into a small chamber fitted with black hangings.

Telana rang a bell.

Belana kissed her. "We'll see you soon."

Then they abandoned her, weak, hurting and alone, in the black veiled room.

□ ■ □

The woman who came through the curtains was similar to Sariah in many ways. She was about the same age, devoid of hair, large with child and as shockingly dressed as she was. She also wore a pair of hand muzzles. The difference was that she could move on her own and that she was smiling.

"I'm Lexia." She helped Sariah to her feet. "I'm going to take you downstairs. You're too far along to be new, but I've never seen you before. Have you just arrived?"

Sariah opened her mouth and found her voice gone. Vexed, she nodded and pointed to her throat.

"You are new. The little vixens took your voice, didn't they? They don't want you speaking to us. Well, at least they didn't take your tongue. Ask Pru, life's tough without a tongue."

They had taken somebody's tongue? Sariah leaned on Lexia and made it out into the strangest of places. A narrow corridor towered above a lower level divided by thick walls into separate spaces. Sariah was shocked when she looked down directly below her. Thirty or forty women were looking up at her, all dressed in the loose-fitting garment, pregnant and hairless like she was.

"The holding pen," Lexia said. "We wait here."

Wait for what? Sariah wasn't thinking very clearly but she managed to point at her belly and then at the women.

"Aye, they're all pregnant or waiting to be bred. What else would you expect at the Mating Hall?"

The Mating Hall. Reality exceeded its foul reputation. The windowless, stark chamber was lined sparsely with cots and tables bolted to the floor. Fires for light and warmth hung high above. The women were mostly quiet, following her slow progress down the steep staircase.

"The men are on the other side of the wall," Lexia said. "Don't ever go that way. They're kept ready, poor chaps. They're no more than high-strung bulls down here. Those are the breeding stalls."

Sariah missed a step.

"Don't worry. You won't be going there for a while yet."

Who had conjured a nightmare like this? She had known the Guild was fickle and devious, but this was beyond reason, beyond indecency and cruelty.

They made it down through two guarded gates. The women glanced her way, a few with a spark of interest, the majority with vacant stares that spoke of desolated minds. Lexia led Sariah to sit on one of the cots and furnished her with a cup of cold tea. Sariah's hands were heavy, painfully stiff and trembling, but she managed a sip. Lexia proved adept at deciphering Sariah's gestures.

"You want to know how long I've been here? About five years, I think, since my master repudiated my lease and I was sent here. They said I had good blood. Look here." Lexia turned and displayed her backside without a trace of modesty. Four vertical lines were etched above her buttocks. "I've earned my keep. I've birthed four wiserlings."

Wiserlings? Is that what they called their babies? She glanced around the chamber, looking for the telltale sign. At the edge of the low-backed garments, most every woman sported at least a scar or two etched on her lower back. Some had many more than two. What of their children's fates? During her time at the keep, there had never been more than two or three children gifted to the Guild each year. What happened to all of their offspring?

"You get used to it." Lexia patted her arm. "It's better than being a beggar, don't you think? Better than being dead?"

There had to be a way out of here. How many guards watched over the pen? When did the guard change? Who kept the padlock's keys?

"There's no escaping this place. Save yourself the grief. If you try, you'll fail. And when they catch you, they'll punish you horribly. Look at Violet over there. The one ready to burst. See? No hands."

Didn't they know that wisers went mad without hands?

"She's already half-mad. They're just waiting for her to farrow and she'll be gone for good. Now sleep. You'll need your strength in the days to come. By the way, not that it matters much down here, but what should we call you?"

Sariah traced the letters of her name on the cot.

"S-A-R-I-A-H." Lexia frowned. "Sariah? Formerly of the Hall of Scribes' sixty-sixth folio?"

How did the woman know her name?

Lexia buried her face in her hands. "If they caught you, what hope is there for us?"

□ ■ □

Sariah lay wearily on the cot, yet unable to sleep. The fires had been put out. Darkness veiled the day's shocking sights. A cot nearby creaked under a heavy body, accompanied by a muted whimper. Unable to wise, cut off from her wiser's core, trapped, humiliated, forgotten. This place was a stonewiser's worst nightmare. What horrors awaited the women's children once born? Sariah corrected herself. This place was foremost, a mother's worst nightmare.

She fisted her aching hands. They throbbed at the pulse of her glowing bracelet. She had to get out of here and fast. But first, she had to restore some of her essential links. Mia's healing practices. Would they work for her too? She closed her eyes and turned herself inward. There was work to do.

□ ■ □

Sariah tapped her fingertips against Lexia's and watched the woman's pupils. There. A slight dilation. Good. The mix was working. By combining the stone tapping she had learned from Malord with what Mia had shown her about stone healing, Sariah had succeeded in restoring at least some of Lexia's essential links.

Lexia's eyes brimmed with tears. "I still can't believe you can do this. How?"

Adding one of her unique skills to the mix, Sariah send a sequence of leveled emotions through her fingertips. *Perseverance. Self-reflection. Concentration.*

Lexia gasped. "Did you just use emotion to speak to me?"

Aye. She had just created an alternative way of communicating with the women. She couldn't tell if Lexia got it completely, but she repeated it, slowly this time, for her benefit.

"Amazing," Lexia said. "All this, with your fingertips only?"

Sariah gestured for Lexia to try it on her. It took Lexia a little while to master the tapping, but when Sariah surged above the pain and finally felt the weak connection come to life in her mind, she grinned. From their usual posts at their respective looms, the rest of the women smiled in quiet delight. Sariah crossed her lips with her finger to remind them that this had to be their secret, but she was as happy as they were, especially when she noticed some of the women's vacant stares flickering back to life.

"Hey, you," a guard barked from the railing above. "Move on, will you? The mistress told us all about you. Don't try your tricks on us."

She walked obediently on to the next loom, carrying along a full basket of black skeins. It was the best pretext she could find to circulate among the women working the Guild's looms. Although it was extremely dangerous, it allowed her the rare occasion to work one on one with each woman.

It wasn't as if she was able to restore the women's ability to wise. The muzzles, combined with the blocking stones implanted in their palms, contained the bulk of the wising functions with brutal efficiency. They also penalized any attempt at fooling the stones with mind-numbing pain. Stone tapping, however, was not a common wising function. Neither were the related finger tapping, the link healing, and the emotion infusions that Sariah had devised. She had wagered that since the Guild didn't teach those, the muzzles weren't designed to restrain those skills. She had been right.

She had only been able to teach stone tapping to a handful of women thus far, but the discovery had changed the chamber's mood. Smiles graced the previously desolated faces, and the occasional giggle could be heard in the work chamber. There was interaction among the captive group, meals shared and secret gatherings after dark where the women tried to revive their truncated links. There were even occasional whispers hidden by the creaks and taps of the levers and pedals that powered the Guild's upright looms.

How strange. Sariah had never once wondered where the black cloth the Guild used to make the stonewisers' robes came from. Now, every day when she followed the other women into the adjoining workshop and sat before her assigned loom, she wondered how many Guild wisers knew that they wore the product of their peers' forced labor and sweat.

"Someone's looking for a paddling today," another guard said from above. "Your loom has been idle too long, woman. You want me to call the mistress?"

No. Sariah didn't need the mistress's attention at the moment. She hurried on to the next loom. She had something else she wanted to do, but the guard was right. She couldn't stay away from her own loom much longer. Failure to deliver the required cloth yield resulted in a paddling proportional to the lapse, ten strikes per yard missing. She knew the sting of the punishment well enough. It was painful, humiliating, and effective. In deference to her bottom's tenderness, she was becoming a most proficient weaver.

Sariah offered the basket to Pru. Pru sank her hands in it as if rummaging for a good skein. Sariah made as if to help, all the while tapping her fingertips against Pru's beneath the sea of yarn. Without a tongue, Pru had not been able to express herself in years.

Perhaps because of that, she had become quite proficient at finger tapping very fast. Sariah braced to try yet a new combination. She called on her imprinting skills, the same process she used to infuse a stone with a tale. Then she shaped the images she needed in her mind, and, testing the tale's reach, tapped it against Pru's fingertips.

Without a stone, the images had no staying power. The tale found no solid lodging and therefore evaporated quickly. But Sariah was counting on the human mind, and more specifically, on Pru's well-honed memory. She allowed the snippets of images to flow. The Guild's Council. Mistress Grimly's face. Master Arron. A short sequence of the bloody battle at the wall. A quick sight of Targamon's bubbling rot. A memory of the fragmented Council meeting at Arron's tent. Then her own thoughts in the form of an opinion: *It's not right.*

With a faint nod, Sariah settled the basket in Pru's lap. Pru understood. It was her turn. She grabbed the basket and went down the loom rows, repeating the process Sariah had created, sharing the images with the others. Sariah returned to her loom as proud as a Domainer teacher.

"This is crazy," Lexia whispered, after her exchange with Pru. "How do you know all that?"

"Is this true?" Lexia's loom neighbor, Celia, mumbled.

"These must be your own projections." Trea said what they were all thinking.

Sariah shook her head. Without their wising abilities fully restored, the women couldn't probe her wising to ensure that she was telling the truth. Instead, Sariah had to find some other way to gain their trust. She put her fisted hand to her heart.

"Wiser's oath?" Lexia whispered. "You're swearing on your stonewiser's pledge?"

"Do you think you're doing us a favor?" Violet stomped on the pedals of her beater violently. It was a wooden contraption that punched the ready weft and tightened the weave, the only job remotely adapted for a woman without hands. "This is too dangerous. If they figure out what we're doing—"

"You're just irked because you can't do it yourself," Lexia said. "This is the best thing that has happened to us in a long time. Please, Sariah, don't take it away from us."

As if Sariah could. Once stimulated, the revived links were active again. Sariah reached out and tapped her fingertips against Violet's arm, issuing a quick burst of emotion. Compassion was most likely what came through to Violet, although Sariah tried to convey a sense of peace as well.

The pain that struck her in the arm left her reeling with shock.

"Keep your hands to yourself!" The guard cracked his lash again, this time against Violet's shoulder. "Or do you want another taste of the lash, dears?"

Sariah rubbed the sting of the vicious welt swelling along her arm, making a conscious effort to stop her body from trembling. She had almost gotten caught. She bent over her loom, nauseous with dread and stole a look at Violet. Violet was beating the pedals as if she were crushing scorpions under her feet.

It was only hours later, during the guard shift change, that Lexia dared a whisper. "Hey. Sariah. Sariah!"

Sariah glanced at the parapet above and then back at Lexia.

"Could these be used as weapons?" Lexia twirled her fingers under her tucked chin.

At last. They understood. Sariah was happy that the women enjoyed their newfound skills, but enjoyment wasn't the reason for her efforts. She stole another glance at the guards, and, finding them busy, she pointed to her fingertips, to herself, and shook her head. Because of the muzzles, alone none of them could create enough of a jolt to stun a guard. But together—she swept her hand in a wide circle—they might be able to do something.

"You mean like escape?" Lexia asked.

That's exactly what Sariah meant. Disable the guards with concentrated communal jolts of power. Escape the keep. But she couldn't dare an attack on the guards with only a few women able to tap. To succeed, she needed to teach all the women.

"We could try," Celia whispered.

"I don't know," Trea muttered under her breath. "They'll kill us if they find out."

"It's a better option than this," Cara said.

"We could flee the keep and quit the Guild. Sariah did it. We could live on our own."

"And eat what? Shoe soles for dinner?"

"At least we'd have shoes."

"I'd settle for shoes," Lexia said. "Hush. Here come the guards."

They waited for the pair to pass.

"We could keep our babies," Celia murmured.

"What would you do with a snotty wiserling?"

"We could wise stones again."

The mere notion silenced the wide-eyed group.

Sariah tapped her temple. They had to think this through. It was risky. They would have to act in concert. She waited until another pair of guards marched over them before reaching out and tapping a few quick images against Lexia's fingertips.

"Outside?" Lexia said. "We need to find out what's going on outside the Mating Hall?"

Sariah nodded. Timing was very important. If they were going to succeed in their escape, they needed to know as much as they could about the keep and its surroundings.

"Information is hard to get in here," Lexia said, but her eyes, along with the other women's stares, were on Celia.

Celia blushed.

"Your guard," Lexia said. "Not that there's much talking when the two of you meet. You could trade your, errr, services for more than apples."

"But I like apples!"

"Think of it," Lexia said. "We could all be free of the Mating Hall."

Quiet fell on the chamber, ominous and expectant.

A small version of Celia's voice broke the silence. "I suppose I could try."

Sariah breathed a sigh of relief.

"Our luck may be changing," Lexia whispered. "Not only have we learned finger tapping, but there hasn't been a summons in days."

A *summons?* Sariah mouthed.

"The sisters. They haven't worked on us at all. With the golden prism?"

Did the sisters use the prism to intimidate these women? Apparently so, judging by the terrified expressions on their faces. Sariah pointed to herself and waved a hand in the air.

"You took it?" Celia gaped. "You couldn't have."

"You're lying," Violet said.

"Is it gone? Are you sure?"

Violet sneered. "It may be gone now, but it'll be back. Those two can't live without it. And the mistress, she'll go after it with a vengeance."

Sariah prayed the keeper was safe and well on his way to the Bastions.

"What's the meaning of this?" Julean stood at the gate, glaring. "Have you all decided that the Guild doesn't need its share of good cloth? Stop chatting and work those looms, you idle sluts."

The women's attention returned to the looms. Except Sariah's. She met Julean's glower and regretted it immediately. His eyes swept over her unabashed, reminding her that she was little more than a sow for farrow. His finger targeted her like a straight arrow.

"Come. The sisters will want you."

Sariah's stomach sank like a stone in water.

Thirty-seven

"WAKE UP, FREAKS, you have work to do," Julean said. When nothing stirred in the far corner of the black granite room, he turned to Sariah. "Wake them up. I can't bear the sight of those things."

Sariah crossed her arms and leaned against the wall. She had no intention of following Julean's orders.

"Feisty, aren't we?" Julean said. "Do you think you have common men like me on the run? I've got no qualms about witches like you. There are thirty men on the other side of that door who would gladly cater to your whore's tastes. Defy me and by the time the freaks wake up, they'll have to unhinge your knees from your ears."

The man's visceral hatred hit her in the gut. But it was about survival now. She went to the other side of the room. A black granite box was built into the corner, almost invisible against the walls. A round hole near the floor seemed to be the only opening. Sariah knelt down. The mere notion of going in there gave her the chills. She peered in and spied the strangest of sights.

The sisters slept in a dark nest of straw and blankets, tangled in each other's arms. Like wintering cubs, they cuddled close together, Belana, an ethereal shape of waning white, wrapped about Telana, her black shadow. It was odd enough to see grown women sucking their thumbs while they slept, but it was even stranger to see that they suckled on each other's thumbs.

Who were these bizarre creatures? Where had they come from? What tragic circumstances had brought them to Grimly's service? It couldn't be easy for them. Julean's contempt was probably the most common reaction they elicited from people. Despite everything, Sariah pitied them.

Balancing on her hands and knees, and reluctant to leave any part of her body hanging out for Julean's insolent perusal, Sariah crawled in the box. Inside, it was warm and somehow moist, rich with the scent of lard and ripe olives, and quiet with an insulated peace broken only by the hushed rustle of the sisters' breaths. The enclosed space seemed smaller by the moment. Sariah's heart broke out into a panicked race.

"*Meow.*" The freckled face of an oversized kitten peeked from under Belana's neck. The black-footed cub climbed on Sariah's lap, a clumsy bundle of fur, huge ears, needle-like claws and enormous yellow eyes. Petting the purring creature settled her nerves. Her hammering heartbeat eased. What kind of cat was it? She couldn't tell.

"Hurry up." Julean's bark sent the kitten scrambling into hiding.

Sariah shook the sisters gently, until Belana's sightless eyes fluttered open. "Is that you, little sister? Sweet awakening, how kind of you."

Telana uncoiled like a mighty python and looked out of the box. "It's back. I can feel it. Julean is here too."

"Sorry, little sister," Belana said. "We have to work."

□ ■ □

Sariah was seriously worried. Belana was leaking black tears and Telana was securing Sariah to the birthing chair as if the belch was coming. Without a voice, Sariah couldn't persuade the sisters from their course. She shook her head. She tried to motion with her bound hands.

"You don't understand," Belana said. "She wants the pain."

"Silly," Telana said. "She wants the progress."

What progress?

"The progress of the Blood, of course." Grimly strode into the chamber carrying a small package that she set to balance on Sariah's belly. "I don't want to hurt your baby. On the contrary, I want to help him."

Help him? Was it vengeance the Prime Hand wanted? If it was, the horror of hurting her baby was the worst possible revenge. But revenge was more Arron's style. The Prime Hand had always been deliberate in her purposes, set on the Guild's grandiose goals. How could killing her baby contribute to the mistress's goals?

"I'm a faithful admirer of creation's beauty," the mistress said. "Yours will be the pinnacle of this generation. Done naturally, no less. I expect great things from you. Do you know what this is, Sariah? Can you guess?"

A trickle of sticky warmth leaked from the packet and dripped down Sariah's side. The mistress cut the twine and unwrapped the bundle. A putrid stench stunk the room.

No. She willed Meliahs. *Please, no.*

It was too late. On her belly, the keeper's blood-crusted hand still clutched the yellow stone prism.

□ ■ □

With the sharp point jabbed in the depths of her navel and the power firing from it, the prism was like a pick to the entrails. The stone was lit from within, shimmering with shifting geometrical patterns as the sisters rotated it against her navel. And the pain. Sariah couldn't stand the pain. It wracked her body with increasing intensity, leaving her rattled and bruised.

Belana held on to the prism with the intensity of a rider trying to tame a bolting charger. "Not too much longer."

Telana's hands were tightly wrapped over her sister's. "Are we making a change?"

"Hard to tell," Belana rasped. "Very opaque in there."

Opaque? Was blind Belana somehow gifted to look into her womb?

"Give it some more," Telana said. "We should've finished by now."

Sariah couldn't understand. The keeper. He must be dead. Why were they doing this to her? The sisters didn't want information from her. They asked no questions; they issued no commands. She thought perhaps the excruciating torture was meant as Grimly's punishment. But why the prism?

She forced herself to pay attention, to function despite the pain. She tracked the stone's power as it rammed through her defenses. She made an extraordinary effort to test the powerful jolt, to taste

it with her mind, just like Kael tasted the water for traces of the
rot with his tongue. The pain seared her as if she had indeed drunk
from the rot, but what she saw in that terrible flash frightened her
beyond pain. How could it be?

The stone's power had both intent and direction. It was directed
at her unborn child. It targeted the baby in a very specific, brutal
way, to grow him, to accelerate him, to change him in ways Sariah
didn't quite understand. She wouldn't allow it. She had failed to
protect the child before. She wouldn't fail now. She strengthened
the protection she had weaved around her womb.

How long had the Mating Hall served as a screen for torture?
How many of the keep's wisers had been born of pain like this?
How many had been murdered here? She wished she could get a
message out to Kael. She needed him to know that she was alive,
but with her wiser's skills muzzled and without access to a stone—
Wait. She had access to one stone and one stone only. The very
stone she needed to wise. Was it possible?

She had to try and quickly, before she lost the unlikely opportunity. A wiser was more than palms, more than fingers and
hands, more than a freestanding core separate from the rest of the
mind. But there had to be some carnal anchor between the stone
and the flesh. No way around that.

She concentrated on her tortured navel, where the prism's
sharp point made agonizing contact. She visualized the spot until
it held preeminence over the rest of her aching flesh. She trapped
the prism's own power on that spot and merged it with the flesh.
Pulse by pulse, she grew it into an elongated cord, a combination
of her own matter and one of her freed links. An amalgamation
of flesh and light crept up her spine, a cold serpent slithering up
her backbone. It was an unnatural creation, a deviance, a feat of
desperate necessity she would have never dared under any other
circumstances. It split at the base of her neck. One string crept
further up to her wiser's core. The other slinked down along the
bones of her shoulders and arms towards her hands like some ma-
lignant ivy.

Between painful spasms, she managed to bring the tips of her
fingers together. There. A sense of contact. A buzz. The prism's

rage seethed in her fingertips, stone power routed to serve as a bond between the link and the flesh. She knew she had it when she felt the curious inquiry of a trance knocking on her mind. She had done it.

She drew a deep breath and gathered her wiser's voice at the tip of the tale. She thought of Mia, of the unique link they shared. She visualized the aberrant connection she had created within herself, hovering over the seal stamped on her wiser's core. She flexed it, aimed it, and flexed it again. Then she rammed it into the seal.

Sariah's body arched like a quaking bridge. Her mind felt shattered. Her brain was bruised. And in that instant the protective weave she kept around her womb flickered, allowing the prism's jolts to get by. But she pulled herself together just in time to restore the weave and enable the heresy. The silent words shot out of her mind like an arrow to her seal. *Keep. Mating Hall. Alive. Beware. Arron's Shield. All around. Amplifying stones. More. When I can.*

"Stop," Belana cried. "Stop."

The prism's point eased away from Sariah's navel. The power quit. The elaborate cord flamed and crumbled to sudden oblivion. Sariah's strung body collapsed on the birthing chair, filthy with her discharges. Her throat ached from her soundless screams. She gasped for breath. Would Mia be able to hear her message?

"Did you feel that?" Belana said.

"Did I feel what?" Telana asked.

"Something, like a bump in the link. Didn't you feel it?"

"No, sister, I didn't. Your sensitive nature must be acting up. Try again."

"But—"

"One last rush. If the mistress senses no quickening today—"

The surge lanced through an exhausted Sariah. She flopped on the chair like a speared fish. The baby jerked, and a cry that wasn't hers echoed in her mind.

Sorry, she whispered wordlessly to her baby.

Sorry. She mourned her dead keeper.

□ ■ □

Sariah was on fire. She turned and tossed in an uneasy sleep, aching, throbbing and buzzing with the remnants of the prism's torturous power, dreaming a nightmare she had once wised out of a tale. In the nightmare, she wasn't a witness in the tale, but rather herself.

The air was thick with steaming vapors. The stench of blood, mixed with the scent of acrid corruption, dilated her nostrils and singed her lungs. She lay on a bed of black rock. Dark blood flowed between her legs. A circle of strangers accosted her. Blurred faces examined her baby's features.

"It is not," Grimly said. Without warning, she cast Sariah's son into a pool of corruption bubbling in the center vault. Like lard tossed on a scalding skillet, the child dissolved. The hissing flow gnawed at the babe's bones until they too melted into the rot.

Sariah woke up drenched in sweat, trembling and gasping for air. She would have been screaming if she'd had a voice; she would have woken the entire keep if her throat had been allowed the luxury of horror.

Against Meliahs' prohibitions, wisers of old had created flesh. They had divided the Blood to make slaves, betraying Meliahs' ways, labor and sweat. It wasn't so different here. Was it?

The baby was the real reason Sariah was still alive. Sariah's purported good blood, mixed with Kael's, son of the powerful stonewiser Aya, was attractive to Grimly. And suddenly she understood what Grimly was trying to do at the Mating Hall, although not necessarily the why or the how.

□ ■ □

The Mating Hall routine ground down even the hardiest of souls. After another long day at the looms, Sariah more or less dragged herself to the tidiness line and stripped her worthless garment before taking her place behind Celia. Celia wiggled her fingers behind her back. News. Sariah shook off the day's weariness. She followed Celia down the stairs and stepped into the cold water of the long cleansing pool. It got crowded at that end of the pool, a perfect opportunity for a brief attempt at underwater finger tapping.

A flash of Celia's lewd deeds filtered through the woman's untrained mind, but after that, Sariah caught a sense of her conversation with the guard the night before. Across the bars, the man was boasting about his cushy assignment at the Mating Hall, gloating because he didn't have to stand guard on the walls day and night like his fellow guards had to do.

The contact broke when Celia's turn arrived. Then it was her turn. Sariah withstood the sponging. She resented the stern hand that forced the washing on her as if she was nothing more than a well-used work beast hosed down after a grueling day in the fields.

She stepped out of the pool and waited for her turn to be dried. She forced herself to focus on the important things. Why were the bulk of the keep's guards posted on the wall night and day? She donned a clean garment and moved on to the table. She downed the tasteless porridge without enthusiasm. The lukewarm gruel was purported to provide all the nutrition necessary to grow wiserlings. It was the only reason to eat it.

She waited until the guards doused the fires to begin her work. Sariah couldn't stray far from her cot, because her bracelet's glow was too hard to conceal. Instead, one by one, the women came to her cot quietly, cautiously, perhaps even faithfully, so that Sariah could try to awaken dormant links and train clumsy fingers into a semblance of rhythm. It was slow, risky, painstaking work, but at least half the women were able to stone tap now, and the other half showed promise.

"Are you sure about this?" Cara whispered when it was her turn. "You said you'd stolen the prism, but it's back and it hurts as much as ever."

Courage, Sariah tapped the emotion against Cara's icy fingertips. The next time, they wouldn't get it back.

Trea was in a nostalgic mood. "Will I ever birth a child and keep it, you think?"

Confidence. Sariah forced herself to convey the difficult notion. She thought of her own child, of the dangers that stood in the way of her son's existence. *Hope.* She visualized the elegant roses etched on her bracelet's link, infusing Trea's mind with the sight of a hundred red buds blooming into stunning, exquisite wreaths. She could almost whiff the sweet scent of her own hope, perfuming both her infusion and her dreams.

Celia's whisper brought her back to the pen's stark darkness. "Don't you think we should try it tonight?"

"Not yet," Lexia said. "We'll get one chance. It's got to be right."

A muted clang sounded by the lower gate. Celia got up and went to meet her guard. Sariah waited impatiently. Time had no true measure in the Mating Hall. The days were long. The nights were endless. Yet the silver haze's advance on her bracelet's crystals wasn't deterred. Every day she spent at the Mating Hall was a day lost.

The prospect of another quickening was enough to squelch any attempts at optimism. Sariah made an effort to think about the things she liked, like flowers, cherries and honey. True, some of those were really Kael's favorites, but she had learned to share in his pleasures. She thought of him, of the memories they had made together. She recalled his scent, dark spices and fresh laurel draping her like the warmest blanket. She sighed like a lovesick maiden. Pathetic. If only she knew that Kael had gotten her message.

After a while, Celia slipped back into her cot.

"Anything new?" Lexia whispered.

"Fighting," Celia whispered back.

"Against who?"

"He's not that dumb."

It had to be Arron. He must be trying to take the keep by force. Sariah had seen him there, massing at the gates, waiting for her. At last, he had gotten tired of waiting.

□ ■ □

Sitting on the birthing chair was an act of pure will. Sariah stilled her trembling limbs and focused on the task ahead. She had lived through several quickenings thus far, each worse than the previous one. But whereas other women returned with their bellies grown by several weeks after each quickening, Sariah's seemed to be growing at a more natural rate. It was her way of defying the mistress, the sisters and the prism's power. And after several failed attempts, a good bit of thought, and much preparation, it wasn't her only way.

"You've got to help us, little sister," Belana said.

"You've got to let us do our work," Telana said.

"Or would you rather the mistress's wrath?"

"For you, for us, the danger is much."

One jolt of the prism had Sariah squirming like a half-stomped worm. She had to fight her body's desperation, before she was able to master her fumbling will. Working through the awful pain was the hardest part. She had already sweated the bulk of her body's water by the time she managed to reestablish the aberrant connection between the prism's power and her flesh, core and seal.

She wasn't sure a tale could transcend time and distance with such flimsy anchors. The seal made it theoretically possible, but only if Mia had heard her before, and if she was close enough and actively listening in the company of her amplifying stones. At best, she might get a glimpse of the tale. Surely Mia would tell Kael. It was Sariah's way of smuggling the tale out of the keep, of sharing her discoveries with someone who might be able to act on them.

She prodded the prism for a trance, lightly, so as to not to alert the sisters to her intention. The stone surprised her. It was swift like an eager harlot. Sariah had to tame the stone's strong will towards visions to keep the wising secret. She reached beyond the painful jolts to grab the trance. It was clear enough, and best of all, it announced a straightforward tale.

The tale arrived with a stormy night. The stink of ozone filled her nostrils and freshened her overheated lungs. She recognized the people right away. The four sages were fleeing through a muddy vale. They carried something heavy in a litter between them. Lightning flashed ahead, revealing a figure standing in the middle of the narrow trail. White hair. Sharp features. Piercing blue eyes. Sariah would have recognized the woman anywhere. Zeminaya—wiser, marcher and First Shield—in her time, before the execration.

"Escape is not the way," Zeminaya said. "The rot has come and the land's dying, but as far as I'm concerned, stealing is still a trespass."

"I've seen what comes." Poe rested his side of the litter on the mud. "This is the only way."

"Fool," Zeminaya said. "We can all see what comes. Dreaming, that's easy. Change, there's a dare."

Vargas aimed her rusty pitchfork. "Step aside. You'll have us go along with this mad journey you propose. The execration. A generation punished for trespasses against Meliahs. Do you really think it will ever be enough?"

"It has to be," Zeminaya said. "We can't survive divided."

Eneis shook his head. "Who speaks unity but the wall's very builder?"

Zeminaya's blue eyes skewered the teacher. "Who takes the stone in the night while I stay with the rot and the circling buzzards?"

The rain trickled like tears over Tirsis's sad face. "We don't undertake this journey lightly, my friend. We know the burdens as well as you do."

"And yet you're still leaving."

"We were dreamed thieves for a purpose," Poe said.

"That could be," Zeminaya said, "except for what you steal." She was upon the sages in one stride. In a swift movement, she pulled off the litter's covers.

Sariah gasped. A large stone sparkled with delicate luminosity where the rain's drizzle touched it. It shimmered with an intense amber coloring that seemed to glow with the light. It was whole, complete and beautiful. It exuded limitless power. The memory of its sweet voice rose above the noise of the sisters' torture to soothe Sariah's mind. *Wise me, wiser, tenderly, bring me to my tale. Don't you know me, child of hers, don't you know my name?*

Dear Meliahs. She should have seen it before for what it was, but she had been too rushed and awed, too needy and ignorant. Poe was right. The dream had dreamed them thieves for a purpose greater than most. It wasn't an old myth, a lie, a legend. It was true.

Grimly's malicious plan coalesced in Sariah's mind, grander than she ever imagined, unholy, maleficent, sickening, not just the what, but the why and the how. How could she?

Another jolt of excruciating pain shook Sariah's fortitude. The sisters increased the quickening's violence. They had found the weaknesses that inevitably developed in the protective weave when Sariah's attention shifted to the wising. Sariah scrambled. She had to finish wising the prism.

"It's not working," Telana said. "We've got to try the other way."

"But I don't like that other way," Belana bleated.

"And you like the mistress's wrath better?"

"All right." Telana jabbed the stone prism in Sariah's navel, but Belana's hands migrated elsewhere. "I'm sorry, little sister."

Sariah hissed. It was only a knuckle, two at the most, but the intrusive presence of Belana's forefinger in her body shocked her. The prism came alight. The jolt struck, doubled with power, skillfully routed from opposite directions to convene at Sariah's center. Her womb convulsed in agonizing contractions. She went into a shuddering rigor.

The jolts flamed through her like fire arrows. She couldn't hold the wising. She had to drop the trance. With every blow, Sariah had to yield bodily control to keep up the shreds that remained of the protective weave. Her mouth dribbled. Her bladder spurted. Even her nipples trickled clear colostrum tears. She was hanging on by a bare string of will that threatened to snap at any time.

We're here, the message arrived with the pain. *We're near.*

Shock. Elation. Agony. She couldn't think beyond the pain. Mia had heard her. She felt a renewed sense of strength. The child was fighting too, rolling and kicking in her womb, throwing up waves of surprisingly effective protection. Sariah waited for a lull in the sisters' assault and managed to issue a rush of hope to travel on the wings of her affection. *Holding on. Together.*

"I haven't seen such great strength in a wiserling before," Telana said.

Belana agreed. "It's got secrets from us."

Sariah found the wherewithal to be proud of Mia, of her baby.

She couldn't help but feel that affection was flowing into her as well, that like her blood, it circulated through her child and returned to her enhanced by their unique bond.

A clear sense of warning rattled her mind right before her eardrums popped. There was a surge in her womb. A bolt of stone power recoiled from within her and struck back. Light burst from the prism, blasting the sisters. The last thing she remembered was her belly, alight with ethereal brightness, and the outline of the tiny bones she glimpsed there.

Thirty-eight

SARIAH TRIED TO ignore the grunts echoing in the chamber. A new wraith of a girl had arrived yesterday and had been put into the breeding stall. Her maddened suitor had gone at her like a stag in rut. She had been loud at first, but now it was just her occasional whimpers and his snorts breaking the hall's silence.

But not even the brutality of her last wising was enough to dampen Sariah's excitement. Mia had gotten her message. Somewhere over the keep's massive wall, Kael was near and pondering, she hoped, the half of the tale she had been able to wise. Would he understand?

It could have been a hallucination. Meliahs knew, she had been in bad shape by then. But she was fairly sure she had received a message, no, better, two. It had to be Mia. Lying there, anxiously awaiting the arrival of Celia's guard, Sariah twisted the bracelet around her wrist. She could swear that time had slowed to a trickle, yet the silvery haze was spreading faster than ever. Courage. Faith. Strength. She would need all of Meliahs' sisters to succeed tonight.

She inhaled a calming breath. Everything had to be perfect. But the wait was hard to bear, and she couldn't keep her mind from drifting back to the amazing wising. The sages and Zeminaya. That stone. Incredible. She had been so close to finishing the job.

She worried about her child. Inasmuch as she tried to block and repair the damage, her belly was swelling bigger, her nipples had grown darker, and cobalt veins crisscrossed her breasts like an engrossment's scribbled lines. Was it nature, working its ways on her? Or were all the changes the quickenings' untimely doings?

"He's come." Lexia whispered from her cot next to Sariah. "After three nights' waiting, he's here."

Sariah squinted in the red-tinted darkness. The outline of a large figure leaned against the bars at the chamber's doors. A faint clanging came from the door. Celia rose from her cot.

"I'll signal when he's at his weakest," she whispered, tiptoeing in the darkness.

Sariah waved her bracelet in the shadows. Muted assents came from the cots. At last, the time had come. Not all the women were capable of stone tapping, and not everyone trained was capable of delivering a stunning jolt, but everybody had agreed to her plan and every woman knew her assigned role.

She figured she could count on the jolt of some thirty sets of fingers. Released at the same time, it should incapacitate the guard, buying them time to steal his keys and work their way to the higher door, where the second guard would be similarly subdued. After that, Sariah would sneak into the black granite room and steal the prism while the rest of the women would release the male captives, set the fires, and wait hidden by the outer doors until the guards came to fight the fire. Lexia swore that if she was able to make it to her pledged hall, her peers would protect them. Sariah wasn't taking any risks. She was counting on the confusion to bolt from the keep for good.

A loud moan overtook all other sounds.

"Hush, everyone," Lexia said. "We need to be quiet."

A commotion ensued a few cots down the line. To Sariah's chagrin, the guards massed around the pen, calling for the fires to be lit. Meliahs curse her rotten luck. So much for escaping tonight.

"It's Violet," someone said. "She's gone into labor."

□ ■ □

Sariah went to her next quickening seething with frustration. Violet's shrieks were fresh in her mind. The woman's labor had gone on for three days. Even though she had been taken from the chamber, the sounds of her agony echoed through the hall, tormenting them all. The guards seemed as agitated as the women, and the fires had been kept high all through the nights, preventing any further attempt at escaping. A couple of hours ago the screaming had stopped. A somber hush had descended on the women in the pen.

When Sariah entered the sisters' chamber, she slipped on a puddle by the door.

"Watch your step," Belana said.

"It's a mess," Telana added.

Sariah struggled to grasp the chilling sights before her. Violet lay dead on the birthing chair, face frozen, eyes round with terror, mouth gaping, maimed arms pleading without hands. And the blood. It dripped from the chair and ran in rivulets everywhere, pooling at her bare feet like a rising tide.

"I never had hopes of anything special from her."

Sariah whirled to find Grimly standing behind her.

"I'm nothing but patient," the mistress said. "She got her time. Such a complicated birth. Handless and all, the wench wanted to live. She had delusions about keeping her baby."

Sariah hugged her belly.

"Some losses are to be expected in the struggle for progress," the mistress said. "That was Violet. Five births, and nothing noteworthy. Do you know what she wanted to trade with me?"

The balmy warmth in the room did nothing to allay the chill freezing Sariah's blood.

"She wanted to trade her baby's life for information about a certain wretch turning wising tricks in my pen and hoping to escape."

Poor dead Violet. She had killed Sariah as well.

□ ■ □

"It's not wise to cross the mistress," Telana said, licking her fingers.

"Now you can't go back to your friends." The corners of Belana's dripping mouth curled down sadly.

Her friends. Surely they wouldn't be harmed while they were with child. Grimly would want to profit from her investment, to bring each pregnancy to conclusion. The women of the pen would pay for her trespasses somehow, but the wiserlings were too important. Grimly wouldn't kill them yet. Would she?

"Finish up," the mistress said. "You have work to do."

Telana stuffed her mouth full. Belana wiped her lips on her sleeve. It was a testament to the sorry state of her wits that only then did Sariah find it strange that both sisters were sitting at the foot of Violet's corpse, eating.

Belana wiped a black tear from her eye. "It's what we are."

Telana chewed heartily. "It's what sustains us."

Sariah looked from one sister to another. A diffusing curtain began to lift from her eyes. The details were coming into focus. Laps wet with gore, mouths dripping with blood; the little body, still bruised and wet from its terrible passage; the tiny head, carefully incised to serve up the brain.

Sariah doubled over and vomited. She wretched until not a drop of bile remained in her body. All the while she pinched herself, trying to wake up from the gruesome nightmare that had taken hold of her life.

□ ■ □

Sariah's body was dead. Just as they had taken her voice, the sisters pressed the prism to Sariah's spine and somehow took away the rest. It was done under Grimly's watchful eyes, both as punishment and precaution. Her eyelids still worked, her throat seemed able to swallow, her muscles quivered reflexively and her innards churned in fear. But her eyes couldn't see, her limbs were heavy as boulders and her joints were rubbery and unwieldy. She couldn't even wiggle her fingers. It was the strangest feeling. She was alive and thinking, able to feel every instance of pain and yet trapped in a body that refused her commands.

"Is this a trick?" A familiar voice gusted over Sariah's face. "Is it really her?"

"Look for yourself," Grimly's unmistakable gruff voice replied. "Isn't that why you came? All those hostages exchanged, all those pledges to ensure your safety, all the arrangements made so that you could witness her captivity. I told you I had her."

He must have leaned over to inspect her face. His breath smelled of dry mouth, of traces of pea and ham soup. She didn't need to see him to know him. It was Arron.

"She's just out of a particularly difficult quickening," the mistress said.

"A quickening?" Sariah heard the repulsion in his voice. "Is that what you call it?"

"Are we playing innocent today? You know as much about my quest as I do."

"So it's not a lie," Arron said. "You did recover the prism."

"Were you hoping it was still at large?"

"And did she wise it?"

"Do you think I'm stupid?"

"Do you know how they punished Adamenes of Hurin when he betrayed the Guild?" Arron said. "They fed him stones, small ones at first, to build up the pain. He died of a rotten, ruptured gut after many days of agony. He passed a few, the stones tell us. The human body's not built for such horror."

The mistress scoffed. "If I eat stones, you'll be dining right beside me. You and I, well, you know."

Arron's strong fingers cupped Sariah's bare scalp and tipped her head backwards, holding her fragile brain hostage. "We're not here for show, Grimly. I've got my dampening stone and so do you. No one else can hear us. What is it that you want from me?"

"It's imperative that the Guild is restored to its former glory."

"And where would that leave me?"

"Restored also. With your lease back and your dignity intact."

"You demand the roast of my table and yet you give me your scraps?"

"She's the strongest wiser we have."

"And you?"

"I'd keep the wiserling. That's all I want."

"You have all of the stones that matter."

"And you'd have the only wiser who can wise them."

Curse them both. They were haggling over her and her baby as if they were meat on market day. Why was Grimly willing to negotiate with Arron? What complicated plotting merited admitting Arron into the keep and allowing him to inspect Sariah at his leisure?

Grimly's tone changed subtly. "Perhaps your reports have been exaggerated?"

"I assure you," Arron said, "there's no exaggeration in my reports."

"Then what we face here is an equal threat to both of us."

"I'll think about it." Arron's boots clicked on the floor as he moved toward the door.

"Why the hurry?"

"A man who values his life is always in a hurry when you're around."

Grimly's laughter was oddly sincere.

"Sariah can stand a lot of pain," Arron said. "It's the humiliation that kills her."

"I'll keep her humble *and* alive for now, but you need to make up your mind soon."

The door clicked shut and Arron was gone.

The mistress wanted Arron to do something else in addition to returning to the keep and rejoining her Council. What was it? It had to do with the trouble Celia's suitor reported at the ramparts. Sariah was sure of it. Perhaps Grimly wanted Arron to desist from an assault on the keep, but if that was the case, Grimly would have lured him into the keep and killed him, despite her oaths.

Nay. Grimly needed something else. She hadn't asked him to quit the Shield or return the Shield's command. In fact, she hadn't spoken about that at all. No. It wasn't so much Arron that Grimly needed. It was the Shield Arron commanded. Soldiers.

A cool ladle of water brushed her lips. Sariah drank eagerly. Grimly's breath brushed intimately against her earlobe. "So you were paying attention, child. Good. A witness is always a good advantage, especially when trapped at the back of a shrewd gaming hand. You won't forget this little discussion between me and Arron, I hope." She pressed the stones on her palms against Sariah's ears. "One never forgets the last sounds one hears."

□ ■ □

Darkness was death's preview and like death, it was both terrifying and forbidding. Pain was keener without light, unexpected and rough. Fear went deeper into her mind's recesses and turned pitch black. There was no sound to Sariah's world, only terrifying, absolute silence. She was drowning deep in her body's wreck, sinking in the loneliness of her inner space.

A slap recalled her from the nothingness. Someone wanted her to obey commands she couldn't hear. The pain of labor struck Sariah as Meliahs' monumental mistake. It originated in the far distance, growing from tiny squeak to thunderous bellow before leaving her for dead. The child was fighting her womb's stubborn hold like a tiger caught in a net, clawing himself out of her dead body. She couldn't blame him.

The stones quaked beneath the sisters' stifling den. The scent of lard and olives overwhelmed her nostrils. A quick brush of fur startled her. It was probably Belana's kitten, fleeing from the box. A vision of the odd sisters flashed in her mind, a sight of herself, strung on the birthing chair and dead like Violet, and the women, nibbling on her baby's brain. The sob got stuck in her throat. The goddess wouldn't, she couldn't let that happen. Meliahs might be hard of hearing, but the goddess was no less of a mother to her than she was to this child. She owed her child some protection.

Someone braced her from the back. Someone else clutched her knees apart and yet a third person pushed on her belly with a giant's strength. The pain. She tried to tap into the remnants of the prism power. It sometimes lasted for a day or two after a quickening, settling into her aching joints, burning through her body like a swarm of stinging scorpions. If she could use it to kindle the aberrant connection she had created, she could establish a beacon for Mia. Kael could retrieve the prism and take it to the executioners. Ars could be saved. She waited for a contraction to pass. There. The connection flared. If she could tie it to herself, it would last for as long as she lived.

She tried to convey her thoughts to the baby. *Not now. Not safe.*

A sense of question filled her mind. *Safe?*

Sariah knew she was hallucinating, but it was true, safety had eluded her child since conception. She tried to patch her protective weave's torn links, to contract her muscles, to persuade the child with her body that it wasn't safe to be born just now. But the baby was barreling down her birth canal like a catapulted stone and there was nothing she could do to change that.

As her body broke, she thought she understood Meliahs' quandary quite well—in death the goddess offered the perfection of her gardens and yet in life her children craved the imperfection of the unknown beyond. When it came to their children, goddesses, it turns out, had as few and as dismal choices as mothers did.

Her hips snapped. Her body failed. Time for partings. *Please, Meliahs, protect them all, because I no longer can.* She thought of the search she would never finish, of the boy she would never know, of his father, the man she loved. With the last of her strength she freed her affection into the dark clouds of nowhere and prayed that it rained upon their faces.

Thirty-nine

SARIAH EMERGED FROM the tenuous depths of nothingness, where life and death blended in a gray haze, where the pain coexisted with oblivion and the faintness of a shallow breath suspended the soul at the crossing. It hurt to draw a deeper breath. Was it a first breath? Was it a last breath? It hurt to think, to feel.

Pain. A touch, ever so tender and tentative. A warm drop on her face, maybe two. A hot breath against her cheek. Was someone crying over her?

She forced another breath. Her lungs rattled like rickety wagons. Smoke scented the air. Was the Mating Hall on fire?

Her limbs were gathered gently. Her body was cradled carefully. She had a feeling of lightness, as if she were flying, separated at last from the sticky trappings of the sisters' nest. How long had she lain there?

Flashes of consciousness intruded in the flickering darkness. Fresh water. Soft linens. Bone-rattling cold. Her hands ached when the leather muzzles were peeled off and the blocking stones were extracted from her palms. Senseless darkness. Unbearable heat. Perfumed oil lovingly massaged into her lifeless limbs. A tap to her wiser's mind, so slight she wasn't even sure.

A touch of healing brought her back to her senses, a cautious probe. She couldn't move, see, or hear, but the stink of burning had eased. She caught a whiff of fresh laurel and spices beside her. It had to be an illusion. Her senses were askew and hardly reliable. A hand guided her fingertips over the scar of a broken eyebrow to the familiar lips that kissed each of her fingers thoroughly. Curse her dreams. They were all too real. Madness was the only fitting explanation to unrequited hope.

But the contact felt real. A hand. The size, the shape, the rough texture of calluses and scars, they were as familiar to her as her own hands. All four of his fingers intertwined with hers in a gentle squeeze.

It had to be him.

The small stone he placed in her palm was smooth and polished. With her palms injured and her links weak and numb, she had to grapple for the simple trance several times before she was able to hold it. It was Kael's telltale imprint, strong, bold, clear. It conveyed no images, only words and a host of his powerful emotions carefully modulated not to hurt her.

"We've come, love, but you know that. It took us too long. The fiery fever got me, but not before the Panadanians were trained and Targamon's rot was contained. By the time we caught up with you, you were trapped. Mia couldn't feel you through the keep's walls. I feared you were dead." Despite his efforts, his pain seeped into the tale like a scalding tear. "Then she said she heard you through her seal. That message, Sariah. I can't tell you what it did to me. I knew I had to get to you, but Grimly had negotiated a truce with Arron and no one was able to make it through to the keep."

Sariah realized at once that more than witnessing the agreement between Grimly and Arron, she had been the object of it.

"We met up with Delis, the keeper and his Hounds," Kael said. "Delis was raging mad at your ruse. The keeper was hurt. He said he lost something you entrusted to his care. He fashioned himself a new claw to fit around his hand's stub once he realized I was set on fetching you."

Poor keeper. To think he had lost his hand because of her. Sariah's heart ached. But at least he was alive. Alive.

"I couldn't find a way in. I swear to you, Sariah, I looked, and I tried, and the damn Shield was waiting at every corner, and the damn keep was sealed like a forbidden tomb. I called on Malord and he came, but he couldn't find a way in either. The others and I, we agreed. We laid siege to the Goodlands and advanced on the keep. Some Goodlanders joined us. Some stonewisers joined us too. The Domain's tribes put out their fair share, and even Mara from Targamon sent some of her newly trained Panadanians. But it was the Hounds who had the ready weapons and the warriors we needed. It is they who scattered Arron and his Shield and now guard the keep's wall. I know what you're thinking." His tale sounded strained and tired. "You're right. I've unleashed the Hounds' Going and there's no stopping it now. "

So much for preserving the peace and keeping the Hounds safe and out of the Goodlands. The world had changed while she was trapped in the Mating Hall. The war they had all feared had arrived.

"If you hadn't led us here," Kael said, "we wouldn't have found you in time. Malord and Mia are trying to mend you, but you must try to rest and get better. Meanwhile, remember that our tales belong to each other. You'll get out of this. You'll be well."

It was just like Kael to command her to health. His words were a welcome reprieve to the silence overwhelming her, a better alternative to her thoughts. But was the prism secured in his possession? Had the baby survived his birth? How much time did they have left?

She tried to issue her own imprint on the stone. She tried to ask the questions. It didn't work. The anguish was like a pillow to her face, like a bull sitting on her chest. *Help yourself.* Kael wasn't going to talk to her about the matters she cared about most in the limited confines of a tale. He didn't know if she was sound of mind and listening, let alone fit to endure his news. No, he would wait until he knew she was conscious. He would tell her face to face. That meant Sariah had to find a way to bust out of her broken body's prison, and fast.

□ ■ □

Sariah resisted Mia's attempt to dose her with an infusion of contrived and youthful calm. She refused to fall asleep. However, she did allow the girl's efforts to soothe her heart's uneven palpitations so that Mia and Malord could resume their healings. She joined their work on her broken links. She kept at it long after they had to stop for the night, overcome with exhaustion.

She had just finished fusing a link when an image suddenly flickered in her mind—a blurry hand, very close to her face. Her

skin was numb as cured hide, but wasn't that the feeling of someone scratching her nose? The hand. Was it hers? She tried to focus
her eyes. They crossed ruefully. She tried again.

The banishment bracelet. It was her hand. It was moving of its
own accord. It made a rustle when it landed on the bed. She heard
that. She tried it again. Aye. The arm answered. It moved.

Slowly, now, old gal. Pace yourself.

A few candles lit the chamber where she lay. She didn't recognize the place, but it was comfortable, with a fireplace that stung
her light-sensitive eyes. She lay on the bed for a moment, gathering her strength, savoring the sounds suddenly available to her,
the roar of the hearth's fire, the bubbling of a pot on the spit, the
voices next door. Then she forced her dazed eyes to focus on the
bracelet.

Eight of the nine crystals glimmered with the opaque film. The
last crystal was already half filled with the silvery mist. Her mind
was like a cart stuck in a rut, slow moving and tentative. She had
left Ars eight and a half months ago. She had been in the Mating
Hall for almost... two months?

She still had some time to wise the prism and find the tale. But
what about her son? Could he have survived his birth with so little
time in the womb? Had he managed to fight off the prism's effects
only to arrive unprepared for the rigors of breathing air?

She pushed herself up and slid off the mattress. Her legs didn't
want to work, but she locked her knees and clung to the bedpost,
trembling like a newborn lamb. The white nightgown she wore
tripped the three tentative steps she dared. She leaned against the
wall, ignoring her muscles' screech for mercy. She could move,
Meliahs be blessed, and she would.

She made a slow progress to the door. It was thankfully half-
opened. She braced herself against the threshold and looked out
into the small adjacent chamber that served as a sitting room.
There were many people milling about, many of whom she didn't
recognize. The ones who mattered were all there—Mia, playing
cards with Rig by the fire; Malord, dozing on a stool; Delis, sharpening her hatchet; the keeper, missing a hand but very much alive;
and Kael, sitting closest to the door with his back to her, studying
a sheaf of parchment and a mountain of maps.

"How?" It was her voice, pathetically hoarse and discordant. The explosion of motion and noise startled her long-stilled senses. Malord was down from the stool, batting the keeper out of his way. Delis was at her feet in two strides but had to hold Mia back. The girl's attempt at a hug toppled Sariah. Kael scooped her deftly, stilling the room with his glower.

"Not now," he said in a tone that defied protest. He took Sariah into the bedchamber, kicked the door shut, and made for the bed.

"No, not there," Sariah murmured.

"You're sick, love."

"I don't want to lie down anymore."

He looked around, then dragged a chair to the fireplace and settled himself in it, arranging her carefully on his lap. Sariah leaned against his shoulder and buried her face in his neck, inhaling his scent, appropriating his warmth, listening to the pulse hammering at the base of his throat. She felt weightless, like a feather perched on his lap, anchored to this world only by the strength of his arms.

He pressed a cloth between her legs. "There's been some bad bleeding. It's better now, but we must be careful."

The shadows in his gaze were much darker than the stain on her nightgown. She fitted her fumbling hand under his tunic and set it against his heart.

"This might not be the best of time for that sort of thing," he said.

"Please?" Her own eyes stared back at her, wide and enormous in the paleness of her face, reflecting in the pools of his black and green gaze.

He kissed her temple. "Go ahead."

It was all there, like a mirror of her soul, the fears, the anxiety, the exhaustion, the hurt, the determination and the blessedly abundant affection.

"Tell me," she said.

"It's not wise."

"Tell me." If she had to wait a moment longer, she would burst from desperation.

"All right." He couldn't hide the dread in his voice.

□ ■ □

The man who spoke was different from the Kael she knew. His face was hollow. His eyes were empty. His voice was strangled and curt. "What was done to you. It was wrong. I can't—for the life of me, I can't stand it. I think I'm broken, Sariah. Broken and mean."

"Kael?"

"What they do. At the Mating Hall. Grimly told me. That they bred you and fostered a... wiserling, she called it, in your womb. That they brewed in two months a semblance of what the goddess grows in nine."

"She said that?" Sariah tried to swallow, but her throat was parched.

"I knew the truth," Kael said. "It wasn't really a baby. It was a foul creature, forged outside of Meliahs' ways. But still, it was hard, because even if it was not of your body, it was the only possible trade."

"It?" Something cold and bitter began to pool at the pit of her stomach. "Trade?"

"It was the only way to get to you. Grimly betrayed Arron, but that was to be expected. She allowed me safe conduct so that she could negotiate with me. She agreed to surrender the keep and you. In exchange, she took the wisers faithful to her, the sisters and the stones."

"Oh, no, not the yellow prism. We need the prism."

"All the stones," Kael said. "She wouldn't trade for less."

"And the baby?"

"She said it wasn't right. She said it was... damaged."

"Damaged? Are you sure?"

"It didn't make it."

The pain punched through her knotted heart like a flaming blade. "Are you sure? How can you know?"

"I saw it."

"The body? You saw a boy? The baby boy's dead body?"

"Aye, Sariah. The witch showed me the little monster."

"He wasn't mine." He couldn't be. "Grimly. She lies. I know she wanted him."

"What I saw—I don't want to share that with you."

Sariah clutched a fistful of his tunic. "Tell me."

"No, Sariah. No."

She sank her nails in his chest. "Tell me!"

He hesitated. "He was there... Next to you. There was... so much blood. His. Yours—"

She clung to hope. "He could've been someone else's." Violet's maybe.

"He was still... connected to you. Grimly. She told the truth. It wasn't... right. He was—the sac—" He couldn't speak the horror reflected in his eyes. "It was yours."

"Where is he?" Sariah said. "I want to see him."

"Grimly took it. It was part of the trade. She wanted to study it—the remains—to see what had gone wrong with it."

The grief struck her like a death blow, like a stoning, like the very last of the killer stones. She crawled out of Kael's lap, ignoring his anguished stare and rejecting his help. He didn't know. What he had done. He hadn't known.

The gush came all at once, a total dissolution of what remained of her, a gush of tears and useless milk and blood that drenched her robe and trailed her to the bed. Climbing on the mattress was as difficult as scaling the Bastions. Kael was calling for help, trying to aid her. He was speaking, but she couldn't hear him. She curled up as tight as her fists.

"Won't you understand?" he said. "Won't you forgive me?"

Her voice was a frail wail. "You won't."

"Why Sariah? Why not?"

"Because that dead wiserling you traded was no misbegotten freak. He was Meliahs' gift. Mine. Yours. Ours. And we forsook him to the Guild like a miserable rotting beast."

Forty

THE WHISPERS STARTLED Sariah out of the depths of her nightmares. Her eyes burned with the sting of sweat pooling on her eyelids. Her muscles quivered with the aftershocks of a rattling fever. She remembered. The prism. Gone. The baby. Gone.

"You're awake." Delis's face came into focus. "Here. Won't you drink a little?"

Sariah batted the cup away from her lips. "Time," she rasped. "How much time do we have left?"

The grim faces of Malord, Mia, Delis and the keeper told her she didn't have a lot of time left. Her arm was heavy as a load of stone, but she managed to lift it to look at the bracelet. Like a creeping mold, the silvery haze advanced on the last crystal. What was it that the executioner had said? *Nine months to honor Meliahs' nine sisters, nine months to find and submit the tale she sought.* Her eyes fell on the tiny tears engraved in the bracelet's ninth link. *But never trust on the last of the nine, Mercy, for she squanders her gifts on others and has little compassion for her bearer.* That was painfully obvious.

"Stones," she said. "I need the stone."

"You need more healing before you start wising again," Malord said.

"Auntie, let me do some more."

"No. Wait. Help me up." Sariah managed to sit on the bed with Mia's aid. "Have you found any other stones at the keep?"

Malord shook his head. "Nothing of value. Grimly took them all."

The mistress had taken a lot more than stones.

"We found these at the Mating Hall." The keeper emptied a small purse on the bed.

"We think they're your stones," Malord said, "the ones you had on you when you were captured."

"I need something more than these." She needed the prism. "Go, for Meliahs' sake. Send out your Hounds. Keep looking!"

The keeper and Malord shuffled out of the chamber. She didn't think they harbored a hint of hope in their hearts.

"Drink, my donnis." Delis was in no mood for disobedience. "You've been very sick. I won't let you die of thirst."

The beaker's wooden nipple intruded in Sariah's mouth and fired its watery load. A good deal of tea ended up down the wrong passage and out her nose. Delis wasn't pleased. She wiped Sariah's face as if she were mopping an old floor.

"Won't you try to mend yourself, my donnis?"

"Aye, Auntie. You need to get well."

She thought about Ars, about the rot loose in the Goodlands, the divided Guild, the breached keep, the restless blood-licking Hounds. How was she going to prevent the bloodshed coming? No, she didn't have time to be sick. Despite their losses, they couldn't give up. Kael. He was the only one who could help her through the haze. Belatedly, she realized he wasn't by her bedside.

"Where is Kael?"

Mia looked out the window. Delis's stare aimed at the floor.

"Well?"

"He picked up his weapons and shot out of here the day you woke, my donnis. He hasn't been seen since."

What had he done? Vengeance. He had gone after the mistress. He was going to kill himself in the bargain. The grief. She couldn't handle the pain of her soul breaking.

"I've got to go after him." She threw the covers aside and rolled out of the bed. Her legs failed as soon as she hit the floor.

Delis caught her. "You can't go after him. You need to mend first."

"Don't you understand?" Sariah said. "I don't have time for mending."

"And without mending you won't have any time left. Back to bed, my donnis. I have no intention of helping you kill yourself."

"Get out of my way."

"Wouldn't that be the same thing as letting you kill yourself? Now be good and do as I say. Remember—you swore me an oath."

"*I* swore you an oath? *You* tricked me into making that daft oath and you know it."

"Daft oath?"

Sariah fathomed she could feel the pain she had inflicted on Delis on her own flesh. "Look, Delis, I—"

"Not another word." Delis grabbed her mantle and marched out the door. "I refuse to be a witness to your suicide on the whim of a daft oath."

The whole chamber shook with the force of the door slamming.

□ ■ □

Delis's faulty reasoning was right on one thing. Sariah was still too sick to be useful to herself. She had to get some strength into her body or risk becoming catatonic and useless.

"I think you're right, Mianina," Sariah said. "I need more healing."

"Good, Auntie. Right away." Mia pressed her hands against Sariah's palms. Her luminous power reached out to repair Sariah's links.

Sariah closed her eyes and tried to help the healing along. Thoughts of Kael kept breaking her concentration. Was he alive? Her heart ached for him. For Delis, too. She guessed a weakling donnis was no prize to someone like Delis. She should feel relieved that the woman was gone, but she was surprised to discover that she was saddened by the sudden desertion. She tried to escape the hurt by focusing on Mia's power, flowing steadily through her links.

Her safety hadn't been neglected. The keeper had replaced Delis by her side. In her current mood, Sariah couldn't help but wonder if she would end up driving him away too.

"How did you lose your hand?" Mia asked the keeper at the same time she was healing Sariah, a testament to her extraordinary power.

"In the battle for the prism," the keeper said. "*Careless are the fools who trust speed over caution.* I tripped the Guild's trap like a tame old goat."

"Does it hurt?"

"*Pain is life's sacred will to endure.* Sometimes it feels like it's still there."

"Rig and I, we could have helped if we had been there."

"You're too young for that."

"Rig doesn't think I'm too young. He thinks I could do it. He thinks he could fight with the Hounds too. You ought to let him join the Hounds on patrol."

"That skinny rail of a boy? He couldn't hold a set of claws straight if he tried."

"Oh, yes, he could. He's stronger than he seems, just like I am. He wants to fight Arron. Won't you order your Hounds to take him along?"

"Perhaps someday, when he's older and has learned the Wisdom—"

"Now," Mia said. "He wants to join the Hounds now."

"*Patience is the sign of wisdom.*"

"*Action is the mark of destiny.*"

"How do you know that?"

"Rig and I, we've been studying the Wisdom."

"*She who learns the Wisdom shatters the world with her knowledge.*"

"That's funny," Mia said. "That Mistress Uma said something similar to me today. And she's not even a Hound."

"What did she say?"

"That she who had the strength would rule the world with her might. She said she had heard about me, that she could teach me more, about healing."

Sariah was suddenly alarmed. She didn't like the thought of Uma near Mia. Mia's particular brand of healing was neither sanctioned nor known at the keep. Mia could inadvertently relinquish many advantages to Uma, but there was nothing Uma could teach Mia, except the Guild's dark and confining ways.

"You seem to have sense beyond your age," the keeper said.

"I'm a freak. Say it."

"I think no such thing."

"That's because you're a freak too, a blood-licking one."

"I might be. Here in the Goodlands."

"People are scared of you. Of me."

"Is that such a bad thing?"

"It is, at least when you are almost thirteen."

Sariah couldn't help but hurt for her young pupil, for all the heartbreak that her extraordinary fate promised.

"I don't think you're a freak," the keeper said. "I'd be honored to drink your blood."

"I'd like that. Can we do it right after this?"

Sariah's eyes sprang wide open. "No blood licking between the two of you. Do you hear me? She's too young to understand the Hounds' ways."

"But I do understand," Mia protested.

"And you, stay away from Uma," Sariah said. "She's dangerous."

"She *is* kind of scary."

"*Noble are the strong for they shall conquer fear,*" the keeper said. "If you'd allow us to cleanse the filth from the land—"

"I'm not granting the Hounds leave to scorch everything in your path," Sariah said. "There are innocent people out there who don't deserve to die by your claws."

"*From the stone we rose and with the stone we shall avenge all heresy.* Let's do it, saba. Let's reclaim the world for Meliahs. *What's anger but the self's denial? What's denial but a swift escape?*"

It was tempting. The keeper was calling on her rage. Stone Grimly to death, quarter Arron, destroy the Guild, eviscerate Ilian and the others for good measure. Would any of it satisfy her anguish, restore her power, save Ars, revive her son, bring back Kael?

Mia's freckles blended with her flush. Her curls trembled with the effort. But she was anything if not determined. Sariah worried she was taxing the girl beyond her capabilities, sucking on the young wiser's strength like an overeager babe at the breast.

But she was experiencing some relief. Her heart was beating more steadily. Her joints were loosening up. She was just beginning to feel the effect of Mia's healing when a commotion ensued outside her door.

"Get your paws off me, you blood-licking lizard," someone screeched outside Sariah's door. "This is my hall!"

There was a bump and a crash, and then Lorian, First of the Hall of Numbers, stumbled through the door. The keeper grabbed her. The tall lanky woman twisted in his grip like a skunk about to spray. Sariah recognized Uma and Olden pushing into the room too, forcing themselves into the chamber like a flock of squabbling ravens.

Lexia came in with the rabble. "Leave Sariah alone. She's ill. She can't cope with this."

Sariah didn't care if they tore into her with bloody beaks, but she cringed when Olden's crooked staff swung at the back of the keeper's knees. Swept in with the crowd, Malord interposed a stool between Olden's staff and the keeper's legs. Olden redirected his staff, clubbing everything and everybody in sight.

The armed Hounds poured into the room. The councilors' followers wielded clubs and knives. She had never seen stonewisers looking like thugs before. Her mind was slow whirling to action, but it seemed that Hounds and stonewisers alike shared in the bloodlust this day. Had the Council members arrived to fetch her for a stoning? Were the Hounds trying to prevent them from seizing her?

"Stop it," she said. "All of you. You're going to kill one another."

No one listened.

"In Meliahs' name, stop it, I say—"

An arch of black flow surged across the room. It left a gaping Olden staring at the handle in his hand, the only part of his once elegant staff not singed to oblivion.

A girl's voice broke the stunned silence. "Auntie said to stop it."

Every eye in the room fell on Mia.

It was a good thing Mia's attention was on Sariah, because Uma mouthed the terrible word. "Abomination."

"I've told them to go away," the keeper said, holding a squirming Lorian at arm's length. "They won't desist."

Lorian slapped the keeper's arm. "Of course I won't desist. This is my hall!"

The keeper cocked an inquiring brow in Sariah's direction. As if she didn't have enough problems right now. But she didn't want more blood spilled in her name. "Release Lorian. Send your Hounds away, and the other stonewisers too. I want no one killed here today."

It struck her eerily strange that everyone did as she asked, not just the Hounds, but the councilors' followers as well. Everybody left the chamber, with the exception of her friends and the three Council members. She tried to make sense of it all. She knew the balance of power had changed at the keep. But this?

"Did you make her?" an incredulous Uma asked.

"Mia is *not* of the Guild," Sariah said.

Olden pointed at the girl with his smoking handle. "You know what should be done with that thing."

Rig materialized next to Mia growling like a faithful mastiff. "Stay away from her, old man. You too, witches."

Sariah hadn't even known that Rig was in the room until this moment, but she was suddenly very glad that the boy stood by Mia with such unshakable grit.

"On my oath," Sariah said. "Target her at your life's peril."

"Is that the proper way to address your masters and mistresses?" Olden said.

Sariah chuckled mirthlessly. "I quit the Guild. Remember?"

"Is it true then?" Uma said. "That you won't heed our authority? That you won't obey us as you pledged?"

"My pledge was to the stone truth, not to your persons."

"Traitor," Olden mumbled.

Mia's recent healing gave Sariah the strength to face the councilors. She steadied herself on her feet and squared her shoulders. She knew she made for a mad if not frightful sight, pale and gaunt like the dead, wearing a blood-stained nightgown and her coldest, most hateful glare. "Is there a point to your excursion here today?"

Lorian actually took a step back. "Lexia and the others, they brought you here. I told them you were trouble, but they begged me. And now you hide in my guest chamber, under the guise of my own hospitality, thumbing your nose at me, at all of us?"

"Sariah's been very sick," Lexia said. "She doesn't know."

"Know what?"

"You haven't heard?" Lorian stared at her in disbelief. "The Hall of Numbers has claimed preeminence at the keep."

"Meliahs save us from the piles of tribute," Olden muttered.

"Preeminence?" Sariah said. "That's a bold step, even for someone as crafty as you, Lorian."

"It's pure maneuvering, that's all it is," Olden said.

"Why should I be blamed if your beloved Hall of Masons scattered to the quarries?" Lorian said. "Is it my fault that Uma's Hall of Healers split? The Hall of Numbers has the greatest say because most of our wisers stayed together at the keep instead of following Grimly or Arron. And that may have something to do with me."

Sariah made a concerted effort to try to understand, even if her head ached and her wits were flowing as slowly as molasses.

"There's no governance at the keep," Lorian said. "We needed some kind of rule."

"How fortunate that you think it should be *your* rule," Olden said.

Lorian's countenance darkened. "Do you forget we tried to solve this problem among the three of us?"

"Tried and failed," Uma said. "What a joy that discussion was."

"The Guild is not used to chaos," Lorian said. "We called a meeting in the Hall of Stones. We couldn't agree on who should head the new Council, so we decided to take a vote."

"A vote?" Sariah was shocked. It had to be a first. The Guild had always appointed their rulers. "The three of you agreed to a vote?"

"It wasn't their idea," Lexia said.

"Our hand was forced," Uma admitted. "The other stonewisers, they demanded a vote."

And the Council members had only agreed to save their necks, Sariah realized, astonished. In Grimly's absence, authority at the keep had deteriorated quickly.

"So we took the vote," Lorian said. "Guess who won?"

"By his bitterness, it wasn't Olden." Sariah hazarded a guess. "You?"

"It should have been me."

"Who says?" Olden fumed.

"*I* had the biggest following."

"By her own account, of course."

"But it wasn't me," Lorian said. "Do know who it was?"

Sariah shrugged.

"It was you."

Forty-one

SARIAH HAD BEEN elected to lead the Guild.

It was surreal, unbelievable, unfathomable. It was laughable, maddening, infuriating.

"You've got to be kidding."

"Do I look like a journey jester?" Lorian's black eyebrows twitched with fury.

Sariah's eyes fell on a skittish Lexia. "Did you have anything to do with this?"

"Me?" Lexia cleared her throat. "Not me. The women of the pen. They're free now, they've returned to their halls. They told everybody. About you, about what you did at the Mating Hall. The Guild. The Council. It isn't right, Sariah. You saw it first. You've got to fix it."

Meliahs curse her rotten luck. She didn't want this. She had quit the Guild. She had never fathomed her attempts to rally the women of the pen would get her into a bind like this. Had they all gone insane?

Yet in a perverse way, everything made perfect sense. She'd had followers all along, other stonewisers who supported her. Grimly had spoken of them as silly people, disquieted by Sariah's adventures. And Arron, in his stone tale message, had wanted Sariah to declare for him to enlist her supporters to his cause. The free women of the pen had galvanized her supporters and spearheaded the vote. Her own actions had brought her to this point. She didn't want any followers. The hefty weight of their expectations bore down on her already burdened shoulders.

"We had to ask ourselves," Olden said. "Why this sudden wave of support?"

"There had been rumblings about you," Uma said.

"Exaggerations."

"And then, poof." Olden snapped his fingers. "You're it. We had to wonder how. Do you care to tell us?"

That's why she wasn't dead just then. That's why Lorian, Olden and Uma were at the foot of the bed, speaking to her, instead of at the head of a stoning crowd. The unprecedented election had inadvertently protected her from the Council's wrath. That, and the Hounds' ferocious claws.

"Must you really do this now?" Lexia said. "Can't you see that she's not well yet?"

"Precisely," Olden said. "She's in no condition to rule. So you'll need to acknowledge the election, Sariah. Then you'll declare yourself too sick to carry out your duties and transfer your election to us."

"You want me to transfer the election to *you*?"

"To all three of us," Uma said. "To the new triumvirate we'll form to shoulder your many duties."

Sariah's eyes shifted from petite and golden Uma, to lanky and raven-haired Lorian, to bold and hunched Olden. They were very different, yet very much alike. She realized what they were doing. A delegated transfer of power. They could be counted on to conceive the most creative solutions on matters of law. They were running their own power sprints. They had been denied rule by their fellow stonewisers, but they were going to seize it regardless.

Sariah had to think fast. What were the chances she could complete her search with these three ruling the keep? Could they provide unity and stability to the divided Guild? Sariah had no doubt about both answers. These three were an omen for destruction.

"Not that I want to rule the keep," she said. "I resigned the Guild, but why would I grant the keep's rule to any of you?"

"You have no choice," Olden said. "Did you think we wouldn't discover your trick?"

"What trick?"

"But we did discover it," Uma said. "And if we tell those stonewisers who remain, those fools who believe in you, you can be assured there will be a stoning at the keep."

"We've been investigating," Olden said. "Who wouldn't, with so much at stake?"

"We probed our respective stonewisers," Lorian said.

"Without their knowledge?" Sariah asked.

"The First of a Hall doesn't need permission to probe her members."

It was pure old Guild thinking, without remorse or doubt.

"Do you know what we found?" Uma said. "Do you know what we found on Lexia and the Mating Hall's women?"

"A seal," Olden said. "We found *your* seal on their cores."

□ ■ □

"My seal?" Sariah's mind spun with the blow. "I don't have a seal."

"The triangle within the oval," Olden said. "Do you remember it now?

Zeminaya's seal. The one she had found on her own core, on Mia's core, the one that created the strange attachment between Mia and her. But how had it spread to the other stonewisers?

"You deceived them," Lorian said. "You told them you were teaching them to stone tap. You did a little more than that."

"That seal is the reason they elected you," Uma said.

"That seal is influencing the stonewisers to your advantage," Olden added.

Sariah raked her hands over her scalp's bristly hair growth. How could she have accomplished something as complex as passing on Zeminaya's seal when she was curbed and unaware? "It can't be. It doesn't work like that."

"Oh, so she admits to it readily," Olden said.

"There's more to it," Lorian said. "Do you know that the seal is spreading? Your seal is contagious, like the plague."

Contagious?

"They could be lying," Malord warned.

Somehow, she knew they weren't.

"How can we stop it from spreading?" Uma asked.

Sariah couldn't figure out how the seal had been passed on

in the first place, let alone how to stop it from spreading. "I don't know."

Olden scowled. "Do you deny the seal powers your followers' fervor?"

"Of course not." It was Lexia who saw the truth first. "Whatever this seal is, it can't possibly affect a stonewiser's judgment."

"How could you know that?" Lorian asked.

"Because Sariah's cause, the stone truth, calls on more than stonewisers. In fact, the majority of Sariah's followers are not stonewisers. Hounds. Domainers. Goodlanders. You've seen them come to the keep to swear allegiance to Sariah and her cause. They have no core. They can't bear a seal. They chose her cause freely. So did the stonewisers."

It was a good argument, but it didn't convince the councilors.

"That's no proof," Olden said.

"What's the seal's purpose then?" Lorian spoke over Olden.

"To control us," Uma said without a trace of doubt.

They started bickering again, belittling Lexia, scorning Sariah, fighting among themselves like rats over scraps. One thing was clear—they were not going to be stopped by something as simple as reason.

"Lexia, I want you to kill these three."

Lexia stared at Sariah, too stunned to speak.

"Kill them, I said."

"You want me to kill the councilors?" Her eyes shifted from Sariah to the alarmed councilors and back to Sariah. "But why?"

"It doesn't matter why," Sariah said. "Just do as I say."

"But—"

"Are you going to kill them or not?"

Lexia stammered. "Well. E-hem. I—No, I don't think I will. I mean, I don't like them, but I don't really think that killing them is right—"

"There you have it." Sariah faced the Council members. "Your proof."

"What are you talking about?"

"I just commanded Lexia to kill you. But she didn't. Did she? She refused my command."

"That just proves she's right of mind," Lorian said.

"It proves more than that," Sariah said. "It proves I can't make her do what I want, despite the seal. It proves that whatever this seal may be, your accusations here today have no merit."

Sariah smiled like the triumphant huntress she was. She had defeated Lorian and the others single-handedly in the briefest of combats.

□ ■ □

Sariah waited until the keeper escorted Lorian, Uma and Olden out of her chamber. They had been temporarily defused, but they would be back, she was sure.

She sat on the bed and closed her eyes, trying to ignore the mounting headache. She had so much to do. She had to go after Kael and figure out a way to recover the prism. But she also had to sort out this mess or risk losing whatever little support she had managed to garner thus far.

The election offered both, an opportunity to finish her search and a chance at surviving her stay at the keep. It was also the reason for the uneasy peace between the remaining stonewisers, the Hounds and their Domainer allies. It kept a fragile balance, one that could be easily shattered if the councilors succeeded in undermining Sariah. She had to figure out what was going on with the seal. But first, she had to get over the shock of hearing words like "Sariah's cause" and "Sariah's followers." Since when did she have a cause and followers?

She thought of Mia, who had been sealed along with Sariah. She thought of Malord, with whom she had worked closely many times. Malord was there, sitting by the fire between Mia and Lexia, clutching what Sariah recognized as one of her amplifying stones. He must have felt her eyes on him, because he turned around. Was he sealed too? He paled under her scrutiny. She had her answer.

"How?" she asked.

"I don't know. It's not much of a seal, nothing as clear or defined as Mia's. It's a newer scar, pretty recent." His voice died midsentence as if surrendering to some kind of betrayal.

"Why didn't you tell me? Is that why you follow me?"

"No, no. I followed you of my own free will. I didn't have a seal that night at Targamon when we found the seal on Mia's core. We looked. Remember? I don't feel like Mia, who needs you and knows where you are. It's only recently that I started to feel as if I wanted to be part of something, I guess. The greater story."

That was a curious way to put it. At least he wasn't compulsively following her. "Can you recall when you started to feel like that?"

Malord thought for a moment. "The seal has nothing to do with how I feel. You were my enemy when you came to the Domain, but you've since proved yourself worthy, as a colleague, as a friend, and now you're like a daughter to me. I'm sorry if that offends you."

Offend her? The words were stuck in her throat so she reached out to squeeze his hand and said nothing and hoped he knew she loved him too. She could feel the strain of the day testing her recovery, but too many questions begged for answers only she could grant.

"And you, Lexia? Do you feel you have to follow me?"

"I'm not compelled to do as you say, if that's what you mean," Lexia said. "I just showed you. No matter what Lorian and the others say, I didn't vote for you out of compulsion. We suffered together in the Mating Hall, and together we'll see the Guild's new dawn."

Until this moment, Sariah had never known that Lexia believed in a notion as ethereal as the Guild's new dawn. "But how, Malord? You weren't there when Zeminaya sealed me with the legacy. The intrusion couldn't have sealed you herself. Could she?"

Malord shrugged. "I don't know."

Mia had been witnessing their exchange in respectful silence, but now she perked up. "The intrusion didn't seal you, Malord. Auntie did."

Sariah's voice was too hoarse for words. "Mia, do you know when I sealed Malord?"

"It was just the other day, when we were healing you, Auntie. You were unconscious, but you did it easily, a quick kiss of links. I didn't think much of it. I thought you knew."

Sariah's brain was boiling. Someone ought to put out the fire in the hearth. Despite the frigid weather outside, she was burning up. She had to face the truth. If she had sealed Malord as Mia said, then Lorian was right and she had sealed Lexia and the women of the pen as well.

It was a lot to consider. The headache didn't make it any easier. What creature was capable of generating something like a seal? What did it take to imprint a seal on another wiser's mind?

Arrogance. The belief that one had the right to intrude in another person's core. She, who had once been a slave, was horrified by the mere notion.

If she lacked the will to do it, how could she have done it in the first place? Was there a trick to the seal or was her wiser's mind able to project it forward at will? Why, if she'd had the seal since her encounter with Zeminaya almost two years back, had she just recently sealed Malord? She had been unconscious, for the goddess's sake. Could the seal propel itself onwards without her leave?

A *self-perpetuating seal.* The notion struck her as fantastic, but it was the only explanation that fit. What was its purpose? What was the extent of its power? And how did the damn thing work? What was it that Tirsis had said at the end of her tale? *Our apologies, stonewiser, for the legacy unleashed, for the burdens bestowed.*

Sariah sank her face in her hands. She had been used. By long dead, recklessly scrupulous people whose ideals prevailed over time and space. Zeminaya. The sages. One had provided the seal. The others had powered it to spread. All she needed was a wising contact with her fellow stonewisers to transfer the seal, and ostensibly, the legacy. Oh, yes, it was pure Zeminaya; it was pure and devious sage wising. The legacy had never been a task to carry out, as she believed. Rather she, Sariah, had been the legacy's carrier all along.

"I'm going after Kael and the prism." She ducked behind the changing screen.

"You can't go," Malord said.

"He's right, Auntie. You're not well."

"She has a fever," Lexia said to the others. "Do you think she could be hallucinating?"

Sariah struggled with a pair of unwieldy leggings and a rebellious tunic. She stumbled out from behind the screen just in time to spy the bewildered expression on Malord's face.

"Perhaps you ought to wait for Kael to return," the old wiser said.

"Wait?" Sariah grabbed her boots. "We have very little time left. How can I wait?"

Her latest discovery reaffirmed what she believed. Her search for a tale to reconcile the Bloods had become much more than a way to save Ars from the executioners' encumbrances, much more than a way to save her life. It had become the only viable part of an ancient effort to unite the Blood, the only remaining way to save a world teetering at the brink of destruction.

It struck Sariah then that she wasn't just working on behalf of Ars and the Domain, on behalf of the refugees at Targamon, or the Hounds, or to preserve the Goodlands. She was working on behalf of the whole Blood, and that included the Guild. To accomplish the legacy, she would have to try to fix the Guild too. It was the last source of order in a putrid world, a critical part of the healing that had to take place if their world was to survive.

Curse Zeminaya and all the sages. What right did they have to use her like that? And what if Lexia had been wrong? What if the seal was designed to influence thinking and free will? Was anything in her life her own doing?

Answers. Sariah needed answers. She needed proof that her life was more than someone else's game, that she was still the mistress of her own fate. She also needed a mantle. She rummaged through the pegs on the wall until she found one that would do.

The stones. She grabbed them from under her pillow. She held the amplifying stone's river-smoothed shape in one hand and her polished memory stone in the other. She had to make sure she had all her facts right. The mere thought of wising stones made her stomach churn. Her palms were healing well enough, but she feared the shock of a sweltering tale decanted into her brittle mind. She gritted her teeth and pressed the stones to her palms.

She got only pain from the touch, a cold jolt to the soul. If that wasn't alarming enough, in a sudden wrench, the banishment bracelet coiled around her wrist. Sariah swore she felt the strike of a single fang on her arm. She doubled over in a flash of body-splitting pain. The room spun like a wobbly wheel.

"What is it?" Malord said.

"Auntie, are you all right?"

The blood in her veins turned cold. Her bones froze. Her skin grew taut and brittle all over. The soft, sensitive plane of her palms thickened and dulled. She couldn't quite put her finger on it, but there was something very wrong with her.

She couldn't understand. A quick check revealed there was still a pure red glow in the center of the bracelet's last stone. She had a few more days, maybe. But what was it that the executioner had said? *When the time comes, Mercy will not hesitate. She'll suck you dry of your essence before abandoning you to die as it's your sworn fate.*

She sought out the power that had fueled her since her break-ing, the persuasive warmth that fired her palms, the heat that streamed seductively through her veins. It wasn't flowing through her core. Instead, it was spouting out of it like brew spurting from a punctured flask.

What was a stonewiser's essence if not stonewising itself?

Terror. Without her stonewiser's power, her body was an empty shell. She had been muzzled before. She had survived. But this was different. Back at the Mating Hall she had known that her power remained in her body, beyond her reach but inside of her. Now, her power was deserting her, too slippery to grasp and too fluid to stop. How long could she live without it?

"What's wrong, Auntie? What's the matter with her?"

A tremor began in her core, a distant murmur growing to a roar, rattling her bones and pounding in her head. Sariah used the last of her strength to bring her thumb to her lips and surrendered to the darkness.

Forty-two

"THERE, THERE, IT'S past now," Lexia said. "You're back and you mustn't be afraid."

Sariah's joints ached like the rot. "Has there been word?"

"No news from your man."

"What happened?"

"You've had your first bout with the prism's darkness," Lexia said. "It happens sometimes. The Council members' visit may have had something to do with it. Stress brings it on. Or anger. It's all that darkness. It stays with us even after the prism is gone."

Sariah sat up. "How often do these bouts occur?"

Lexia shrugged. "No one knows for sure. It's different for everybody. There's nothing you can do but stop what you're doing when you feel it coming, find a safe place to stand it for a few hours, and bite down on leather to spare your teeth. But it's over now."

"How long was I out?"

Lexia hesitated. "A few days."

Sariah clenched. She tried to keep in her frustration, she tried and failed. She groaned like a wounded beast. "Why do you do this to me?"

"Me?" Lexia stared at her with puzzled concern.

"Sorry. I wasn't talking to you." She was yelling at Meliahs, the fickle goddess, who knew very well how much Sariah needed the time she had just lost.

The bout had left Sariah exhausted, but that wasn't the worst of it. The prism's darkness had struck her at the same time that the bracelet had unleashed its lethal sentence. Lexia didn't know that. Neither did the others.

Sariah dragged herself out of bed and stumbled to the wash

basin. Her reflection in the mirror shocked her. What a frightening mess she was. Too pale, too skinny, too weary, with her razor-short hair spiking like a nest of thorns. She splashed water on her face and neck and then scrubbed herself mercilessly, as if by washing her body she could cleanse her soul's filth.

So this is what it felt like to be ordinary, empty and cold inside, exposed to life's inclemency and bare of all protection, helpless, destitute, powerless. She had often fantasized about living an ordinary life. But how did normal people exist without the goddess's divine touch, without the stone's authority ennobling their lives, with such a fragile sense of the self?

Lexia hovered like a bee over a hive. "Look, I know how you feel. It's always tough afterwards. Sadness sometimes follows a difficult birth. You had a hard birth, plus the prism's darkness. There's also Violet's betrayal. The gall of the wench, to tell the mistress you were turning wising tricks in her pen. But the body heals, sometimes slowly, but it heals. I've lost four, Sariah. It doesn't get any easier."

Sariah couldn't imagine enduring four times the pain.

"I get to keep this one." Lexia patted her belly and smiled. "You should hear the debate at the Hall of Numbers. But I'm going to keep her even if I have to quit the Guild, move to the Domain and eat the soles of my boots."

Sariah dried herself, blotting her watery eyes as well. "The others," she said. "Do you ever—?"

"Rumors about a wiserling nursery are just that. We looked everywhere. I think they kill them if they're not gifted."

Images of Violet's dead baby flashed in Sariah's mind. She held the bile down.

"I'm not really helping, am I?" Lexia said. "I thought perhaps you wanted to talk."

Talk? No. She needed to *do*. Something. But where to begin?

Lexia took a deep breath. "Sariah, you can't waste your time looking for the prism. You can't even think about leaving the keep right now. The halls are leaderless. The councilors are scheming. No one knows what or who to believe. You've got to assume your election."

"My election?" She felt like cackling. If the other stonewisers knew that she couldn't wise, they wouldn't be so sure about her election. Would they? She had a vision of blood splashing the Hall of Stones' walls; of Hounds slaughtering stonewisers by the hundreds and Goodlanders hunting Domainers by the pound of flesh.

The prism, the baby, Kael. It was as if all of her life's losses had coalesced into a monstrous cudgel that beat down on her soul with crushing finality. She feared the end of Ars, the war, the rot. She feared she was going to live long enough to hear firsthand the news of Kael's death.

Mercy is a fickle friend when it's all self-pity, a tidbit of Tirsis's Wisdom echoed in her mind. She glanced down at her bracelet and traced the tiny tears etched on Mercy's link. Sariah had once found the strength not to cripple Kael with her sorrow. Could she do the same for herself?

"You can start by taking this back." Lexia pulled something out of her pocket and put it between Sariah's hands. It was round, heavy and cold between her fingers, but by the way her hands tensed around it, it could have been stinging hot.

Her stonewiser's brooch. Lexia must have retrieved it from Grimly's abandoned quarters. In contrast with the brooch's coldness, the round onyx stone embossed at the center was pulsing with warmth. Sariah couldn't have managed a word through her constricted throat if she tried. With the exception of the last two years, she had worn that brooch all her life, a symbol of her faith, a sign of her obedience.

She traced the intricate lines of the ivy of knowledge edging the brooch, the intertwining vines of light that radiated from the black onyx, the four garnets on the subsidiary bosses, the honeycomb of silver filigree. She craved the brooch's presence between her breasts, the cold metal standing like a shield to her battered heart.

She shoved it back into Lexia's hands. "I don't ever want to see that thing again."

"But Sariah—"

"The answer is no, Lexia, and no again."

"But the stonewisers, they took a huge risk, they voted for you. Won't you at least think about it?"

"I can't come back to the Guild. I just can't."

"Sariah, we need you. Those Hounds are ready to slaughter us at any time. We don't know what to do about the Domainers streaming into the Goodlands. The chill is never ending, the crops are sure to fail. And then there are those stories..." Lexia actually shivered.

"What stories?"

"There are tales, that stonewisers are no longer welcomed in some places. They say that Meliahs' own, the stone eater, has returned to clear the land of stonewisers. They said Grimly sent a party to investigate the claims. They never returned."

"Rumors. Who can believe anything that Grimly does or says?"

"Things aren't as they used to be," Lexia insisted. "The world's changing. We're changing too. Think about it. Maybe that seal just gives stonewisers courage."

Courage? Not when panic was running rampant and the keep boiled with frightening, improbable tales. The seal wasn't giving Sariah any courage at the moment either, but then again, she wasn't really a stonewiser anymore. Was she?

"You taught us to stand on our own," Lexia said. "Did you know we made our own way out of the Mating Hall?"

Was that true?

"We took advantage of the siege," Lexia said. "We followed your plan. We lit the fire at the height of the last attack. It wasn't the keep's guard we met at the courtyard. It was those creature warrior things—"

A knock startled them both. Lexia went to answer the door.

"I've got a message for Stonewiser Sariah," she heard a man's voice say.

"I'm sorry, but she is sick and can't receive you." Lexia began to close the door.

"But it's urgent," the messenger said.

"I'm fine, Lexia." Sariah stepped to the door. "What is it?"

"Mistress Lorian summons you right away."

What did the witch want with her now? Sariah couldn't hazard a guess, but she had her own reasons for wanting to see Lorian.

"I'll go. Do you know what this is about?"

The grim expression on the messenger's face chilled whatever little warmth remained in Sariah's body.

"Something bad has happened," he said. "The mistress says it's something terrible."

□ ■ □

"I'm not sure you should be up and about," Lexia said.

"It could be a trap," the keeper grumbled. "*She who walks without caution risks the final tumble.*"

"You and your men are my caution," Sariah said. "And I'm not going because Lorian summoned me. I have questions for her and her friends."

Sariah, Lexia, the keeper and her Hound escort were following Lorian's messenger down the keep's busy main lane. Sariah was having trouble keeping up with the others. Her breath was short, her heart was faltering, but she had to find a way to secure the keep while she figured out the rest. Sariah didn't know what was more surprising—the sheer numbers crowding the keep or the astounding mix of people bustling about despite the frigid weather. Hounds, Domainers, Goodlanders and stonewisers were living together in an uneasy truce, a miraculous if nerve-racking sight.

The hostility among the different factions was palpable in the air. But the changes in the keep were almost shocking. Above the gates, the Guild's usually lonely black and gold standard was flanked by the Hounds' five-bladed slash banner and the blue gonfalon of the house of Ars. Even if Kael wasn't there, the sight of his pennant warmed her heart. It was surrounded by other Domainer banners, including the yellow one with the three embroidered tupelo trees. The forester was playing her game. The green banner with the massive "T" on the oak's trunk gave it away as Targamon's new standard. Good old Mara. She had taken the legacy to heart. When had it all come to this?

Lorian met them in the back alley as high-strung as a charging bull. "No one must know. Do you hear me? If this gets out, we're doomed. Doomed."

"Know what?" Sariah said.

"This is a day of penance and lamentation." Olden appeared out of nowhere with Uma in tow. "Meliahs weeps at the sight of our wickedness. We must leave, before it's too late."

"Leave?" Uma asked. "You mean abandon the keep?"

"Hush," Lorian said. "Someone might hear you. How did you two find out about this?"

"About what?" Uma asked.

"It's all her fault." The point of Olden's newly sculpted staff aimed at Sariah.

"He's right." Lorian clutched Sariah's arm and dragged her along. "If you hadn't gone on about lies in the stones, if you hadn't caused a war and brought all these strangers to the keep, this would have never happened." She halted abruptly before a crack in the cobblestones and yanked Sariah to her knees. "Look!"

Sariah couldn't believe her eyes.

"Are you happy now?" Lorian said. "For the first time in the Guild's history, the rot has breached the keep."

□ ■ □

The rot had breached the Guild's keep. With the wall so powerfully wised, it didn't seem possible. Sariah stared at the small lesions bubbling faintly among the cobblestones. At least it was the weaker kind of rot, the easier form to contain, like the lesser lesions she had seen at Targamon. Sariah struggled with the notion. The rot had defeated the wisings of generations and now simmered like an innocent little rain puddle just a few steps from the Hall of Stones?

She wondered if Meliahs and all her sisters had abandoned the land for good.

"Saba?" The keeper gestured with his head to one end of the alleyway.

Sariah's throat barely managed a dry gulp. A large group of Uma's stonewisers were blocking the way.

"I said nobody should know about this," Lorian spat. "Why are they here?"

"Olden told me we might need them," Uma said defensively.

Sariah eyed the other way out of the alleyway. Her hopes were for naught. Olden's stonewisers blocked her path with hefty chunks of stones in their hands. She wasn't sure she was going to get to ask her questions after all.

"Stone her," someone cried out from the crowd.

"She's brought the rot to the keep."

Sariah's voice was a hoarse whisper. "Keeper?"

"*Wise is he who survives the trap, for he shall never be caught again.*" The keeper's whistle strummed Sariah's eardrums.

The window shutters on both sides of the alleyway flew open. The few doors opening onto the narrow lane blew from their hinges. Armed Hounds were everywhere, inching down the lane with their backs against the walls, deploying at either side of Sariah, perched on the window sills, standing along the distant rooftops wielding claws, arrows and spears.

A massacre. That's what Sariah had on her hands. One wrong move, from anybody, and the uneasy truce that held the keep together would be over. Panic bubbled in her belly like a ready stew. She surveyed the faces in the alley. The stonewisers were angry, resentful and bitter. The Hounds stood rigidly, ready for the fight.

"Wait," Sariah said aloud. "We can fix this."

"Fix the rot?" Lorian said. "How?"

"There's a group of Domainers trained to fix this weaker kind of rot," Sariah explained. "They're from Targamon. Some of them might even be here. We don't have to abandon the keep."

"Are you sure?" Lorian asked. "Will you swear?"

"On my stonewiser's oath."

"Can't you see that she's lying?" Olden said. "She brought the rot to the keep. What are you waiting for? Stone her!"

"So you still believe the old legends?" Sariah let the question hang in the air for a moment. "Please, Olden. Times have changed. We all know that the rot doesn't travel on the bottom of the Domainers' feet. We can fix this. All this time, you've been playing your own game."

"This might be a game to you," Olden said with an aggrieved look on his face. "Me, I'm for the good of the Guild—"

"Save it." She had to sound confident. "I overheard you at Arron's tent."

"Overheard me?"

"At Arron's tent?" A few gasps came from the crowd.

Sariah was thinking on her feet. "I was there the night that you, Uma and Lorian visited Arron in his camp. What was it that you promised Arron after the others left his tent? Ah. Yes. You promised you would try to talk some sense into them."

"Preposterous. I'd never try to—"

"You have been trying to persuade them to join Arron all this time, and when that failed, you tried to empty the keep of stone-wisers, a move that could only weaken the defenses here and allow Arron to retake the keep. That would have been a sweet triumph over me, not to mention Grimly."

It was Lorian who bit on Sariah's lure. "How exactly has he been trying to empty the keep?"

She had only a few moments to transform a convoluted turn of events into irrefutable proof. How? Tell the story. Quickly. Make the case.

"This place that I just mentioned, Targamon. It's a farm out in the borderlands. The family there never looked kindly on Arron's Shield. One day, the rot's shallow lesions appeared in the backfields. There had been no earth tremors, no failed fields, no indications of rot until that very day."

"What happened then?" Uma asked.

"Even as the rot arrived in Targamon, it was a lighter version. The bushes continued flowering and the soil was fertile. Still, the farm was ruined. The laborers left in droves. In lieu of the orders, the Shield came and took the last of the seed. Coincidence, you think?" She met the riveted stares. "I don't think so. Instead, I ask, how come the farms and villages that refuse to help Arron have a higher incidence of this lesser version of the rot?"

"How does this have anything to do with what's happening at the keep?" Lorian asked.

Instead of answering Lorian's questions, Sariah asked her

own. "How was Olden so quickly informed when you found the rot? Did you send a messenger to him?"

Lorian's head swiveled on her wiry neck. "No."

"Then how did he know to show up here? Why did he bring Uma along, and all these other stonewisers?" She didn't wait for a response. "Because he knew. Because he decided to use the same strategy Arron has been using to control villages and farms—planting rot roots on the lands of those who defy him. It was Olden who carried the rot root into the keep, the only possible way of bringing the rot inside these thoroughly wised walls."

"Olden planted a rot root in the keep?" Lorian's mouth wouldn't close.

"How else does this lesser version of the rot make sense?"

The crowd went into a stunned silence. A gust of icy wind blew through the narrow lane, chilling Sariah and the crowd. Anger rose from the alleyway like vapor steaming from a boiling pot. It happened suddenly.

"Stone him! Stone him!" the crowd began to chant.

"He should be quartered first," someone else yelled.

"Wait," Sariah said. "What you want is justice—"

An irate Olden confronted his followers. "Are you so stupid as to believe her word over mine? Did I not tell you about the seal she forced on you? Can't you see this is not your own doing, but rather the seal working its strange power on you?"

Sariah couldn't let the notion go any further. "Did I call you here today? Were you forced to come to this alleyway and stone me out of a sudden compulsion? Did you hear strange thoughts in your head? Did you experience some sudden decrease in will that made your actions possible? No? Neither did I."

Olden tried to speak. "But—"

"I came here because Lorian called me, with words, brought by a messenger. She called me. Somebody called you here as well, not with a mysterious seal that somehow affects your reason but with words, with rumors, perhaps even with innuendos. Why? Because someone wanted you to kill me. I ask you, why would I try to command you to kill me? How will that serve my purposes? And if I have this power over you through this mysterious seal, why are we here at all? Why haven't I asked you to kill Olden instead? Or Lorian, or Uma for that matter?

"Because I have no sway over you. And if you're feeling persuaded in any way by my words or my actions, then chalk it up to your reason, not to the seal."

"She's right," someone said.

"The seal didn't bring us here."

"Olden summoned us."

"He planted a rot root in the keep."

The stone that hit Olden was followed by others. Uma dove into the crowd. Lorian took cover beneath the eaves. Sariah's voice was drowned in the uproar. Olden stumbled under a hail of rocks, but managed to stay on his feet.

"I am a Guild councilor," he bellowed. "You'll refrain from such disrespect."

A jagged rock sliced open his forehead and drenched his face with blood.

"Stop!" Sariah shouted. "Stop!"

Her Hound escort closed ranks around her like a human shield.

"Let me out!" Sariah pounded on the Hounds' backs. "Move, you oafs. Move!"

"But why, saba?" the keeper asked. "Why would you want to protect that fickle man who wanted to stone you?"

"Protect him? Nay, I don't want to protect him, but this is not justice, this is murder—"

"He deserves it," Lexia said.

Sariah tried to squeeze herself between the tightly linked Hounds. "Let me pass!"

"And where would those stones go if you tried to stop them?" the keeper said. "No, saba, we won't incur the stonewisers' rage for no reason. You said we have to make friends. This man is their problem. *What is blood drawn but blood unleashed to freely flow?*"

The keeper was right. The angry crowd would turn against the Hounds in a heartbeat if they intervened. Once attacked, the Hounds would exterminate every stonewiser in sight with compulsive efficiency, unleashing the massacre Sariah feared. To make matters worse, she didn't have any stone power to help persuade anybody to do as she willed. She couldn't even make a simple stone burst.

But just beyond her escort's fringes a man was dying a terrible death. He was a crooked man, a fickle soul, perhaps even a man who deserved the stoning sentence. Yet he was dying a death without justice within the land's last bastion for justice.

Sariah tried to stop the stoning. She tried to shout above the crowd's noise. She tried to push the Hounds out of the way and then she tried to crawl in between their linked legs. But the Hounds stood with unshakable determination, her strength was ebbing steadily, and so was her hope. She winced at the memory of Kael, who had once been unfairly stoned. She remembered his pain, his nightmares. Kael and Olden were hardly similar men, but all men, good and bad, felt pain and injustice just the same.

Olden's heavy body crashed on the ground. The stones kept raining on him, a deadly hail of granite against bursting flesh. Through a forest of legs, Sariah saw Olden's face, contorted in a grimace of pain. There was a sickening crack. The brain began to ooze from his broken skull, spilling onto the ground. Hands grappled with her limbs, but Sariah was unable to tear her stare from the gruesome spectacle. Even as the Hounds retreated in silent synchronicity, dragging her away from the carnage, she spotted the dark flow of Olden's blood trickling between the cobblestones and joining the bubbling rot pools.

Justice had no hope in a world where stones killed propelled by rage.

Her heart dropped into her stomach when she spotted Malord knuckling his half-body through her escort, coming toward her at top speed.

"What is it, Malord? What's wrong?"

"I have news," he wheezed. "You never told me. They've come. They're here!"

"Is it Kael?" Sariah's heart raced. "Has he come back?"

"A last chance," Malord said. "You've given yourself, all of us, a last chance."

"What are you talking about?"

"Metelaus has arrived," Malord said. "The executioners are here."

Forty-three

THE SHOCK AND grief on Metelaus's bearded face when he set eyes on her confirmed what Sariah already knew—that she looked as dead as she felt, that all hope was lost. But his expression changed when Mia landed in his arms like a whirlwind of affection, as if her kisses revived his weariness and her laughter restored his hope.

Metelaus beheld his daughter adoringly. "You've grown taller by a head."

"Wait until I tell you about Rig and my Hounds," Mia said.

"You and I have a lot of catching up to do," Metelaus said. "But first, might a dutiful daughter find some fare for a weary traveler in this whole grand keep?"

Mia scurried out the door of Sariah's chamber. Metelaus watched her go with a measure of pride. When she was gone, he took a stool next to Sariah and squeezed her hand. "I'm sorry about your loss. We lost a baby once, Torana and I. Only Meliahs knows the purpose of pain like that."

"Did they tell you Kael's gone?" Sariah asked.

"He'll be back. I promise you that."

"I don't think so. Nobody wants to tell me, but I think he's dead."

"My brother's not dead. No one's heard from him for a time, that's true, but he's a roamer. He knows how to take care of himself. You can't think the worst."

As if the worst hadn't already happened many times over. "If he isn't dead, then why isn't he here?"

"He might not be finished with his task," Metelaus said. "Or perhaps he encountered some unexpected complications."

"Unexpected complications?"

Metelaus sighed. "I might as well tell you. There's a Domainer delegation scouring the Goodlands for Kael."

"As in *armed* delegation?"

"They mean to return Kael to the Domain, by arms if necessary."

"Why? Kael hasn't broken any Domainer laws."

"No, but strange things are happening in the Domain. People are scared. Every day messages come for Kael. Marchers want him to take a look at their water, at their demesnes, at the strange animals they're finding in the Barren Flats. It's the same thing at Ars. We had a flock of geese land on the Crags the other day. Geese! The honking devils scared the crap out of the goats. You think we should all be glad for Meliahs' small favors—they taste pretty good, those geese—but people are scared, especially about the weather."

"Has it been bad?"

"Seasonal variations are fine, but this chill seems to have no end. Worse. I got lost in the Barren Flats the other day. Me. A marcher. Lost! And before I left, we measured a full span of new growth at the Crags. The dead water is somehow retreating from the Barren Flats, only it's not possible. The flats are a closed geography. There's no draining the dead water, which means—"

"That the rot is on the move?"

"That as it seeps elsewhere, the dead water's volume is going down."

"Is it because the wall is broken?"

"It's possible. Before, the wall contained the bulk of the rot in the Domain. With the wall broken, things could be changing."

And not necessarily for the better.

"I've brought water samples and stones with hundreds of reports for Kael. But Domainers want explanations for all these changes. Kael is the only one who might be able to give them."

"And you think they might have caught him?"

"I doubt it," Metelaus said. "But it's a possibility."

Sariah regretted it was she who had taken him away from his people.

Metelaus pulled a rumpled parchment from his bag. "This is

making its way through the Domain. I can guarantee that it's not the only one."

Sariah recognized it immediately. "I have no idea how—"

"How it got there doesn't matter. What matters is what you're going to do about it. Keep it, if you'd like. I've got no use for it. I'm here, am I not? You've got to rally, wiser. You've got to fight back."

"I don't know what to do, Metelaus. The peace at the keep can break at any moment. There was a stoning at the keep. A stoning. Arron's out there, harrying the Goodlands. Grimly took the stones and I have no way of completing my search. Worst of all, I haven't told anybody else, but—I can't wise."

Metelaus frowned. "What do you mean you can't wise?"

"The bracelet. It's sucking my wising essence. I can't wise stones and every day that passes I'm getting weaker."

"It's frightening. I'll admit it. It's bad. But you can't give up hope, sister of Ars. You've got to figure out a way. You've done it before. There must be something you can do."

"I swear I've tried, but nothing is working. I was trying to find a way to secure the peace at the keep today. Instead, I got a man killed."

"That man killed himself, Sariah, and only after he tried to kill you."

"Still, everything I try goes wrong."

"Not all. Look. I've done all you asked."

"I didn't ask for you to bring the executioners here."

"Not in those words, you didn't, but when you left the Bastions you sent me a message with those Hounds of yours—mind you, their appearance caused quite the commotion at Ars—telling me to do my best to persuade the executioners to come as close as possible to the wall. You didn't think you would have the time to travel back to Ars and you didn't want to risk missing the deadline. That was clever, Sariah. You anticipated the current situation quite accurately. So I tried. And when the executioners wouldn't heed my arguments, I resorted to kidnapping."

Sariah's jaw dropped. "You kidnapped the executioners?"

"Not the entire tribe, of course not, just Petrid and his seconds, enough to conduct a proper witnessing and make a decision if necessary. Mind you, the tribe is livid and threatening blood. We've got just a few days left before the deadline, and the executioners aren't happy with their lodgings at the keep's cages. So here's the deal. I made war on the executioners. I crossed the broken wall. I fought the Shield and came clear across the Goodlands. Now it's your damn turn."

□ ■ □

Metelaus was right. She couldn't give up. It wasn't in her nature, despite the bad odds.

"I think Auntie needs more healing," Mia said. "Go ahead, Daddy. Get some rest. I'll stay with her and infuse her with some of my strength."

Sariah was thankful for Mia's generosity.

"What is it, Mianina?" she asked when Mia's nose wrinkled in puzzlement.

"I don't know, Auntie. It looks like your core is, well, kind of dim or something." Mia closed her eyes and tried again. "Your links are slippery. It's like you're getting worse instead of better."

That was a good description of her life at the moment. The girl was doing what she could, but Sariah's links were withering. Despite Mia's impressive healing skills, Sariah couldn't feel the child's luminous presence in her mind.

Sariah drew in a deep breath. "Mianina, I want to thank you for everything you've done for me. I'm sorry I've put you in danger and dragged you so far away from home. I'm sorry you've grown up so fast and I haven't been able to help you as much as I should."

"But you have helped, Auntie. Lots. You taught me everything I know. Well, maybe not everything, but almost. I figured out the part about the honey all on my own."

"Honey?"

"Your craving fulfills my craving," Mia said. "As long as I have honey, I can control my need to be with you and check my power. The honey makes the distance between us bearable."

"How—?"

"Malord said the craving led me. The farther you traveled from me, the more I needed something, although at first I didn't know what. Thank Meliahs you craved honey." The blue and green eyes sparkled with mirth. "'Cause green sprouts would have meant the Goodlands' doom for sure."

The smile that tickled Sariah's lips felt rusted and crooked, but it was a smile. "Your thoughts kept me sane, Mianina. I can still hear the words in my mind. *We're near* and *we're here.*"

Mia's face tilted to one side in puzzlement.

"What is it?"

"Uncle Kael told me to say *we're near.*"

"And?"

"I never, ever said *we're here.*"

Forty-four

MELIAHS HELP HER. *We're here.* The baby had spoken to her. It wasn't a pain-induced delusion or a wistful creation of her feverish mind. It was a true contact. She thought about the boost of strength she had felt during the quickening. It had been no coincidental revival of her battered senses. It had been *him*, her tiny courageous son, adding his incipient strength to hers.

The revelation confirmed what she had suspected all along—that the child was powerful beyond the norm, self-aware well ahead of his time. And if there was one thing Sariah knew for sure about Grimly, it was that even damaged, she wouldn't allow a wiserling treasure like him to pass her by. The thought dazzled her mind. Could her child be alive?

A deafening crash startled her. Something large thrashed in the hallway and then in the waiting chamber, scattering stools and tables before crashing like a battering ram against the door. The bedchamber's door exploded. Delis strode in, dirty and bloody like the executioner she used to be, sporting a new torque of fresh ears and noses. Her face was streaked with dirt and her hair was matted with mud. A contusion bruised her cheek. Aided by quite a few Hounds, she dragged something huge and ferocious behind her.

She snarled. "Get out of here!"

Mia and the Hounds scuttled out of the room, fleeing Delis's wrath.

"I won't have it anymore." Delis slammed the huge sack against the wall. "I haven't come halfway across the world for this. I'd do it. You know I would. But I'm not the one. Am I? You!" Sariah recoiled from the dirty finger. "Stop toying with your damn life."

"And you." Delis kicked the sack. "I don't care what you think you have to do or why. Fix her." She dragged a battered man from the sack and hurled him against the bed. "Fix her now!"

The bed quaked with the force of the impact. The hangings collapsed to one side and tipped over the basin. Sariah stood with her back against the wall in disbelief. Then Delis was gone and the door slammed shut, leaving a bruised Kael sprawled against the foot of the bed and Sariah gaping.

□ ■ □

Signs of life came from the bedside. An uncouth oath. A groan. "I'm going to kill the bitch." A large hand grabbed the blankets and pulled, followed by Kael's battered face.

Sariah had to will the air to flow through her faltering lungs. He was alive. He was back. He was here. His mere presence was as fortifying as a year of healing. She wanted to cry from relief. She wanted to cackle like a mad woman. Instead, she fell on him like the most thorough of healers. His bones seemed whole, the blood on his face was dry, his pupils looked normal.

"Are you hurt?"

"I think she broke my ribs."

"They're just ribs. They tend to mend on their own."

The broken eyebrow went up. "Unless they puncture your lungs."

"You don't have time to be pierced and done."

She dipped a sponge in the basin and tossed it to him. She groped through the chest, throwing things out of the way until she found a long cloth. Without waiting for him to finish washing, she wrapped it around his ribs. Then she threw the window open, grabbed a chunk of ice from the sill, bundled it and pressed it against his bruised lip.

"What's going on, Sariah?" he mumbled through the cloth.

"We have to hurry. You'll have to kill Delis some other time."

"I'm thinking today."

"Not when she did right."

He yanked a clean tunic into place. "So you thought it wrong that I left?"

"Only on one count."

"And that is?"

She rose on the tip of her toes and kissed him on the lips. "That you left without me."

The kiss he gave her in return was fresh salve to all her sores. He embraced her with such passion that, for a moment, Sariah feared for his ribs and hers. It was the only luxury she allowed herself.

"Did you find Grimly?"

"I almost did. I was so close—"

"Did you see any signs of a baby when you tracked her?"

"A baby? Nay. But I never caught up to Grimly herself—"

There it was, the spark that had been missing from his eyes, the green-eyed boyish look of wonderment that never failed to steal her breath. "Please, Sariah, tell me. Are you thinking he might still be alive?"

"Maybe—"

"What about the body I saw?"

"There was this other baby. Violet's baby. It was dead."

"You think the witch staged everything and showed me some other child?"

"She's capable of that and more."

"If he's as strong as you say, the witch will want him alive."

"The prism," Sariah said. "Does Grimly have it?"

"Not anymore."

Sariah's back collided against the wall. In Kael's hand, the lifeless yellow prism reflected the candlelight with a macabre golden glow.

□ ■ □

Kael dropped the accursed stone. "Are you all right?"

Panic was rising through her veins like boiling magma.

"You said we needed it, that's why I brought it back."

"We did," Sariah said. "We do."

"Should I toss it? Should I bury it? What is it, Sariah? Tell me."

She kept her eyes on the stone as if it were capable of launching itself and striking at her navel.

"Is this the thing they used to—"

"It was misused," she said for her own ears.

"How do I destroy it?"

"You can't." Her voice was steadier this time. "How did you get it?"

Kael's face went blank. "They had fallen behind the others. They were running from the sunlight, I think, and they took refuge in the shade. She had it in her hand when I killed her."

"Who did you kill?"

"The black one. I killed the black sister."

□ ■ □

Meliahs help them. Kael had caught up with the sisters and killed Telana, and there wasn't a trace of regret on his face. She knew he spoke truth. Only death would have wrestled the prism from the dark sister's hands.

She was afraid to ask. "What happened to the other sister?"

"I would have killed her too. Except that Delis showed up."

"You mean Belana is not dead?"

"Delis caught her and dragged her along. I could tell by the ungodly screams. The woman's mad. She's likely at the cages."

"At the cages?" One thought fell systematically behind the other. Belana was near. The prism was here. Kael had returned. The babe was alive. The whole world came back into focus, ripe with possibilities, renewed with purpose. She had to wise the prism. Right away. But how could she wise the stone without her stonewiser power? An idea began to take shape in the back of Sariah's mind, a dangerous, desperate thought.

"I have to see her." She snatched her mantle from the peg and made for the door. "I have to speak to her."

She stopped dead in her tracks and retraced her steps to fetch the prism from the floor. She hesitated, but she couldn't let her fear of it prevail, so she grabbed it. It was lifeless and cold in her hand, a far cry from the sinister tormentor she remembered. Perhaps if she tried… She pressed her palm against the stone and willed her mind to reach out to the trance. Nothing. She tried again. Not even a twinge or a tickle.

"Malord." Sariah called from the door.

Malord knuckled himself into the chamber.

"I need to know if this stone can be wised." Sariah held out the prism. "It's a very strong stone. It can be dangerous. You've got to act with care."

Cautiously, Malord tapped his weathered fingers against the stone. "I don't feel anything." He laid a careful palm against the stone. "Nothing at all. There's a wising in this?"

It was disappointing but expected. It confirmed Sariah's theory. The prism could only be wised when active, and even then, like with the seven stones, its final trance would only engage the one stonewiser who had managed to wise Leandro's game and the sage's statues, namely her. Damn. It was back to her dangerous idea.

"Thanks, Malord," Sariah said. "Come on, Kael. We've got to go."

They startled the people loafing in the antechamber with a swift passage.

"Find Mia," Sariah said to Delis in passing. "Bring her to me."

Lorian dropped her counting tablet. Uma tried to ask, "Where are you g—"

The Hounds guarding her door deployed themselves to detain the others. A half-dozen Hounds fell behind Sariah and Kael, as if they had been escorting the pair all their lives. They made it down the stairs and into the keep's main lane, where the wind sliced through her clothing as if she were a ghost without substance. She didn't care. She had forgotten about the pain, the weakness, the crippling sorrow. Her mind was clear with purpose and sprinting like the strongest runner. They were within sight of that horrible place by the time the notion struck her.

"Grimly must have thought them unnecessary," she said. "She wouldn't have left the sisters behind if she still needed them."

"Does that mean that—?"

"Grimly must think that she already has what she wants."

Her *live* child.

□ ■ □

No one had ever termed the Guild's cages as comfortable, especially not Kael or Sariah, who had spent time in the misery of the wretched place. They rushed from one cage to the next, looking for Belana among the dejected prisoners crowding the upper cages.

"Stonewiser!" A voice thundered from one of the cages. "How could you stoop so low as to bring us here by force?"

Sariah spied the trio of red robes among the defeated keep guards.

"It's about that time," Petrid said. "Have you been bitten yet?"

He must have seen Sariah flinch. He cackled quietly, an odious chattering eerily similar to that of the monkey perched on his shoulder. "You can't wise anymore." He laughed even harder.

Sariah rushed to the floor below. Curse the executioners. They had loaded their dice to win and were ready to collect their earnings.

"Is it true?" Kael said. "What he said? About you not being able to wise?"

"It's true."

Without a word, he moved on to the next cage. Sariah appreciated the reprieve, because at the moment, even a kind word could have tripped her fickle emotions.

The cage they sought was in the deepest and gloomiest part of the keep's many dungeons. Ultimately, it was the wailing that led them to Belana. The woman was balled in the darkest corner of the foul-smelling cage.

"Open it," Sariah said to the guard.

"Are you sure? She bites and scratches like a wild cat."

"I'm sure." Sariah stepped into the cage, scattering the rats with her cautious steps. "Belana? Are you all right?"

The creature who struck from the shadows wore horror's face. The ashen pallor, the gruesome snarl, the guttural growl that turned into a hiss through bared fangs sent Sariah tumbling against the bars.

"Don't hurt her." Sariah stopped the guard. "Your light. It bothers her."

"The woman's blind, my lady."

"But the light hurts her."

Indeed, Belana was clawing at her eyes as if the torch were a relentless sun.

"Is that better?" Sariah asked when the guard withdrew. "I've brought what you need."

"Do you have it?" Belana sniffed the air like a she-wolf. "Did you bring it?"

"Right here." Sariah placed the prism in Belana's anxious hands. The sister clutched the accursed thing against her breast and sobbed like a weeping widow. Sariah hesitated before patting the wretch's back. Despite the spectrum of her terrible memories, Belana seemed frail and alone in the cage's darkness. Her arms locked around Sariah's waist. Kael was by her side in an instant, but Sariah waved him off.

"She's dead," Belana whimpered. "Little sister's dead."

Sariah didn't know quite what to say.

"It was awful. We felt it. It hurt. He killed her." Belana's nostrils flared in Kael's direction. "That putrid stink of a mongrel killed her. We'll scratch his eyes out, we swear."

"No, nay, please don't." Wordlessly, Sariah pleaded with Kael for forbearance. "He thought Telana was my enemy, you see. He thought you wanted to kill me."

"We didn't want to. I promise we didn't want to."

"I know, but he's my mate. He thought you hurt me."

Belana wrinkled her nose. "Stonewisers don't have mates."

"I do," Sariah said. "I couldn't tell you before, because I couldn't speak. Remember? He went looking for Grimly, but he found you and Telana instead."

"The light," Belana said. "It hurt. We needed the prism. We had to have it."

"You have it. You're fine now."

"We were one in the womb, all alone with the stone. What will we do now?"

"It's all right. I'll take care of you."

Kael mouthed a soundless but definitive no.

"You won't like us." Belana sobbed. "The mistress said it. What we need. Nobody but she will give it."

Grimly had probably been right about that.

Sariah stilled her churning stomach. "We'll have to find another way. A little cream, perhaps some cake?"

"Cake tastes nice to the tongue," Belana said. "But it does nothing for the belly's growl. We are what we are."

That's what they had been raised to believe. This poor oddity, how could she believe otherwise? Why would she consider herself anything other than what Grimly said she and her sister were? And even if Belana tried, could she, Sariah, overcome her own revulsion to keep an oath?

She held Belana's grisly face between her hands. She stared at the ghoulish complexion, at the bizarre sightless eyes, at the feral expressions on her quasi-human face. She inhaled the scent of ripe olives and lard, seeking her senses' acceptance. It wasn't easy. The woman's smell provoked her bile. She had lost so much to the sisters. She asked so much of Belana. Could she give in similar measure?

Compassion. Sariah summoned it, from where, she didn't know.

"Oooooooh." Belana's lips puckered in wonderment.

"We can be who we want to be," Sariah said.

Belana's hot tears soaked through Sariah's tunic and drenched her belly. All Sariah could do was cradle the odd creature who was going to help her to find both the tale and her son.

Forty-five

"TELL ME AGAIN," Sariah said. "Where was the mistress going? What did she intend to do? Did she travel with my baby?"

"Baby?" Belana grimaced a puzzled frown.

"Wiserling. Did Mistress Grimly travel with my wiserling?"

Belana turned to Kael, fangs bared in a chilling smile. "More, please?"

Sariah cautioned herself not to look, but her eyes meandered to Kael's bloody hands, picking the brains of a slaughtered piglet and offering Belana a share.

"No core?" Belana asked.

"No core," Kael said.

"Shame." Belana pouted. "A wiserling's core is the best part."

Sariah stumbled to the bucket and wretched.

"Sorry," Belana mumbled through bloody teeth.

"It's hard for Sariah," Kael said.

"It's delicious for us," Belana said.

Belana's feeding was the foulest of spectacles, one that evoked memories Sariah would rather forget. But Belana had been starving and Sariah knew that the woman couldn't be of any use unless her basic needs were satisfied. If she would just finish quickly. A sliver of pure red was all that remained in the bracelet's ninth crystal, a tiny dot filling up fast. Sariah was hard pressed to restrain her urgency. But at least Belana was calm now, looking much better.

They had found a small, dark storage room in the Hall of Numbers' cellar. It was clean, warm and rodent free. Fresh straw piled with clean blankets in a corner to make for a comfortable nest and the single light of a shielded candle didn't bother Belana's eyes. The food selection had been Kael's idea. It wasn't to Sariah's liking, but it was a damn good choice considering the alternatives.

"I think you've had plenty." Sariah wiped Belana's face with a wet rag. "About the wiserlings. Where's Grimly going?"

Belana shrugged. "Bright place. Cold, wet, bad. We cried and cried with the hurt. We needed it." She kissed the prism in her hands and turned to Kael. "We think your eyeball would taste good. We'd eat it, if you give it to us."

"No, thanks," Kael said. "I think I'd rather keep it."

"Thirsty." Belana squeezed Sariah's breast. "Is there any left for us?"

Sariah fought the urge to slap her. Instead, she took a deep breath and removed Belana's hand from her breast. "My milk's long dried up."

"Pity. We liked mother's milk. We drank it all the time. From the stonewisers. It goes sour when they die."

Sariah gagged.

Kael intervened. "How do you grow the wiserlings?"

"We were made for it. Before us, the stone was only a hound for the blood. But the mistress, she found a new way."

It was just what Sariah had concluded that fateful night at the Mating Hall. Grimly had adapted the stone's unique power in an attempt to create the powerful stonewisers she coveted. It was a trespass as old as the execration, a foul deed prohibited as early as Meliahs' pact. Sariah had felt the prism's struggle in her own flesh. She didn't dare consider the effects of that struggle on her child.

"Will you let us grow more wiserlings for you?" Belana asked. "We can grow them good. We promise. We make only a few mistakes."

It was Kael who answered. "No more growing wiserlings."

"Will you kill us then?" The sightless eyes were trained on Sariah's face.

"Growing wiserlings is not the only thing you can do," Sariah said. "We'll find something better for you to do, something that doesn't hurt people."

"You think we could do that?"

"That and more. But right now, I need you to help me."

"How?" Belana asked.

"Can you wise stone?"

Belana's lips curved down in a sad expression. "We can't. The stone doesn't like us that way. What we do is more like the opposite of wising."

It was a strange way of putting it, but Sariah suspected it was the truth. "It's fine, Belana, don't be sad. Even if you can't wise stone, you can still help me. I must ask a great favor of you." She whispered the rest.

"You want me to do what?" Belana croaked. "Are you crazy, little sister?"

"This is very, very important."

Sariah sat on the cellar's floor and braced herself against the wall. She wished she had a different alternative. She also wished Mia was around for a loan of strength. But Delis hadn't come back yet and Sariah couldn't afford to wait any longer.

Belana shook her head. "But you didn't like it before—"

"There's no other choice."

"What do you mean to do?" Kael knelt by her side. "Is it safe?"

It was far from safe. But what else was she supposed to do?

She lifted her tunic and exposed her navel. She took the stone from Belana, who let go of it reluctantly. Sariah's hands were shaking. She wasn't able to aim the prism's sharp point, mostly because of pure terror of the thing. She was liable to pierce herself badly if she kept at it.

"Hold this." She gave the stone to Kael. "Place it against my navel's center. Here."

"I want no part of this. If this is going to hurt you—"

"Please, Kael. Ars. Our son. This might be the only way."

His eyes were storming with doubt, but he bit his lips and steadied his hands. The point of the prism hovered over her navel's deepest fold, a contact so slight that Sariah could barely feel it.

"Hold it steady," she said. "Now you."

"But we don't want to," Belana said.

Not even in her wildest nightmares had Sariah fathomed that she would ask for it. "Belana, a lot is riding on this. Please. I need you to hurt me."

□ ■ □

The first bolt of the prism's power left Sariah's ears ringing. The second jolt reminded all corners of her body of the meaning of pain. By the third bolt, she had broken into a cold sweat, her belly button was oozing blood, and she was in danger of losing consciousness.

Belana begged. "We don't want to do it no more."

"One more time." Sariah wiped the sweat from her brow. "I'll catch it this time."

Damn the stupid bracelet. It had been sapping her wising essence for days now, emptying her power from her core like a sucking drain.

"This is the last time," Kael said. "Do you hear me?"

"Do it," Sariah said, before her body rebelled and ran away from her mind's tyranny.

The jolt zapped her like lightning. Her arms and legs jerked. Her joints echoed the power's buzz with a throbbing ache. The world went dark. A single glimmer of power uncoiled from her depths and slithered at the very edge of oblivion. Sariah pounced on it. She rode it like some unwieldy massive serpent. She held on to it, spurred it, until it sparked one of her links to life, and then a second and a third.

The scent is a spark of reckless life, she remembered Tirsis's words. Sariah was using the prism's torturing jolt to spark her sputtering stonewiser's power. In turn, her own wavering life force was fueling the stone. It was an uneven exchange, one that could kill her at any moment, but it was worth the risk if it yielded the tale.

It wasn't working too well. She had to modify her approach to compensate for her lack of power. She collected the remnants of the prism's power humming in her joints and slung them back into the prism. She held her breath. She hoped the prism wouldn't refract the huge blow back to her.

A deep amber light flickered in the stone and strengthened with her body's contact. Slowly, the glow stabilized, sustaining a shimmering luminosity. Thank Meliahs. All she had to do now was keep the stone going, stay alive, and of course, wise the damn tale.

□ ■ □

Sariah embraced the stone's trance with a lover's passion. The prism's optical prowess extended to her eyes and this time, she didn't have the need or the strength to curtail the visions. Fantastic lights projected onto the black screen of her closed eyelids, toying with her pupils to match the stone's phenomenal patterns. When she opened her eyes, the tale she saw flowed through the prism and projected onto the cellar's floor. The three-dimensional images of the four sages and Zeminaya took shape from the light. The tale began where it had stopped the last time. In the stormy night, the sages faced each other over the most beautiful stone Sariah had ever seen.

"That stone," Kael said. "Can it be?"

"Aye," she said. "The stone of creation."

It was the stone Meliahs used to fashion the world, to give life to the Blood, to make stonewisers. It was the very stone stonewisers of old had misused to break Meliahs' prohibition, to make simmering fire and flesh. Again, in Grimly's hand, a portion of it had been used to repeat the mistakes that led to the execration, to fashion wiserlings.

In the tale, the stone's extraordinary call reigned supreme over the stonewisers' senses. It was hard for the four sages and Zeminaya to withstand such seduction while keeping to their purposes. It was hard for Sariah too, but if the others had done it, so could she. She shook herself out of the stone's subversive influence and concentrated on the tale.

"This is as much desertion as it is thievery," Zeminaya was saying. "Here I am, trying to prevent catastrophe, yet you steal life and destruction as if it were nothing but mule baggage."

"It won't do any more damage," Poe said.

"You've seen what comes, dreamer," Zeminaya said. "It's not just the five of us."

"Zeminaya's right," Tirsis said. "As long as the stone is whole, the Blood will be divided by the power it wields."

"What are you saying?" Vargas said.

"A partition for the sake of unity," Tirsis said. "A way to enable creation and discourage destruction."

"A way back for the Blood," Zeminaya said, "if the Blood ever wants a way back."

"Come, my friends," Tirsis said. "We have a hard night of wising ahead, our last together. For we too must part, and like the stone, break for good."

□ ■ □

Sariah struggled to hold on to the trance. It was as slippery as an oiled hand. Or was it her core failing instead? She knew she had this one chance to wise the stone. Her body couldn't endure one more of the prism's torturing jolts and survive. Her frail hold on the trance weakened with every moment that passed. The images failed. Her focus faltered. She gathered whatever little power simmered in her joints and tried again. This time, she was able to return to the tale.

A workshop took shape from the light. Tirsis labored over the stone. It was still warm from the recent wising, puffing golden vapors like a dragon's breath. Tears dripped from Tirsis's eyes as she tapped her mallet over her chisel with a steady thump.

"She was of the Hall of Masons tradition," Kael said.

Aye, a wise sage like Tirsis would have been.

In the tale, the stone cracked open into two uneven parts. Tirsis gestured to the larger portion and addressed Poe. "To you we entrust the greater part of the whole, so that it may be worshipped for Meliahs' pleasure, so that it might escape destruction and persecution."

"And so it shall be," Poe said, bowing formally.

Tirsis handed the smaller portion to Vargas. "To you we entrust this smaller part of the whole, so that it may disappear and thus become the last of all assurances. You're destruction's last warden."

"And so I shall become." Vargas pressed her pitchfork against her breast.

"A stone divided into two parts is still easy to put together," Zeminaya said.

"Patience, my friend. We're not done yet." Tirsis wiped the tears from her face and bent over the larger part of the broken stone. She began to harvest the druses from the geode's center at random, chiseling the ones most likely to remain whole, a good lot of them. She wrapped the pieces in a silken cloth with great care and gave them to Eneis.

"To you we entrust this part, further divided but together, so that it can only be found by the witted studious."

A mixture of disbelief, despair and sadness darkened Eneis's homely face as he beheld the broken pieces in his hands. "Who can puzzle out faith and destruction if not the witted studious?"

Sariah's mind slipped from the tale like a climber dangling from a larded rope. Not yet. She needed a few more moments. She focused all her strength on the tale and somehow made it back.

"We need a fourth part," Zeminaya was saying. "Four parts will daunt even destruction's greatest seekers."

The veins in Tirsis's hands bulged. Her chisel glowed with her sight engraver's power. An issue of soft white light carved a section out of the stone's core. Carefully, she pulled out the newly chiseled piece. It was still sparkling with the light's refraction. Several flat, highly polished surfaces met in a triangular base that thinned out into a point as sharp as a whalebone needle.

"What will you do with this last part?" Zeminaya eyed the stone on Tirsis's lap.

"This stone I'll wise myself," Tirsis said. "But she who wises this stone cannot be its warden. So you, Zemi, you who'll remain in the world at large, you'll be its warden. It must be found by those who search for the truth, even though it must be protected, foremost from greed."

Tirsis closed her eyes and imprinted the stone for a long while. After she was done, she ran the tips of her long delicate fingers over the even edges of her newest creation. She cried out when she pricked her thumb at the tip.

A beam of symmetrical light shot up from the newly carved stone to project a kaleidoscope of brilliant light on the ceiling. It grew to tremendous complexity before it was done. It was beautiful, an elegant combination of geometrical and scrolled shapes which shifted three times before its final flare was imprinted on the ceiling.

Kael gasped. "By the rot—"

The image of Tirsis returned to command the tale. She was smiling, beholding Zeminaya and the others. "A part to be worshipped, a part to thwart destruction, a part to lead the way to the truth, and a part to stand witness to the Blood. We've done our best. Meliahs save us from the rest."

□ ■ □

Sariah was stunned. These five sages had wielded the goddess's courage to split more than stone: themselves. Friends and foes, allies and opponents, they had conspired together and reached across the generations to grant the Blood the possibility of a future. In the process they had touched Sariah with the miracle of their Wisdom.

A new realization rattled her. "Grimly wanted the stone whole."

"To gather not just the prism's power," Kael said. "But all of the stone of creation's power."

She had found and wised three out of the stone's four parts. How close had she come to doing Grimly's bidding?

Kael's touch was as soothing as his voice. "Don't fear, Sariah. She can't do it. We have three of the stone's four parts."

Aye, but the close call didn't make her feel any better.

The stone of creation had been divided, like the Blood, but it was real. The largest part dwelt among the Hounds at the Dome of the Going, to be worshipped. The second part was lost, thank Meliahs, entrusted to Vargas precisely to avoid an ill-intended unification. The third part, recently reunited with the first, were the carved druses, cleverly disguised by scholarly Eneis as Leandro's game. The last part was the prism carved from the stone's center by Tirsis herself, the stone Sariah held in her hand. Sariah knew that Grimly had refashioned it to serve her own interests.

What's pure but stone? Eneis had said. *What's more credible than proof, more credible than action and moment, but substance itself?"*

At last, Sariah knew with certainty what she needed to do to furnish the tale.

□ ■ □

Sariah stood up in too much of a hurry to mind her aching joints. "We've much to do."

Belana clung to her leg. "Don't leave us, little sister."

Meliahs grant her patience. "You won't be alone."

Kael opened the door and beckoned Malord, who had been instructed on the subject of the white sister. Malord had seen his share of bloody deeds during his long life, but still, when he saw Belana picking at the piglet's remains, he blanched.

"This is Malord," Sariah said. "He and some of my Hounds will stay here with you. Do you promise you'll be nice to him?"

Belana sniffed Malord and then tentatively reached out to probe his truncated limbs. "Did somebody eat your legs?" she asked. "Were they good?"

Forty-six

SARIAH FOUND DELIS drinking more than ale in the keep's old guardhouse. Several off-duty Hounds waited around for a trade of tastes.

"What do you think you are doing?" Sariah whispered, furious.

Delis had the gall to look completely unabashed, even as she wiped the blood off her mouth with the back of her sleeve. "Didn't you send me to find Mia for you? She is with the Hounds. They went to fetch her. So I'm making the most out of waiting."

"Would you like some of my blood, saba?" One of the Hounds extended his arm with impeccable courtesy.

"No, thank you." Sariah managed to smile.

She dragged Delis aside, away from the Hounds' appraising looks. "For Meliahs' sake. Why would you take up blood licking?"

"Isn't it obvious, my donnis?"

"Don't tell me. You think that when you offer your blood, your life's continuance is assured in those men's veins? You believe that when you take their blood, they live on in you?"

"I don't know about that." Delis shuffled embarrassedly. "But you said we had to make allies, and the Hounds are restless creatures. There's no surer way of making friends with a Hound than blood licking. You should try it, my donnis. You need all the friends you can get."

Sariah didn't know if she should scold or praise Delis, but by any account, she didn't have time to decide. "I need you to do something for me."

"Of course, my donnis."

Sariah told her.

"Now?" Delis asked. "My donnis, you're not well yet and the toad wisers—"

"The who?"

"Toad wisers." Delis flashed a quick grin. "That's the Hound's nickname for the black-robed fools croaking in this crowded pond."

Sariah fought the smile tickling her lips.

"In any case," Delis said, "the toad wisers won't let you. They need you. I don't even know if the Hounds will have it either—"

"They don't need to know."

"It might be too soon—"

"Or too late."

Delis thought about that. "Do you think it can be done?"

"I think that if anyone can do it, it's you. Something without entailing toxic fumes would be nice."

"Aren't we getting picky these days?" Delis said. "And the old wasp?"

"He knows."

"Should I be pleased the man is back?"

"Very pleased." Sariah squeezed Delis's hands. "I'm sorry if I hurt you before. What I said, about the oath, I didn't mean it like that—"

"I know."

"You were the one who realized what—no, *who* I needed. You fetched him for me. The truth is that no one has been a better friend to me than you."

Delis's blue and violet eyes considered her thoughtfully. "Still, he's the one you trust the most."

Sariah didn't miss the chagrin in Delis's voice. "But I'm donnis only to you."

"So if it wasn't him...?"

"Aye," Sariah said, and she didn't think she was completely lying.

☐ ■ ☐

The simple sight of Kael warmed Sariah's heart. But it was the warrior in him who joined her hurried march across the bailey towards the Hall of Stones, in command of an escort of twenty Hounds who blended with her own escort seamlessly.

"Metelaus?" she asked, without missing a step.

"He knows what to do," Kael said.

"So you talked to him? You know about the changes in the Domain?"

"Briefly. He showed me the reports. The rot is acting in strange ways. The weather is crazy everywhere, including here." He surveyed the darkening skies and inhaled the cold air. "Can you smell it? A storm is coming. It smells like a whiff of the belch."

"That would be a first. The belch has never reached beyond the wall to the Goodlands."

"Whatever is happening is affecting the entire land."

"Great." Sariah grimaced. "We're all going down. Together."

"I wish I had the time to study the changes," Kael said. "All that time wasted dodging foes and friends alike—"

"So the Domainer delegation did find you?"

"Find me they did, although not for long."

"You got away from them. Didn't you?"

"Not that I don't want to help them, you know, but we have so little time."

Sariah could see that the land-healer in him was fascinated, curious and eager. But he knew they had to live through today to gain a right to tomorrow.

"What are the odds your plan will work?" he asked.

"Half and half."

"Not very good."

"Yesterday, I had no chance at all."

"Are you sure you want to do this?"

"To secure the tale and to find my son, I would bet on worse odds. So yes, I'm sure."

They had almost crossed the bailey when a group of Hounds trotted in through the gates carrying an oxen-skin-wrapped bundle. At the head of the group, Sariah recognized Torkel, the keeper's brother. A wail echoed in the bailey, and it wasn't just the wind screeching.

Kael frowned, then slowed down. "The patrol is back early."

Sariah halted.

Torkel's eyes went wide when he saw her. "Saba, really, I didn't think much of it. It was just a patrol around the walls. He wanted it so much. It's all my fault. I wanted to please her."

Sariah was faintly aware of Kael's hold on her arm. The Hounds parted to allow her to pass. She came to a dead stop and knelt before the bundle laid on the ground. She took a deep breath before she uncovered the face.

Rig. His young face was partially gone and his eye had sunk into his crushed skull, but his irrepressible black curls stirred in the cold breeze as if he were still alive. The wind cut through Sariah like a set of the Hounds' claws. She didn't have to ask how. Mia and Rig had eroded Torkel's resistance and persuaded him to let Rig go on patrol.

Sariah's heart ached with angry grief. The war. The destruction. They seemed worthless compared to the young life lost. A small crowd was assembling around them. Metelaus had just arrived. The keeper was glaring at his brother with both fury and concern.

Her mind suddenly registered the familiarity of the heart-wrenching wail. She looked up to see Mia restrained in Metelaus's strong arms. Her curls were crusted in blood. Her face was covered with tears. Black flow leaked from her fisted hands. She was screaming like a bolt-stricken fiend. Her wailing haunted the sunset and became the sound of Sariah's most perturbing nightmares.

□ ■ □

Sariah walked with the weight of a thousand boulders on her back. She couldn't delay her meeting with the executioners and there was nothing she could do to console Mia. She felt like the coldest wench in the world. She felt selfish too. She would have wanted the child with her for what was to come. But Mia was in no condition to help. Sariah left her in the care of Celia and Pru and marched on to meet her fate without delay. The night had arrived with the storm. When the sun rose tomorrow, atonement would be over.

But Torkel was not easily appeased. He planted himself in her path and offered her one of his claws. "*He who errs shall be maimed from his sorrows.*"

"Stand aside," Sariah said. "I'm not going to maim you because you made a mistake."

"But saba," the keeper said, "it's the law."

"For my honor," Torkel pleaded. "*What's respect but trust in the blood?*"

"I think your anguish is enough punishment." Sariah side-stepped Torkel and strode on toward the Hall of Stones.

"I'll speak to her later," she overheard the keeper muttering to his brother, before he fell in with the rest of her escort.

"Perhaps you should have punished Torkel," Kael offered quietly.

"So you too think that everything we do should be tainted by blood?"

"Sometimes people can only be comforted in their own strange ways."

"I can't even afford the time to console poor Mia and you want me to stop and punish Torkel? I should have stayed with Mia. Torkel, he is a grown man. Sooner or later, grown men need to learn to comfort themselves."

Kael's silence diffused Sariah's fury. A slushy drizzle crunched beneath her quick steps. The stink of ashes scented the courtyard. Poor Rig. Poor Mia. Poor Torkel. Maybe Kael had a point after all.

Lexia was waiting for them at the Hall of Stones' entrance. "What's this I hear? You're meeting with the executioners?"

Sariah couldn't help but notice that Lexia was well-informed. "Domainer justice." She kept up the pace through the hall's cavernous vestibule. "It shouldn't take too long."

"Did you tell Uma and Lorian?"

"I didn't see the need to complicate things."

Lexia halted. "I think things are already complicated."

The Hall of Stones' massive doors were thrown open to reveal the jet stone aisle crowded with a host of black-robed stonewisers. Lorian and Uma stood framed by the ornately sculpted doors, waiting for Sariah like Meliahs' weeping twins—plague and slaughter.

☐ ■ ☐

The sheer length of Lorian's gangly limb transformed the sweeping motion of her arm into an even grander gesture. "You'll enter the Hall of Stones and account for your actions."

"Let's do this later. I have something very important to do and very little time."

"Whatever you have to do can wait," Lorian said. "The Guild always comes first."

"Not this time." Sariah marched on, knowing herself free from the Guild and secured by her escort's claws. She had taken three steps away from the doors when a dull thump stopped her advance. She pushed against an invisible wall. It yielded some, but then contracted as if she was caught in an invisible net.

Kael ran his hands over the unseen obstacle. "What by the rot is this?"

The surprised gasps coming from the keeper and his Hounds announced they too felt the barrier when they tried to step away from Sariah.

"Saba?" the keeper said.

"This fight requires a different set of weapons." Sariah faced the two councilors. "It's just a guess, but I believe one of you has a wising trick in progress."

"We tire of hearing exclusively about your wising prowess," Lorian said. "We too can wise a good trick or two."

"What kind of trick?" Kael asked.

That would have been an easy question to answer, indeed, a quick problem to solve, if she hadn't lost the bulk of her stonewiser's power to the banishment bracelet. As it was, she didn't even have enough strength left to probe the wising. Trapped. She didn't need this right now.

"Look," Sariah said. "Domainer executioners have come for justice. I have to respond to their law before it's too late—"

"Their laws are no good here," Lorian said. "They can't kill

you or take you by force, not here, at the keep, where they're out-
numbered by stonewisers and Hounds."

"They might not be able to take me just now," Sariah said.
"But they can harm an awful lot of Domainers if I don't deliver
what I promised." She didn't tell them that her life was at stake
too. No sense in adding to their advantage over her.

"You forget there's rot in the keep, disorder in the Guild,"
Uma said.

"I wish I could forget," Sariah said. "Let me go."

"You'll yield your election to us," Lorian said. "Else you'll be
trapped here for the rest of the night, for the rest of your life, if
need be."

Time was the one thing she didn't have. The night was advancing fast. The silver haze had almost filled the last of the crystals
and a strange numbness had settled on her right hand's fingertips.
Was it a last warning? Or was it the beginning of the end? She
didn't have her stonewiser's power to counter the councilors' wising, and as good as Delis and the Hounds were at spilling blood, a
fight would not release the wising that held them there. She had to
think of something and fast.

Sariah considered the Council members. She had an idea. Of
the two, Uma was the more secretive, Lorian was the more reac-
tive. Did she know enough to do as she proposed? She didn't want
to do this here and now, but the fools gave her no choice. They
didn't know they were clamoring for their own destruction. As
pressed for time as she was, Sariah understood that they required
nothing less than total defeat. *Plunge the ax deep into the timber
to split the future's kindling*, the words echoed from her stores of
Vargas's bloody Wisdom.

Quickly then. She had resisted any involvement that could
splatter her with the Guild's dung, and yet here she was, charging
at the future with the Guild's fate stuck in her reluctant claws.
Somewhere in Meliahs' gardens the sages must be laughing, not
just at the dubious notion of a Guild election, but at the sheer irony
of *her* election.

Forty-seven

"LEXIA, GIVE ME the brooch," Sariah said.

"What?" Lexia stared at her, openmouthed.

"The brooch," Sariah said impatiently. "Do you have it?"

"Oh." Lexia fumbled through her pockets until she found it. "Yes, here it is."

It was Kael who took the brooch from Lexia. "Are you sure you want it?" he asked. "You've fought so hard to shed it."

Sariah met his stare. "I am what I am. And this is the only way I know."

Kael's kind green eye dominated his gaze when he relinquished the brooch. Sariah felt like a fake. Here she was, accepting the brooch, when she didn't have a lick of stonewiser power running through her veins. She wasn't wearing a stonewiser's robe, so instead of pinning the brooch between her breasts in the usual fashion, she clasped it on the mantle knot over her shoulder. It felt strange, heavy and baroque against the fur-trimmed mantle. But it was firmly on.

Then, as if she hadn't done herself enough wrong, she walked past the Council members, through the massive doors and down the jet aisle, the only route allowable by the wising trick entrapping her. Her friends followed. Lorian and Uma tripped over each other as they scurried to catch up.

She stopped short of the dais and turned to face the restless audience. Once, the Hall of Stones had been filled to capacity with black-robed wisers and pledges. Now less than a fourth of those remained, scattered in small groups among mostly empty benches. Their smaller numbers were no consolation to Sariah. The last time she had spoken to this crowd she had gotten a man killed. She had never formally addressed her fellow stonewisers, never dreamed she would, least of all on a day when she was nothing more than an ordinary woman forsaken by Meliahs and deserted by the stones. She was suddenly very frightened of the stonewisers before her, of the expectations she spied in their eyes.

"Go on." Kael stood behind her like one of the sages' statues. "They're listening."

She didn't have a lot of time for talk. She took a deep breath and tried to suppress the tremor from her voice. "Do we all agree that this election is binding?"

"It was fairly done," someone said.

"We voted freely," someone else added.

"You said you didn't want to rule the keep," Uma said.

"I said that, and I meant it. But if I've been—" the word got stuck in her throat "—elected, and if we all agree, then it follows that my decisions should be accepted by all the stonewisers in the keep."

"That's why we elected you," Lexia said.

"But you rejected rule," Uma reminded her.

"I might have been a bit premature."

Kael's broken eyebrow climbed high on his forehead.

The fingers on her right hand had gone numb. She needed the goddess's touch as much as she needed a hefty drink to steady her voice. In the absence of both, she resorted to pure confrontational bravado.

"And you?" She challenged the stonewisers in the chamber. "Do you agree to stand down and follow my directions?"

It was a testament to the direness of the Guild's situation that the majority of the stonewisers present murmured a muted assent.

"Very well, then. In my capacity as the keep's first elected ruler, I'll pronounce my first decree." There. She sounded firm enough.

Kael stared at her in open puzzlement. Lexia, the two councilors and the rest of the stonewisers were perched on her every word. Even the keeper and the Hounds seemed interested, an astonishing break in their usually stoic demeanor.

"In accordance with the Guild's laws, I'll appoint one of the councilors as my deputy."

She managed to shock them into total silence for a moment or two. Then Uma and Lorian exploded into questions.

"One among us?"

"Who?"

"The one best suited for the task," Sariah said, sounding more assured by the moment. But who would that be?

"I swear to do as you say," Uma pledged, forestalling Lorian.

So it was to be Uma first. Sariah didn't have time for a long elaborate argument, so she went for the kill right away. "I suppose you'll have to stop courting the little girl Mia then. She's just that, a little girl. Her kind of healing has nothing to do with yours."

The words were as effective as bursting stones.

"Did you approach the abomination?" Lorian's brows knotted in a fearful frown. "Did you speak to that misbegotten thing? We agreed that no hall would pursue new pledges."

Uma stuttered. "I didn't—"

"*She who has the power will rule the world with her might,*" Sariah said. "Isn't that what you said to Mia?"

Lorian hissed. "You did approach the accursed girl!"

"She's a natural healer," Uma said. "She belongs in the Hall of Healers."

Sariah seized the opportunity. "Who can blame Uma for promoting her hall's interests? It's only natural that wisers of the same hall stick together to protect their hall. The Hall of Healers is famous for hunting in packs. Do we remember to which hall Grimly belonged before becoming the Prime Hand?"

It had been nothing more than a hunch, but she knew she had hit home when Uma's golden complexion paled to silvery gray.

"Did the Prime Hand ask you to join Lorian and Olden so she could keep tabs on them?" Sariah asked. "Are you reporting to her about the situation here? Did she leave you behind as a plant to do her bidding?"

Gasps and whispers filled the hall and grew into outrage.

"Grimly's minion," someone cried from the stands.

"We don't want a traitor at the top," someone else said.

And just like that, Uma's chances were squelched. It was amazing how the facts had come together like the pieces of a wooden puzzle. Sariah had considered all she knew about Lorian and Uma, her observations, her hunches, the sequence of events.

"Uma should be stoned and quartered," someone shouted.

Sariah's blood drained from her veins. She didn't want another execution, least of all in the Hall of Stones.

"We're charged with the stone truth," she said with steel in her voice. "You might decide after a proper hearing that this woman should be punished for her actions, but we can't afford to repeat the same mistakes. No more mob lynchings. We must return fair rule to the keep with the justice of our actions."

A murmur of agreement swept the hall. Uma was taken into custody, but she wasn't harmed or dragged away. Sariah experienced a new thrill—her voice had been heard and heeded. A sense of power flushed her body with warmth almost as seductive, sweet and pervasive as the heat of a stone trance. Then the bracelet squeezed tighter and her whole hand went numb from the wrench.

"So it is to be me." Lorian tried to conceal the triumph in her voice.

No time for dillydallying. No inclination for mercy. Sariah shot to kill. "How long have you known about Grimly's trials at the Mating Hall?"

"Me?" Lorian stammered.

"My guess is you've known for a while. I think you knew as soon as Leandro's game disappeared from the Hall of Numbers."

"Leandro's game?" Lexia asked.

"Only a brilliant mind from the Hall of Numbers could have created a wising as precise and logical as the one found in Leandro's game. I should think that since you've been the First of your hall for over twenty years, Lorian, you know what I'm talking about. Did you notice it gone? Was it stolen from you? Or did you give it to Grimly to aid her cause?"

"Is she in cahoots with Grimly?" Lexia's question was an accusation.

"It appeared so," Sariah said. "Until I started thinking. What could the First of the Hall of Numbers do if her hall's sacred treasure disappeared under her watch? Denouncing the theft would be an admission of stupidity, gross neglect and incompetence. It would also cost someone like Lorian not just her position as the First of the Hall of Numbers, but her Council seat."

"Did you lose the teacher's treasure?" Lexia asked. "Answer

me, mistress. I belong to the Hall of Numbers. We have a right to know."

"A right?" Lorian scoffed. "What has happened to the Guild when a ragtag wiser like you thinks *you* can question *me*?"

"Times have changed," Lexia said. "We must all adjust."

The chamber rallied behind her, including Lorian's own escort.

"I'm not incompetent," Lorian said. "I didn't neglect the vaults. I've been a good First for my hall. When all the halls have scattered, the Hall of Numbers endures whole. Will no one see that? I didn't give the game to Grimly. She took it. It was there one day when we toured the vaults together. It wasn't there the next. I couldn't very well go to the hall and announce that our treasure had disappeared, but I couldn't accuse the Prime Hand either. So I did the next best thing. I started looking for it."

And for her, Sariah realized. Lorian would have gone after Sariah, because she suspected Grimly wanted Sariah to find the teacher's treasure. It made sense. Grimly had stolen Leandro's game, Eneis's carved druses, from the Hall of Numbers and put it into play precisely because she wanted the stone reunited. Sariah had been Grimly's tool all along.

Beware of he who plays the stone and not the game, the old crone in Alabara had said. *His tales are your demise.* A caught Domainer roamer would have been easy to turn for someone as cunning as Grimly. It was all becoming clear. Grimly's scam. Arron's catch.

She met Kael's eyes. He had figured it out as well. Grimly had turned the Domainer roamer Leandro and forced him to take Eneis's game into the Domain to bait Sariah. The ordeal caused Leandro to go mad, but still, he put the tale out there and Sariah followed it dutifully. Arron must have discovered Grimly's plan, at least in part. He knew enough to track Leandro. So he sent his Shield into the Domain to find Leandro, and once found, held him prisoner as evidence of Grimly's plot.

"Ilian took you to see Leandro," Sariah said. "Uma and Olden went with you. But Leandro is completely mad now, and you weren't convinced."

"And now, after playing all your games, you want to rule the keep?" Lexia was unable to conceal her contempt. "I don't think so, mistress. There's no vote that will ever elect you."

A murmur of agreement rose from the stonewisers in the hall.

It struck Sariah hard how quickly allegiances changed in the keep, how fast Uma, Lorian and even Lexia had positioned themselves for a quick ascent to power. It must have struck Lorian even harder, because her head hung low on her stringy neck.

Sariah had succeeded at splitting Vargas's proverbial timber, but so far she had only managed to speed destruction's crafty ways. She was keenly aware of the time. The numbness was advancing up her wrist. The little she had gained could be lost in a moment's balance.

On the other hand, what would happen to the Goodlands if the Guild crumbled? What would happen to a leaderless Guild? How could she favor the Domain over the Goodlands or over the land beyond the Bastions without a trace of remorse? Could she just let the Guild die?

In that instant, she had the wherewithal to wonder if the seal was influencing her thinking, propelling her to protect the lives and livelihoods of stonewisers across the centuries. She supposed anything was possible when considering Zeminaya and the sages. But she was different from them, and seal or not, her thoughts and emotions were clear. The Blood could only thrive in unity.

She might have been sealed with someone else's legacy, but looking at her fellow stonewisers' expectant faces, she realized that she had her own legacy to impart. She believed in the power of a united people—Domainers, Hounds, Goodlanders, stonewisers—to defeat the rot, restore the land and return to Meliahs' ways, labor and sweat. She had been elected by her fellow stonewisers. Elected. That was no intrusion trick, no sages' meddling.

She made up her mind. She took the wrinkled parchment out of her pocket and held it up with her left hand, because her right hand wasn't working anymore.

"Do you know what this is?"

No one spoke. There was no room for long explanations or lengthy discourse. She had to do this now and move on, or risk forsaking everything she had pledged to protect, everything she cared about.

"This is an old-fashioned document. It was addressed to the Council, yet I have a copy of it, and others, apparently many people, have copies of it as well. I wonder—is there a person in this hall who hasn't read it yet?"

Nobody met her gaze. She unfolded the parchment and read it aloud.

"I, Sariah, free stonewiser of the one Blood, formerly of the Guild's Hall of Scribes' sixty-sixth folio, hereby swear and affirm that I have wised the seven twin stones before credible witnesses and that the tales confirmed that we are all of the one Blood. It is a discovery which frees all of us to reconcile, to stop the bloodshed, to build a new tale together; for what is the call of the stones if not justice for all?"

Absolute silence met her reading, until at last Lexia cleared her throat and broke the chamber's tense stillness. "Anybody who had access to the Council could have copied that document."

"Are you saying that you know who copied it?" Sariah asked.

"I've been in the Mating Hall for five years," Lexia said. "I couldn't have."

"Yet you knew of it."

"No—"

"When we first met you told me you had hope until they caught me. Perhaps your hope came from reading this?"

"My hope came from word of mouth, rumor."

"As you once said to me, information was hard to come by at the Mating Hall."

"The goddess spare me, Sariah. I'm your friend. You don't think I could have written all those copies, do you?"

"I'm trying to make a point. Somebody capable of commanding hundreds of copies thought of it. The head of a hall, perhaps?"

Uma started. "But that would be—"

"Treason?" Sariah smiled. "Aye."

"Do you know what could happen to a treasonous hall?" Lorian said. "It could be disbanded, scattered, ruled out of existence."

"Yet someone thought the message in this document was important enough to run such risks."

"How does this have anything to do with who rules the keep next?" Uma asked.

Why were they so obtuse?

"The person who copied and released this document wasn't working with Grimly or Arron," Sariah said. "It makes both Grimly and Arron look like divisive warmongers. To ensure that the parchment would survive the rot, many copies were made. To make sure the message reached everybody, including people who were not stonewisers, parchment was used instead of stone. The person who commanded those copies was willing to risk status, position and hall. Whoever did this wanted to put a stop to the bloodshed and had the Guild's best interest at heart. Sometimes treason is not a choice. It's a responsibility."

Uma didn't hesitate. "I must confess. It was I who commanded those copies."

Someone cried out from the benches, "For all anyone knows, I commanded them."

Lorian's pronounced Adam's apple bobbed up and down her throat. "It can't be."

Lexia snapped. "We're back where we began."

"Not quite," Sariah said. "Lorian, will you care to explain?"

An uncertain hush fell over the hall. Sariah could almost hear the wheels of Uma's mind creaking as she tried to come up with a credible tale, but it was Lorian who spoke up first.

"It was a fair exchange," she said.

"Go on." Sariah's forearm was completely numb. "Quickly now."

"I heard through my..."

"Spies?" Sariah offered.

"Helpers." Lorian gulped. "I heard through my helpers that the mistress had received a stone from you. It was addressed to the Council, you understand. We had a right to know what it said. Mistress Grimly had stolen my treasure, so I stole the stone from her desk, copied it and put it back. I knew the sorry state of affairs. Your stone message wasn't going to be addressed by the Council. Arron and Grimly were warring. I had to find another way."

"Oh no, not her," Lexia said. "How can you know she tells the truth after so many lies?"

"Proof, yes," Sariah said. "The bane of our time. I can call on some of that. It's the ink, you see. The Hall of Scribes favors spider webs for thickening. The Hall of Epics likes sparkling sand. The Hall of Numbers prefers a composition of heavy lead mixed with water soluble gum which comes from the sap of the Domain's enduring wood, the bulbous tupelo. It has a very dark reddish tint and a particularly fragrant and distinctive smell, sweet but citrus-like."

Sariah waved the parchment before Kael's nose.

He inhaled. "Very nice. Lemons, I think."

"All this time," Lorian said. "You knew?"

"I suspected it when I saw the first copy, but now, it all makes sense. You sent your Hall of Numbers' agent to the Domain's forester. It was easy to combine his two tasks, masking one with the other. Let's not pretend we're all appalled at the thought of a Guild hall doing business with the Domain. We all know it happens. As usual, your agent went to the forester to trade for the gum the Hall of Numbers uses to make its ink. While there, he persuaded the forester to set a trap for me."

"The forester set a trap for you?" It was Kael and he wasn't pleased.

Oooops. Sariah went on. "Lorian's agent pretended to come from Grimly in order to conceal her identity and protect the Hall of Numbers. She was looking for me, just like Arron and Grimly."

"Should I have abandoned the Guild to succumb to Grimly and Arron's ambitions?" Lorian said.

Sariah considered the woman before her with new eyes. In a time of greed, a little loyalty couldn't be harmful. Sariah didn't like Lorian, but all she knew about the woman suggested she cared about the Guild, at least enough to refuse both Arron and Grimly. During these troubled times, Lorian had chosen to stay at the keep. She had tried to keep the rot's appearance a secret to protect the Guild. She had risked her neck and her hall to copy and distribute the call. Considering the circumstances, those were no small feats.

But Lexia was nowhere near as forgiving. "Lorian isn't fit to rule. She lost the teacher's treasure. She conspired with traitors. She must be expelled from the hall."

A murmur of approval suggested Lexia had won over Lorian's followers. Given the mess at the keep, change had become attractive to these weary stonewisers. Sariah couldn't blame them. They would be much more willing to support the woman who had busted out of the Mating Hall and challenged Lorian, than the mistress who had led them for twenty years. But the choice wasn't theirs. Not yet. It was hers. And it needed to be made swiftly.

The burden pained Sariah. She thought of Lexia's long stay at the Mating Hall, of her own time in the horrible place, of the friendship Lexia had offered, of the comfort she had taken in that friendship. She remembered how Lexia had cared for her through her recent sickness, how she had defended Sariah when she couldn't find her own voice. Then she steeled herself for what she had to do even though she didn't like it. It was a day of truth, a day to tackle all lies.

"Is a lie always a betrayal?" she asked.

"Of course it is," Lexia said. "What else could it be?"

"A way out."

Lexia was suddenly subdued. Fear glowered in her stare, but tears dampened her eyes as well. She realized that Sariah knew.

How? her eyes asked silently.

A memory of the words that Grimly had said the day Violet died flashed in Sariah's mind. *The gall of the wench, to tell the mistress you were turning wising tricks in her pen.* Lexia had used the same exact words offhandedly just a few days ago. How did she know something Sariah had never told anyone?

Sariah was sure that Lexia had seen the parchment before, not just because she could spy the truth in the other woman's eyes, but because Grimly had likely showed it to Lexia when recruiting the woman to assist her. Grimly, who never left anything to chance, had handpicked Lexia to escort Sariah to the pen, to befriend her, to watch her. Sariah should have seen it all before, but she had been too sick to put it all together. It was strange. Sariah didn't doubt Lexia liked her. But it didn't change the facts. It wasn't Violet who had told Grimly about Sariah's plans. It was Lexia.

"Sariah, I—"

"Don't say anything, Lexia."

"But—"

"Don't fret. We both know it can't be you. Not yet."

"You won't—?"

"No, Lexia. I won't."

"But why not?"

She wiped a tear from Lexia's cheek and whispered. "To save my baby's life, I might have done the same."

□ ■ □

Time to end it. Sariah turned to face the stonewisers before her. She knew their anguish, the conflict between blind obedience to the Guild and loyalty to the self, the struggle between service to the stones and compassion for others. Need it always be so?

"She who issued the call of the stone should be the first to follow it," Sariah said. "I appoint you to the task."

Lorian jerked. "Me?"

"You had the right idea. But remember, Lorian, it's the stonewisers who make the Guild, not the other way around. You'll do fine if you learn to care for your stonewisers as well as you care for the Guild. If we can all learn to care for each other as much as we care for the stones, we'll be all right. Do you think you can do that?"

Lorian gazed over the stonewisers in the hall. "I think perhaps, until things are settled, if Meliahs wills it, and if they want it, I could try."

"I trust you will hold the Hall of Stones to the highest standards of justice," Sariah said. "For Domainers, Hounds and Goodlanders. Now, rescind your wising and let me go."

Lorian groped through her pockets. "Sorry, Sariah, I had forgotten—" She found the stone she sought, shut her eyes and pressed it to the nearest wall. "You're free to go."

"Not quite yet," Sariah said, sprinting out the doors.

Forty-eight

SARIAH MADE IT to the soaring vault of the Hall of Stones' antechamber. Just as her eyes fell on the gigantic candle-clock that lurked over the gates' high arch, the banishment bracelet compressed around her wrist with a third wrenching coil. Her entire arm went numb from the yank. She stumbled to a halt and dropped to her knees. Her quivering legs were unable to support her weight.

"What's wrong?" Kael skidded to a stop beside her.

Sariah stared at her wrist. The bracelet was changing before her very eyes. The same silvery flow which had built up in the crystals seemed to be pouring out of the bracelet now. She had a bad feeling that the lethal discharge was somehow seeping directly into her veins.

"Sariah, what's the matter?" Lexia's concerned face was joined by Lorian, the keeper and the bulk of the Hounds who were now forming a human chain to prevent the rest of the stonewisers from following Sariah.

"Time's up," she mumbled. "It's dawn. I'm done—"

"No, you're not." Kael half-dragged her to the Hall of Stones' massive gates. The doors were opened out into the bailey. The wind hit Sariah in the face, acrid with the scent of fire and death. The air moaned a morbid chant that froze everything—ear, nose, soul. The clouds rushed by pregnant with lightning. Heavy chunks of muddled slush plopped to the ground. It was cold and chilling, as if the goddess had vacated the world and forsaken her vows.

"That trinket may say otherwise, but the sun's not up yet. Look!" Kael barked against the sounds of the storm. "The night's black with ashes. That was the deal. Until the sun comes up."

"I can't—"

"Find a way." Kael yanked her to her feet. "Do you hear me? Find a rotting way!"

Leave it to Kael to carve time out of the darkness enveloping them. He helped her down the stairs and through the lesser law chambers. Lexia and the keeper hovered around her. Lorian followed, wrapped in her black mantle, fighting the drafts like one of Meliahs' ill-omened crows.

She was helpless and empty inside without her stonewiser's power. She had tried and failed. There was no way that she, an ordinary woman confronting extraordinarily bad odds, could do anything to change her circumstances. Was there?

Ordinary people did it all the time, she realized, astounded. They relied on impossible emotions—Meliahs' sisters—Pride, Faith, Courage, Hope and the rest, to defy the darkness and build lives and selves. They did more than just endure. They grew strong, they toiled hard, they thrived without the stone power. They lived full lives and died powerful deaths. They had reason, will and emotions to light the way and warm their days. They had each other. She glanced at Kael, at her unlikely friends. She had that too.

A great calm came over her, the peace that stemmed from accepting death and life at the same time, from understanding hope only after thorough defeat. The consecutive arches of the Hall of Stones' cellars paraded above her like the final markers of her winding trail. Sariah knew what she had to do. She just didn't know if she had enough time left to figure out how to do it. Before she knew it, they arrived at the small law chamber where the executioners waited with Metelaus. Delis was there and so was Malord, with Belana, just as Sariah had requested.

"Where have you been?" a visibly anxious Metelaus said. "Do you have any idea how little time we have left?"

"We had some complications," Kael said.

"She's been struck." Petrid noticed the bracelet's draining glow. "Her time is done."

"It's still dark," Kael said. "You swore she had until sunup. The bracelet may say one thing, but the weather says different and as long as she can do what you asked, she's within her rights. I've never known an executioner to break his word."

Petrid's smile was as confident as ever. "We haven't come all this way to lose our assurances on a technicality. She's drained and the sun will come out any time now."

Kael started to speak on her behalf. Sariah flashed him a grateful look, but she steadied herself on her feet and stepped forward.

"Forgive my ways, executioners, I meant no harm or disrespect. I acknowledge your right to kill me. Everyone has a right to make a living in the Domain and yours is no less than mine."

"How can any man's right be respected when he's captive?" the executioner said.

"You're right," Sariah said. "These proceedings have no bearing unless you're free. So you are free. On my word, no one under my command will stop you if you choose to leave."

The chamber fell deadly quiet.

"Give them their weapons."

"But, my donnis—"

"Their weapons."

The men accepted their swords with trepidation, no doubt expecting a thrust through the gut at any time.

"Can we leave now?"

"You can. Or since you're already here, you can hear me and assess what I have to offer. I'm alive and present. You cannot claim the assurances unless you hear my proof. Am I right?"

The executioners exchanged troubled glances with each other. Somewhere in the Domain, their tribe was packing up for the jubilant trip to the Crags. They would do nothing to jeopardize such triumph.

Sariah's eyes fell on Belana, tucked of her own accord in the chamber's darkest corner. She called her to her side. Like a wild beast, Belana crawled out of the shadows, blind gaze trained on Sariah's face.

Delis elbowed the slacked-jawed executioners. "Didn't your mother teach you not to stare?"

Sariah was keenly aware of the time, of the numbness, of her weakness. Her life's wick was burning down to the end, but she refused to give up without assuring the future of Kael's kin, her kin.

"You really don't have to endanger yourself to humor their primitive laws," Lorian said.

"But I do have to honor their laws," Sariah said, "as the Guild will have to do if we're to restore peace to the land. Whatever happens today, for good or bad, from now on, anyone who comes here for justice shall receive it, including Domainers. Remember? Justice is the call of the stone."

Lorian opened her mouth and closed it several times before she could speak. "You mean to establish—"

"A record of justice," Malord said.

"For Domainers?" Lexia croaked.

"For everyone."

The executioners looked taller and more at ease for the distinction. Outside, the wind groaned with renewed urgency. Sariah felt the cold in her bone marrow. She knew daylight was straining to break the night's hold as surely as the poison in her veins was grinding down her body's weary defenses.

"Do you have it, Belana?" Sariah caressed Belana's fair hair. "I need it again."

The woman relinquished the prism she clutched to her breast.

"Who will stand for the Domain?"

Kael stretched his arm before Sariah. He understood precisely what was required next. She was counting on all she had learned about the stone, from the sages, from her terrible experience with the prism, from the sisters. It was time to give the hound a fair scent.

A little wobbly on her feet, Sariah braced herself. "Only a tiny prick."

She used her left hand to turn the prism's point in the blood pooling at the base of Kael's wrist in the same way she remembered the sisters turning the point over her navel. Nothing. She added her useless right hand and tried again. Nothing. She had not a drop of stonewiser power left to spare. Corrupted by the bracelet's poison, not even the last of her vital force was enough to power the thing.

"Take it from me." Kael placed her hand over his heart. "Take it all. Without you, it matters naught to me."

Tears stung Sariah's eyes. She couldn't accept his precious gift because her palms were numb to his emotions. But she thanked him with a brilliant smile, a smile which brought the furious grin she loved to his face, a fitting last sight to her heart.

They went to their knees together, she leaning on him, he steadying the both of them onto the cold floor. She rested her forehead on his shoulder and listened to the steady beat of his heart, marking the last moments of her ebbing life. She had been lucky, she knew. She had known the stones, freedom and him. She thanked Meliahs for all three favors.

Forty-nine

THE NUDGE FELT shaky at first, a tentative trickle of strength, a contribution of a few more seconds of life, coming from the rhythmic taps on her shoulder. Then the infusion doubled with the addition of a steady rapping against her shoulder blade. She craned her neck. Lexia and Malord were tapping with concentrated expressions on their faces.

"How do I do it?" Lorian also began to tap. "Like this? Is it working?"

It was working. Their strength was sweeping through her body like a rising tide, warming her core and heating her muscles, animating her limbs—even her right arm—compelling her organs to function. She channeled the joyous infusion to her core and from there, to the prism. She gasped when the stone lit up in her hands, a wink of yellow glow that gained brilliancy with her sustained effort.

There was no time to lose. She returned the prism's point to Kael's wrist and turned it slowly in his blood. A light shot from the prism. Sariah ducked to one side but held on to the increasingly unwieldy prism. It was hot and heavy in her hands, difficult to turn. It was like trying to move one of Meliahs' hulking pylons. The light flickered on the ceiling before dying down. She had managed to power the thing, but she didn't know quite how to use it.

"What's wrong?" The strain was showing on Kael's blank face.

"I'll try it again."

"We'll do it." Belana's ghoulish face came into Sariah's field of vision.

Of course. Why hadn't she thought of it? Belana was the natural choice.

"This is different from what you've done before," Sariah said. "It could be dangerous."

"We were made for the prism," Belana said. "Our blood remembers."

"You're very brave."

Belana placed her hands on top of Sariah's hands, unleashing a harsh issue of smoldering heat. Sariah surrendered to the contact's intimacy, to the striking sense of oneness emanating from the strange union. Her palms began to sweat over the prism's increasing glow. The prism turned with more ease. The point ignited with a particularly bright shade of orange.

It happened then. Colored shapes shifted within the prism and projected upwards. An ornate symmetrical pattern emerged as Sariah and Belana rotated the stone in the tiny pool of Kael's welling blood.

"It's working." Sariah smiled. "It's working!"

The light flared three times and then died, leaving an intricate pattern carved on the stone ceiling, a decorative rosette similar to a delicate carbon drawing, something that could have been sketched by a most talented artist. Sariah couldn't believe it.

"You did it, Belana."

"Is little sister pleased?"

"More like delighted." Sariah hugged Belana. "More like mad with happiness."

"This isn't proof of anything," the executioner said.

"Not yet." Sariah caught her breath. "But soon. Who will stand for the Goodlands?"

"I will," Lexia offered.

"No, no, let me," Lorian said.

Sariah and Belana pricked a point of Lorian's blood on her wrist and then repeated the process, until the kaleidoscopic array projected from the prism and flared three times before stamping itself on the ceiling.

Sariah understood that it would match Kael's, but the sight of the twin rosette felt like rapture to her soul. She giggled like a wide-eyed girl. "See? They're the same. The same!"

"I don't understand." Petrid scratched his head, a caricature of his tiny monkey.

Lorian narrowed her eyes on the ceiling. "Are they—?"

"Blood prints," Malord said. "We're looking at blood prints. This is a tale beyond my wildest dream, beyond redemption."

"It's an ancient notion," Lorian said when she saw that the executioners were still at a loss. "It's a stone practice believed lost generations ago."

"Is it like a pennant for a creature's kind?" Metelaus asked.

"Exactly," Sariah said. "In a world where greedy stonewisers had broken the pact, the prism was created for the very purpose of recognizing Meliahs' Blood."

"Extraordinary."

Yes, it was amazing, but Sariah knew she couldn't afford to delay. "Who will stand for the Hounds?"

"My blood is yours, saba." A visibly excited keeper endured the puncture without trepidation. His blood's pattern fit Kael and Lorian's in every way, to the last three light shifts and the matching rosette imprinted on the ceiling. And so did the blood prints of the rest of the men and women in the room.

"It's true," Malord whispered when his turn came.

Delis couldn't take her eyes off her blood's print. "So my blood is no fouler than yours?"

"We're all of the same blood," Metelaus said. "Sariah's been saying that for a long time."

Everyone in the room was staring at the prints on the ceiling in awe. The chief executioner, however, was perturbed. "This is quite remarkable. But how can I trust this is not a wiser trick when there's no comparison to be had?"

It was a fair question. "Here," Sariah said. "Lend me your monkey."

"What?"

Sariah called the little beast. It climbed up her arm and perched on her shoulder, chattering all the while. She cradled it in her arms like a baby. The creature yelped and gnashed a yellowed set of tiny fangs when Sariah and Belana pricked it with the prism, but a tickle under its chin calmed its irritation. The prism flashed briefly and only once before the monkey's blood print embedded itself in the ceiling.

"You see?" Sariah said. "Your monkey's blood print is different from the rest. If we were to apply the prism to every animal in the land, each kind of animal would share the same print. Yet as you can see, the pattern is quite different when comparing it to yours."

Petrid was neither appeased nor content. "Not so fast, wiser. The prism's blood print is proof that there were *things* created beyond the Blood's purity, things beyond the Old and the New Blood, abominations. But the tale you've wised out of it in no way serves to unite the Bloods. As I see it, all of these patterns could be of the wrong blood. We could all be abominations in this room. Couldn't we? So you see, wiser, you've furnished nothing helpful, nothing as agreed."

Sariah wondered if Petrid understood what he proposed. He was willing to cast the abomination spectrum over his people and himself to claim his assurances and fulfill his greed. But of course, his tortuous argument made perverse sense. What harm was an accusation of bad blood to a people who saw themselves as foul-blooded when they stood to gain so much? Sariah realized that all her efforts had been in vain, unless she could somehow shut down Petrid's objections once and for all.

Sariah remembered Grimly's prized scroll. She recalled the sisters' reverence when they spied her name on it. She didn't want to open that door, but a measure of clarity was trying to break up the storming night. The sun would come through the clouds and ash any time now. Her hand was trembling as she put the prism's point like a blade to her wrist. Little sister, they had called her. Could it be?

"We'll do it." Belana grabbed the stone and pricked her own wrist. "We're the tale you seek, little sister."

□ ■ □

A culture of blood took shape before Sariah's very eyes: the Hounds' revolting worship; the Domainers' relentless quest to redeem themselves from the execration's accusations; the Goodlanders' obsessive preoccupation with their blood's own purity. It all came down to the generations' ingrained distrust in their own ability to contain the crime of creation as the ultimate temptation. They had all been right.

Belana's blood justified their skepticism. The fantastical light patterns that shone from the prism were a distorted version of the others. The colors blurred; the tonalities were opaque. It shifted six times instead of three. It left a different print on the cellar's crowded ceiling—a muted, blunted geometry lacking the others' elegant complexity.

Lorian whimpered. "What have we done?"

Sariah's voice failed. "Who was your mother, Belana?"

"The mistress," Belana said. "She said never to say it."

"You can tell me."

"We were grown in the stone's belly. The prism is my father. The stone is my mother."

Sariah's throat was too tight to make words. "Belana, little sister, how old are you?"

Black tears spilled on her face like blotched ink. "We were nine as of the last chill."

□ ■ □

Sariah cursed her own blindness. She cursed Grimly too, for taking her macabre explorations beyond the boundaries of cruelty. In retrospect, Belana's nature should have been obvious to her. She had confused the woman's oddity with her youthful soul. Lost in her own troubles, she had neglected to see Belana's tragedy. In doing so, she had wronged Belana and her dead sister greatly.

Petrid muttered a curse. "Horror of all horrors."

Sariah put her arms around Belana's shoulders. "What gives you the right to judge her blood as worse than ours? You, an executioner of all things. Don't you know how it feels? She's of Meliahs' just the same."

"She's sin turned to flesh," Petrid said. "She was made beyond the bounds of the Blood."

"But with her blood she's proven that Goodlanders, Hounds and Domainers are of the one Blood," Kael said. "You have your proof, executioners, a tale that can unite the Bloods. And we have plenty of witnesses. Now lift your edict and go."

Petrid's pinched face quivered in anger. He opened his mouth to protest, but Malord spoke first.

"The Domain's gathering will be most interested to hear of your reaction here today."

"The Guild certainly considers the tale Stonewiser Sariah has furnished as sufficient for a record of justice," Lorian said. "You wouldn't want to break a first record of justice, would you?"

The incensed flush in Petrid's weathered face was mild compared to the ire flashing in his eyes. "This is an evil place. We'll go now."

"Not to Ars, you won't," Metelaus said. "We're free of your encumbrances and safe."

"And call off your stinking mob," Delis added.

"Aren't you forgetting something?" Kael said. "Your bracelet. Take it with you."

Petrid eyed Sariah. "I assume you want it off?"

Sariah chuckled. Caught in the moment's excitement, Malord, Lexia and Lorian had been distracted from the vital tapping that had deferred the effect of the bracelet's poison. It was strange, this ebbing of strength that surged and receded like a leaden wave, reminding her that although the tale had been delivered, her life was very much at stake.

"It's not so bad to live like you," Sariah said. "A little cold and brittle inside perhaps, but one could get used to it. Are you asking me if I have good reasons to live or are you asking me if the bracelet will kill me?"

"Perhaps you'll survive the bracelet as cunningly as you've survived us," Petrid said.

"Poison is poison," Sariah said. "Take it off, executioner. I want to live. And I want my stonewiser powers back. They may be foul to you, but it's what I am."

The chief executioner approached Sariah cautiously, as if she could bite him, as if she and Belana could turn into venomous species at will. Petrid's monkey was not afraid. He climbed on Sariah's shoulder and licked her ear, chattering like a plague of crickets.

Sariah set the prism aside and watched the executioner intently. She had missed the vital moment before. She wasn't about to miss it again. Petrid mumbled a ritual prayer in the old language, just as he had done when he had invested Sariah with the bracelet. This time, she caught a quick glimpse of the sharp, iron-capped tooth in the very back of his mouth. He clenched subtly, and brought her hand to his mouth. He bestowed a passionate kiss on the bracelet's closed-eyed clasp.

Sariah might have missed the quick lick of blood if she hadn't been watching so carefully. She gathered Petrid had pierced his own tongue with his iron-capped tooth. Unbeknownst to the rest, he smeared a lick of his blood on the clasp when he kissed it. She should have known. After a day like today, she should have guessed that only blood could harbor liberation.

It was surreal. In one subtle pulse, the hinges reappeared on the bracelet. The clasp's silvery lid lifted to reveal the glowering eye. It yielded with a muted hiss. With a twist and a turn, the pin was out.

Sariah had to smile. The bracelet's designer had either a preference for irony or a knack for consolation. One by one the links lifted from her wrist, first Pride, then Courage, then Strength, followed by Hope, Shrewdness, Loyalty, Generosity, Faith, and last, perilous Mercy. She thanked each of Meliahs' sisters. They were all the company a banished traveler might need to endure the journey's hardship, if one ever looked beyond the bracelet's curse. She had never been truly alone in her banishment.

Sariah's arm felt obscenely bare and impossibly light. Nearly a year of torture and despair was suddenly gone. The strength returned first to her body, a surge of vitality which flushed her veins with healthy vigor and returned the sensation to her limbs. Then it traveled to her wiser's core, jolting it out of stillness with a shudder and a shake, until her core was pumping steadily. She basked in the warmth flooding her mind and body, and decided privately that she was after all better suited to exist as the hot-blooded creature she had been born to be.

Kael welcomed her back to the living with an embrace. "Well

done, wiser," he murmured in her ear. "You're the stone's bravest heart."

Ars was safe and Sariah had been true to all her debts.

She was just rising to her feet when she spied one of the Hounds slipping into the chamber and talking urgently to the keeper. Shock flashed on the keeper's face. At that moment, Sariah knew that her reclaimed world was far from mended.

"It's Mia," the keeper said. "They're leaving."

Fifty

THE SIGHT THAT welcomed Sariah to the keep's main lane was horrifying and oddly familiar. Despite the time, dawn was lost to the penumbral darkness. The frantic torches cast more shadows than they gave light, illuminating a chaotic scene of frenzied motion and gleaming weapons. She thought she had seen the long epic line of armed Hounds heading to the keep's massive gates before, the brisk-walking snippet of a curly-haired woman leading the terrifying procession.

"Mia!"

"What is she doing?" Kael asked.

"Stand aside, Auntie. I'm going to war."

Meliahs help her. The child had gone sick with grief.

"You can't go to war, not you, Mia. You don't understand what's happening here."

"But I do, Auntie. The evil Shield is loose upon the land and you won't challenge your former master. He kills people and wastes the Goodlands and you do nothing to stop him."

"It's not like that—"

"I can't let him kill any more good people." Mia's luminous eyes were strangely blank. "Not anymore."

"Mia, if this is about Rig—"

"Rig died," Mia said. "Arron killed him."

"Is it true?" Lorian arrived, an unsettled jumble of long limbs and gasping breath. "Is she mad? We have effective ways to deal with rebellion in the Guild."

"Ways I hope you're about to revise," Sariah said.

How was she going to keep Mia safe?

She spotted the keeper, arguing with some of the Hounds. "Keeper, command your Hounds to stand down."

Shock was etched all over the keeper's face. "They won't listen to me. It's Torkel. He's of Vargas's line. He's convinced a good number of Hounds to follow him."

"Where is he?" Sariah found Torkel directing his Hounds out of the gates. "Torkel!"

Torkel signaled and a line of Hounds stepped between Sariah and him.

"Let me pass."

They didn't move.

"Torkel," Sariah called out. "What are you doing? Stop this. She's just a grieving child."

"She's a wise one," Torkel said without meeting her eyes. "*Wise is he who finds wisdom in the clash of orders. Wise is he who chooses as Vargas would have chosen.*"

Sariah had a mind to impale Vargas on her pitchfork and slap the man to his senses. She knew better. Words would not dissuade Torkel. Sariah had denied him the retribution he needed, and guilt had persuaded him best. He had made up his mind and convinced a great number of Hounds wielding Vargas's violent wisdom as his divisive weapon.

"But Torkel, your oath—"

"Is *to redeem the worthy and forsake the frail, to lead Meliahs' restoration or perish*," Torkel said. "*Who are we but the fist that waits in the shadows to unleash the blow?*"

"It's not that time yet."

"It's past that time."

As if any Hound would choose anything other than blood when readily offered. Sariah didn't know what was worse—the thought of Mia leaving her to wage war or the notion of the Hounds loose upon the Goodlands.

She turned to Kael and the others. "What can we do?"

Kael surveyed the deserting Hounds with expert eyes. "We'll have a bloody fight on our hands if we try to rush those Hounds. It could be a near thing. It will be bloody. And if Arron figures it out while we are at it—"

"This has to be stopped," Lorian said. "If the Hounds leave, the keep will be left unprotected."

"There are some Hounds here who remain loyal to Sariah and the keeper," Kael said. "Lorian, call all the stonewisers you can get to take the place of the deserting Hounds on the walls as fast as you can. Call all the standards in the keep to duty, Domainers and Goodlanders alike. Get those guards who are willing to swear fealty to the keep out of the cages and onto the wall. Let's hope the Shield doesn't realize what's happening just yet."

Lorian took off for the cages like a wrangling raven.

The keeper released and retracted his claws compulsively. "Saba, give me your leave and I'll kill Torkel. He's dishonored my pledge to you and given me cause for battle."

The Hounds were split. Brothers were ready to beset each other for their tortuous Wisdom. "I won't have us killing each other to Arron's benefit today," Sariah said.

Metelaus arrived at the gates, carrying Malord. "I don't understand. They said that—what's happened to Mia? Is it the urges again?"

"No," Sariah said. "Not the urges. She thinks she should lead the Hounds in the fight against Arron."

Metelaus faced his daughter. "Mianina, you can't do this. You're a girl, not a warrior."

"Sooner or later we all have to grow up, Daddy."

"Think of your mother," Metelaus said. "She'll be so sad."

"Sad," Mia said. "Like me."

"I'm your father. I forbid you to go."

"Sorry, Father, but I'm sabita now. I will lead."

"Over my rotting body," Metelaus said. "I won't let you—"

The Hounds standing between Metelaus and Mia released their claws in unison.

"Will you command harm against your own father?" Metelaus said, incredulous.

"Only if you try to stop me," Mia said. "Tell him, Auntie. Tell him that we all have our obligations."

"This is not your duty," Sariah said.

"It is. Rig told me. In the dream."

"That's just your grief talking, Mia. Let me help you get through this."

"Won't you believe me, Auntie? It's inscribed in the Dome of the Going, that I have a duty, that I'll lead my Hounds in the final battle."

That's where Sariah had seen the image! On the frescoes formed on the Dome of the Going when the sages' statues transformed to color and paint.

"Is this prophesy?" Malord asked. "Has it been ordained?"

Ordained to the rot pit, Sariah couldn't care less. This was no mysterious feat of the sages, no mischievous intrusion intervention. This was her Mia, leaving her, leaving them all, to go fight a war that wasn't hers.

"Mia, please."

Sariah had never seen the cold sneer that overtook Mia's face. "You don't believe me. You never do, Auntie. You should, you know. You made me what I am."

The accusation struck her like a low clobber to the gut. She recalled the day she'd had to break Mia. She remembered how thoroughly she had slashed at the remains of her common nature, how savagely she'd had to tear her old connections to allow her stonewiser's links to thrive. She had known then that Mia would hate her one day. She just hadn't realized how brutally that hatred would strike her.

Metelaus came to a quick decision. "Lazar will take care of Ars in my absence. I'm going after Mia. She won't kill me. I have to believe that."

"But you'll need us," Sariah said.

"You can't come," Metelaus said. "We both know what you have to do."

"Kael, I can't just let her go."

"Trust Metelaus to do right by Mia. He's her father."

"She's been through so much." Sariah beheld the beautiful little girl flanked by Torkel and the horror of his best Hounds. It was a contrast too strong to stomach. The pain was rife in her soul, the infectious stab of staggering loss and betrayal. She had expected it from the Guild, from the councilors, from almost anybody at any time. But from Mia?

"Don't do this." Sariah took a step toward Mia and then

another. "There's much work to be done yet. The time to face Arron is not now."

"I said stay away." A shot of flow gushed from Mia's palms, turning the space between her and Sariah into a trail of ashes. Sariah staggered back, shocked.

"Don't try to stop us again," Mia said. "Good-bye, Auntie. May you die well."

Sariah watched Mia go, reeling like a mortally wounded woman. Mia walked through the gates without looking back.

□ ■ □

"What by the rot happened to you?" Kael said.

Sariah turned to see who he was talking to.

Delis stumbled toward them. Blood crusted her nose and flowed down her chin. In her arms, Belana was barely conscious. Kael relieved Delis from her load and settled Belana on the ground. Sariah rushed to Delis's side.

"Are you all right?"

"My donnis, I was going to fetch you, but those wily rot spawns rushed me. When I next knew, I was knocked out flat on my back and those foul mongrels had escaped."

"It's fine, Delis, as long as you're not harmed, the executioners served their purpose. They were free to leave as they wished. Are you sure you're not badly hurt?"

"No, my donnis, you don't understand. They took the stone with them, the prism."

Fury and disbelief flattened all of Sariah's emotions. "Why?"

"They said that it belonged to them." Delis rubbed her head. "They said even if they had been robbed of Ars and all the assurances, they could at least reap some gains from the prism."

"Benefiting from the might of the stone?" They didn't even know how to work it. It was preposterous. It was dangerous. It was pure, greedy profiteering. It was not so different from what the Guild had done since its inception.

She looked up to see Lorian returning from the cages with Lexia in tow. "The wall's secure," she said, "at least for the moment."

"Sariah?" Kael called.

It would be nothing less than irresponsible to leave the prism in the executioners' inexpert hands. "We'll have to retrieve the damn stone—"

"You better look at this," Kael said grimly. He was crouching by Belana, propping up the woman in his arms.

Sariah knelt next to them. "What happened?"

"Are you free, little sister?" Belana asked.

"I am, thanks to you."

"Good." Belana's eyes lost their luster. "Us too."

It was then that Sariah noticed the blood bubbling fluidly from the tiny puncture in Belana's wrist, the purple-black stream trickling over the ghastly pale skin and pooling on the ground like a vast lake.

◻ ◼ ◻

Belana was cold and heavy in Kael's arms. Grimly's creation, Meliahs' forsaken, wiserlings' nightmare, Sariah's torturer and little sister was dead. Sariah caressed the ghastly face and lowered the lids over the milky eyes. The pain. In her heart. Was she grieving over one lonely child who never got the chance to grow up or two? Was she grieving over thousands or millions?

Disregarding the others' spooked whispers, Sariah swiped her finger on Belana's spilled blood, closed her eyes and licked it.

"*What I was to you, you are to me,*" she whispered. Who could tell apart the goddess's wishes from her myths?

Malord inspected the puncture on Belana's arm. "She wasn't made to heal."

"Grimly's cunning," Lorian said. "This poor creature was made to destroy the very evidence of her existence if she was ever probed."

Why was Sariah's heart aching like a gouty joint? "She was just a child."

"Come on." It was Kael, gently shifting Belana out of his arms and helping her up.

"She gave up her life," Sariah said. "For mine?"

"So that we could know," Kael said. "For sure. All of us."

Sariah was suddenly very tired. "We have to bury her."

"It will be done," Lorian said.

"Like a person," Sariah said. "Like the child she was."

"We'll take care of it, little sister," Lexia said.

"Aye." Sariah clung to Lexia's hand. "Little sisters of the prism we are."

□ ■ □

Sariah watched the sun fight the darkness and win. It was a weak sun and a tenuous triumph, a late start to a short day that had begun in ashes and smoke. But it was a new day, and despite the bad odds and the night's losses, she had to believe that it still held promise.

The sights from atop the keep's wall were deceiving. The land looked peaceful. The keep seemed orderly. And yet Sariah knew better.

The smallish cloud on the horizon was the last trace of Mia and her Hounds, a storm of blood spewing from a young girl's rage. Metelaus would not be far behind. Delis would be that speckle on the western road, chasing the executioners to make sure Ars's encumbrances were duly lifted and charged with retrieving the stone. West and South, Mara, her Panadanians and a few thousand more were hunkering down to fight both the rot and the Shield. Lorian huddled in the Hall of Numbers with Malord, debating justice pertaining to all the Blood. Lexia had just started her labor. Sariah regretted she couldn't stay for the birth. In the courtyard, the keeper had assembled his remaining Hounds to chant the Wisdom's lament. The morbid bass echoed beyond the keep like battle drums beating a somber retreat.

Sariah felt lonely. Just as it had happened with the stone of creation generations ago, the friendships that had brought her this far had broken up into separate pieces. Life had scattered them like seed in the wind and the crop was far from assured.

Kael came up to stand beside her so quietly that Sariah felt him before she heard a sound from him. He was a commanding sight, shouldering the bags Delis had prepared for them, dressed for traveling and fully armed, Meliahs' treasure.

"How did you figure it out?" he asked. "How did you know to use the stone in that way?"

"Remember when I wised the tale of the stone of creation? I realized that we were looking at Tirsis's blood print then. In the tale, Tirsis said that the prism's purpose had been to be a witness to the Blood. Belana had told me that before Grimly, the prism had been only a hound for the blood. That's when I realized that the tale I sought, the proof we needed, was the blood print itself."

It was her turn to ask. "Would it matter to you if my blood was just like Belana's?"

"You mean if you were one of Grimly's creations?" He thought about it. "Would it matter to you?"

Sariah shrugged. She was so many things that she never thought she would be. She was stonewiser and mate, friend and mother. She was teacher, foe, aunt, wall-breaker, rot-fighter, sister, seal-spreading plague and who knew what else. Some she had dreamed of, some she had never wanted, yet fate didn't make a distinction. "What's one more brand for the iron-kissed?"

"You're thinking about the lines on that parchment that Grimly had," Kael said. "I can't know how they connected or not as they approached your name, but this you ought to know—you are Meliahs' own, made by her command and for her pleasure, an excellent sample of her fondness for beauty."

Sariah smiled. "*Wise is he whose tongue spreads joy, for he will taste happiness.*"

"The goddess is sparse with her blessings," Kael said. "Whatever you are made of is great and fair to me."

He kissed her and she knew the answer for sure. No. He didn't care.

"Will you really walk away from all of this?" he asked.

"This?" Sariah surveyed the hectic keep, the crowded roads, the bustling town, the burning countryside. "Easily."

"You know what I mean." Kael straightened the brooch on her shoulder. "You've been elected. You've got houses pledged to your name, troops sworn to your command. You are the Bastions' anointed saba. You could reclaim your Hounds and send them to search in your stead."

"If I thought the Hounds would give us some advantage, I wouldn't hesitate to bring some with us. But numbers will not help this hunt. Stealth will. Besides, this is my duty, my search."

"*Our* search," Kael said. "You might yet find some advantages to rule."

"There are many others well suited for this kind of thing. I'm not walking from it, I'm more like running."

"They'll have a tantrum when they find out."

"They're all needed here."

"Still, Lorian will be livid. Malord will be even worse. The keeper, well, I can't even begin to imagine the howling."

"That's why we're not telling them." Sariah pulled the hefty ladder out of the sack she fetched from the stone gutter. "That's why I asked Delis to plan our escape."

"The wench did well." Kael hooked the ladder on the cleverly disguised iron spikes protruding from the crenels. "An old-fashioned escape. No one would expect that at the keep. Won't the wising in the wall be a problem?"

"It would be, if our bodies were to make contact with the wall directly. The wall is wised to repel human flesh. See this?" She ran her fingers through the ladder's thickly padded sides. "Domainer gutweed. With a little bit of care, it should keep us clear of the stone."

"She did well, our Madame executioner. But how did Delis manage that?" He gestured towards the guardhouse, where the extraordinary sight of four Hounds snoring placidly would have shocked Meliahs herself.

"She fed them her blood, fortified with a large dose of sleeping oil rubbed on her skin. Blood is the one temptation Hounds can't resist."

Kael was still laughing when he dropped the ladder. It unraveled against the wall for quite some time. "It's a high wall. Are you sure you can handle the climb down?"

Sariah sighed. "*What's rest but a short reprieve?* I'll be fine."

"We'll find time for you to regain your strength on the road."

"No, nay, no. We've got to hurry, Kael. She might be hurting him. She might break him. She could kill him, or worse—"

"She could turn him into one of hers." He knew the risks as well as she did. He shared her fear as well, the dread lodged in the pit of her soul.

"But he's strong," Kael said. "He'll fight the witch. I know he will."

"He's just a little child."

"I can go. I can travel fast. I can do this on my own."

"Not a chance."

He grinned his furious smile. "I thought you might say that. Are you ready, then?"

Sariah took the hand he put out, brought it to her lips and kissed it. "I'm ready, love. Let's go find our son."

The End

A LOOK AT THE CONCLUDING BOOK
IN THE STONEWISER SAGA,

STONEWISER
The Lament of the Stone

Prologue

DESOLATION AWAITED KAEL at the top of his steep climb. The trail he had been following for the last few days ended abruptly in a barren landscape. He crouched at the edge of a sloping crater. A sterile field of shattered stone sprawled beneath him. The stones were strewn in all directions, as if crumpled by a giant hand. But it wasn't only the gray vision of fractured rock blending with the leaden sky burdening his senses. It was the silence, the total absence of movement and life stifling the air. Doom had a silent way of claiming its territory. Death stalked this place like a curse, hovering over him like an ax ready to split his skull.

He followed the footprints to the stone field. The drizzle had washed away some of the tracks, but he was well practiced in the sport of the hunt. A few days. That's all that stood between him and the beast who had stolen from him. He crouched when he spied the sandaled footprint. Not only was it smaller than the others, but it was also fainter, as if its owner walked above the rest of mankind, as if she deigned not step over the same path everyone else followed. She could not run forever. And he would be waiting for her when forever ended, preferably tomorrow or the day after that.

He surveyed the trampled place where the party split. The bulk of the warriors had waited here, although for what, he wasn't sure. There were no signs of camps or fires, no traces of idle lingering or carelessness. But there had been a late addition to the group, a man who had traveled here from a different direction. Someone of means, Kael noticed, examining the prints of a pair of doubly stitched soles that sported the faint outline of the Guild's master cobbler's seal. It was this new man who had gone into the barren stone field accompanied by a guard. It made perfect sense. She would have never taken the risk herself.

What did Grimly expect to find there? Kael knew firsthand the folly of trying to guess the cunning crone's purposes. The Guild's former Prime Hand was the most dangerous foe a man could face; driven, devious, brilliant, as skilled at intricate deception as she was brutal. He couldn't afford to guess Grimly's game. He had to do better. He had to *know* her game.

The stones crunched under his cautious steps. The one-way tracks led him into a deepening gulch and stopped at the gully's end, as if the men had suddenly vanished. Kael inspected the rocks. They were crammed together and solid. There were no dragging marks, no signs of struggle, no indication of hidden entrances.

He ran his hands over the harsh granite. He was no stone-wiser. Like most people, he was deaf to the stones. But the curse of his Domainer blood offered a slight advantage. Because he was a Domainer, he was able to imprint the stones with tales. Moreover, after years of rebelling against the Guild's brutal rule, he had developed the common skill into a rare but convenient talent. These days he was able to imbue the stones with his most violent emotions making them burst at will.

He wagered he could adapt his singular talent to try to trick an answer from even the sneakiest of stones. That's what he did now, carefully imbuing the piles with a pulse of measured curiosity to unmask the wised stones hiding among all that senseless rock. The stones would never grant him a tale, he knew that, but maybe they would react to his query, betraying their presence and confirming his suspicions that he treaded in wised territory.

Had he been someone else, he might have missed the stones' discreet reply. It came in the form of a smoldering flash, so quick and sudden it could have been his body's own doing. But he was not easily deceived. Born to a stonewiser and mated to another, he was accustomed to the stones' mysterious ways. The heat that flashed through his body reminded him of his lover's fiery embrace. Loving her was like loving the flame. He craved the fire's sizzling blaze. A lick of that familiar flare had taunted him a moment ago. These stones were wised. He was sure.

But even he was surprised when a small burrow began to open

up at the foot of the shifting rocks. It hadn't been there a moment ago. His modest skills with the stones couldn't begin to account for the widening passageway. Could they?

Nay. There was something else in play here, something dangerous. He examined the opening carefully. The footprints disappeared into the darkness. He cringed when he caught a whiff of the foul stink. A revolting scent lingered in the stale air, sweet, noxious and repellant. He listened carefully before he started down the passageway. No noise came from the inside. The only sound he heard was the drizzle, tapping a steady rustle on the rocks, whispering a warning for his ears alone.

Kael proceeded with caution. Wised stone could be gift or curse, friend or foe, wonder or deception. Like Grimly, wised stones could be treacherous too. He crawled along a narrow tunnel, until it widened enough for him to stand beneath a small arch marking an entrance of sorts. He tested the lintel, running his fingers up and down the ledges, finding no ropes, door traps, or hidden mechanisms. His steps made no sound as he advanced down the sloping corridor.

The stagnant air grew steamy as he descended, damp and rich with the foul scents trapped below. A hint of soft, diffused glow issued from somewhere ahead, allowing him to make out the outline of the long winding stairs his feet negotiated. Where was the light coming from? Opaque shadows paraded in his peripheral vision. He ran a hand over the dilapidated paintings that had once decorated the walls. A dank coating of mold feasted on the decrepit plaster and smeared his fingertips.

This had to be an Old World ruin, one of those abandoned places occasionally discovered in the Goodlands, a wreck of the past, a reminder of all that had been lost and destroyed. What was it doing here, so far removed from other known sites? And why was Grimly interested in this place?

The luminescent glow spilled from what appeared to be a larger chamber at the bottom of the stairs. Kael flattened against the wall. With his twin swords poised, he crept down the last few steps. His heartbeat remained steady. Fear had long since been silenced by determination. The child of his heart deserved nothing less than freedom and care. To retrieve the son he had lost, he would challenge Meliahs herself.

The chamber was an ode to destruction. Huge beams fractured the ancient walls. Bursts of long blades skewered the mountain like enormous swords, creating a striking garden of dark fallen stars. The beams had crushed the tiered marble benches, decapitating the gilded statues and shattering the ruined frescoes. Kael's trained eye identified a pattern right away. The jagged beams seemed to radiate from an unseen center. The footprints he tracked veered in the same direction.

At last he was able to identify the source of the strange glow. The place was alight with an odd phosphorescent gleam emanating from the beams. He ventured a touch. The surface was warm to his hand. Remarkable. Were these giant formations made of rock? And if they were indeed stones, were the light and warmth they offered indications of a powerful wising?

He scratched one of the radiant beams with his blade. A thin lustrous layer broke off into a long, smooth plane, a perfect cleavage. The glassy surface reflected the puzzle in his green and black eyes. It was soft and flexible between his fingers. It didn't feel like any rock he knew.

The land healer in him wished he could linger to investigate the odd beams. The roamer in him wanted to survey the entire, extensive place. Observation was a prolific teacher, always willing to speak to the attentive pupil. Not today. He snapped the sample he had taken into smaller pieces and tucked them in his pouch. Perhaps someday he could come back to investigate this place. Right now, his life was pledged to one purpose only—to find his son.

Kael made his way through the beams. The humid heat was hard on the lungs. A man would do well to shorten his exposure to such hostile conditions. He was sweating by the time he reached the ruins' center. The bulk of the columns radiated from a single point, a hollow core, an empty space marked by a low sheaf of needle-sharp blades bursting from the earth. Light issued from these blades, a purple glow pulsing in the sheaf's center. The footprints stopped before a pile of ashes, the source of the awful stink permeating the air.

Kael poked at the ash pile with the tip of his sword. A scorched, brittle pike point clinked against his blade. A charred skull had managed to retain its form. The guard had died a sudden, fiery death. This place was not just treacherous. It was deadly.

The distant clunk of wooden soles heightened his alarm. It seemed impossible, but the sound appeared to be coming from the sheaf itself. A tiny shadow distorted the light's dark hue. A miniscule shape reflected on the blades, a vision of bustling skirts growing in size with every step, gaining color and definition. Kael was hard-pressed to believe his eyes. A woman sprang from the sheaf and marched toward a rustic farm table that materialized out of nowhere in the ruins' center.

Kael clutched his swords with a battle grip, yet the short, stout, middle-aged woman who strode past him with a massive basket perched on her hip seemed harmless. She looked more like a cranky, overworked peasant than a dangerous foe. A cursory glance at the heap of ashes reminded him that he trampled in the stones' perilous territories.

"You'd think two are enough after all this time," the woman muttered in a shrill, grating voice. "But noooo. I get to do it again. Are you as ignorant as the others were?"

The others? Was she talking about Grimly's men?

Kael surveyed the woman's pinched face. A stern pout dominated the lines of her brooding mouth. Little astute eyes burrowed in the wells of furrowed slits. Her massive forearms were as sturdy as the heavy plough they must have wielded in the fields. The dirt-stained hands were topped with callous sausages for fingers. A man different from Kael might have concluded that she was a hallucination of his oxygen-starved, heat-baked mind. Not Kael.

He steeled himself for the uneven confrontation. Since he wasn't a stonewiser, his life would be of no consequence to her. But it could be tricky. He needed the information only she could provide and, other than his wits, he had no way to deflect or defuse her dangerous powers.

The woman huffed. "Don't tell me you don't know who I am."

Kael had an idea, but he saw no advantages to discussing his suspicions.

She slammed the heavy basket on the table. "What kind of fools are we growing these days? Are the likes of you supposed to be the bright future of mankind? If you don't know who I am, then what by Meliahs' stinking pits are you doing here?"

"I'm looking for someone," Kael said. "He came this way. I'd like to know why."

"Why?" She laughed, a screech almost as unpleasant as her voice. "Who gave you the right to ask questions? *I* get to ask the questions around here. Do you know why you are here?"

He endured her glare wordlessly.

"Great," she snapped. "Just great. And a damn mute to top it all. I suppose it doesn't really matter, does it? After all, what's time for a simple creature like you?" She grabbed an ear of corn from her basket, ripped off the husk with a sequence of angry tugs, and tossed the stripped ear into yet another basket.

Kael was sure the new basket hadn't been there a moment ago, and neither had the three-legged stool upon which the woman plopped down. He had grown accustomed to expect surprises from the stones, but this was beyond anything he had experienced before, too real to be false, too eerie to be real.

His blade sliced the air where the basket's tough weave should have stopped it. He could feel the faint resistance of its presence on the table, but when he reached out, the image crumpled, only to rearrange itself around his hand. The air was growing hotter. His lungs were laboring like slaves. He needed to finish his business and get out, before it was too late.

"The men who came here," he said. "Did they come for stones?"

"Do you see any stones here?"

"Not the kind I expected. Perhaps they stole them from you?"

"I might look harmless, but no one can take anything from me that I don't want taken." She eyed him thoroughly. "At least you're burly enough to do the job. I can tell you're skilled. You were taught well. You honor labor and sweat. He didn't." She pursed her lips in the general direction of the ash heap.

"Is that why you killed him?"

"Do you mind a life lost? Aw. How sweet of you. He was nothing to me." She tore into another corn husk.

"Did you kill the other man as well?"

The woman's double chin quivered with indignation. "Do you think I'm a common murderer? Only the ignorant and the unworthy need to die."

"Then where is he? Where did he go?"

"There is only one way to me and one way from me. I don't know where he went. He might have mumbled something about going to the coast."

"Did he mention the woman who sent him here? Do you know of a mistress called Grimly?"

"Now why would he do that? And why would I care about this mistress anyway? Why would I care about *any* of you pitiful mongrels?"

"You were interested enough to allow those men in here," Kael pointed out. "Am I right to think that you had something to do with opening the way into this place?"

She grinned an enigmatic smile. "At least you're not so conceited to think *you* did it."

"Was there a child with the men?"

"A child? Of course not."

"A young one, a baby in arms," Kael insisted. "Perhaps he stayed outside, with the woman?"

"I don't have to answer your daft questions."

"True. On the other hand, I would be most grateful if you could tell me what you know."

"Grateful?" She threw her head back and cackled like a bickering crow. "As if *I* had gone through all *this* just for the purpose of easing *your* puny existence."

Kael swallowed his frustration. Creatures like her were seldom helpful except to themselves, but this one was as infuriating as they came and testy to boot. As far as he knew, there was no reasoning with the stones. A stonewiser might have found this encounter fascinating, but he was pressed for time. He had been gone too long. His camp's safety was at stake and he couldn't afford to lose Grimly's fresh trail.

"Don't look so concerned." The woman flashed an insidious dimpled smile. "What's a life but a few pints of blood for the goddess?"

"Spoken like the warring sage."

"So you do know who I am!"

"You are—"

"Don't you dare speak my name."

"—as intractable in the stone realm as you were in life."

"And even more accomplished now than when I lived." She laughed again. "Smarts. Mankind's single redeeming quality. You're looking better and better for the job."

"What job?"

"Why, the job you came to do, of course."

"I'm afraid you have me confused," Kael said. "I'm no stonewiser. I'm just a man seeking justice. If you're not going to help me, I might as well leave."

As soon as he turned away, a sprout of dark blades burst from the ground to block his path. Kael was vexed. He knew from experience that the woman would be interested only in stones and stonewisers. What could she possibly want with him?

"I didn't say you could leave yet." Her eyes narrowed. "You might be an ordinary mutt, but the stones like you well enough. After all, they allowed you in here, didn't they? Shall we find out why the stones think so highly of you?"

The sensation that scoured Kael's mind was as odd as it was unnatural, sudden, unpleasant, invasive and disturbing. He could feel her mind's eye scouring his brain, her claws raking his skull even though the woman's hands were nowhere near him.

"A land-healer, are you?" the woman said. "Convenient. Of course, there's hardly ever such thing as convenience when it has all been carefully ordained."

Ordained? What by the rot was the woman talking about? He was having trouble breathing, let alone thinking, but he trained his eyes on her and tried to kick her out of his mind.

"It's a fair effort you're making to boot me out," she said.

"Notable but useless. You're also a roamer, I see. That's just good training. Yet there's more to you than meets the eye. What is it?" A sly smile overtook her face. "Of course. You've got wiser blood in you, don't you? It's diluted enough to grant you passage, but strong enough to make you ideal. Was it your father? No, no, allow me." She tilted her upturned nose towards Kael and inhaled deeply. "Your mother? How delightful. She was a stonewiser. A pure one. The maternal line is always strong to perfume the blood. I bet your blood would be... delicious."

The sight of her fat little tongue sweeping over her lips had every hair on Kael's body standing on end. Whoever—no—*whatever* she was, the woman knew way too much about him. Kael's senses homed in on the escape route he had identified from the outset, a quick leap over the beam to his right, then a sprint through the outermost formation—

"Don't even think about it," the woman warned. "You, I'd like alive."

It was alarming news, but defiance was a better option than submission or fear. He needed to keep her talking. Whatever little knowledge he could gain from this encounter could make the difference between finding his son and losing him forever.

"I don't understand," he said. "What good can the life of an 'ordinary mutt' be to you?"

"Cocky, aren't you? Mocking me so easily. You've got steel for guts and granite for a backbone. I'll give you that. But I was never a kindly soul and even courage can be reckless."

"I mean you no offense," Kael said. "I simply find your interest in me surprising, that's all. Why would a powerful creature like you cling to a common man like me?"

"Because I need you to do the goddess's bidding."

"The goddess's bidding? Or your own?"

"They are one and the same."

"Somehow, I doubt it," Kael said. "I want nothing to do with you or your stones."

"What if I told you that doom is coming?"

Kael scoffed. "Predicting doom is always the surest bet."

"It doesn't frighten you?"

"Doom is the coward's argument, the fear monger's tale, the easy victory."

The woman's face darkened. "Are you so careless as to provoke me with your insults?"

"I'm not insulting you. I'm making a point. Sooner or later we all die. Sooner or later, what we are, what we built, what we treasure, it all passes. Doom is unavoidable and therefore, irrelevant."

"Irrelevant? In all my years I've never heard anyone say that. But I'll admit it—yours is an intriguing notion."

"Seeing all that's wrong with the world is not so difficult," Kael said. "Seeing all that's right with the world and growing it, now that's a chore."

"Reason and sense to match brawn and guts." The woman whistled. "I see now why it must be you. Oh, yes, my wager is most definitively on you."

"And what race will you have me run?"

"The goddess's own."

"What if I said no?"

"You can't say no."

"The goddess would give me a choice."

"Choice?" The woman laughed. "What little you know of stones and goddesses. I need you, Kael of Ars. And you will serve."

"I don't bend the knee to any man, or woman, for that matter."

"Who says I'm either one of those?"

The pain that struck Kael was as sudden as it was devastating. His muscles cramped. His joints gave way. His knees hit the floor, sending jolts up his spine. He could have sworn that stakes had skewered his calves, pinning him down to the floor. He had experienced more than his fair share of pain in his time, but this was excruciating. He curled over his stomach, bit down on his lips and swallowed the scream surging up his throat.

The woman was laughing so hard that tears were streaming down her face. "Forgive my methods. I favor suffering over persuasion any day. Let's get this done. I might have forever, but you don't."

"What do you want from me?" Kael rasped.

"Her," the woman said.

"Who?"

"She who will defy the stones and destroy the world."

The realization hit Kael like a kick to the balls. She wasn't after him. He should have known better. She wanted who she needed, the only one who might be capable of mustering the power to do her bidding, the only woman he'd ever called his own. His mind was spinning furiously. He wasn't going to surrender her. Not her. Not ever.

"What if I told you that a day will come when nothing but you will stand between her and the end of times?" the woman asked.

"I wouldn't believe you." He tried to rip his aching knees from the floor but failed. He took a deep breath, succeeding only in scalding his lungs. He had to think clearly. He had to keep his wits straight.

"You'll know the signs," the woman said.

"The signs for what?"

"It has all been told before. Her name will become the path upon which the faithful will travel. She will make life from death, think with her heart and feel with her mind. She will lie with the truth, cheat with devotion, lose to win and win to lose. Her life will be the goddess's last stand, but her death, now... her death will be the world's last blessing, bringing future to past."

"You can't sway me with musty old tales," Kael said. "The Wisdom is nothing to me."

"The Wisdom is everything to you. You'll do what you must to make it happen."

"To make what happen?"

"Her demise, of course."

The words punched the breath out of his lungs. "No."

"It's too late," the woman said. "Her death is already in you."

"No," he said again, but a sight flashed before his eyes, an indisputable vision of Sariah dead in his arms. A sharp pain twisted his heart and squeezed his throat. Terror inched on his mind's fringes like an avenging army, cold and unforgiving. "I would never—"

The smile on the woman's face was just another omen for

disaster. "Fate is not always arbitrary. Common sense. You can always rely on it to finish the job."

"I can't—"

"You know her better than anyone. Who better suited to kill her than you?"

"I won't—"

"Oh, but you will. She must die. Like we did. Like *I* did."

He knew it couldn't be. He wouldn't do it. Meliahs knew he would never be able to survive her death, let alone cause it. Yet he also realized that the present and the future had been woven together in a tangled knot to bring about disaster, true, unavoidable and done.

Kael's mind raced. Had the woman invested others with the same task? What could he do to prevent what he'd seen from happening? A sense of pragmatic logic prevailed. He and Sariah had defied worse odds before. Together, they had been able to overcome the most lethal of troubles. Together, they would be able to beat this newest challenge as well.

"I don't think so," the woman said. "You won't be able to share this news with her."

"What?"

"You can try, of course. You will. But you won't be able to. You'll see."

Kael refused to believe the woman. She didn't understand the indestructible bond that he and Sariah shared. After all they had been through, nothing could keep them from each other, not even the stones and their damn tricks.

"Dare you think your bond is stronger than the might of the stones?" The woman snorted. "You're in for a hard, rough road."

Kael considered his options. What if the woman's outrageous rantings turned out to be true? He could kill himself to avoid killing Sariah, but then he'd only be surrendering her to someone else's blade. He couldn't begin to fathom killing her, but if she died he would die of grief all the same. Or he could try to defy the stones, knowing himself lethal to the stonewiser he had pledged to protect, the enemy who against all odds had conquered his prejudices and claimed his heart, the woman he cherished.

By the rot. He had always lived life by his own leave. Was he ready to relinquish his will to the stones' fickle creatures? "Do you know why the stones grieve?" the woman said. "Not for a soul, I'll tell you that much. The stones don't grieve for the passing of a lowly woman or the madness of a smitten man. They don't mourn death, or lost love, or broken dreams, or loneliness or despair. Yet you will make them wail. For you, the stones will weep."

"You will not command my will," Kael swore, to her, to Sariah, to himself. "You can't."

"Have you ever heard the stones cry?" The woman shook her head sadly. "It's a ghastly wail, a soul-killing sound, a hope-ending affair. All will be done when you hear the lament of the stones. She will be done as well."

The cavern's ceiling retreated, revealing the somber gray sky and allowing the drizzle to dampen his face. It felt like defeat raining on his cheeks, like misery drenching his existence. The ground rumbled beneath his knees, gathering in an imminent explosion that would eject him out of the ruins, hurling him toward the fate he dreaded.

"I won't do it," Kael spat between clenched teeth. "Do you hear me? I won't."

"Farewell, my newest Wisdom maker," the woman said. "May you die well."

Acknowledgments

As always, my sincere thanks to:

My awesome family, for the huge amounts of love and the steady supply of support; my editor, Peter Gelfan, who is not afraid to cut through my writer's density with a shear of clarity and perspective; my friend and proofer, Linda Au, whose passion for writing is only matched by her passion for writing perfectly; the folks at Mermaid Press, for their hard work and commitment; Debbi Zimmerman, whose patience with both printer and writer is legendary; my doting husband, who insists he can cook just so that I can write; my patient son, who will eat what his father cooks with resigned humor; my audacious daughter who takes matters into her own hands with a much appreciated kitchen coup d'état; and especially to my brilliant readers, who share in my mind's adventures with such generosity and enthusiasm.

The Author

Dora Machado is the author of the fantasy novel *Stonewiser: The Heart of the Stone*. She graduated Phi Beta Kappa from Georgetown University, but thinks that motherhood is by far the more challenging and rewarding of her accomplishments. Although she was born in Michigan, she grew up in the Dominican Republic, where she developed a bilingual fascination for writing, a preference for history, a sobering perspective of the human condition that permeates all of her stories, and a taste for Merengue. As a teenager she had the honor of meeting Mother Teresa while volunteering with her charities in the barrios of Santo Domingo. After a lifetime of straddling such compelling but different worlds, fantasy is a natural fit to her stories. She lives in Florida with her indulging husband, her two extraordinary teens, her awesome exchange students, three very opinionated cats and a gold fish. She loves to hear from her readers and can be contacted at Dora@doramachado.com